Francesca Scanacapra was born mother and Italian father, and her ch between England and Italy. Her adul nomadic with periods spent living ir Senegal and Spain. She describes her..... as unconventional and has pursued an eclectic mixture of career paths – from working in translation, the fitness industry, education and even several years as a builder. In 2021 she returned to her native country and back to her earliest roots to pursue her writing career full time. Francesca now resides permanently in rural Lombardy in the house built by her great-grandfather which was the inspiration for the *Paradiso Novels (Paradiso, Return to Paradiso* and. *The Daughter of Paradiso*). Francesca is also the author of *The Lost Boy of Bologna*, published by Silvertail Books. *The Sardinian Story* is her fifth novel.

Also by Francesca Scanacapra

The Paradiso Novels:

Paradiso

Return to Paradiso

The Daughter of Paradiso

*

The Lost Boy of Bologna

The Sardinian Story

By Francesca Scanacapra

SILVERTAIL BOOKS • *London*

For all the Leonoras, wherever you might be.

PART 1

THE LITTLE HOUSE ON THE MOUNTAIN

CHAPTER 1

The cold had forced its way inside at the beginning of October and had remained like an unwelcome visitor. Still now, almost at the end of February, it was showing no inclination to leave. A whipping blizzard raged outside the little mountain house and a vicious, window-rattling wind threatened to suck it from its very foundations.

To Dante Bacchetti it seemed to be getting colder every winter – perhaps because the ravages of old age were taking over his body, or maybe because as each year passed he had less meat on his bones. Previously, lighting the range had been sufficient to warm the whole house. After all, it was a very small house – just a kitchen and a store on the ground floor and an attic bedroom above – but for the past three winters he'd had to light the open fire too. Dante had made up a bed in the kitchen because the attic room was so cold that the curtains froze rigid.

He'd brought the goat, Gineprina, inside. Dante couldn't have left her alone in her shelter in this wicked weather, and anyway, it was pleasant to have a little company. Her mate had died suddenly during the preceding autumn of some mysterious goat affliction. Now Dante and Gineprina were two widowed souls together.

The goat was tethered up in a well-fortified pen in the corner of the kitchen, which Dante had been obliged to re-enforce twice. The first time Gineprina had got out and polished off the last of the carrots. The second time she'd chewed the arm-rest off the chair.

Dante poked at the flames and arranged his gently-steaming socks, which he had just washed and hung out to dry on a string in front of the fire. The soup which was simmering on the range gave the occasional languid pop as the bubbles rose and burst in slow motion. Dante breathed in the promise of supper. How good it smelled, and all it was made from was lentils, onions and a piece of mutton shoulder.

'A carrot or two would have been nice,' he said, addressing the goat reproachfully. 'Still, the aroma is surprisingly meaty considering there was only a vestige of flesh left on that mutton bone. But any food is good if you cook it patiently and if you're hungry enough to appreciate it, don't you think, Gineprina?' The goat did not reply, as was usually the case.

Dante rarely ate during the daytime, except in spring and summer when he grew things in his vegetable plot and foraged for wild fruits and berries. He found that it suited him well enough. In any case, he couldn't afford to eat breakfast and lunch as his meagre administrative pension didn't stretch that far.

The wind was whipping up and the shutters were shaking. This, Dante could ignore, but the chimney pot was rocking and the noise was travelling down the wall, amplifying the sound. *Clonk. Clonk. Clonk.* Dante hoped that the storm would subside before he retired to bed, or it would keep him awake.

He lit the oil lamp, took his seat by the fire and put on his reading gloves, fashioned from a pair of socks which were worn past darning. With the sheep fleece covering his knees, he opened his book, knocking out his bookmark in process – not that it mattered where he had left off as it was a collection of poetry and he had read it so many times that he knew every verse by heart.

Dante continued to leaf through the pages until the clock announced that it was six, which was probably more or less correct. This far up the mountain there was no radio signal to set the time by exactly, but punctuality was the least of his concerns.

4

Hunger was making his belly rumble, so Dante went to peel two potatoes to add to the soup. Always better to put them in near the end, or they'd disintegrate. He set the peel aside to give to Gineprina later.

As he was stirring the pot he heard a noise coming from the porch where he stored his firewood. Dante stopped and listened. Silence, then scratching and shuffling. Something was out there – a wild cat, or a fox maybe. Perhaps the door had blown open.

When he pricked up his ears again, he heard a cough, and it was definitely human. But who on earth could it be on a wretched night like this? The snow was chest-deep and the track to his house was impassable. He'd been marooned for over a month.

Dante climbed into his sheepskin and grabbed the poker from beside the fire, just in case the intruder was not friendly in nature. He put his ear to the door and heard the cough again.

'Who is it?' he called out and a deep, trembling voice said, 'Please, let me in.'

Gripping the poker in his hand, Dante tentatively pulled back the bolt and opened the door just a crack. Standing in his porch was one of the most enormous men he had ever seen. The giant was hunched over and shivering and dressed in an inappropriate coat – the oiled, waterproof kind one might wear out at sea, not half way up a mountain. His eyebrows, eyelashes and nostril hair were frosted. His nose and ears were so red that they glowed.

'Are you Dante Bacchetti?' Asked the big man through his chattering teeth. His accent had a hint of foreignness about it.

'Who wants to know?'

'My name is Jubanne Melis Puddu.'

'That's an unusual name.'

'Not unusual where I come from.'

'And where might that be?'

'Sardinia.'

'What's a Sardinian doing in the Apennine Mountains on a fiendish night like this?'

'I'm here to see Dante Bacchetti.'

The huge man stepped closer and Dante shrank back, tightening his grip on the poker and shielding himself with the door, although in truth he did not really feel threatened. This stranger, despite his gargantuan size, did not seem menacing. If anything, he appeared nervous, and half frozen to death.

The Sardinian said, 'I wrote to you about your daughter.'

'All the correspondence I ever receive, with the exception of letters from the tax office, is about my daughter. You'll have to be more specific than that.' The jaded tone of Dante's voice gave the impression that whatever this visitor had to say, the old man had probably heard it before. Over the years he'd encountered more than his fair share of fantasists and crackpots, all keen to share their fanciful theories about Leonora's fate.

Jubanne Melis Puddu gave Dante a quizzical look. 'If one of my children had disappeared and someone knew something, I'd want to know. Don't you want to hear what I have to say? I've come a long way to talk to you.'

'Do you know where my daughter is?'

'No, but I know where she *was*.'

Dante loosened his grip on the poker, then said, without disguising his irritation, 'Well, I'm not sure how that's going to be of any use, but I don't have the heart to send you away in this weather, so I suppose you'd better come in.'

The big man dipped his head as he stepped through the doorway. The light from the fire and the oil lamp cast a flickering glow over his ruddy, cold-mottled skin. He was somewhere around fifty-five years of age, perhaps a little more.

Now Dante felt awkward. He shouldn't have been so standoffish. Despite the unexpected nature of the visit and the inevitable pointlessness of it, there was no need for bad manners.

'Forgive me,' he said. 'I did not want to seem rude, or unwelcoming, but your sudden appearance in my porch on a night such as this came as quite a shock. It's rare for me to have any visitors here, even at the height of summer. And being of the size you are, I'm sure that you're well aware of what an alarming first impression you give.'

The big Sardinian gave a contrite nod. He was standing in the centre of the room and taking up a considerable portion of it. The ice and snow were melting off his oilskin coat and dripping puddles onto the flagstones.

'First things first,' said Dante adopting a deliberately convivial tone. 'We need to get you dry. If you'd like to take off your coat, I'll hang it by the range. And would you mind stamping the snow off your shoes? A man of my advanced years can't afford to slip on a wet floor. Or better still, you should take them off and dry them by the fire. They're soaked through. Not really the right footwear for trekking up a mountain, if you don't mind me saying.'

Jubanne Melis Puddu placidly did as his host asked. Dante hung the coat on the hook by the range. It was the size of a boat-sail.

'Good, good,' said Dante, arranging the biggest pair of shoes he had ever seen by the fire, beneath his drying socks. 'Please, make yourself comfortable. Unfortunately I am ill-prepared to entertain. I can't offer you any grappa or suchlike as I don't keep any in the house and I have no coffee left. I haven't been able to go down to the village for six weeks, almost seven in actual fact, and last time I did, the shop had run out. Getting supplies up here is always a headache. I do have goats' milk though. I was saving it to make cheese, so it's slightly turned, but don't let that put you off. It's an acquired taste, but very good once acquired

7

in my opinion. Some object to the goaty smell, but personally, I can no longer smell it. It's particularly delicious with a little honey added, and I have plenty of that. A former neighbour in Montacciolo keeps bees and furnishes me with several jars of his fine honey every year.'

Dante busied himself with preparations, glancing up occasionally at the big man warming himself facing the fire. Despite the strange circumstances and his initial reticence, he was pleased to have some company. Nobody had been to visit him since the early autumn, and then it had only been the neighbour delivering the honey, but he wasn't the talkative type. There was only so much one could say about bees. He'd had more stimulating conversations with Gineprina the goat.

When at last the Sardinian turned round, His eyebrows had thawed and he was no longer trembling with the cold.

'Here,' said Dante, handing him a bowl of hot, sweetened milk. 'This'll warm you from the inside too. Please, take a seat. I apologise for the state of the arm rest. It was chewed by my hungry goat. Well, I say hungry, but she might just have been bored. Understandable really. There have been times when I myself have felt so woefully lacking in stimulation that munching the furniture might have seemed like an entertaining way to pass the time.'

The Sardinian settled his enormous frame into the chair, which creaked under his weight, and began to sip the steaming milk.

'So,' said Dante. 'You say you wrote to me last year?'

'Yes. But I didn't send my letter here. I sent it to the village of Montacciolo.'

'I moved out of Montacciolo a long time ago. People do still send letters there and I collect them myself when the weather allows and I can get down the track. Other times the postmaster gives them to the goat-herder, Ermenegildo, to drop off if he's coming this way. So things arrive eventually, one way or the other. But how did you know where to find me?'

'I went to the village and I asked in the bar.'

'And someone told you?' Tutted Dante. 'Really, some people can be terribly indiscreet.' He didn't ask who had divulged the information. He could guess. They wouldn't think twice about sending Satan, or an axe-wielding madman his way. 'But I must say how astonished I am that you managed to make your way to me as this place can be tricky to locate at the best of times, and now all the tracks are snowed under. It's quite remarkable, particularly as you're so unsuitably dressed for the conditions. Just as well you're such a strapping fellow, or you'd have frozen to death and we wouldn't have found you until the spring. I'm afraid to say that last winter a chap went out to check his traps and when he didn't come back, his brother went out to look for him. He didn't come back either. They were found weeks later – dead as doornails of course, and somewhat gnawed by the wildlife. How's the milk? Is it sweet enough?'

Jubanne Melis Puddu nodded and continued to sip from the bowl.

'It's good, thank you,' he said, 'Did my letter reach you?'

'I'll have to check. You say you wrote last year. Do you remember when approximately?'

'In the spring.'

'And kindly remind me, what exactly was the nature of your correspondence?'

The Sardinian stared wide-eyed at the old man through the milk steam.

'I told you that I knew where your daughter went after she disappeared.'

Dante stroked his long beard and tilted his head to one side.

'I will have to ask you to be more specific. You see, many people have written to me over the years claiming to know my daughter's last known movements, and with theories concerning her disappearance and her supposed death. I also receive accusations, confessions and reported sightings of both a mortal and ghostly nature.'

Dante went to the far end of the room, where the wall was shelved from floor to ceiling and crammed with neatly-stacked document boxes.

'See here? This is where I file everything concerning Leonora. Assuming your letter reached me, it will be archived here somewhere. Under which category would you say that your correspondence falls?'

Jubanne Melis Puddu surveyed the wall of paperwork, looking baffled.

'I'm not sure,' he said. 'What are the options?'

'On the top shelf are the confessions, divided into two categories – *Credible* and *Questionable*. Only one box for *Credible*, and there's never been much in there. Six boxes for *Questionable*. Originally I had begun to file them chronologically, but trying to sort them like that is tricky. Not everybody who chooses to correspond with me is too punctilious about details such as dates. They're more concerned with the gory and salacious aspects of how Leonora supposedly met her fate. Nevertheless, it never ceases to surprise me how many men are willing to confess to a murder that they clearly haven't committed, or which may not have been committed at all. Claims of culpability used to be very frequent. Fewer now that so much time has passed since Leonora disappeared, but I hold onto them all, just in case.'

Now even more astonished, Jubanne Melis Puddu asked, 'How many men have confessed?'

'To date, twenty-two. And it would seem that not one of them is guilty. There is just one claim in the *Credible* box, which I placed in there more out of hope than certainty, but it was disproven some time ago. It's only still in there because I haven't had the wherewithal to move it. Getting up to that top shelf is problematic for me. I have to stand on a chair and my balance isn't what it used to be-' and then, with a look of sudden realisation, as though something had just dawned on him, Dante asked, 'Would you mind getting that box for me? A fellow of your size can reach without even standing on his tiptoes.'

Jubanne Melis Puddu rose to his feet and joined Dante.

'Which box?'

'Far left. And if you could also grab the third one along from it, I'll move the contents into that one.'

The big man did as he was asked and Dante re-arranged the files, muttering, 'That's better. It's been bothering me.'

'But why would people confess to something they hadn't done?'

Dante shrugged, 'Leonora's disappearance was a high profile case. I suppose that some people just wanted to be part of the circus, to have a few moments of fame, or notoriety. I assume you saw all the reports in the newspapers?'

'I saw some.'

'There was a time when you couldn't pick up a newspaper without reading some new piece of speculation. Even the foreign press reported Leonora's disappearance and her supposed murder.' The old man shook his head, indicating a dozen further document boxes, 'But the confessions are far outnumbered by the allegations from third parties.'

'Third parties?'

Dante nodded, 'On this shelf are letters written by people who suspect, or claim to know, that a particular person committed the murder of my daughter. There were two hundred and sixty-two at the last count, although seventy-four of those are from the same woman who was trying to pin the blame on a neighbour. But just like the confessions, to date these allegations have all been unfounded. Most are malicious in nature – spurious accusations from scorned women, cuckolded husbands and suchlike. Others are straightforward vendettas, and often revenge for trifling disagreements. To my knowledge, not one has been in any way reliable.'

'But don't you pass any of this on to the police?'

Dante made a dismissive *pffft* sound.

'The police!' He snorted. 'Their uselessness has only been surpassed by their apathy. I used to inform the authorities every time a letter arrived and insist that they investigate each claim. But none of their inquiries ever reached any useful conclusions, so I stopped. After the police mothballed the case, I hired a team of private investigators hoping that they could shed some light on what had happened to Leonora, but all that succeeded in achieving was a year of all expenses paid travel for them and financial ruin for me.'

Dante gestured towards the remaining boxes and added wearily, 'I also receive correspondence from psychics and fortune-tellers who claim to have seen apparitions of my daughter. I'm certain that their authors are perfectly well-meaning, but nothing has led to anything. They claim to know all sorts of things – the circumstances and manner of Leonora's supposed death, where she is buried, or otherwise disposed of. These tend to be less specific as to who did it, although they always refer to a male perpetrator and generally the motive is a matter of the heart.'

The old man sighed wearily and concluded, 'And in these boxes here are the letters which claim that Leonora is still alive. Some say that she has been kidnapped, others that she has disappeared of her own volition and is living in secret in a foreign country. Nepal seems to be a popular choice, and I did write to the police commissioner in Kathmandu on two occasions, but never received a reply. I'm assuming that it was because he didn't speak Italian and couldn't understand the nature of my inquiry. Some people have been kind enough to enclose photographs of women whom they suspect to be Leonora, but none of them have been my daughter.'

Jubanne Melis Puddu stared at all the boxes before him and said, 'I'm not sure which file you'd have put my letter in.'

'Hold on a moment,' said Dante. 'You said you wrote to me in the spring of last year? From Sardinia?'

'Yes.'

'Ah yes! I do recall receiving a letter with a Sardinian postmark. I believe that it reached me late last summer. In late July, or early August 1989. I filed it under *General*.'

'*General*?' Repeated the big man with a clear note of disappointment in his voice.

Taking note of the Sardinian's reaction, and not wishing to offend a man of such imposing stature, Dante was quick to redress. He wouldn't mention that he had also sub-categorized it under *Unsupported/Speculation*, where he filed the letters which he considered hardly worth the paper they were written on.

'Please don't think that I didn't take your letter seriously. But please also understand that so far nothing has shed any light on what happened to my daughter. All this correspondence has led to is confusion, dead ends and many, many wild goose chases. Who knows? Perhaps the answer to the riddle of Leonora's disappearance *does* lie within one of these files, but perhaps it doesn't, and all this paperwork is good for is to light the fire.'

The Sardinian still had about him a look of despondency. Dante reached up, patted his big shoulder reassuringly and said, 'However, it cannot be ignored that not only did you go to the trouble of writing to me, but also you have come all this way to see me – a long and complex journey by anybody's standards. And what's more you've trekked up a mountain in the depths of winter in truly deplorable weather, and woefully under-dressed for the conditions. I apologise if I did not give your letter appropriate consideration at the time I received it, but I can assure you that you have my full attention now.'

Satisfied that his guest had been placated, Dante took the letter from its file and beckoned Jubanne Melis Puddu to take a seat by the fire again, then slipped the letter from its envelope. As he thought, it had reached him in August of 1989. He was certain of that because he had written the date himself on the top left-hand corner, as was his habit with correspondence which arrived undated. He began to read the single paragraph, written in a carefully-formed but childish hand on a single page.

'You say you met my daughter in April of 1973, when she came to work at your guesthouse in Sardinia.'

'That's right.'

'But you are aware that the last confirmed sighting of Leonora was in Pesaro, on mainland Italy's Adriatic coast, in October of 1972?'

'Yes.'

'Then why, may I ask, has it taken you eighteen years to write to me to say that you knew of her whereabouts after her disappearance?'

'When she came to Sardinia, I didn't know that anybody was looking for her. I hadn't read any reports then. And when I did see some, they weren't recent. I came across them by chance in some old newspapers. It's only then that I made the connection.'

'So now you've travelled all the way here to tell me everything that happened when a young woman whom you believe to be my daughter was in Sardinia?'

'Yes.'

'Why, when you could have written it in this letter?'

'Because there's a lot to explain. I couldn't write a letter that long.'

Dante had come to the end of the paragraph, and therefore the end of the letter. He put the page down and paused to gather his thoughts. When at last he spoke, his tone was grave.

'You understand that everything I read concerning my daughter, Leonora, whether it be true or false, proven or unproven, brings back to the surface indescribable anguish and suffering? I am now, in my way, at last resigned to never knowing what happened to her, but it has taken a truly herculean effort to reach this point. My dear wife went to her grave in a state of torment caused by the uncertainty of our daughter's fate and I have no wish to go the same way. I will be seventy-three years old soon, and I know that the end of my days on this earth is not far away. In truth, I'm rather surprised to have made it through this cold spell. Therefore I ask you, are you sure of what you have to say? Is what you are about to tell me something you have lived, or seen with your own eyes? Are you certain that the young woman you have come all this way to speak about is really my daughter, Leonora?'

'Yes.'

Dante inhaled deeply. 'Well, then I suppose you had better enlighten me.'

Drinking the last of his milk and honey, the Sardinian began his story.

CHAPTER 2

Jubanne Melis Puddu considered that life had dealt him a very favourable hand. He had many blessings to count, and he counted them often.

What man alive would not be grateful to have a wife as fine as his? Signora Melis Puddu was blessed with innumerable good qualities – kindness, intelligence, fortitude, to name but a few. Not only that, she was also strikingly beautiful, of unmistakably Mediterranean appearance, brown-eyed, dark-haired and olive-skinned.

Jubanne had been utterly taken with her from the moment they had met but had been shy about making his feelings known. Surely such an exceptional woman, one endowed with such elegance, class and sophistication, would not be interested in a great lumbering bear like him? Had she not made the first move, he might not have had the courage to mention that dance – but she had inquired whether he had any intention of asking her, and when he had mumbled 'yes' she had smiled and said, 'I'll consider myself invited, then.'. From that moment, he had never looked back. They'd got married only six months later. Everybody had been thrilled for them, saying what a good match they were.

There were those who couldn't help but remark on the couple's considerable difference in height. Jubanne didn't mind if people mentioned the fifty centimetre disparity, but those who cracked off-colour jokes, or made any kind of innuendo, were immediately reprimanded. He was very proper when it came to things like that. This adherence to good manners had been instilled into him by his grandmother, the venerable Nonna Maria-Annoriana.

The Melis Puddus seldom argued. Both worked on the premise of being considerate towards one another. There was nothing that Jubanne would not do to make his wife happy.

The fruit of this content and successful union was two children, a boy and a girl. That summer they were eight and ten years old respectively. Jubanne would gladly have had more children, but had agreed with his wife that a large family would be too much to deal with. They already had enough on their plates running the business.

Their guesthouse, Villa Zuannicca, had come from Signora Melis Puddu's side of the family, but when she had inherited it, it had been a sorry place – out-dated and shabby, and lacking any sort of modern amenities or indoor plumbing. Over the years Jubanne and his wife had worked tirelessly to make something of it. Now Villa Zuannicca was a fine establishment, clean and well-appointed with three bathrooms on each of its three floors, plus separate WCs. There were fifteen guest rooms in total, each equipped to lodge between two and four people. The Melis Puddus served their guests good, wholesome food, and plenty of it – home-made pasta, traditional local *fregola* made from semolina, and fresh fish brought in daily off the boats, as well as the finest Sardinian lamb and suckling pig. The wine from the neighbouring vineyards flowed plentifully.

Every Friday night a band would come to entertain the guests and there would be dancing on the terrace. Sometimes, if she was not too busy and she felt that way inclined, Signora Melis Puddu would agree to sing, for aside from all her excellent qualities, she was blessed with a beautiful voice. Her repertoire comprised a wide range of traditional Sardinian folk tunes, and sometimes she took modern songs and gave them a folkish twist. The guests were always an appreciative audience. Jubanne would watch and listen, tapping his foot and swelling with pride – unless his wife sang '*Amore Mio, Amore Mio*', before which she would say, 'I dedicate this song to my husband,' – in which case he would have to move discreetly to one side and pretend that he had something in his eye.

Since Jubanne and his wife had taken over Villa Zuannicca it had earned an excellent reputation, and the proof was that people came back year after year – and not just Italians. The Melis Puddus welcomed guests from other countries too. During the high season it was rare for them to have any vacancies.

Villa Zuannicca was situated in the north-east of Sardinia, tucked within its own private cove, overlooking a bay where the sea changed from sapphire blue to emerald green, depending on the weather and the time of day. On clear days, the wild, uninhabited island known as Isola Spargi could be seen in the distance.

The building itself was anchored to a rocky crag, with a broad terrace and a garden filled with aloes, prickly pears, roses and lavender. From there, stone steps lead down to a half-moon of sandy beach. A wooden walkway stretched further out to where the water was deeper, and it was there that Jubanne's boat, his beloved *Lavandula*, was moored.

She had previously been a traditional Sardinian sail-boat, but Jubanne had fitted her with a motor when he had restored her. He tended her with great care, always ensuring her seaworthiness, although what with work and the children and one thing and another he didn't take her out as often as he would have liked. The most time he spent aboard was sleeping there in the summer. Being such a big man, Jubanne suffered terribly with the night-time heat and rather than tossing and turning and disturbing his wife, he would often decamp from the marital bed and go to the *Lavandula*. The coolness coming from the sea and the rocking motion always did the trick. Jubanne never had a better night's sleep than when he was cradled on the little boat bunk, lullabied by the lapping of the water.

There was no time for a leisurely boat trip today. The tourist season was about to start and with just a few days to go before re-opening, and being short –staffed, Signora Melis Puddu was fretting that some things wouldn't be ready in time for the first guests' arrival. The restaurant, in particular, still needed so much attention.

Villa Zuannicca's isolated position was its selling point for guests who wanted to holiday somewhere quiet and out-of-the-way, but its seclusion was a problem when it came to finding staff. There was no shortage of potential manpower in the next town, but that was fifteen kilometres away. Most people didn't have transport and there weren't enough spare rooms in the guesthouse to accommodate all the employees needed to keep the place running.

Added to this geographical inconvenience was the fact that whenever possible, Signora Melis Puddu preferred to hire female staff. Women, she maintained, were severely disadvantaged when it came to employment opportunities, particularly in that underdeveloped part of Sardinia. She would never take on a man to do a job if she could find a woman capable of doing it.

Jubanne's wife had mentioned that a girl by the name of Nora was coming to work at their guesthouse, but he hadn't really been paying attention as he'd been occupied with something. When Signora Melis Puddu appeared on the terrace looking flustered and complaining about the mountain of preparation still outstanding, Jubanne had asked, 'What about that girl you said was coming to work? Where's she?'

'Nora's been delayed.'

'How come?'

'I told you, she's flying in from America.'

'What? Someone would come all the way from *America* to work *here*?'

His wife gave him that exasperated look, reserved for times when she had to repeat something because Jubanne hadn't been listening when she'd said it the first time, or maybe even the second time. It was a look he was seeing more and more of these days.

'Yes, I explained to you that she's been working on a private yacht. She was held up by bad weather in the Caribbean and they only docked in Florida last week, so that messed up all her flights.'

Jubanne took in the information, but he was absolutely certain that his wife hadn't mentioned it before because he would definitely have remembered something so exceptional.

'Well fancy that, she's coming all the way from America!' He chuckled. It seemed so strange to choose their modest little guesthouse in a remote corner of Sardinia over a private yacht which had just travelled the Caribbean.

'How did you find her?' Asked Jubanne, but he received no reply as Signora Melis Puddu was already hurrying away, clearly far too busy to furnish him with any further explanations.

He began to inspect the stone slabs on the terrace. Some of them were loose. They were trip hazards. He needed to take them up and re-lay them right away.

Jubanne was a practical man who could turn his hand to most things. He had spent the winter months re-whitewashing all the bedrooms, which had seemed like a never-ending task. After that, he had repaired and replaced several sets of shutters. He had also grubbed up a section of scrub at the end of the garden which had been spoiling the view to the sea. He'd intended to plant another rose bed there, but hadn't got round to that. The following winter, his wife wanted him to build a wooden veranda backing onto the dining room. There was a fig tree in the way and it would be a shame to have to cut it down. Perhaps he could incorporate it somehow. He'd have to have a good look to see whether it was feasible. Still, that would have to wait. He had those loose slabs to sort out as a matter of urgency.

As he was turning over the cement in the wheelbarrow, Jubanne happened to glance up and see the young woman walking towards him. The sun was at her back and threw a shimmering golden aura around her. Jubanne was instantly dumbstruck by the vision. She was probably not much older than twenty. Her eyes were very large and her hair, which must have reached past her waist, was being lifted gently by the sea breeze. For a moment Jubanne was reminded of his wife, but the way she was years before, when they had first met. Perhaps it was something in the girl's eyes; or perhaps it was those thick waves of shining, onyx-black hair. But there was something more to this young woman. To Jubanne, she was beyond beautiful.

How prettily dressed she was, in a long, loose dress printed with multi-coloured flowers. She wore sandals which were barely more than three thin leather straps criss-crossing her toes. Around her neck and on her wrists were strings of big, bright beads.

'Hello,' she smiled, 'I'm Nora,' and Jubanne found himself unable to speak, like some daft teenaged boy. All he could do was to gaze at her, but rather than be put off by his stare, she met it and gazed right back.

The way those deep brown eyes connected with his made him feel as though the ground beneath his feet was about to give way. In that instant he felt something which could only have been described as deeply spiritual – an other-worldly connection, as though some invisible force was drawing them together. He could feel it, not just coming from him, but coming from her too. He was overwhelmed by the certainty that he already knew this young woman called Nora, that somehow they had met before; although of course, that was impossible.

Jubanne averted his gaze. He didn't want her to think he was some dirty old man who gawped at pretty young women. But in those few moments something powerful had happened between them, and he knew that they had both felt it.

Clearing his throat, Jubanne adopted business-like manner. 'You're here to work in the restaurant, aren't you? You'd better go and speak to my wife. She'll show you round and tell you what needs doing.'

'Can't I stay out here with you?' Nora asked.

'Re-laying slabs is no job for you, young lady,' Jubanne found himself saying. 'Run along inside and find my wife.' Then he cringed at the patronising tone of his voice and choice of words because he had sounded as though he had been talking to one of his children when they'd been disobedient.

Nora hesitated. Clearly she was reluctant to go, but finally she gave a little shrug said, 'All right. But I'll come and see you later.' Then, quite unexpectedly, she stepped towards him, looped her arms around his neck and kissed him on the cheek – and Jubanne was so overcome that his legs shook and his size forty-nine feet almost fell away from under him.

Nora turned and made her way towards the guesthouse, and although he had told himself not to look, Jubanne could not help but watch her walk away. He wanted to cry out, 'Come back!', but he bit his lip and kept the words inside him. When she glanced over her shoulder and smiled, he suppressed the urge to wave. Instead, he pretended not to have seen her.

Once she had vanished from view, Jubanne was compelled to sit down before he fell down. A combination of euphoria and exhaustion overwhelmed him. The feeling that something truly momentous and life-changing had just happened pulsed through every cell of his body. It was so powerful that it gave him a headache. He rested his elbows on his knees and cradled his throbbing head in his hands, trying to make some sense of what he had just experienced. How was it possible, he wondered, to feel such a profound connection to a stranger?

It would be easy to explain it away as just a wave of lust. Nora was, after all, conspicuously beautiful. But Jubanne wasn't a man of lecherous temperament. Of course he could appreciate a lovely-looking woman, and there was no shortage of them at the guesthouse during the season, and often they weren't wearing much; but he was never one to leer at them, or ogle like some hungry dog drooling after a bone. He might not be a high-born or educated man, but that did not stop him from behaving like a gentleman.

Most importantly, there was the matter of his wife. Never before had he disrespected her by paying improper attention to another woman. From the day he had met his wife, other women had ceased to exist for him in *that way*. It had certainly never crossed his mind to cheat. When occasionally he had an erotic dream which didn't involve the lovely Signora Melis Puddu, the guilt would stick to him all day.

Although there was still so much to do, Jubanne felt too dazed to do anything but remain seated on the terrace. The slabs would have to wait. Unable to fight the wave of deep fatigue, he fell asleep in a chair.

It was Nora who woke him some time later. She arrived carrying a tray with a jug of cold lemon tea and two glasses, one of which was one quarter filled with crushed ice and mint leaves. Signora Melis Puddu must have told Nora that was exactly the way he liked his tea.

'You found my wife then,' said Jubanne.

'Yes,' replied Nora with a wry smile. 'She's a slavedriver. She put me to work straight away getting the restaurant ready. I've just ironed forty tablecloths.'

She pulled up a chair and sat down beside Jubanne, in an easy, familiar way, as though she had been doing it all her life.

This young woman feels it too, thought Jubanne. She feels this *thing*, this sensation that we've met before – no, it's more than that – this certainty that we've known each other for ever; that we are somehow part of each other.

'You've come from America then?' He said, and Nora nodded as she began to pour the tea.

'Yes, I was meant to fly from Palm Beach to Barcelona, then from Barcelona to Rome and Rome to Cagliari, but the first flight was re-routed via Atlanta and that messed up all my connections. I should have been back here in three days, but instead it's taken me seven.'

'Holy Carrots! You've been to more places in seven days than I have in my whole life.'

Nora smiled at the strange exclamation, then continued with, 'I've been to lots of other places – to most of the Greek islands, from Corfu and round the peninsula to Skyros, then down to Crete. I've sailed around the Turkish coast too. Two years ago I spent a season sailing all around the Mediterranean and we stopped at several North African ports. I've spent the last winter in the Caribbean. That's the furthest from home I've ever been.'

Jubanne doubted whether he'd even know where to look for half of those places on a map.

'Amazing,' he said, and he found himself repeating the word after everything Nora said, because everything about her *was* utterly amazing to him.

He was trying not to stare at her too much, but it was impossible. He felt compelled to study her; every expression on her face, the way her eyelashes cast shadows on her cheeks when her head was tilted just right. Watching her talk, her lips moving, her eyes gleaming, her hand as it swept back her hair. It all enchanted him.

'I know it sounds terribly glamorous,' she was saying, 'but believe me, it's no holiday when you're part of the crew on one

of those yachts. The owners and their guests are very demanding. They pass their time clicking their fingers and giving orders
whilst the crew runs around making sure everything's perfect
for them, day and night.'

'Sounds like this place, but at sea.'

'It's much worse. At least here you can get away from them.'

'I suppose you'd have to jump overboard, or throw a guest
over the side,' said Jubanne, and to his utter delight, this made
Nora laugh.

Even her laughter affected him. It vibrated inside him, giving
him a strange buzz in his ears, followed by and a peculiar sensation, as though they had already had this exact conversation
before.

Nora hitched her long skirt above her knees to sun her legs.
She had a fine gold chain around her ankle, attached to which
was a pendant in the shape of a rose.

'That's pretty,' said Jubanne.

'My rose?'

'Yes.'

'Mamma's friend gave it to me. It came from a market in
Marrakesh. It was her good luck charm, and now it's mine.'

Jubanne realised that he probably shouldn't be looking at
Nora's legs, so he respectfully averted his eyes and concentrated
on the conversation. As Jubanne continued to listen to this mesmerising, cosmopolitan young woman, her stories, descriptions
of exotic people and places, he was overcome by an absolute
conviction.

Before that day, his life had been a desert, and now it was a
garden in full bloom.

CHAPTER 3

Dante had been paying close attention to the Sardinian's story and could not deny that he was moved by this candid and emotional account. However one chose to define the feelings that Jubanne Melis Puddu had described, there was no question that they were genuinely felt. Nothing had been said so far which could prove beyond doubt to the old man that the young woman described was his daughter, Leonora; but neither was there anything indisputable to confirm that she was not.

His daughter had indeed been given a pendant in the shape of a rose by a friend, which she had worn around her neck; although Dante had no knowledge of where it had come from originally. Being a relatively commonplace item – the type of trinket you'd find for sale at a thousand different market stalls – it could have come from Marrakesh just as easily as from Montacciolo.

Dante turned over these new facts in his head. After her reported disappearance from the town of Pesaro in October of 1972, had Leonora in fact found employment on a private yacht, as the Sardinian claimed? Had she travelled as far as the Caribbean, and to America? It was not implausible. But why had she left without saying anything, or taking all her things? And most importantly, why had she never been in touch again?

'These stories of travel to the Caribbean and to America on a private yacht are news to me, but I cannot claim to know every place which my daughter visited,' admitted Dante. 'Leonora had certainly travelled to Spain and France, and Greece too. Of that I'm certain because she wrote to us from there. She also spent some time in the Maghreb region of North Africa – Morocco,

Tunisia and Algeria. After she left home, her life was somewhat nomadic and she never stayed in one place very long. Her correspondence was inconsistent, due partly to the irregularity of her lifestyle, and partly to the unreliable postal services of those countries.'

The old man shook his head and an expression of regret fell across his face. 'Leonora, I fear, kept a great deal of information from her mother and from myself. She didn't want us to worry, I suppose. Travelling as a young woman, mainly alone, carries its risks...' Dante's words trailed off. 'It is a cruel irony,' he mused after a moment's contemplation, 'that through her travels, Leonora hoped to find herself, but eventually that is how she came to be lost.'

'I don't understand.'

Dante twisted his beard in his hand, seeming to choose his words carefully.

'From an early age it was clear that my daughter was different to other little girls. There was a restlessness about her. She was what one might call a "free spirit" these days. Leonora was a clever child, and she could be sweet and funny. But I cannot deny that there was another side to her. She was also wilful and disobedient and took great pleasure in making a nuisance of herself. Leonora was not always an easy child to raise.' Dante paused for a moment and his face crinkled into an indulgent, yet mournful, half-smile. 'She was, I confess, not dissimilar to me in character, except that I learned to curb my boisterous traits. If truth be told, my spirit was beaten out of me, first by my father and then at school, where I learned that life was less troublesome if I conformed.'

Dante sat forwards and poked at the fire, sending a blizzard of sparks fizzing up the chimney, and continued with, 'I myself was born in Montacciolo, and my family goes back generations in this area of the Apennines. My father and his father before him were stone craftsmen, skilled in quarrying, stone-cutting and masonry. They built this little house before I was born. My father, although he was not formally educated, was a very astute and forward-thinking man. He knew that the end of the traditional mountain trades was nigh. As he saw within me a glimmer of promise, he decided that I should receive an academic education. Somehow he found the money to send me away to school, to a Jesuit academy, where the instruction was both rigorous and brutal. He hoped that eventually I would become a priest. In those days one's son becoming a priest was the pinnacle of many parents' ambition. I was indeed accepted to the seminary in Pistoia, but quickly realised that a life in Holy Orders was not for me, so I trained as a schoolteacher and found employment at a school of excellent reputation in the city of Ferrara...'

Dante Bacchetti's words slowed before fading away entirely. Jubanne Melis Puddu waited for him to collect his thoughts and continue, but all that ensued was a period of silence. Eventually the Sardinian prompted Dante with, 'But you went back to live in Montacciolo?' and the question made the old man look up with a start.

'Oh, forgive me. I became quite lost in thoughts which have not occupied me for a very long time. Yes, I returned to Montacciolo. I had always come back for the summer break, and often for Easter too if the weather permitted, although not entirely by choice, I confess. Whilst my colleagues spent their holidays going on tours all over Italy and beyond, I felt duty-bound to visit my ageing parents. And yes, I was a touch resentful about it. In those days I still carried with me the self-importance of a young man who knew he had done better than his peers – a misplaced egotism, of which I am not proud now – but it would be disingenuous of me to claim that I always came to visit my family willingly. Every time that I returned, the village was a little emptier; more people had left, or died; a few more houses were closed up and abandoned. Then there was the earthquake in 1940. That impelled people to leave who might otherwise have stayed. At the time of my birth in 1918, the population of Montacciolo numbered four hundred and forty-seven. Thirty years later it was barely two hundred souls, and so it was not a stretch to suppose that within a few more decades there would be nobody there at all. My father had been absolutely right. The old mountain trades were dying out, but even more quickly than he had foreseen. As there were no jobs, the exodus of young people from Montacciolo was quite comprehensive. Life was bleeding out of the village. It was clear that the handful of remaining children would not be able to live there for their whole lives if that was what they wished.'

The old man adjusted his spectacles. 'My apologies,' he said. 'It was not my intention to digress in such a maudlin way. It's just than not having had any company for several months, speaking to another human being has come as a rather unexpected relief, and you are a very good listener, Signor Melis Puddu. Now, where was I?'

'You were telling me why you came back to Montacciolo.'

'Ah, yes. Well, one summer I returned to find that there was talk of the village school having to close. The schoolmistress had worked past what would be considered a reasonable retirement age and finally gave up due to failing health. No replacement could be found. Nobody wanted to work in such an isolated spot, nor in such a small school where all the pupils between the ages of six and sixteen had to be taught within the same classroom – a system which came burdened with many logistical difficulties. Without a new teacher, the children would have to be sent away to boarding schools.'

Dante swallowed hard and his voice became strained, 'I myself had experienced the horrors of boarding school, and I could not allow it to happen those poor children. Suddenly my eyes were opened and I saw Montacciolo not as just some inconsequential huddle of houses clinging to a remote mountainside, but as a struggling place in dire need of help. All ambitions of career advancement left me and I saw my true vocation in life. The village of Montacciolo, and most importantly the *children* of Montacciolo, needed me.'

A gentle smile spread across the old man's face. 'So I returned. And then I married my dear wife, Ortensia, a true Montacciolana born and bred, and she would never have dreamed of living anywhere else, so as far as I was concerned, the path of my life was firmly set and my destiny was to remain anchored to my roots here in the Apennine mountains.'

Dante inhaled deeply, as though refilling himself with the emotion he had felt at the time and half-rose in his chair as he stated, 'For the first time in my life, I experienced a sense of having done the right thing for the right reason. I made it my mission to impart to the children not only the basic academic requirements of reading, writing and arithmetic, but also the importance of their heritage; to teach them the history of the area, to acquaint them with the old skills and trades of their forefathers, and for those things to be celebrated, not consigned to some past memory of a primitive time. I wanted my students to understand that Montacciolo was not a backward place, but one steeped in precious folklore and tradition which had taken centuries to establish, and that unless this culture was recognised and honoured, it would be lost forever.'

The old man shrank back into his chair, breathless from his impassioned address.

'That was a kind thing to do for all the children,' said Jubanne Melis Puddu. 'They must have been grateful not to be sent away from their parents.'

Dante raised an eyebrow and made a *hmm* sound before replying.

'Not quite all of them,' he said. 'It became clear very early on that this education, however broad-based, was not enough for Leonora. She was an exceptionally bright student – by far the most intelligent amongst her classmates – and I claim that not through the biased viewpoint of a parent, but as a teacher who has taught many children during his career. Leonora was sharp, imaginative, full of potential, but...' The old man stared into the fire, as though searching for the rest of his sentence somewhere in the flames. '...but Montacciolo was too restrictive for her, the people too small-minded. She sensed that there was more to discover in the world beyond the village. From a very young age Leonora spoke of leaving, and even before she had caught a glimpse of the sea and had only read about it in books, she developed an obsession with it, for the sea could take her far away. She would indicate the globe in the schoolroom and say "Look, Papá, you can't go all around the world by land, but you can go all the way around it on the sea.".'

The old man moved his chair closer to the fire. 'I tried to explain to her the paradoxes of the human condition. The human condition is to want something other than what we have, at least, when we are young. But as we grow older, if we have some sense, we learn to accept our lot. With a bit of luck, we might even grow to love and appreciate it. And if age endows us with a little grain of wisdom, we might understand that more often than not, our malcontent is rooted in desires which can never be fulfilled. In our youth, the grass is always greener elsewhere, not just on the other side, but again on the other side beyond that.'

'That's a complicated thing to explain to a child.'

'Leonora was no ordinary child. She understood perfectly. But my words were of no help at all in calming her wanderlust. And as each year passed she grew more disgruntled in Montacciolo. The winters were the worst, when the village would be cut off for months. "I'm not made for the cold, Papá," she would say. In fact, after she left, it was no coincidence that she gravitated towards sunny climates. In those temperate places I believe she found some level of contentment for the first time in her life. She certainly found inspiration, for it was in there that she wrote some beautiful poetry.'

Dante reached across to the book he had been reading before the Sardinian's arrival. He held it reverently, stroked its cover and said, 'This volume contains Leonora's poems. After her disappearance, when at last her personal effects were returned to us, amongst those things were several notebooks of poems. I took the most complete of them and had them printed and bound.'

The old man offered up the book to his companion, who understood the preciousness of this object. He took it delicately in his big hands and read the words printed on the front.

The Little Boat

'That is the title of one of Leonora's poems, the longest of them, in fact. One might call it a saga,' explained Dante. 'It is autobiographical. Within it she embodies the little boat. She refers to Montacciolo and its mountainous landscape and begins by saying that a boat has no place on a mountain. A boat needs the sea to fulfil its purpose. Then she speaks of her need to seek new places, new people and new experiences...'

The old man took the book back and ran his fingertips over the words embossed on the cover.

'To this day, my anguish is undiminished. Perhaps if I had dealt with my daughter differently, she might not have rebelled and left in the way that she did. Or at least, she might have left in less dissolute company.'

At this point Dante stopped, seemingly embarrassed by the openness with which he bared his soul to the stranger sitting opposite him. He hung his head remorsefully and said,

'Hindsight is a fine thing, is it not? We can all look back and say, "If only".'

Jubanne Melis Puddu was not satisfied for the explanation to end there. 'What do you mean by "dissolute company" Who did your daughter leave with?'

Dante removed his spectacles and rubbed his eyes until they were red. Swallowing hard he said, 'During the summer of 1965, when she was seventeen, some outsiders came to the village. And that was the beginning of the end of Leonora's life in Montacciolo.'

CHAPTER 4

The village buzzed with speculation. Some strange people had moved into the old place on the western boundary – that house which had been empty since the charcoal-burner had died over a decade ago. His son had never lived there. Like so many of the younger generation, he'd left home to find work elsewhere and nobody had seen him since his father's funeral. The house had been for sale for a while, but it was nigh on impossible to sell houses in a village like Montacciolo. All the villagers lived in homes handed down from generation to generation, or in houses that belonged to relatives. They had neither the need nor the money to purchase property – most didn't even pay rent.

It was unheard of that anybody without a family connection to the village should choose to spend the summer there. What was more, the people who had arrived were unlike anyone who had been seen in Montacciolo before, and therefore they were greeted with acute mistrust. They were odd types – four men who wore their hair long, like women, and four women who walked around with necklaces and bracelets made of flowers. They all wore peculiar, wildly patterned clothes.

Dante Bacchetti was not just Montacciolo's schoolmaster. He was also its deputy mayor – a position burdened with far more responsibility than it should have been. The mayor, never having mastered the art of reading and writing, did very little. It was therefore Dante who was charged not only with all deputy-mayoral duties, but also with most of the mayoral duties – and as Montacciolo was such a small place, he also had the role of head of the council, general secretary, treasurer, and when necessary, policeman and tax collector.

Some villagers afforded Dante the title of 'King of Montacciolo', which he considered to be an affectionate nickname. In fact, he played on it, always making a little joke about the onerous responsibility of Royal governance, whenever anybody said it to his face. It was a given that 'King' Dante should go and make contact with these new people and to see what they were about.

As he approached the charcoal-burner's house, dressed in his best suit and armed with a clip-board, a pen and three sheets of council-headed notepaper, he heard music and stopped for a moment to listen. It was rather lovely – just a guitar and women's voices – unusual, but so pretty and melodious. He found its source to be a group of four of the newcomers, who were sitting in a circle on the grass outside the house. They stopped when they saw him, clearly surprised to see a man in such a formal suit carrying a clip-board, but initially they were not unwelcoming.

'Good morning. Can I help you?' Said the man with the guitar. Dante introduced himself with a formal flourish and explained that he had come to take their names. Immediately their expressions changed from friendly to suspicious.

'Why would you want to take our names?' Asked one of the women. 'We're only here on holiday. Do you always take people's names when they're visiting?'

'Well,' explained Dante, who was already feeling wrong-footed, 'As nobody has been here on holiday before who was not in some way related to one of our residents, we have no precedent to go by.'

The group, although maintaining their expressions of mistrust also looked at him with an air of amusement, as though standing there in his best suit and holding a clip-board, he was some kind of joke. It was then that a further two people emerged from the house and were told the reason for Dante's visit.

'He's come to take out names, has he?' Said one of the new arrivals. 'What's the problem, Signore-from-the-council? Do you think we're her to cause mayhem in your little village?'

Although these people did not seem to be physically threatening, this out-numbering made Dante extremely uncomfortable. He cleared his throat to steady his voice and said in his best official tone, 'The requirement for your names is purely an administrative matter – something which is necessary in case of emergencies, or if anything was to happen to any of you.'

'Such as?'

'An accident, for instance. Or say if you got lost along one of the mountain tracks, which is not unheard of. Even locals get lost out there. And much of the terrain is extremely tricky. Then we'd send a search party out, but they'd have to know who they were looking for.'

Satisfied that he'd given the best answer he possibly could under the circumstances, Dante took out his pen. 'So, if you wouldn't mind...'

'Actually, we would mind,' said the man who had just come out of the house, crossing his arms defensively across his chest. 'Because who we are, or what we're doing here, is our business, not the business of some busybody from the council. We're here with the house owner's permission. Feel free to contact him and ask him. We're doing nothing illegal. We're not being a nuisance. We're just *being*, and last time I checked, that was still allowed.'

There followed a very heavy moment of silence, eventually broken by one of the women.

'I don't mind giving you my name,' she said, although Dante sensed an undertone of mockery in her voice. 'It's Wild Rose of the Emerald Island, but you can call me Wild Rose.'

'And mine's Earth Star,' added another, and her tone was similarly derisive. 'I'm originally from planet Zhog.'

'I'm Mighty Oak,' smirked the man with the guitar. 'Protégé of the Great Yambini of Kabul.'

Dante forced a smile and hovered his pen above his clip-board, aware that now he was definitely being treated as a joke.

'Well? Aren't you going to write our names down, Signore-from-the council?'

Feeling that he had no other option, Dante wrote down the names he was given – Wild Rose, Earth Star, Mighty Oak, Moonbeam, Raindrop and Forest Wolf. He was told that Silver Fox and Bigfoot had gone for a walk and wouldn't be back until later.

Then, as he could think of nothing else to say which wouldn't lead to an even more awkward situation, Dante thanked the visitors for their time, wished them a pleasant sojourn in Montacciolo and hurried away from the charcoal-burner's house feeling somewhat embarrassed by the fact that he had dealt with the situation so badly.

What had he been thinking, turning up in an official capacity like that? He must have looked such a pompous prig. If he'd just sauntered up to the house to give a friendly, welcoming hello and hadn't worn that suit things would have got off to a more favourable start. The newcomers would have told him their names (their *real* names) just as ordinary people did in the course of a normal introduction. The clip-board was definitely a mistake. Anyway, what was done was done, and it was too late to change it now.

An extraordinary general meeting of the council took place that evening in the village bar and was attended by all the Montacciolani. What had Dante found out about the strangers, the villagers wanted to know. Of course, there was very little Dante could tell them, apart from the names they had given him, which clearly were false. However, he said, he saw no reason to consider these people a threat. Perhaps it would be best just to leave them alone to enjoy their holiday in peace.

The Montacciolani were not impressed by Dante's reconnaissance mission, although it was generally agreed that the strangers should be given a wide berth. But when someone suggested that the two commerces in the village should refuse to serve them, the proprietor of the bar and bakery, and the shopkeeper who was also the postmaster, protested.

'You think I can afford to turn down a single paying customer?' Scoffed the bar owner. 'Perhaps I might if some of you lot paid your tabs. And if my wife didn't give some of you her bread for free, you'd go without.'

'The same applies for me,' grumbled the shopkeeper. 'You folk have never got two lire to rub together. You all beg for credit and I'm obliged to give it to you or you'd starve. I owe my suppliers so much money we're lucky we're getting any groceries at all up here.'

There followed a heated discussion concerning who owed what to whom and why it hadn't be paid, with lack of money being the overriding reason for the outstanding debts. The bickering was interrupted before it could get out of hand by the priest, Don Generoso, who had hitherto remained silent. When finally he spoke it was to say that he *could* not and *would* not refuse these unusual people entry into church. After all, had Christ not sought out society's outcasts? He further stated that he would be most displeased if any of his parishioners were rude to these newcomers within the House of God and reminded them that the parish of Montacciolo was in much the same dire financial position as its commerces. A handful of new worshippers putting a few extra coins into the collection tins over the summer would benefit them all. He then added that what happened outside the House of God was beyond his jurisdiction.

That first Sunday was rather tense. The congregation gathered, waiting for the arrival of the group, but nobody came, which rather irked Don Generoso. At the end of the service he ushered his flock out quickly and went directly to the charcoal-burner's house. Like Dante, initially he was given a friendly welcome, offered bergamot tea, which he refused, and invited to sit down, which he accepted.

The priest announced that he was there in his capacity as a most humble servant of God to welcome them to the village. He then explained that their attendance at Mass would be most appreciated.

The group thanked him for the offer but told him that they did not follow his religion, or believe in his God. Their religion – if that's what he wanted to call it- was the worship of nature and its inexhaustible bounty. Don Generoso was alarmed.

'You're Pagans?' He gasped.

'We don't feel the need to give ourselves any particular label because we are free of mind, spirit and soul,' said the man who had called himself Forest Wolf. 'But would it matter to you if we were? After all, countless elements of the Catholic Church are based on far more ancient beliefs, and it still incorporates many Pagan symbols and customs into its ceremonies.'

The priest spluttered impotently. His mouth had gone dry. He was totally unprepared for such a discussion, unlike the man seated before him, who was clearly very well-informed.

'The worship of nature in one form or other has been around since the dawn of mankind, but your church did not exist before the Edict of Milan issued in AD 313, and when it was established, one could argue that it was more of a business arrangement than a vehicle of faith,' continued Forest Wolf. 'And let's not ignore the fact that the Roman Catholic Church built many of its churches on former Pagan sites. Judging by the iconography and the wall-carvings, your own village church is one such example.'

'W-what?' Stammered Don Generoso.

'Your village church is very likely built on an ancient Pagan site. That's why there's a Triquetra above the door – those three interlaced arcs have a spiritual history going back millennia before the supposed birth of Christ.'

The priest leapt to his feet and crossed himself so fervently and so fast that his hand became a blur. Forest Wolf appeared to find this reaction rather amusing.

'Even that Sign you're making now is based on something which long precedes the crucifixion. The vertical and horizontal axes illustrate the cross of the zodiac, which represents the winter and summer solstices and the spring and autumn equinoxes.'

Confronted with this heathenish information all Don Generoso could think to do was to continue crossing himself and to call repeatedly upon the protection of The Father, The Son and the Holy Spirit, lest something of these Godless infidels should possess him.

'*In nomine Patris et Fillii et Spiritus Sancti. In nomine Patris et Fillii et Spiritus Sancti. In nomine Patris et Fillii et Spiritus Sancti...*'

Forest Wolf, who was very much enjoying the priest's discomfort, added, 'In any case, I find it morally abhorrent that an institution such as the Catholic Church should hoard obscene amounts of wealth whilst the majority of its followers live in need. Just look around you. Up here people are dirt poor and can barely afford to feed themselves, but they're still expected to feed your church collection tin on a Sunday. Are you familiar with the nineteenth-century English text by Alexander Hislop which argues that the Catholic Church is the Babylon of the Apocalypse?'

This was too much for Don Generoso. He left the charcoal-burner's house almost at a running pace and locked himself in the church, where he remained in devout prayer for the rest of the day.

The priest denied being the source of the rumour that the group were disciples of Satan, but once the speculation started, it spread like a pestilence. People began to allege all sorts of things about birds falling dead out of trees, missing cats, the cadavers of dogs being found nailed to fences and suchlike. One woman claimed that her white hen had turned black and laid an egg filled with blood. Another, believing herself possessed by some evil eye cast upon her by the godless newcomers, collapsed screaming and gnashing during Sunday Mass. Don Generoso was booked in for more exorcisms in one week than he had been over the past six months, which was an unforeseen way to bring a little more money into the parish coffers, so certainly not unwelcome.

Dante thought this speculation to be unhelpful and initially did his best to quash the hearsay, but it was like trying to return smoke to a fire. The superstitious chatter was out there, and a village such as Montacciolo, where nothing ever happened, was fertile ground for gossip.

Nevertheless, the newcomers remained in the charcoal-burner's house that summer, seemingly not put off by the hostile, suspicious villagers, or by their interactions with church and state.

CHAPTER 5

Dante sat back in his chair, the emotional strain of recounting the story of the arrival of the group showing clearly in his expression.

'So who were those people?' Asked Jubanne Melis Puddu.

'They called themselves "The Collective". They had no fixed base and spent their time travelling around Italy and overseas, staying wherever they could and with whoever would put them up. They didn't believe in the ownership of property, or in amassing material possessions. They would have done without money entirely, but of course, that was impossible in the real world. None of them had regular jobs. Some would take on casual work and the money would be pooled and they would all survive on that. They had no religious or political affiliations and didn't believe in the authority of any government, or agree with war.'

The old man paused to give his companion a moment to absorb the information. He then gave a little shrug of his shoulders. 'Of course, on the surface, none of that appears sinister. Marginal, perhaps. Over-optimistic, definitely. But many of those principles are sound. One could easily argue that money and material greed, religion and politics are the root of all the world's problems. And only a fool would claim that war is a good thing. But it quickly became clear that these noble beliefs were simply a front behind which lay something altogether more perverse.'

Gazing at a spot somewhere in the middle-distance, as though imagining the character he was about to describe was standing there, Dante went on, 'Their self-appointed leader was the man who had called himself Forest Wolf, although I was later to discover that his real name was Fernando. He was a charismatic individual, scholarly and informed, in his own way, and very controlling of those around him, who were drawn to him like moths to a candle.'

Dante sucked his breath in sharply through his teeth, which remained tightly clenched as he hissed, 'That wicked, immoral man seduced my daughter – not just in the literal sense of the word, but in other ways. Not only did he take her innocence, as if that was not enough. He plied her with alcohol and drugs and he filled her head with notions of rejecting society's rules, of living free from life's obligations. And being only seventeen, and dissatisfied with her life as it was, my daughter was ripe for being turned.'

Jubanne Melis Puddu saw a flash of anger break through the wretchedness of the old man's expression.

'It wasn't just Fernando. If anything, Leonora's friendship with the woman who called herself Wild Rose was even more damaging. That woman, I believe, was gypsy in origin – a swarthy type, garishly-attired and covered in baubles and bangles. It was she who gave my daughter a pendant in the shape of a rose. She too filled Leonora's head with upside down ideas. She convinced her that women were repressed by society, by marriage, by the morality imposed by the church. She said that all the policies of the government were weighted in the favour of men. And Leonora, being so young and impressionable, believed everything that she was told. Wild Rose turned Leonora against everything that my wife and I represented. Any affection or respect she had for us was eradicated by The Collective.'

A look of loss returned to Dante's face and he cast his eyes downwards.

'At the time, I reacted to this indoctrination with anger. How could they? I thought. How *dare* they take Leonora and wash her brain of everything my wife and I had ever taught her?

Worse than that, in fact. How could they make her believe that until that point everything in her life had been misguided? And for my wife, Ortensia, being a deeply religious woman, what torment it was to watch her only child be corrupted right before her eyes! This caused my dear wife unspeakable shame from which she never recovered.' The old man lowered his voice. 'Are you familiar with the term "free love"?'

The Sardinian nodded, 'Yes, I think so.'

'It was not a term with which I had been acquainted before that summer. But I soon learned that it was the underpinning precept of The Collective's way of life – although I would argue that the word "love" is an ugly misrepresentation in this context. They did not believe in monogamy, or marriage. Both the men and the women were allowed, I would go as far as to say *encouraged*, to take as many casual lovers as they pleased, both from within their group and from outside, and they were not discreet about this libertine behaviour. So you can well imagine that once this information filtered into the village, it took the gossip and speculation to a frenetic level.'

The old man made a grunting noise and wrinkled his nose in disgust.

'And that sensationalist fool of a priest, Don Generoso, did nothing to help the situation. Before that summer, his sermons had been so dull that he might as well have been reciting the telephone directory. But suddenly it was all impassioned readings from the Book of Revelations and any biblical verse which might be interpreted as having a sexual connotation. If there was any allusion to intercourse, or bestiality, or sodomy, he found it and he preached about it. It was the most obscene form of titillation, but of course people sat up and listened. Oh, how they listened! Men went either red, or white, and women fainted. I quite expected the four horsemen of the apocalypse to come charging through the church.'

Dante had talked himself breathless. He stopped and reached for a handkerchief in his pocket and dabbed the perspiration from his brow.

'I confess that despite the passing of time, it is still a very testing matter for me to recall,' he declared. 'Speaking of it is painful, even now, after all these years. The way Leonora, my child, my *only* child, was taken and used by those people and turned into little more than a sexual accessory to The Collective's depravity causes me physical agony. Thinking of it sends a shot of anguish into my heart.'

The old man pressed his hands against his chest, inhaling, holding and exhaling each breath slowly, as though trying to ease the pain he felt. 'And of course, Ortensia was deeply affected. For her, the torment was unbearable, and made all the worse by the gossip which began to spread through the village. It became that summer's sport for certain villagers to congregate at the boundaries of the charcoal-burner's house at night and to watch the spectacle of The Collective. What the group called their "ceremonies" were simply gratuitous acts of debauchery. There would be alcoholic drink and concoctions of goodness-knows-what passed around, with the women dancing bare-breasted around a bonfire, and lewd and Sapphic acts taking place right there in the open air. And Leonora in the midst of it, prostituting herself to the desires of whoever wanted her. Oh, it was a godsend for the gossips! The shame of this, for my wife and for myself was intolerable. How dearly we paid for our daughter's rebellion.'

Jubanne Melis Puddu listened in respectful silence as the old man continued his lament, describing how he and his wife became objects of ridicule. All manner of abuse was levelled at them. Dante had been forced to resign as deputy mayor and his council powers were removed from him.

'It was only the fact that it was up to the Ministry of Education and not to the villagers of Montacciolo that I retained my job as schoolmaster,' he said.

Now the old man's voice became full of hatred as he described how he awoke one morning to find that a most odious insult had been painted on the wall of the school. Somebody had taken the common affront of *Figlio di Puttana*, son of a whore, and amended it to *Padre di Puttana*, father of a whore.

'Following that heinous act, my poor wife, Ortensia, locked herself in and would no longer leave the house – not even to attend church on Sunday mornings, which had always been so important to her. It was a true cataclysm in our lives.'

Dante paused, sucked on his moustache and proceeded to assure his visitor, 'I feel I should point out that until that summer, Leonora's reputation was unblemished when it came to involvement with the opposite sex. Of that I am certain, for I would have known. In a small village such as Montacciolo, where everybody knows everybody else's business, any improper behaviour would have been brought to my attention immediately.'

'I worry about boys showing interest in my daughter,' concurred Jubanne Melis Puddu.

'As every good father should, particularly in this day and age, when society's moral boundaries are dissolving. But when it came to The Collective, there were no moral boundaries whatsoever.'

The big Sardinian sat forward and a dark scowl creased his forehead.

'If my own daughter was ever involved with such people, I would wring their necks,' he growled, cracking his knuckles, as though preparing himself for the task.

'That is easy for you to say, being a man of such imposing structure,' replied Dante shrinking back, for sitting there, dwarfing the chair on which he sat and in such a menacing pose, the

Sardinian looked very frightening indeed. But when the enormous man spoke again, there was no threat in his voice, just concern.

'Why did you allow your daughter to leave with those people?'

'*Allow?*' echoed Dante. 'As if my permission had anything to do with it and as if anything I could have said or done would have stopped her! Even if I'd locked her in her room, Leonora would have probably climbed out of the window and then accused me of unlawful imprisonment. It might seem like a terrible thing to say now, considering what happened subsequently, but when Leonora announced her intention to leave with The Collective, it was a *relief* to me. My wife begged her not to go, but I did not say anything to discourage her. Of course, I did say to her that if things didn't go the way she hoped, and if she ever needed to come back home, she could. But even that she threw back in my face. She said that she would sooner die than spend one more minute of her life in Montacciolo, and that when *I* died, I should not expect her to return for my funeral. I fear that those words might have been uncannily prophetic.'

The clock struck seven as the old man finished his sentence and he seemed relieved to halt the conversation there. He rose to his feet and went to see to the soup.

'You will be staying to dinner, won't you?' he said to his guest as he stirred the pot. 'There's plenty enough for two and we still have so much to talk about. Could I ask you to set the table? You'll find spoons in the basket on the dresser.'

Before long the men were sitting opposite one another with two bowls of hot soup steaming before them.

'*Buon appetito!*' Exclaimed Dante. 'I apologise for the fact that there's no bread. Since my dear Ortensia passed away I have had to learn to cook for myself, but unfortunately my culinary talents do not stretch to baking my own bread. I did have

47

a go, but my loaves came out of the oven as hard as house-bricks.' He paused for a moment and contemplated the soup. 'Leonora, on the other hand, was rather skilled in the kitchen. I hoped that one day she would make something of her talents, but I fear that they were utterly wasted.'

The Sardinian seemed untroubled by the absence of bread and began to eat his soup.

'Forgive me,' said Dante. 'I fear that I have commandeered the conversation, and I would ask you excuse me for that. You were describing to me the arrival of the young woman whom you presume to be my daughter.'

Jubanne Melis Puddu nodded, but his answer missed the point. 'Yes. She was a very capable employee. She ran the restaurant as though she'd been doing it for years.'

'That must have been a relief for both your wife and yourself, considering the difficulties you faced with staffing. But you mentioned certain feelings earlier; your reaction on first meeting this young woman?'

The big man hesitated, as though he was counting back through different events and trying to pick the right one to recall.

'Yes,' he said at last. 'Those feelings I'd had when I first met her wouldn't go away. They grew so big that it felt as though my head would burst.'

'Did you act on those feelings?'

'No, no! Another man might have tried to take advantage, but I kept myself under control. But then everything changed when Corrado came along.'

'Who's Corrado?'

'A young man who worked at our guesthouse.'

'Well then,' said Dante, blowing on his soup to cool it. 'I suppose you had better tell me about Corrado.'

CHAPTER 6

Jubanne had always been extremely fond of the boy to whom he was related, not by blood, but through Signora Melis Puddu's side of the family. Corrado would often come to help at Villa Zuannicca, doing odd jobs for a bit of pocket money. Whenever he needed an extra pair of hands on his boat, Jubanne would call upon young Corrado. The previous summer the lad had worked as a waiter in their restaurant and had saved all his money to purchase a Vespa.

School had finished early that year for Corrado, for he had just sat his final high school exams. There was talk of him continuing his education at the university in Cagliari if his grades were up to scratch, which they were bound to be. He wanted to study engineering.

Corrado was a cheerful youth, blessed with an affable manner which people often commented on. And to cap it all, he was good-looking, with a big, white-toothed smile to contrast his crop of curly black hair. He was tall, but still fresh-faced and boyish. He hadn't quite finished filling out yet.

Of course, he noticed Nora immediately, and there was no mistaking that he was in awe of her. Jubanne observed, trying to discern whether the attraction was reciprocated, but Nora was just friendly towards him. She ordered him around and teased him fondly, usually about the fact that he didn't have a girlfriend, like a big sister would a little brother, and Corrado took it all in good humour.

It was not long after Nora's arrival that Jubanne was resting in his favourite shady spot under the fig tree. From there, he could see in through the open dining room windows. He didn't have a full view of the room, but just enough to glimpse Nora and Corrado passing as they went about their work. The lunch service had come to an end and they were busy clearing the tables and re-setting them for dinner. Jubanne could hear little snippets of their conversation over the sounds of crockery being stacked and the clinking of glassware.

Nora came into his direct line of sight, although she had not noticed that he was outside because she was three-quarters turned away from him. She was folding napkins. Jubanne's eyes fixed on her. Her hair was tied into a single braid, as thick as a rope, and she was wearing another of those pretty floral dresses. The thin fabric fluttered as she moved.

How utterly wonderful you are, Nora, thought Jubanne, although in that instant he was so mesmerised that he might have said it out loud.

For a moment he was tempted to find some excuse to go inside and lend a hand, just so that he could be closer to her, then he told himself that he must not. The way he felt must stay hidden from view, so he too must stay hidden from view. He shrank back a little further into the shade of the fig tree. If Nora came out onto the terrace and spotted him, he would pretend to be asleep.

But then Corrado must have said something which Nora found funny, because her laughter rang out through the open window and rippled through Jubanne. He craned his neck for a better look inside the dining room. Nora was play-chasing the boy around one of the tables, flicking a napkin at him and still laughing. Jubanne clutched his stomach as a clammy, prickly feeling began to percolate through him. What could Corrado have said that might have amused Nora quite so much? She was still laughing, and it was bothering Jubanne more than was reasonable.

There had been no obvious signs of sexual attraction between these two beautiful young people before this moment, but could that last? Was that initial sibling-like affinity now morphing into something more? It was not possible that Corrado could be blind to Nora's allure; nor was it likely that Nora would be impervious to such a good-looking youth. Perhaps what Jubanne was witnessing was the opening scene of a summer romance, or more, even? He could hardly bear to think about it. Drops of sweat began to trickle down the back of his neck. Now Corrado no longer felt like the amenable boy of whom Jubanne had always been so fond, but like a rival – a rival against whom he couldn't compete. This thought boomed through his brain and would not be quiet.

Jubanne would be the first to admit that his experience with women was limited. He'd never been a ladies' man. He'd had a couple of girlfriends before getting together with his wife, but those were more innocent times back then. You'd have to court a girl for months before she'd even hold your hand, and then you'd have to (at the very least) mention marriage before she'd agree kiss you, and then there were always conditions attached, as well as watchful mammas, and papás who'd kill you for even daring to breathe too close to their daughters. Trying to spend any time alone with a girl required planning, subterfuge, and a minimum of two accomplices to agree to give you a cover story. It wasn't like that now. Things were a lot more liberal. You couldn't go into the local town at night without tripping over a necking couple.

He heard Nora say, 'Do you want to go out somewhere this afternoon?' and Jubanne's heart stopped. But Corrado replied that he'd promised to run an errand for his mother. The relief was so intense that it was only then that Jubanne realised he had been holding his breath.

How he would love to be able to say, 'Do you want to go out somewhere this afternoon?' and for Nora to reply, 'Yes.'. They could drive up to that beauty spot by the lighthouse and look out across the sea to Isola Spargi, or even better, he could take her out in his boat.

Then he felt guilty for thinking about it, and was glad that he felt that guilt. It was proof that he had a hold on his feelings. Imagining Nora that way was wrong. Think of your wife, Jubanne, he said to himself. *Think of your wife.* He did, and it was very pleasant. He thought about her that first evening when they'd gone to the dance. She'd worn that blue satin dress. Jubanne paused, lost in the memory. Oh, that beautiful blue satin dress. That dress would look lovely on Nora. She'd fill it out differently. Her legs were longer. She did have very lovely legs, made all the more enticing by the rose pendant on her ankle and those sandals of shoelace leather. And her hair, he pictured flowing loose, like on that first day she'd arrived. *Stop, Jubanne, STOP!*

He told himself to turn his mind to something else, yet his imagination kept coming back Nora. But was there really anything so wrong in *thinking* about her? A bit of fantasy never hurt anybody, and he wouldn't think of anything crude – just the pleasure of Nora's company and being able to look at her, to kiss her at most. He could give himself a time limit. Five minutes; no, ten. Yes, ten was reasonable. Jubanne glanced down at his watch. He had until seven minutes to three.

Oh, lovely, lovely Nora. She was perfection in every way. Any man would be lucky to have her attention. Jubanne couldn't help but wonder whether those thoughts strayed into Nora's mind too. Did she fantasise about him – that big, strong, older man?

Then reality turned up and brought vinegar to the party. What was the likelihood of a fabulous young woman like Nora being interested in him in that way? Who was he trying to kid? His fantasy came to an abrupt end, and it was only twelve minutes to three.

Jubanne made his way to his bedroom, which he knew would be empty as his wife was in the kitchen planning the week ahead's menu with the cook. He took off his shirt and stood before the mirror to inspect himself.

Although he knew he wasn't ugly, nor had anyone ever told him he was handsome, not even his wife as far as he could recall. She told him he looked smart when he put on his suit, but that was only for weddings and funerals. People were usually just impressed by how big he was, and their comments were the closest he ever got to a compliment. He'd always been a strong man, the sort of fellow who people called upon when something heavy needed moving. Over the years that had become a bit of a badge of honour. In his twenties he'd been crowned regional arm-wrestling champion four years running. He could easily have won a few more titles, but was satisfied with the glory of four wins, and he'd met his wife by then, so he had better things to do than arm-wrestling. He still had the medals in a drawer somewhere.

Jubanne had been over two meters tall since his late teens, and thickset with it. That physique came from his maternal side. Family legend, according to his grandmother, Nonna Maria-Annoriana, stated that their origins had been Sicilian, and that their Phoenician and Byzantine blood had been mixed with the Vandal blood of the fifth century invaders, then subsequently with that of the Viking marauders who had landed in the year 860. Jubanne's impressive size had been the consequence of various episodes of land-grab, rape and pillage; but the result was that although he felt as Sardinian as Cannonau wine, he was far more Nordic in appearance that Mediterranean.

He turned his attention back to the mirror. To tell the truth, he'd been in better shape. Years of good guesthouse food and wine had thickened his middle, and his sweet tooth hadn't helped the situation. If he held in his paunch, drew his shoulders

53

back and puffed out his chest, he didn't look too shabby, although admittedly some angles were more flattering than others. Maybe he should work on getting a bit of a sun tan, but he wasn't blessed with skin that browned well. He probably had either the Vandals or the Vikings to thank for that. Usually he went from white to red and ended up a slightly patchy pink, apart from his forearms, which did go brown. He moved to a position where he could look at his reflection over his shoulder. Holy Carrots! When had all that hair sprouted on his back?

Jubanne got dressed again and went downstairs where he found his wife alone in the kitchen taking an inventory. He stood watching her, trying to arrange the words of the question he wanted to ask in his head. She didn't notice him at first, but when she did, he startled her.

'Good God, Jubanne! Must you creep up on me like that?' She exclaimed. 'How does a man your size move about so quietly?'

Jubanne apologised. It was a question his wife had asked countless times. He didn't do it on purpose. Although he was such a big chap, he was light on his feet. 'Sorry. I didn't mean to scare you.'

His wife picked up the inventory which she had dropped and said, 'What is it?'

'Do you think-' he began; but that wasn't the right way to phrase it. He needed more than just a 'yes' or 'no' answer, so he made a second attempt, 'What do you think-' but still, the question felt awkward and he came to a halt.

'Is this urgent, Jubanne? I have a thousand different things to do.'

Before he lost his nerve entirely, Jubanne blurted, 'What do you think about the way I look?'

His wife peered into his face for a few seconds before replying, 'I think you look all right. Why? Are you feeling unwell?'

'No, no. I didn't mean it like that.'

'What do you mean then?'

'I mean, well, I suppose I mean, do you think I'm a good-looking fellow, or not?'

Signora Melis Puddu half frowned and half laughed.

'Where's that come from, Jubanne?'

'It's just something I'm wondering. It's not a hard question, is it?'

'Well, no. It's just a bit odd. You've never asked me anything like that before.'

'So, what do you think?'

'I think you look fine.'

'Just "fine"?'

'Are you fishing for a compliment? Do you want me to tell you're the handsomest man in the world?'

'I'd settle for the truth.'

'You look good to me, and you always have done.'

'So you thought I was good-looking when we met?'

Signora Melis Puddu paused to consider this for longer than Jubanne would have hoped.

'Your size was the first thing I noticed about you, and I think that's probably what everybody notices. You're hard to miss.'

'It was just my size then?'

'No, of course it wasn't just that. Lots of things appealed to me, but they were far more than skin deep. I'm not so shallow as to judge you, or anybody else, just on appearance. What attracted me when we first met was your dependability, and I consider that to be far more important than having movie-star looks.'

'Dependability,' repeated Jubanne flatly, unable to disguise the note of disappointment in his voice.

At this point it was clear that Signora Melis Puddu considered the matter resolved and that she had greater concerns than her husband's sudden silly insecurities.

'I'm going into town to pick up some clams and prawns because we're serving a seafood *fregola* tonight. Nora suggested it and I think it's a good idea. I'd probably better get more semolina too,' she said.

'Do you want me to drive you in?'

'No thanks,' she smiled, giving his hand an affectionate brush with her fingertips. 'It's kind of you to offer, but I'll drive myself. I'll take Nora with me. You stay here and keep an eye out for the sea-urchin seller. If he turns up whilst I'm gone, take everything he's got. Those *spaghetti al riccio di mare* were really popular last week. And if you get a moment, can you check the bathroom at the top of the stairs on the second floor? One of the guests reported a bit of a funny smell coming from the basin. Oh, and can you remember to change the beer kegs before this evening please? That group of Germans has been drinking the bar dry.'

As she gave him a quick kiss which didn't quite touch his cheek, Jubanne assured Signora Melis Puddu that he would see to everything. His foremost quality was, after all, 'dependability'. He also felt a certain relief that Nora would be spending the afternoon in town with his wife. It would keep her away from Corrado.

With so much to do throughout the tourist season, Jubanne rarely had much leisure time. Whenever he did have a spare hour or two, which was usually after lunch, during the hottest part of the day when most of the guests retired to the cool shade of their rooms, he liked to go to his boat. He didn't necessarily take the *Lavandula* out to sea, but he would give her a clean, polish the brass-work and wax the wood. He found keeping her ship-shape very therapeutic.

That day, which was a week or so after the exchange with his wife in the kitchen, he'd completed all his guesthouse duties. Signora Melis Puddu had said that she didn't need help with anything else until later, so he thought he'd take the boat out.

He wouldn't go far, just round the headland to give the *Lavandula* a bit of a run, and then maybe drop anchor and take a quick nap. But when he started the boat, she made a noise which wasn't right.

'Blasted Beetroots!' he muttered to himself, switching off the engine. He knew what the noise was. There was something stuck in the pump again, probably some piece of rubbish. Last time it had been one of those plastic slip-on shoes that the tourists left lying about on the beach and which were always getting washed into the sea. There would be no jaunt out onto the water today.

The pump wasn't a difficult thing to fix, as long as he had an extra pair of hands to help him lift it out of its housing and slot it back into place. Even a man of Jubanne's size couldn't manage it alone, because it wasn't just a matter of strength – he'd need four arms. Although it was Corrado's afternoon break, he wondered whether the boy might want to earn himself a bit of extra money helping him for an hour.

The Vespa was parked by the kitchen door, so Corrado couldn't be far, but there was no sign of him inside the guest-house. Thinking that he might have gone to the beach, Jubanne made his way down and found the only people there were a handful of crazy English roasting themselves lobster-red in the scalding sun.

When Jubanne asked his wife if she'd seen Corrado, she replied, 'He's gone for a swim.'

'I don't think so. I've just been down to the beach and he wasn't there.'

'He hasn't gone to our beach. He's gone to Baia Sanna, with Nora. That's where they've been going the past few days. It's nice and quiet down there.'

'Oh, Baia Sanna,' repeated Jubanne lightly. 'With Nora. That's nice.' The word 'nice' came out squeaky, high-pitched and hoarse.

He turned away, gnashing his teeth. *That's where they've been going the past few days?* How had he missed *that*?

Baia Sanna was the next cove along from Villa Zuannicca – the very place he'd intended to take the *Lavandula*. Lovely though it was, it wasn't a spot any tourists frequented, or any locals for that matter. There were only two ways to access the beach – one was by boat, and the other was via a precipitous cliff path, much of which was in perilous condition. Even the sign which read 'DANGER OF ROCK-FALL' had succumbed to the erosion. Its dented, rusted remains were visible at the bottom of the escarpment.

Jubanne hadn't ventured down to the Baia Sanna beach for years. The last time had been when the path was still more or less intact. He'd gone with his wife, but before they were married. They'd gone there for a bit of privacy – not that they'd done anything they shouldn't have. Those were different times and going too far before you were joined under the eyes of God, whether you believed in Him or not, really wasn't the thing to do.

But this recollection of the pleasant afternoon spent at Baia Sanna with his wife all those years ago bothered him and he felt that prickle at his nape again. Had Corrado and Nora gone there for a *bit of privacy*? The thought made his heckles rise. The pounding of his pulse in his temples was almost deafening. When he put his hands over his ears, it was worse, like a base drum thumping through his skull.

He hurried through the pinewoods which rose beside Villa Zuannicca, all the way up to the top of the cliff. The view from there across the sea was spectacular – deep blue dotted with little white sail boats. Isola Spargi was clearly visible in the distance. Under different circumstances, Jubanne would have stopped to admire it, but he was too distracted to pay any attention to a pretty vista. Instead, he followed the cliff edge for two

58

hundred meters, then veered off, down through the scrub where years before there had been a discernible path. Now that path was so overgrown that it had all but disappeared, but he could see the route that Corrado and Nora must have taken as some of the gorse branches had been snapped and the rough grass was trodden flat.

It was very, very hot that day. He could feel the sun blistering his skin. Jubanne's sweat-soaked clothes stuck to him and even his eyes were stinging with perspiration. It was as he reached to dry them with his shirt that a section of path crumbled under his foot and he almost went head over heels down the cliff-side. He was saved by a gorse bush, which hooked into him, breaking his fall and driving two dozen thorns into his arm. Jubanne cursed. Corrado was a reckless idiot for taking Nora along such a dangerous route.

He came to the part known as the 'Balzi', a series of huge stepped rocks which were relatively easy to clamber down, but he wasn't as nimble as he had been the last time he'd tackled them. Those few extra kilos he was carrying around his middle made a difference.

Finally he reached a narrow plateau, and it was from there that he first heard Nora and Corrado's voices. As he rounded a jagged outcrop, he saw them, some twenty to thirty meters below, swimming in the transparent shallows and knocking a ball back and forth between them. He stood and watched, half-hidden by the rocks, waiting to discern what their motive for this trip to the secluded beach was; but they weren't close, like two people fooling about. In fact, they were quite some distance apart and Nora was counting each time one of them hit the ball, as though she was keeping score. Jubanne observed them for what might have been ten or fifteen minutes, until they emerged from the water, towelled themselves dry and sat side-by-side on the sand. There was no physical contact between them at all.

Jubanne felt an overwhelming sense of relief. They really had just gone for a swim. It was all perfectly innocent. Good. Now they were sitting wrapped-up in their towels, so Nora wasn't giving Corrado the opportunity to ogle her half-naked. The yellow swimsuit she was wearing was a very modest full one, as opposed to one of those skimpy two-piece numbers that some women wore these days – not that Jubanne had anything against those. He was just glad that Nora wasn't wearing one.

Then Nora let her towel fall open and lay back with her arms stretched above her head. Was that provocative pose an invitation? Jubanne held his breath, 'Don't you dare touch her, you dirty little bastard,' he snarled, but Corrado took no notice of Nora reclining so seductively. The boy had turned his attention to something in the sand, which he began to dig out with a stick.

A short time later they were both on their feet and getting dressed. They gathered their things and made their way off the beach. Jubanne scrambled back up the cliff and hurried back to the guesthouse. Corrado and Nora arrived at Villa Zuannicca soon after him. He heard her say, 'See you later,' and head up the stairs to her room.

'Ah, Corrado, there you are,' smiled Jubanne, feigning surprise. 'I've been looking for you. I was wondering whether you could give me a hand on the boat tomorrow afternoon. There's a little problem to fix and I thought that after it's sorted, we could take her out. I'll pay you for your time, of course. What do you reckon? I thought Nora might like to come too.'

Corrado agreed to help and said he'd mention it to Nora.

'Splendid!' Grinned Jubanne, patting the boy on the shoulder. 'After the lunch service is finished then. Shall we say around half past two?'

He walked off with a spring in his step, feeling very pleased with himself. He knew exactly where they'd take the *Lavandula* the following day. Less than half an hour out, to the North of

Isola Spargi, was a horseshoe-shaped reef where the water was shallow and warm. It was an excellent swimming place and if they were lucky they might even catch sight of a few dolphins.

Jubanne fetched himself a drink of lemon tea with crushed ice and mint and went to his shady spot under the fig tree where he sat thinking about the boat trip, although in his fantasy, there was no Corrado. It was just him and Nora. She wasn't wearing her modest yellow swimsuit, but one of those barely-there two-pieces made of nothing more than four tiny triangles of fabric – the sort which could be undone, top or bottom, by the pulling of a cord.

If the wind was right, he'd switch off the engine and unfurl the sail. He imagined asking Nora whether she wanted to steer the boat, and how he would put his arms around her and guide the rudder with her. How good it would feel to clasp her around that slender waist, and to feel her body against his. And she in turn would feel his strength, the solidity of his big physique. Then they would reach the horseshoe reef, anchor the *Lavandula* and dive into the water, naked perhaps...

Jubanne's reverie was shattered by his wife, who appeared looking displeased.

'Corrado just told me you offered to take him and Nora out on your boat tomorrow.'

Jubanne replied with an indistinct, 'Hmm?' as though he hadn't quite heard and took a nervous sip of his tea.

'Well, did you?'

'Did I what?'

'Did you say you'd take Corrado and Nora out on your boat tomorrow afternoon?'

'Uh...I only said we'd give her a quick run out after we've sorted the pump. There's something stuck in it. Might be one of those plastic shoes again. I was thinking, we should probably put a sign up asking people not to leave them on the beach-'

'Never mind the plastic shoes!' Interrupted Signora Melis Puddu. 'Did you say you'd take Nora too?'

'Er...I might have mentioned it. Anyway, would it be a problem if I did?'

Jubanne smiled, but he knew it didn't come out quite right. It was more of a graceless grimace, and it made his wife all the more cross.

'Explain to me why you would take them out instead of your own children, who you know very well would love a trip out on the boat and have been looking forward to you to taking them for weeks.'

'It's different.'

'Different how?'

'Well, for a start the children aren't helping me fix the pump. And if I were to take the children, they would need constant supervision and we could only go out for a short time, so they'd probably sulk all the way home and for a whole week after that.'

Then his wife read his mind, which really was a most inconvenient talent of hers.

'All you want to do is to leer at Nora in a swimsuit.'

Jubanne made a strangled noise which expressed utter indignation. '*Leer?* What? Don't be so ridiculous! What's got into you? If I want to see a woman in a swimsuit all I have to do is to walk to the edge of the terrace and look at our own beach.'

Signora Melis Puddu's eyes narrowed, as though she was focusing her gaze like a searchlight right inside her husband's head.

'Watch yourself, Jubanne,' she warned. 'If I catch you messing about I'll feed you your own balls for breakfast.'

Jubanne knew better than to argue when he was in the wrong, so he got up and stomped away.

Despite his wife's disapproval, he did take Nora and Corrado out on his boat the following day. The conditions were perfect, with hardly a ripple on the sea. At the horse shoe reef they were delighted by the spectacle of a pod of dolphins frolicking in the water. Nora and Corrado stripped down to their bathing suits and jumped in, but Jubanne remained aboard the *Lavandula* fully-clothed and just watched them swim. He'd lost his nerve. There they were, all youthful, brown-skinned and athletic. And there he was, a big, old, lumbering lump with sunburn, a spare tyre and a hairy back. He felt like an idiot.

CHAPTER 7

Leonora's departure from Montacciolo with The Collective could not have come too soon for Dante. At last, after the most nightmarish summer of his life, he could breathe again – although the anger that raged inside him made it feel as though he was breathing fire.

Ortensia remained deeply traumatised and was staunchly refusing to leave the house, but Dante was determined that he would gather what was left of his dignity and resume as much of a normal life as possible. He didn't have any choice in the matter. He had to make a living and couldn't afford to lose the only job he still had. He was already feeling the pinch from the loss of his modest council salary.

There was no hiding from the fact that the villagers treated him differently. Nobody referred to him as 'King' any more. Whenever he walked through the village, some Montacciolani avoided him altogether by disappearing into their houses; others cast their eyes sideways and whispered things to each other behind their hands. Amidst this pervasive antipathy, the best Dante could hope for was a false, watery smile; or a perfunctory greeting; or some banal observation on the weather.

He was in no mood for small-talk, anyway. His outrage was so all-encompassing that it was hard to separate the fury he felt towards his daughter, from that which he felt towards The Collective, from that he felt towards the Montacciolani. It burned inside him, like a swarm of a million hornets, where every individual hornet represented a wrongdoing, an insult, an affront, an accusation, a let-down – from the smallest irritation to the most egregious assault on his dignity and reputation.

Night after night he awoke drenched in sweat, frantically beating at his arms and legs, convinced that he was being consumed by insects.

He felt betrayed by the villagers whose children he had educated and whose mundane little lives he had kept running for so long. Who had successfully campaigned for the connection of Montacciolo to the electrical grid? Dante Bacchetti. Who had ensured that the roads remained in a usable state of repair and had overseen the clearance of snow and fallen trees year after year? Dante Bacchetti. And who had organised the Christmas lights and the village festivals? -The very same, Dante Bacchetti.

All of these things, one could argue, were expected of a school teacher, deputy mayor and councillor, but they made up just a part of the infinite number of services which he had undertaken for the people of Montacciolo. He couldn't walk from his house to the piazza without somebody asking him for something.

There had been countless eleemosynary acts – school supplies purchased from his own purse for children whose parents couldn't afford them; communion and confirmation celebrations organised by him for families in abject need; and a thousand other charitable gestures. How many stricken and injured Montacciolani had he loaded into his own car at any hour of the day or night and driven down into town to the emergency doctor in town? And not to be forgotten were the monetary loans made to villagers in desperate circumstances, many of which he had never claimed back. He could go on *ad infinitum.*

And for each of these selfless acts, what recompense had he ever received? It would not have taken much, Dante surmised, to make some small gesture of gratitude. He wasn't talking about anything which involved a financial expenditure, of course. There were so many ways to say thank you which cost nothing at all. It would have been nice to have opened his door to find an appreciative Montacciolano with a basket of blueberries, which grew in such abundance on the mountainside every year that many spoiled on the bushels; or a pannier of hazelnuts; or a posy of flowers; or even just, 'Thank you, Dante, we really appreciate what you've done for us.'

Yet this, *this* was the reward for years of service? To be turned into an object of mockery and mistrust – a pariah.

But what else might he have expected from such backward folk? These were the sorts of people who needed a scapegoat to distract themselves from the endless tedium of their isolated lives. Maybe it was a way for them to feel better about their own transgressions. There were plenty of unsavoury things that went on behind closed doors in Montacciolo. It was no secret that Pierino Ciocca shared the same father as his own mother. Those bruises on the bar owner's wife weren't all from slip and falls down the bakery steps. And Germano Pozzo, despite being innocent of any involvement in the crime, was still commonly referred to as 'the rapist's brother'.

Nevertheless, Dante knew that the Montacciolani were also a fickle lot. Whenever they found an object of mockery, hatred, or mistrust, they'd mock and hate and mistrust them for a while, then they'd get bored and move onto some new distraction. With a bit of luck before too long there would be a child born out of wedlock and nobody would own up to the impregnation; or there would be more than one potential father. That should change the direction in which the tongues wagged.

There had been an incident one night in 1963 when a newborn baby had been left on the church steps, but nobody had noticed, and when the priest had gone to open the church the following morning, the infant was dead. Initially it was not known whose the baby was, or even whether it had been left by one of the Montacciolani. Speculation abounded. A week or so later a girl called Tina, one of Dante's pupils aged only fifteen, was found hanged in the chestnut woods. Nobody had suspected a pregnancy, but two and two was put together, and whichever way anybody looked at it, the result was four. This was confirmed by the doctor who examined the girl's body and found evidence of recent *partus*. The identity of the baby's father had never come to light. Dante put the tragic saga of Tina and the baby out of his head. Now was not the time to be thinking about all that sorry mess.

Although things could never go back to the way they were, Dante knew that the scandal over Leonora and The Collective would blow over eventually. Hopefully then he could return to some sort of bearable existence.

He had come to terms with having been stripped of his deputy mayoral and council duties, and now part of him was glad not to be burdened with all the petty administration. There had been a hastily-organised election to appoint his replacement, which succeeded in being hasty, but not in being organised. It had been impossible to decide on a clear winner, despite the hundred and fifty or so votes being counted and re-counted.

Dante himself had abstained from voting, not through any feeling of sour grapes, but rather because there was nobody he could bring himself to vote for. On learning that his former roles were to be shared between three men because no single candidate wanted to shoulder all the responsibilities alone, Dante had tried not to laugh out loud. Those three stooges, whose ignorance knew no limits, couldn't compile a shopping list between them – not even during the half hour in the morning when they were relatively sober. It wouldn't be long before things fell apart. The village would be in administrative chaos by Christmas. Maybe then the Montacciolani would appreciate all the work he had done for them. Maybe one day they might even thank him, but he wasn't holding his breath.

Dante returned to his only remaining job, promising himself that that the personal struggles he faced would have no negative effect on the professionalism of his teaching. That would be unfair on his students and there was no reason why their educations should suffer. Tempting though it might be to make the children pay for the behaviour of their parents – and a schoolmaster of lesser moral fibre might well have been swayed to do it – he must lead by example. After all, would that not be a version of the situation in which he found himself, as the innocent party being made to pay for the sins of another?

Dante had painted over the offensive graffiti and was relieved that it had not reappeared, either on the schoolhouse wall or anywhere else in the village. Although he had no proof, he had a good idea of who the perpetrator was – Enrico, a former pupil.

It was the irregular joining-up of the double 't' in *Padre di Puttana*, and the way the author had capitalised the 'p's in a poorly-proportioned way and with a slight backwards slant that aroused Dante's suspicions. He never forgot a pupil's handwriting and he recognised those foibles in style as Enrico's. Still, he had no appetite to start going round levelling accusations which he couldn't back up with proper evidence; and even if Enrico admitted to it, or it could be proven, there would be no consequences. Whoever had daubed those pithy words on the wall, whether it was Enrico or some other wag, had made their point and he hoped that they were satisfied with their moment of glory. At least the spelling had been correct. Praise be for small mercies, thought Dante.

Keen for the new school year to feel like a fresh start, Dante spent the two weeks before the beginning of term sprucing up the schoolhouse. He sanded down all the desks, including his own, and gave them each a gleaming coat of varnish, then ensured that all the chairs were in a good state of repair and knocked in a few nails where necessary. He took the dusty and sun-yellowed old pictures down from the walls and replaced them with new ones, all of which he had acquired the previous year, but had never gone to the effort of putting up.

He was particularly pleased with a large topographical chart of the Apennine mountain range. This detailed map depicted the land contours and the heights of various landmarks, as well as showing the names of every town and village, including Montacciolo. The highest mountains were illustrated in the palest green, with deepening tones for the lower slopes and valleys, all latticed with fine blue lines to represent the rivers and torrents. Dante stood back to admire his new chart. It was as beautiful as it was instructive.

However, the beginning of term was not the new start he had hoped for. Even the smallest children, those with no comprehension of the summer's scandal, had been turned against him by their parents. It was a disgusting thing, thought Dante. Little minds could be so easily twisted.

Those who had never caused any trouble before misbehaved. The younger ones aped him and pulled faces behind his back. They flicked ink and spat little missiles of spit-sodden blotting paper across the classroom. The older ones played more elaborate practical jokes and invented offensive nicknames for him, drawing upon more imagination than they ever found for their essays. They tormented him and tried his patience in every way imaginable.

Dante Bacchetti, having been the recipient of innumerable beatings from his Jesuit schoolmasters, often delivered for as little as an error in spelling or calculation, was a staunch opponent of corporal punishment within the school establishment. At its worst, he believed it to be a sadistic abuse of power. At best, it was a symptom of incompetent teaching. Frequently it was a combination of both. Dante had written several articles on the subject for various academic publications. One had even made its way into a national press, onto page twelve of the *Resto del Carlino* newspaper, along with a photograph of schoolmaster who wasn't him.

But by the end of the first week of term Dante's principle of non-violence was being seriously tested. As the second week drew to a close, he would happily have taken a leather belt, or a whip, or a club studded with rusty spikes to those little demons. Drowning in boiling oil, flaying and burying alive and various inventive methods of suffocation had also crossed his mind.

When one pupil thought it a great jape to pull down the new topographical chart of the Apennine mountain range from the classroom wall, badly tearing all four the corners in the process, Dante grabbed him and shook him, then threatened to nail him to the blackboard by his ears. His outburst was met with derision by the other students. Maestro Bacchetti dismissed his class early that day.

Dante already felt shattered by the ordeal of the summer, but these daily sessions, which were no more than exercises in self-control and behavioural containment, wore him down further. This exhaustion made him bad-tempered. His fuse was short and it took only the smallest spark to light his touch paper. He seriously considered applying for a new post elsewhere, a long way away from Montacciolo, but Ortensia wouldn't hear of moving away. She cried about it for days and it worsened her fragile condition. Dante wished he'd never mentioned it.

Faced with no other choice, Dante continued with his everyday routine, trying (and often failing) to do his best. Rather than diminishing his anger, this charade of trying to assume a normal life was making it worse. He questioned the wisdom of having returned to the village all those years ago; of having given up a good job with prospects to replace it with what was little more than charity work and paid less than a third as much as before. Such a foolish sacrifice to have made!

He felt his contempt spread to Montacciolo itself. It was not just the inhabitants he despised now, but the village itself. Every grim grey stone that made up every horrid little house; every crooked, grubby, rat-infested alleyway; even the church offended him.

All his campaigning to save the heritage of the village and all those trips to the Regional Council to beg for funds on behalf of villagers who couldn't afford to have their shoes repaired, let alone their houses – what a waste of time and energy all that had been! And it wasn't just the government he had been obliged to shake a begging bowl at. It was *he* who had secured the emergency payment from the diocese for repairs to the church roof. That should have been the priest's job, but that Bible-blabbering imbecile had been too busy praying that he could borrow enough buckets to catch the rain to try to do anything practical to deal with the leaks.

Now Dante did not care if this pit of a place didn't survive; if within a generation it was left inhabited only by those too old, too drink-addled or too stupid to leave.

Maybe there would be an earthquake again, twice the force of the quake of 1940. That could see off the last few stragglers; finish the job that the first quake started. Tremors were not uncommon throughout the region. They rarely did more than knock off the odd chimney pot. People regarded them as nothing more than an occasional annoyance and something to talk about for a few days. It was a different matter that Sunday morning in June of 1940. At around eleven-thirty, whilst the Montacciolani were busy at their worship, the big earthquake had struck. At first, all the congregation had been aware of was a rumbling sound, like a storm in the distance, but it was soon followed by a most terrifying noise – the cracking of beams and tearing of masonry; the crashing of buildings falling to the ground; and then a sound which could only be described as the earth screaming.

Frantic prayers were said. Everybody looked upwards, expecting an imminent catastrophe and supplicating God to save their souls. But the church roof did not fall on the congregation. There was nothing – no movement at all; no trembling, or aftershocks. Not one drop of holy wine was spilled from the chalice, which remained steadfastly on the altar.

When at last the villagers summoned the courage to emerge from the church, the scene that met them was apocalyptic. The earthquake had destroyed a dozen houses in a matter of seconds, and the mountain had swallowed a whole street. Yet quite unbelievably, not one person was hurt.

Had the disaster happened at any other time than between eleven and twelve on a Sunday, when everybody was in church, there would have been casualties. If the earthquake had struck at night, at a conservative estimate, forty villagers would have perished in their beds.

'*The Miracle of Montacciolo*' the newspapers had called it. That report had appeared on page two of the *Resto del Carlino*.

Thinking back to that day, Dante found himself reciting a couplet from Leonora's poem, *The Little Boat*. '*Let the ground shake and the thunder sound. Let this godforsaken place fall into the ground.*'

Dante repeated it over and over again as he stuck together the torn corners of the topographical chart. How old had she been when she'd written that? Thirteen, perhaps? He had reprimanded her for it at the time and given her that tired old lecture about appreciating what you have. He was eating his words now. *Let this godforsaken place fall into the ground.*

He stood back to inspect his repairs. He didn't have the right glue, but his patching-up would have to do. Dante ran his eyes over the chart, then slid his fingertip along until he reached Montacciolo. There it was – the smallest possible dot on the second-to-palest green mountain. It was like fly shit on the map.

CHAPTER 8

The *Lavandula* still had her mast and her rigging in working order, but Jubanne rarely sailed her the old-fashioned way. The winds could be fickle around that part of Sardinia. Switching on the engine was so much easier and it meant that Jubanne could come and go whenever was convenient to him, without having to wait for a favourable wind.

He was careful to keep the boom, which was the horizontal pole used to control the angle of the sail, secured. He always verified that the blocking peg was pushed in fully, because if it worked its way loose, the heavy wooden boom might swing round and knock him into the sea. It was one of those pre-outing checks that he carried out without fail. He often checked twice as it was wise to be extra prudent. He'd heard about a fellow who'd been killed by a swinging boom, so he had a bit of a thing about it.

That afternoon he had gone down to the boat with no particular plan in mind, except perhaps sneaking a quick nap after he'd checked her over and given the brass-work a bit of a buff.

Stepping aboard was the very last thing Jubanne could recall. He had no memory of any of the checks he carried out, nor of taking his brass-cleaning kit from below deck. He certainly didn't remember the boom swinging round and hitting him on the side of the head.

Nobody could be certain how long after the accident he was found, but he must have been lying unconscious on the deck of the *Lavandula* quite a while, because by the time the alarm was raised, the pool of blood around his head had been burned black by the sun.

Jubanne woke up in hospital with a headache so severe that it felt as though someone had his skull in a vice. The pain was so blinding that he couldn't even see where he was, but he sensed his surroundings by the smell of disinfectant and a woman's voice saying, 'He's coming round. Get the doctor. Ask if it's all right to call his wife yet.'

He made some sort of noise which must have expressed that he was in pain. The woman's voice went softer. First she confirmed that he was indeed in hospital because he'd had an accident, then she said, 'Try not to get yourself in a state, Signor Melis Puddu. I'm going to give you a shot for the pain and you'll feel better very quickly, I promise. The calmer you are, the quicker it will work. Breathe. Breathe slowly. There. That's good. There...'

Sure enough, no time later, when Jubanne opened his eyes the pain was bearable; and when at last he could focus his vision, a wax-whiskered doctor in a spotted bow tie was standing over him, with a stethoscope hanging from his ears, checking his pulse.

'Good morning Signor Melis Puddu!' He said cheerfully. 'Welcome back. You had everybody worried.' He then raised his index finger and began to move it closer, then further away from Jubanne's face and having done this repeatedly, seemed satisfied that whatever Jubanne's reaction was, it was the right one.

'That's good,' said the doctor. 'Now, how's the head?'

Jubanne wanted to say, 'Fuck the Virgin Mary! It hurts like buggery!' which was not language he would normally have used, particularly to a respectable professional like a doctor, and certainly not in the company of a female nurse. But for some reason he felt compelled to swear. Every obscene, blasphemous and profane word he knew ran through his mind, but his mouth was so dry that his tongue was stuck to the roof of his mouth, so the sound that came out was indistinct. The doctor understood.

'Nurse, would you give Signor Melis Puddu a drink? Then I think another two milligrams should sort him out.'

Jubanne felt a sponge on his lips, a syringe in his neck and within moments the compulsion to swear dissolved. The pain was gone. In fact, it was better than gone. His head fizzed very pleasantly, as if someone had poured Spumante into it, and he became acutely aware of his body, which felt light and rather wonderful. Just as well that there was a blanket covering him and weighing him down, or he might have floated away.

'What happened?' He asked. Even the sound of his voice felt altered, as though he could hear himself talking from another room.

'You got a whack on the head from the boom on your sailboat, Signor Melis Puddu,' replied the doctor. 'Quite a common accident, I'm afraid to say, but you were very lucky it only knocked you out.'

'How long have I been here?'

'Ten days.'

'*Ten days?*'

Jubanne's wife arrived shortly after, looking years older and ravaged with worry, and she cried more than Jubanne had ever known her to cry, continually excusing herself for the fact she couldn't stop.

'It's the shock,' she sobbed, 'I've been so worried!' Then she cried some more.

Jubanne held her hand and assured her that he was fine, promising he'd be home very soon. He was sorry for having been so careless. How were they getting on without him at the guest house? Was she managing? How were the children, Corrado and Nora?

His wife assured him that they were coping. The children were fine and he mustn't worry about anybody but himself. All the staff had really pulled together. Everybody sent their best wishes. But he must concentrate on getting better and not be unduly concerned about the guesthouse.

Suddenly Jubanne was assailed by panic. If the boom on the sailboat had hit him because it hadn't been properly secured, or perhaps because the peg was broken, it might yet hit someone else. He thought about his children in particular, because sometimes they liked to play on the deck. One whack had been enough to lay a big man like him out for ten days. He couldn't bear to think what might happen if it hit one of the children.

'Have you checked the boom?'

'What?'

'The boom on my boat. Have you checked it?'

At this point the heart rate monitor began to beep quicker and louder. Jubanne heard the nurse say, 'You should let him rest now, Signora Melis Puddu,' and he felt the familiar prick of the syringe. Then the tranquilizer kicked in and Jubanne was no longer awake.

The days which followed might have been weeks. To Jubanne they were just a haze of conscious and semi-conscious fragments of time. Usually when he awoke he was by himself in his unremarkable hospital room. It was painted a very pale green. His bed had bars on both sides, like a protective cage, so that he couldn't fall out. There was a window, but all he could see through that was the sky, and only when the blind was up. The nurses kept it down most of the time because the sunlight made his eyes hurt, but they said that was normal and his eyes would re-adjust eventually.

On one wall there was a cork board with papers pinned to it, where the nurses would write their observations for the doctors to read. Whenever the doctors looked at them they wouldn't say much. They'd just make noises like *hmm* and *ah* and talk about dosages of medicines with complicated names. On the other wall there was a print of a traditional Sardinian sailboat, identical to the *Lavandula*. How ironic that was, thought Jubanne.

When the door was open he'd hear the general buzz of hospital activity in the corridor beyond – greetings and instructions being exchanged between medical staff and the clatter of trolleys being wheeled past. He'd learned to recognise the different trolleys by a series of subtle differences. The medicine trolleys clinked. The food trolley was preceded by the smell of boiled meat or steamed fish. The cleaning trolleys moved in fits and starts, but most of the cleaners whistled, so that always gave the game away. Gurneys made a different sound depending on whether there was a patient aboard. When they were empty, they rattled. When they were carrying someone Jubanne was aware of a sort of sucking noise their rubber wheels made on the tiled floors. Then there were footsteps – the nurses were the quietest, a brisk pitter-patter at most. Some hardly made a sound, as though they were levitating down the corridor. The firm tapping of the doctors' leather-soled shoes had an air of determination about it. He knew when it was visiting hour because that was the only time he'd hear the click-clack of ladies' heels. He never heard children though, but someone had told him that children weren't allowed onto his ward. Who'd told him that? He couldn't be sure. But that was why he hadn't seen his children. It was just as well, he thought. Seeing him laid out in his hospital bed would be very upsetting for them.

When he awoke at night, the hospital was almost soundless. Jubanne didn't mind the quiet, which wasn't really quiet because the rhythmic beeping of his heart rate monitor seemed amplified a hundred times. He found it a friendly, comforting sound.

Sometimes his wife was there. She'd really let herself go, but he didn't like to say. He thought he might have seen his brother-in-law a couple of times, and a few other people he knew, but

77

his recollections of them were very vague. The nurses insisted on medicating him before visiting hour so that he wouldn't get too excited. That usually resulted in him being too groggy to know what was going on, which made the whole visiting thing pointless.

Different nurses came and went. They were motherly and good-humoured and always asked the same questions. *How are you? How's the pain? Another two milligrams?* They seemed to know exactly what he needed, even when he couldn't speak, because sometimes the medication disconnected his brain from his mouth. The wax-whiskered doctor often appeared too, each time wearing a different bow tie. Jubanne liked to play a game called 'Remember the colour of the last bow tie', which was played exactly as the name suggested. Although he knew they'd been introduced, he couldn't recall the doctor's name, so he simply called him 'Doctor Bow Tie'.

Sometimes he pretended to be asleep in order to listen in on the doctors' and nurses' conversations. They seemed astonished that they had managed to keep him alive.

Once he'd had a strange conversation with one of the nurses. She had asked him whether he'd experienced anything whilst he'd been unconscious. It was not uncommon, she claimed, for patients to have spiritual, or religious, revelations. They spoke of being led down a tunnel towards a light, of being reunited with loved ones who had passed away, and even of coming face-to-face with God. Others, despite being in a coma, were aware of everything going on around them. Some had had out of body experiences and were able to watch themselves from the corner of the room, or from the ceiling. Even more astonishingly, certain people maintained that whilst their bodies remained in their hospital beds, their spirits had travelled to other places, both known and unknown to them.

This all sounded very entertaining and Jubanne wished that

there was something he could have told the nurse, but there was nothing. The time had had spent unconscious had been a void – nothing but a long, deep, dreamless sleep.

There had been one strange incident, not long after he'd regained consciousness, but he didn't want to share it with the nurse. He had woken up to the sound of singing – a distracted humming with a few words thrown in. Although he had not heard that voice for many years, there was no mistaking that it was his grandmother's. He had turned his head and there, sitting on a small chair beside his bed was Nonna Maria-Annoriana. She was embroidering, as she often had done when she was alive.

Jubanne's grandmother glanced up from her work and raised an eyebrow at him over the rim of her spectacles, then looked back down and continued with her stitching, still murmuring her half-hummed song. Now a little wry smile curled the corners of her mouth, as though she was having trouble keeping a straight face. Jubanne felt her say, 'Ha ha! Aren't you surprised to see me!'

Without saying it out loud, Jubanne replied 'Yes,' and Nonna Maria-Annoriana looked up again, then tilted her head to one side and he felt her say, 'You've been in the wars, eh Jubanne?

This unspoken but perfectly-understood conversation continued. *You daft donkey, Jubanne, getting yourself hit on the head like that.* I know, Nonna, I know. *Well, you'd best be concentrating on getting better now, my boy.* I've let my family down, Nonna. *Nonsense! You've had an accident, that's all. You're strong as an ox. You'll pull through.*

Of all the dead people who could have dropped in to visit, Jubanne was glad that it was Nonna Maria-Annoriana. She had more or less brought him up, not because he was orphaned, or had feckless parents, but because his mother and father ran both a tavern and a general store and worked very long hours, leaving no time for parenting. He had never resented them for it because given the choice he preferred the company and the cooking of Nonna Maria-Annoriana.

Nonna Maria-Annoriana claimed absolutely all the credit for Jubanne's impressive height, partly for having passed it down, and partly because she had nourished him so well during his formative years. Nonna herself had been one meter eighty-six tall and proud of it. She carried herself with poise – shoulders back, straight and confident, as though she had a broomstick for a backbone. By the end of her life, she had shrunk by three centimetres, but still claimed that she measured one meter eighty-six if anybody asked. She dressed exclusively in black and powdered her face with a pale peach-coloured *cipria*. There was always a dusting of it caught in her eyebrows and moustache.

Jubanne's grandmother was a woman who commanded great authority and had what people referred as a 'strong character', which could be taken either way. She loved *mungeta* snails cooked in white wine, traditional Sardinian wrestling and Jesus – but above all, she loved Jubanne. He was her favourite grandchild and she did not mind it being known.

Nonna Maria-Annoriana was a staunch advocate of good manners. It was because of her that Jubanne never swore, or threw his weight around. 'Big dogs don't need to bite,' she would say.

They didn't speak much that day, although there would have been plenty to talk about. It just felt good to be side-by-side after all this time. They had always been like that, so comfortable in each other's presence that being in the same room was enough – they didn't need to fill the space with chatter. That moment reminded Jubanne of the time he'd been sick with mumps and Nonna Maria-Annoriana had sat by his bedside for a week, just as she was now, singing absent-mindedly to herself whilst occupied with her needlework.

The chair was low, and Nonna Maria-Annoriana's legs were long, so she sat slightly folded over, with her body at an angle of forty-five degrees to her thighs. After a while, she adjusted herself, stretched and rubbed her back.

'Are you comfortable, Nonna?'

'Getting a bit uncomfortable now, so I'd best make my way. But I'll come and see you again.'

'Bye then.'

'Bye,' and she was gone. So was the chair.

It was then that Jubanne's thoughts returned to the day that Nonna Maria-Annoriana had died. He had gone to call in on her and found her slumped over with her sewing work on her lap. She had been embroidering Jubanne's initials onto the shirt he was due to wear for his wedding.

Having received this unexpected visit from his beloved grandmother, Jubanne willed his parents to come to see him too, but what came to him was more of a dream than a vision. Images of his mother and father floated past him like ribbons caught by the wind. They were smiling; they were pleased to see him; then they vanished.

It was funny, thought Jubanne during a moment of lucidity. These two appearances corresponded to how things had been when these ghosts had been alive. Nonna Maria-Annoriana had always been at his side, whilst his parents had been distant figures. He had never doubted their love, but their commitments to the businesses which they ran day and night took precedence over the business of parenting. They had laboured with the goal of a comfortable retirement, invested, scrimped and saved; but what neither had accounted for was that they would work themselves to death years before that retirement. Jubanne's mother had died aged fifty-two and a year later, aged fifty-four, his father had followed her.

Whenever Jubanne asked Doctor Bow Tie when he could go

home, which was every time he saw him, the doctor would give vague replies such as, 'We'll have to see,' or 'It's too soon to tell,' or 'All in good time.'

'But I have a business to run!' Jubanne would protest. 'And guests to look after.'

'You've also suffered a skull fracture, Signor Melis Puddu,' the doctor would say as though he had repeated it many times before. 'And a significant bleed on the brain. We can't let you go until we're sure you're mending properly.'

Then, to stop him getting upset, he'd give him another two milligrams of whatever it was they injected into his neck, and under the influence of that Jubanne didn't mind being in hospital at all.

These in-and-out moments gradually settled to a pattern which was more in than out and Jubanne found that he could stay awake for longer periods of time. This was all very well, but it meant that boredom set in. He was brought a radio, but he could only tune into two channels – one broadcast from the Vatican, which sent him to sleep with its monotone sermons and chanting. The other played some awful music and talked about football and politics, which interested him even less than religion.

One morning Doctor Bow Tie appeared with a chart and asked Jubanne whether he could read the words which were printed on it in large capital letters. *BREAD – BALL – DOG – CAT*. Jubanne felt utterly insulted by the simplicity of the task.

'Of course I can read that!' He exclaimed. 'I might not be a highly-educated man, like you, but I'm not illiterate!'

The doctor then hid the chart behind his back and asked Jubanne whether he could recall the four words which he had just read, and whether he could repeat them in order, to which Jubanne replied confidently, 'Ball, dog, house, mouse.'

Doctor Bow Tie thanked him for his participation and left, but feeling that he should make a point, Jubanne requested some reading material from the nurses. From that moment on, he always made sure that he had his nose in a newspaper whenever the doctor came on his rounds; although in reality, he couldn't read much at all. He could manage headlines and larger print, but anything smaller just quivered and blurred. Eventually he mentioned this to the doctor, who suggested that he might need reading glasses now. It was not uncommon for sight to diminish at his age. *At his age.* The cheek of it! He was about to protest, then he realised that he couldn't remember exactly how old he was and he felt rather stupid about it, so instead he assured the doctor that there had been absolutely nothing wrong with his vision before the accident. He could have read the small print on the back of an aspirin box from across the room. It must have been the bump on the head which had affected his sight. The doctor concurred that he might be right, then passed him his own glasses to try. The print was crystal clear, so Doctor Bow Tie lent Jubanne his spare pair. But now, even though he could see the print, he found it difficult to retain the details of anything he read. Much of it was gibberish. Why did people bother publishing nonsense?

One day a physiotherapist turned up with a wheelchair and informed Jubanne that they were going to start his physical rehabilitation, which apparently he'd been told about, but he had no recollection of.

'It's time to get you up and about and walking again, Signor Melis Puddu,' smiled the young man pleasantly.

'What?' Scoffed Jubanne. 'I don't need help with walking. I only banged my head. I didn't break any bones.'

The young man gave a sort of half-smile, as though he knew something that Jubanne didn't.

'You haven't stood on your own feet since your accident,' he said.

'It's not because I haven't wanted to. It's because they've told me to stay in bed. I've even had to do my business in a bed-pan.'

Suddenly Jubanne was overcome by that urge to swear again. *Piss in the bed-pan. Shit the bed. Fuck this. Fuck you. Bugger the Pope and all the Cardinals.* He pressed his lips together to stop the words leaking out of his mouth. Just as well Nonna Maria-Annoriana wasn't there. She would have been horrified.

'You'd be surprised how quickly muscles lose their strength when they're not used, Signor Melis Puddu. But you were a fit, strapping fellow before, so I'm sure you'll be taking your wife dancing before you know it.'

Although dancing was a bit ambitious, Jubanne could raise himself into a standing position unassisted within a couple of weeks, and not long after that, he began to walk again – slowly, tentatively, and not very far – but everyone seemed delighted with his progress. They praised and applauded him, as they would a little child who had just taken their first steps.

Then, after giving him a list of rules and conditions as long as his arm and a supply of enough pills to medicate a small army, the doctor told Jubanne that he could go home.

CHAPTER 9

'At first, being back at home was much harder than I thought it would be,' said Jubanne Melis Puddu, slurping a spoonful of soup into his mouth. 'I thought that within a week or two I'd be working again – just light duties, a bit of helping out – but it wasn't easy. It was a terrible time.'

'Well, clearly you'd had a serious accident.'

'I'd had an operation too, but I didn't realise until I got home. Nobody had told me when I was in hospital.'

The Sardinian lifted the hair on the side of his head to reveal a thick, raised scar in the shape of a cross.

'Good grief!' Exclaimed Dante. 'They cut your head open?'

'They used a drill to release the pressure from the bleed. And apparently that's what had affected my balance because I wasn't too steady on my feet. The doctors were afraid I'd fall and hit my head again. I had to be careful and I wasn't allowed to use stairs. So my wife made up a room for me on the ground floor, but that was worse than being in hospital. My wife was busy all the time, so I hardly saw her, or anybody else. I was just lonely and miserable by myself. And at night, my wife slept in our old room up at the top of the house – not that I expected her to sleep in my bed when I was ill – but it just meant that I never had much company, and sometimes it would have been nice to have some.'

'What about your children? Didn't you see them?'

The big man's bottom lip trembled, and he shook his head.

'They kept telling me I'd seen them, but I couldn't remember. They must have brought them to me when I was doped up to my eyeballs. But when I got back home, no, they were staying at my wife's sister's. We used to send them there every summer during peak tourist season. My wife's sister and her husband ran a farm a little way inland. It's where we used to get our lamb and pork from for the guesthouse. Their kids were the same age as ours, so all the cousins spent the summer together on the farm. But my kids stayed there a lot longer that year. I don't think my wife wanted them to see me in the state I was, and I couldn't blame her for that.'

Jubanne Melis Puddu stopped talking abruptly and looked across at the clock.

'Is that the right time?' He asked.

'More or less.'

The Sardinian reached inside his shirt and took out a folded note and a screw of paper. He opened out the note and consulted it, then slid it across to Dante.

'Does that say "blue round and white diamond with dinner"?' He asked.

'Yes, it does,' confirmed Dante, scanning the contents of the note, which was written in the same carefully-formed, child-like hand which he recognised from the letter.

The big man carefully undid the screw of paper, inside which was a rainbow of different coloured pills. He picked out a round blue one and a white one in the shape of a diamond, put them in his mouth and swallowed them down with a spoonful of soup, then screwed up the paper again and slipped it back in his pocket along with the list of instructions.

Once again Jubanne Melis Puddu retracted into his own thoughts and stared down glumly at his supper. After a while he said, 'She was different when I came home.'

'Who was different?'

'My wife.'

'How?'

'I felt that she didn't really want me there, that I was in the way. Sometimes I thought that she wished the accident had killed me.'

'That's harsh. But perhaps your perception was skewed? You said that you were on a lot of medication.'

'The medication was to stop me having seizures, and it made me sleep a lot. But when I was awake I was perfectly aware of everything and I could tell that my wife was different. She even looked different, and she was distant and irritable. I just felt like a burden to her, which I was, really. Before the accident we'd been a great team. People used to comment on how well we worked together. Some husbands and wives couldn't do what we did without being at each other's throats, but we weren't like that. We each had our own set of jobs and chores and everything ran smoothly. But after the accident, when I wasn't useful anymore and she had to take on all the responsibilities, I felt that she resented me for it.' He then added bitterly, 'I had lost my *dependability*.'

'It must have been hard for you both,' said Dante, trying to offer some consolation. 'But you seem very well recovered now. You don't give the appearance of a diminished man. Quite the opposite, I would argue. The fact you made it up an impassable mountain track in wholly insufficient clothing is surely testament to how you have regained your vigour.'

Jubanne Melis Puddu's expression changed suddenly, as though something had lit the darkness of his thoughts.

'I got better thanks to Nora,' he smiled. 'If it hadn't been for her, I would have given up. Nora could see how awful it was for me, being stuck in that room, so she set up a lounging bed for me on the terrace under the fig tree and she would come every morning after the breakfast service was finished and she'd help me get up and she'd take me to the terrace. Being outside was like being reborn after all that time spent inside.'

The big Sardinian tilted his chin up, as though in the fire-lit semidarkness of the little mountain house he could feel the Mediterranean sun on his face.

'It was nice being on the terrace. I'd just watch the world go by and look at the boats out at sea. I liked seeing the guests too when they were in the garden, or heading down to the beach, so even when I was by myself there I didn't feel lonely. And whenever she wasn't working, Nora would come and keep me company. At first I was scared to talk to her because my memory was still shaky and I didn't want to make a fool of myself by saying something stupid. Some things I could remember like they were yesterday, but other things just wouldn't stick, or if I did remember them, I wasn't sure if I was remembering them right. Then I'd panic about it and get this strange noise in my head and nonsense would come out of my mouth before I could stop it. That was frustrating, but I wasn't supposed to get agitated, so Nora would calm me.'

Despite the difficulty of the situation of which he spoke, clearly Jubanne Melis Puddu was enjoying the recollection.

'Nora had a way of helping me to make sense of things,' he continued. 'She told me not to get into a state if there were things I couldn't remember because eventually they would come back if they were important enough. She said that my brain was like a china cup which had fallen on the ground and broken. Now we had to put the pieces back together again, but it didn't matter if there were a few pieces missing, or if the repairs showed. Expecting that cup to be exactly the same as before it was broken was pointless, because it could never be. But it could be repaired and it would be a cup again. And even if it leaked a bit, that was all right. And the mends were just part of it. There was no point trying to hide them.'

'My daughter was extremely fond of metaphors,' commented Dante, nodding fondly.

'Nobody had ever talked to me the way Nora did. And I could

say things to her that I couldn't share with anyone else.' The shadow of a slightly bewildered smile spread across the Sardinian's face and he said, 'I could smell things after my accident.'

'You couldn't smell before?'

'I could, but like an average man. After my accident I gained a nose like a Sardinian Jàgaru dog. I'd always been able to smell the scent of lavender and roses in the garden, but suddenly it was ten times stronger. And the lemon trees, well, I could smell the lemons a long time before they were ripe, when they were no bigger than walnuts. Then there was the sea too. It came in bursts, as though each wave that landed on the beach was sending me a blast of salt.'

Jubanne Melis Puddu pushed aside his bowl and sat forwards with his elbows resting on the table.

'But it wasn't just that. And I couldn't have told anyone except Nora, because they would have thought I was mad, but I could *see* those smells. The scent coming off the lavender was like a very thin, greyish smoke. It was pink for the roses and yellow for the lemons with a sort of silvery sparkle that caught the light. And the salt coming in off the sea was a pale green colour most of the time, although sometimes it was more blue. And I told Nora this and she said that being able to see smells had a name. But it was a long, complicated word. I can't remember it now.'

'Was it synaesthesia?' offered Dante.

'Yes, that's it!' The Sardinian opened his mouth to repeat the word, but it seemed to have slipped from his head already.

Dante sat up. Until that point, he had been ready to dismiss his visitor's claim that the girl called Nora really was his daughter, Leonora. A great part of him wanted to. After a time with no news, the 'missing' label had been officially amended to 'missing presumed dead', and once that presumption had been made, Dante had resigned himself to it. Even when letters had

89

arrived claiming that Leonora was alive and well, he hadn't once been convinced.

But now he was doubting his doubts and coming round to the idea that this girl called Nora really could be Leonora. That word, 'synaesthesia', surely was too unusual to be coincidental, for that was a word he remembered teaching to his daughter, and one which she had used as a title for one of her poems. *O, Synaesthesia, how can it be, that I can taste the colours I see?*

'Did she ever mention her parents?' Asked Dante.

Jubanne Melis Puddu pondered for a moment, as though he was seeking a diplomatic answer, then replied, 'Whenever I asked about her family, she would change the subject, so I stopped asking. She never mentioned the village of Montacciolo either, not that I can remember, anyway.'

Clearly the Sardinian's answer came as a disappointment to Dante, but not as a surprise.

'It pains me greatly that she still harboured such hostility. There was a time when things were good between us. I thought that with the passing of time and with the distance, perhaps my daughter might recall the affection we once shared. Our relationship was not always an embittered one.'

'Are you still angry, like your were after she left with those people?'

'No, no, that anger has been replaced by other feelings over time, but I cannot deny that it was a very difficult obstacle to overcome. Neither can I deny that some of those subsequent feelings were not equally testing, in their own way.'

Dante, who had finished his soup, set aside his bowl.

'To begin with, I was so saturated with rage that I thought I might never feel a different emotion again. I must confess that when Leonora's first postcard arrived, about a month after her departure, from some small seaside town in the South of Italy, I was tempted to tear it up and throw it away. The only thing that stopped me was that doing so would have upset my wife and I really did not have the wherewithal to cope with yet another crisis.'

That first postcard comprised just a few lines and no return address. *It's beautiful here. We're heading for Greece. Looking forward to a warm winter without snow.* There was no 'love from', or any such nod to affection – just Leonora's name scribbled at an angle.

The use of the plural added a further layer of irritation to Dante's anger. Leonora was officially one of 'them' now; part of The Collective. She was no longer an 'I', but a 'we'. 'They' were off to Greece for the winter. How very jolly.

'I know I wasn't the first to read it,' remarked Dante drily. 'The postmaster had probably informed the whole village of the postcard's contents well before it was delivered into my hand. After that, Leonora sent postcards more or less monthly, but it was rare for two to come from the same place. My wife pinned them to the dresser in the kitchen and would stand in front of them crying, sometimes for hours. When she wasn't crying, she was praying. Sometimes it was hard to differentiate one from the other.'

Dante shook his head mournfully, 'My poor wife,' he lamented. 'She had always suffered with her nerves. When I met her, she was such a timid little thing. Ortensia had been orphaned very young and was not a worldly woman, but she had a charming innocence about her which I found appealing. I hoped that through my protection and my love she might grow more confident, but it was never the case. Following Leonora's birth she suffered from a type of post-partum instability which inflicted upon her a permanent melancholic state.'

Dante shut his eyes, as though recalling something which he first wanted to recite in his head, then said, in a dream-like voice, *'The winter is upon us, but behind its cosy fires, Are secrets that we have to keep and cold nights filled with cries.'*

'Cold nights filled with cries?' Repeated Jubanne Melis Puddu, furrowing his brow.

'Those are two lines from Leonora's epic poem, *The Little Boat*. What Leonora refers to as "the winter" is an allegorical reference to her mother's state of mind. During her worst episodes, Ortensia rarely slept at night, and she would cry out incessantly – the most desperate howls, which still echo in my mind whenever I think back. Nothing could be done to soothe her. Eventually, usually between four and five o'clock in the morning, she would cry herself to exhaustion and fall asleep.'

'And what did your daughter mean by secrets behind fires?'

'Ah, the reference to secrets that we have to keep hiding behind the cosy fires, well, that describes the lengths I went to in my attempts to try to give an impression of normality to the outside world, for Leonora's sake. But as she made clear in her poem, she was not fooled by my efforts. She understood that we lived hidden behind a mask.'

Dante sighed heavily. 'That first winter after Leonora's departure was a winter in every sense of the word. My wife's mental state was in such upheaval that I questioned whether I too might end up crying all night, or howling at the moon.'

'How did you not go mad?'

The misery of the old man's expression gave way to a look of serenity. 'I was saved by the mountains. And by this little house'

CHAPTER 10

The lengthening days and the first signs of spring had a stabilising effect on Dante's wife. Ortensia was sleeping better, and consequently, so was he. He could be assured five hours of sleep most nights. During the daytime, aside from the wailing prayers and intermittent weeping, the house was quieter.

His nightmares about the insects had stopped and had been replaced with the same recurring scenario, where Dante would be walking through a field of long grass and notice blood on his hands and cuts on his legs. He would realise that what surrounded him was not blades of grass, but the blades of countless knives sticking out of the ground. Dante was so used to the tedious regularity of having nightmares that he would simply wake himself up, check that he was not really bleeding, have a drink of water and go back to sleep.

Spring was particularly fine that year. The primroses were a glory to behold. They burst into bloom in clusters of joyous purple, pink and yellow, not just in the meadows and on the borders of the woodlands, but all over the village. By means of some climactic fluke which had rendered the conditions perfect, seeds which had lain dormant for decades germinated everywhere – between the cracks in the cobblestones; in the gaps where the pointing had fallen out of walls; out of rocks where there could be no more than a few grains of earth for them to sink their roots. It was a spectacular display.

The scandal of the previous summer was no longer quite so gossip-worthy. People had started talking to Dante again and he was beginning to feel a little less ostracised. Some villagers had the temerity to ask him to help them out with administrative matters. Each time, he declined politely, explaining that he was no longer vested with the necessary official powers and they should ask one of the new councillors. This last piece of advice was given with little attempt to hide the sense of vindication that he felt. As he had predicted, the three men who had taken over his responsibilities were not up to any one of the tasks. New councillor number three had resigned following a fist fight with new councillor number two during one of their council meetings in the bar.

As Easter approached, Dante felt compelled to do something which he had not done for many years, and that was to go walking in the mountains. Those long ago summers, when duty had brought him back to Montacciolo to visit his ageing parents, had been made bearable, even at times enjoyable, by his daily walks. Back in those days he had the legs of a young man who could bound up and down the tracks as though he had cloven hooves. Now, being almost three decades older, he exercised prudence to begin with. The first few times that he ventured out he kept his walks to no more than half an hour each way, which he increased to forty, then fifty minutes, and finally to an hour. He no longer had the boundless energy and sturdy legs of his youth, but he was still quite physically fit, and naturally, the more he walked, the more his stamina increased, and the stronger his legs became.

During the Easter break he trekked from Montacciolo to a place by the name of Santa Croce, where a tall wooden cross had been erected when he was a small boy. Dante could not fathom, then or now, what purpose it served in that remote spot two hours from anywhere, where nobody except the goat-herders ever passed. As a young lad he had lacked the courage to ask his father, who had accompanied him to Santa Croce, along with the village priest. He had not dared to ask the priest either, for Don Generoso's predecessor had been a bombastic man, prone to giving long-winded explanations to any question asked of him, and often to questions not asked of him too.

Signor Bacchetti had volunteered his son to carry all the things necessary for the cross-blessing ceremony – a very heavy incense-burner and two brass candlesticks which were each a meter forty high, not including the candles; and a bell which ting-a-linged with every step he took.

It was on that auspicious day that Signor Bacchetti had decided that his son should become a priest. A vision had come to him, he claimed, the moment the cross had been blessed. The message was clear. Dante's destiny was to join the priesthood.

Perhaps Signor Bacchetti had thought that carrying that burden of liturgical accessories might in some way prepare his young son for life in Holy Orders, for Dante was obliged to lug the incense burner, the candlesticks and the bell back down the mountain too.

As they descended, and as the boy struggled to keep up, his father and the priest were engaged in an intense discussion concerning the moment of revelation which had just taken place at Santa Croce. The more Signor Bacchetti re-told his experience, the more definite the will of God became. What had started as a feeling turned into a voice speaking to him directly from the clouds.

Delighted at having been present at such a miraculous event – of having been instrumental to it, one could claim – the priest quoted several chapters from the book of Genesis, where Abraham, so keen to show God his devotion, had agreed to sacrifice his only son, Isaac. The parallels between the events of that day, centuries before the birth of Christ, and what had just occurred at Santa Croce were clear, the priest concluded.

Signor Bacchetti, who was still in the grips of his religious fervour and desperate to impress the priest, had stated that in Abraham's position, he would have done the same.

Dante realised that by being offered up for the priesthood he was getting off considerably more lightly than poor Isaac. Nevertheless, it bothered him that his father had not asked him whether he actually *wanted* to be a priest. But then, Isaac was never consulted on the matter of his own murder – just popped up on the sacrificial alter and given a last minute reprieve by God, who'd masterminded the whole tasteless prank in the first place. How could you ever trust God after He'd played a trick like that on you?

All the way back to the village Dante's father made solemn oaths with the priest as his witness, avowing that he would make a pilgrimage to Santa Croce every year on that day, even crawling up on his knees if the priest thought it appropriate. He would also increase his offerings to the church. The priest replied that a yearly pilgrimage would be a marvellous thing. Perhaps, once the word had spread of this heavenly visitation, other pilgrims might join him – although he saw no need for Dante's father, or anybody else, to go up on their knees. Feet would do just fine. In fact, he would recommend the wearing of sturdy boots. Of course, increased offerings would be very welcome. He would not be in the least surprised if Signor Bacchetti experienced further visions, for clearly God saw him as a channel.

This had impelled Dante's father to cry out in zealous ecstasy, 'Heavenly father, I am your channel! Fill me with your everlasting light!'

When they arrived home, Signor Bacchetti was still so enraptured that he threw himself at his wife's feet and wept, and for the first time in their fifteen-year marriage, almost admitted out loud that he loved her.

That day at Santa Croce had been life-changing, not only for Dante's father, but also for Dante. The priest had said that if the boy was to take his vows, he would first need to be prepared by means of an appropriate education; and there was no better preparation for the priesthood than the Jesuit academy. Thus the following September, aged eight, Dante had been packed off to boarding school to fulfil his imposed vocation. Had that event not happened at Santa Croce that day, Dante would never have received anything beyond a basic village education.

Now, standing at the foot of Santa Croce, Dante contemplated the wooden cross. It was smaller than he remembered and it was looking a bit weather-beaten.

'I regret to inform you,' he said, addressing the cross, 'that I was never able to realise my father's ambition. Although I passed the appropriate exams for entry into the Seminary, it was not the place for me as I did not meet one of the fundamental requirements – that of believing in God.'

Dante waited for a flash of light, or a voice from the clouds, or a bolt of lightning that would reduce him to a pile of smouldering cinders. There was nothing.

From where he stood, there was a good view of Montacciolo on the mountainside opposite. Dante could see the scar of the earthquake, running like a sharp curve with a jagged end on the eastern boundary of the village. How the church had been spared was quite unbelievable, unless you believed that God had spared it, in which case it was a miracle; and this, the villagers accepted as fact. Just as amazing was the fact that Don Generoso' predecessor hadn't tried to claim any glory and put his name forward for canonization, considering he'd been present not only at the moment of the earthquake, but also during Dante's father's vision. How many miracles did it take to be considered for sainthood? Was it two, or three performances?

On his way back home Dante took a detour via the lake known as Lago Stretto, a long, narrow ellipse of water which had been created centuries before by the flooding of a stone quarry. He's swum in it as a boy. Dante tested the temperature of the water with his finger. He definitely wouldn't be swimming today. The water was so cold that it turned his finger red.

Although he was not tempted to take a dip, he did spend a little time indulging in other boyish pursuits. He skimmed shards of flat stone across the surface of the lake, just as he had done in his youth, then picked through the heaps of quarry rubble, scouring for ancient treasure. He found two stone-cutting tools, both still sharp, and half an axe head.

Following the Easter break Dante crossed off the days on his calendar, counting down to the beginning of the summer holiday.

Despite several attempts, he had not been able to locate the track which led up to the little house which his father and grand-father had built. Most of the Montacciolani seemed to have forgotten about it too. Dante had asked a few, but only those whom he trusted not to send him on a path to nowhere, or over the edge of the nearest escarpment. The villagers concurred that it would probably be best to ask the goat-herder, Ermenegildo. He was the only one who ever ventured up that high, but he'd already gone to take his animals to the pastures. Nobody could say when he was due back.

Dante thought it prudent to wait for the goat-herder's instructions. Trying to get to such an out-of-the-way place without directions would be foolhardy.

Admittedly, the construction of the little house had been a bit of a mad caper. Many people had questioned who in their right mind would choose to go to such a remote place, let alone go all that way there to sweat and toil. But the Bacchetti menfolk had been desperately short of work at the time, and the project had been undertaken both as a way to occupy themselves and as an opportunity for Dante's father to learn essential building skills from his own father. The house had taken them three summers to complete and had been constructed from the materials available on site. There was no shortage of stone and wood up there. All they had had to bring with them from the village were some basic tools, plenty of rope and a few bags of nails.

The little house had been used regularly as a hunting cabin whilst Dante's grandfather was still alive; less so after his death. Dante's father would have gone up there more often if he'd had the time, but his work situation had improved by then, and with his son's education and those increased church contributions to pay for on top of everything else, he didn't have much opportunity for leisure.

In his younger days, Dante had trekked up to the little house during his summer holidays and had continued to make daytrips even after he was married. He'd never managed to convince Ortensia to accompany him. She didn't have the constitution for lengthy physical exertion. Occasionally he had taken Leonora with him. She'd usually made a fuss.

When at last Dante was able to speak to Ermenegildo, the goat-herder drew him a rudimentary plan on a stone with a piece of charcoal.

'When did you last go there?' Asked Dante.

'Would have been last year, end of the summer.'

'Is the house still standing?'

'Oh yes. Looking a bit sorry for itself, but all in one piece. Built to last, it was. Your pa and his pa sure knew how to put a house together.'

Dante ventured out the very next day, equipped with a transcribed plan, some provisions, a claw hammer and a hunting knife. He found the track that Ermenegildo had indicated, although it seemed a lot steeper and narrower than it had previously. Clearly it was a path that few feet trod. When he turned off, as directed by the goat-herder, Dante found himself in locations he struggled to recognise. But of course, he thought, the landscape changes over the decades. New trees grow, old ones fall. The snows bring boulders down the mountainside. Streams and torrents carve new routes. And maybe, after so many years, his memories were flawed.

By the time he had been walking for two and a half hours and had not seen anything which was familiar to him, he questioned whether he had turned off in the wrong place, or copied down the plan incorrectly, or simply been given misleading directions. Then, when he was close to giving up and retracing his steps, he emerged from an area of tall ferns into a sweeping, sunlit glade, carpeted thickly with daisies the size of fried eggs.

This place was not forgotten. This was a place he knew.

He was immediately transported back to a day, so many years before. Leonora, aged six, was running through that very daisy-meadow. He had carried her much of the way up on his back. He didn't mind the extra effort, although sometimes he would huff and puff and pretend it was a chore.

'I'm tired. Can you carry me, Papá?'

'But I'm already carrying all our things, Leonora.'

She glanced up at him slyly, with that look she gave when she was trying to out-fox him. 'I'll carry our things if you carry me.'

'But then I'd still be carrying everything!'

Having been unable to trick her father, she resorted to saying 'please' repeatedly and tugging on his sleeve. Dante scooped her up and in a well-practiced move, swung her round onto his back and trotted off, making a clip-clop noise like horses' hooves.

Now back in the present, Dante was smiling, and the tears which had sprung into his eyes were not of rage, but of joy. If there was one moment of his life that he could go back to, which he could physically live through again, it would be that day with Leonora in the field of daisies. And if he could, he would stop time right there and then.

A realisation hit him suddenly, like a bright light being switched on right in front of his face. This was the first time since goodness-knows-when that the thought of his daughter had aroused in him a feeling of paternal fondness, and the notion that fatherhood could be joyous and wondrous, and filled with a thousand marvels. There had been a time, all those years ago, when he was certain that Leonora had loved him.

He could remember the details of that day perfectly. As he made his way across the meadow, he conjured the vision of Leonora dancing amongst the flowers. She'd been too tired to walk up the mountain, but now she had plenty of energy for dancing. She was making up a song about the daisies. Those funny songs about everyday things were her first poems.

'Daisy, daisy, don't be lazy! Daisy, daisy, don't be lazy! Daisy, daisy, don't be lazy!'

She had repeated it over and over again, louder and louder, then stopped suddenly.

'What else rhymes with "daisy" Papá?'

'Hmm...let me think now. How about "hazy"?'

'No. Find a better one.'

'Maybe "crazy".'

And little Leonora had gone whirling with her arms wide open across the field singing at the top of her voice, *'Lazy daisy you're so crazy!'* and then she had made herself dizzy and had fallen down hooting with laughter amongst the lazy and crazy daisies.

Dante had gone over to check that she was all right. His little girl was lying on her back with her arms and legs spread out like a star. Every part of her was coloured gold by the pollen. She was wearing a look of concentration, as though she was questioning something.

'What are you thinking?' Her father asked.

'I'm thinking about the pollen that's gone in my mouth.'

'Does it taste like honey?'

'No. It tastes like yellow,' Leonora had replied with great certainty, 'But how can things taste like colours, Papá?'

'It's called synaesthesia. It's when your senses get mixed up.'

'Synaesthesia,' she repeated, and Dante knew she would remember the word, even though she was so small and the word was so big. Leonora had an astonishing capacity to learn new words.

He had dusted her down and tried to show her how to make a daisy chain, but her little fingers fumbled, and his big fingers struggled too, so he used the tip of his knife to pierce each stem. Leonora watched him wide-eyed, quivering and hardly able to suppress her delight at what was being created in front of her. This delight had escaped from her as an excited squeal when he had looped the finished chain around her neck. Then, or course, she had needed bracelets, and a tiara, and a second necklace, and a daisy loop for each of her buttonholes.

At the house he had lit a fire outside in a ring of stones and cooked a string of sausages on a makeshift grill. Oh, the mouth-watering aroma of that thick, savoury smoke which burst forth with every spit and sizzle! The sausages were too hot to pick up, and Leonora couldn't wait to eat. Dante broke a sausage into bite-sized pieces, carefully wrapping each one in a leaf so that she wouldn't burn her fingers, and blowing on each one before he fed it to her.

Once they had finished their food Leonora had gone inside to play house, leaving her father preparing his coffee, a process which took a good twenty minutes on the open fire, but it was always well worth the wait. That coffee, made with mountain spring water and left to percolate slowly over the embers of the fire was hard to beat. Dante had sat savouring it, but then, thinking it suspiciously quiet, he had gone into the house to see what Leonora was doing. He had found her curled up on the bed like a little cat, sound asleep. He contemplated her for a while. How lovely she was, he sighed, and how quickly she was growing up. He had things to do, but they could wait, so he had curled up beside her.

Dante had not slept. He had just lain quietly, synchronising his breathing with Leonora's and wondering what the future held for his funny, clever little girl. He had been questioning the wisdom of having returned to Montacciolo for some time now. The place frustrated him, although he tried not to show it. There was nothing in that intellectual desert to stimulate his mind, and he feared that it would not be too long until Leonora felt that same frustration. They could never move away, to a town or a city where there were libraries, theatres, museums, art galleries, well-equipped schools and all those other places where one could expand one's mind with new knowledge and different ideas. That was what Leonora deserved, but Ortensia would never agree to leave Montacciolo.

As the images of this memory faded in his mind's eye, Dante reached the boundary of the daisy field. The path to the house should be beyond the next line of trees and over the next meadow. Back in the daisy-chain days, the chimneys of the house had been visible from as far back as where he stood, but now the trees had grown too tall.

He made his way through the pines and came out on the other side onto what had once been a pasture, but clearly the goat-herders seldom brought their animals up this far these days, for now it was covered with wild raspberry bushes. The canes were laden with green fruit. What a bounty that would be when it ripened!

Then Dante saw it – a little higher up and half-built into the rock face was his grandfather's house. The plateau on which it sat was so overgrown that the house appeared to be growing horizontally out of the rock.

Considering the snowstorms and the vicious gales which assaulted it every winter, it was astonishing that anything was left of the house at all. Now it was covered in ivy and creepers, yet its walls and roof were intact and its two chimneys were standing as straight as the day his father and grandfather had built them.

'Unbelievable,' marvelled Dante.

Although he was no more than five minutes from his destination, Dante felt unready to walk the last few meters just yet. He was overcome by a deep, reverential, appreciation for all that was around him. The expanse of raspberry canes with their soft leaves quivering in the breeze; the great elevations of pinewoods rising behind them, broken by lines of rocky escarpments down which small waterfalls trickled, firing off flashes of refracted light. In the distance, on the higher mountain tops, the ice-covered peaks caught the sun like shards of broken glass. And the birdsong, oh, the birdsong! How loud those birds were in this otherwise silent place – the trilling of the bullfinches; the punchier whistles of the chaffinches; the speedy, high-pitched calls of the wrens, and the to-and-fro melodic calls of other birds, as yet unknown to Dante, but no less extraordinary.

If one was looking for proof of God's existence, thought Dante, surely this would be an excellent place to start. He might even become convinced of it himself. For the first time he thought back to his father's vision at Santa Croce not with ridicule, but with a new understanding. It would not be difficult to translate this spectacle of nature into something divine. Up in the mountains one could not help but feel possessed by an omnipotent power, as though one could feel the breath of God. If one looked hard enough, one might even glimpse heaven's gates in the sky.

Dante's senses were so saturated with this quasi-religious sensation that he felt compelled to lie down. Instantly the heat of the earth rose into his back, yet it was more than just heat. The only way he could think to describe it was like a powerful fluid energy being poured upwards into his body. And the more it filled him, the more he realised how empty he'd been until that moment.

He was a man of the mountains, just like his father and grandfather and their fathers and grandfathers before them. The mountains were not just in his blood, but in every fibre of his being. Over the years, being so snarled up in the administrative hum-drum of work and the domestic anguish of his daily existence, he had forgotten this – or maybe it was only now that he was able to understand it.

At last he opened his eyes a crack and squinted up at the sky. It was clear, with the exception of one solitary cumulus cloud, which was so white and fluffy and archetypally cumulus-cloud-like, that it was almost like a cartoon drawing. Dante was reminded of a thought-bubble, as one would see in a children's comic book. Its position, hovering just above one chimney of the little house, amused him. What was the house thinking? he wondered. *Who's this coming to see me after all this time?*

How he envied its position, so far away from the loathsomeness of people and all the grief they caused. In this beautiful, wild, isolated place there was time and space just to think and to be. Here a man could either lose himself, or find himself...

Accessing the house took significantly longer than the five minutes Dante had predicted. The path was choked with overgrowth. Tree roots had dislodged the stone steps which his grandfather had set into the steep incline, so in some places there was no path left at all. The hunting knife which Dante had brought with him was a woefully inadequate tool with which to clear a way through, but eventually, after well over an hour, he made it.

The house had not been built to any plan. His father and grandfather had used what was available to them and had let the materials dictate the construction. This squat, pot-bellied little place with its sharply pitched roof was certainly not without its charm. It would not have looked out of place in a book of fairy tales.

The stream beside it was still running, although not as freely as it had previously. Dante could see that it was dammed by a fallen tree further up. Probably just as well, or it might have flooded the house.

Dante had feared that perhaps over the years others might have stumbled across the place, or heard about it, gone looking and found it. There had been incidents of groups of youths camping in the goat-herders' cabins and causing deliberate damage, or making off with the few bits and pieces which the goat-herders kept there for emergencies, just for sport. Fortunately, Dante was certain that the last hands on the planks which barred the door had been his own. He took his hammer and clawed out the nails. They were rusted, but came out straight and intact. They were old-style, wedge-shaped clout nails, probably made in Montacciolo. There was still a village blacksmith back then.

Inside, the place was like a time capsule, shrouded in cobwebs as thick as blankets, but everything was just as it had been left. There was some basic kitchen equipment – tin plates and cups, some cutlery, a couple of pots, a frying pan, a coffee percolator, and general household things, such as buckets and brooms. The bedding had seen better days. Clearly at some point a colony of mice had moved in.

The house was furnished very basically with a rustic table and benches, a couple of beds and a rudimentary dresser. All this had been fashioned from trees felled to make room for the construction. There was no denying that Dante's forefathers had been capable men. It was a tragedy that skills such as theirs were dying out, and in many cases had already died out. Dante himself was the perfect example. If he was tasked with building a house, he wouldn't know where to start.

The only large item which had not been rustled up from the surrounding area was the range. His father and grandfather had brought that up in pieces and re-assembled it. The story of moving the stove had achieved the status of family legend. Each time it was told, the stove became a few kilograms heavier.

First the flue pipe and fire box had been carried up, then one cheek, then the other, the back, the front minus its doors, then the doors, until finally what was left was the cast-iron plate – the heaviest part, which could not be broken down into smaller pieces. Dante recalled his father telling him what a labour that had been. They had tried to load it onto a mule, but it was impossible for the poor beast to balance such a cumbersome burden. In the end, the men had hauled it a few hundred meters further up the mountain with each trip. Once they had moved it as far as their strength would allow, they would stash it away in the undergrowth until the next time. On several occasions they had forgotten exactly where they had left it, which had caused some very heated arguments. It took two years for all the parts of the stove to be reunited at the top of the mountain.

When Dante, aged around thirteen, had listened to his father recounting what he referred to as his 'Calvary', it had reminded him of a story from Greek mythology which he had studied during a lesson at school. Hoping that his father would be impressed by his knowledge of this classical subject, he had narrated the story of Sisyphus, punished the God Zeus and forced to roll a boulder up a mountain for eternity.

Signor Bacchetti probably wouldn't have paid any attention if the story hadn't involved a stone and a mountain, but to begin with he was intrigued and interrupted with lots of questions. *How high was the mountain?* Dante was unprepared for this, but surmised that as three hundred meters above sea level was the minimum height to classify as a mountain, it must have been at least that. *And the boulder? How big was that?* Dante wasn't sure, but it must have been pretty big. *What type of stone was it? Granite? Sandstone? Limestone? Marble?* Dante said that wasn't specified in the story. *What shape was it?* Again, Dante didn't know. *Did Sisyphus use ropes and wedges and levers?* No, he had to push it with his bare hands. *That wouldn't be possible. Nobody could move a boulder uphill like that. This Greek mythology business all sounded a bit far-fetched.*

Irritated by his son's lack of detail, and clearly having run out of patience with the improbability of the story, before Dante could get to the end, his father demanded, 'So did Sisyphus manage to get the boulder to the top of the mountain or not?'

'Yes, he did.'

'What happened then? Did that clear the air with the Zeus fellow?'

'No. The boulder just rolled back down and he had to start again.'

'Who made him start again?'

'Zeus.'

Dante's father had spat on the ground.

'Pah!' He'd exclaimed. 'If I'd been that Sisyphus chump I'd have told that Zeus to stick his boulder where the sun don't shine.'

Signor Bacchetti then questioned, as he did frequently, what this fancy education he was paying for was really teaching his son.

Dante came back to the present and found himself smiling as he cast his eyes over the old stove. He'd been so caught up with all the recent angst that he didn't think about his father as much as he should. They'd had a few squabbles over the years, but that couldn't be helped, being such different characters and living such different lives. There was no denying that his father had been a hard man to please, but he had mellowed with age. His bellicose nature and had softened to a more endearing curmudgeonliness over time.

That first day Dante spent just a few hours at the little house, re-acquainting himself with its nooks and crannies and reminiscing about past times spent there. He wished he could have stayed longer, but did not want to risk being out on the mountain after dark. Nevertheless, as he left, he knew that something of the angry knot inside him had loosened. His mind, which was always so wracked with rage and frustration, had found a few hours of stillness and quiet and almost – yes, very, very nearly almost – a little speck of happiness.

The summer ended. Autumn came and went. The winter was not as cold as others had been. Spring was wet, but mild. As a new summer approached, Dante counted down the days to the holiday again.

That school year had been marginally less arduous. Before everything had fallen apart, Dante had cared so much for each pupil. He had stayed behind every day to give extra help to those who were struggling, or to encourage those who showed promise in a particular subject. He had even held extracurricular classes on Saturday mornings, unpaid and in his own time. But since the debacle with Leonora, Dante had reduced his workload to the bare minimum and always left within five minutes of dismissing his pack of brats. All that he cared about was that his salary was paid. He felt not the slightest twinge of conscience about it.

Life at home had improved slightly. Ortensia had begun to cook and to do a little housework, which was a positive sign, but she refused to open any windows. The house looked cleaner, but it stank.

With the new summer's approach Dante watched the charcoal-burner's house with trepidation, hoping that it would not fill up again with undesirable tenants; but then a postcard arrived from Leonora, sent from the Spanish island of Mallorca to say that 'they' were spending the summer there living in a rural smallholding which she called a *finca*. It was beautiful, she said, set within acres of almond groves. 'They' would help with the harvest.

Dante wanted to spit. An intelligent mind wasted almond-picking, like a peasant! Had Leonora's education counted for nothing? Still, he felt relief that 'they' were a long way away. The charcoal-burner's house remained closed up. No outsiders visited Montacciolo that summer.

Returning to the solace of the mountains occupied Dante's mind. He planned trips to Santa Croce and to Lago Stretto, but most of all, he thought of going back to the little house. Perhaps he would take sausages with him and light a fire outside in a ring of stones, just as he had done all those years before; with a slowly percolated coffee made with spring water and patience to follow. And he would certainly be feasting on this year's crop of wild raspberries when they ripened.

He should tidy the house up a bit, he thought. Just a few days of cleaning and airing and some good old-fashioned elbow grease would make it useable again. He should probably start by sorting out the access and dealing with the ivy and creepers. There would be even more of them now.

Dante didn't bother with trips to Santa Croce, or to Lago Stretto. On the first day of the summer break he was once again on the mountain track, heading for the little house, equipped with branch-cutters and a handsaw. Then again, two days after that, this time carrying a new brush-head for the broom, oil for the door hinges, a chisel and a wood-plane. And so it continued, through that first month of the summer holiday, Dante would go to the house every few days and spend as long there as the daylight would allow, cleaning and fixing up all the things which needed cleaning and fixing up.

Each time he would take something to leave there – tools and utensils and household things. He also began to carry up tins of food, which he never ate, but left there for future trips; then candles and blankets with the thought of staying overnight. Just one night, but maybe two, or longer if there was a good moon –

a week perhaps, if provisions allowed – although no, he couldn't leave Ortensia for that long. He would have to satisfy himself with a couple of nights at most.

With every trip, the route to the house grew more familiar and its features became recognisable landmarks, like milestones. Reaching the ivy-covered oak signalled that Dante had been walking half an hour. Then, after another half hour he would take the zigzag path which climbed sharply between two high walls of rock. At the end of the path was a towering maple tree, still living, but hollowed-out by lightning. Next came the series of waterfalls known as the *Tre Sorelle*, the Three Sisters, although since they had been christened, a new waterfall had emerged, thus making the three sisters four. Here, Dante knew that he was half way and would rest a while on a mossy rock, carved by time and weather into an almost perfect armchair. Sometimes he would cool his feet in one of the pools. In between these markers were ancient pits dug by charcoal-burners, grottos in which people might have lived once, and occasionally the ruins of a crude man-made structure.

Then at last he would arrive the daisy field, where he would always take himself back to the day with Leonora. Sometimes he would sing under his breath, '*Daisy, daisy don't be lazy. Daisy, daisy, you're so crazy...*' and other times Dante would sing it at the top of his voice, over and over again, just as Leonora had done.

When he reached the raspberry canes his heart would soar. There was the little house! He felt welcomed by it, like a long-awaited friend. Its higgledy-piggledy prettiness never failed to enchant him.

The first thing he would do was to get a fire going outside in a ring of stones and he would cook up whatever leftovers he had brought from the pantry at home. Then, using the ancient percolator, which was so tarnished that it was black, inside and out,

Dante would brew his coffee. There was never a more enjoyable coffee than that first cup, sipped whilst sitting on the front steps of the little house. As the coffee soaked into his system, he would feel the quickening of his heartbeat. But these were not anxious palpitations. They were a reminder that being alive could sometimes be bearable.

This place, so far away from everything, filled him with a dizzying sense of freedom, and the clearing and arrangement of the house seemed to have a corresponding effect on his mind. Bit by bit the suffocating grip of his anger was loosening. Dante's mind was emptying of all those furious thoughts, and within the newly vacated spaces, other feelings were taking their place.

The more time he spent at the little house, the more he felt at one with it. He began to wonder whether solitude might be the answer to the troubles of his life. Still, he couldn't remove himself from his responsibilities, however tempting it might be. He had to think about Ortensia.

As the summer progressed, Dante felt an ever-stronger pull towards self-examination, and it was during one of these introspective moments that he felt the regret and a sense of *mea culpa* begin to seep in. At first it was uncomfortable and he pushed it aside, but he knew that just like his anger, it must be dealt with if he was ever going to regain some sort of equilibrium in this life.

Now that a little time had passed since Leonora's departure Dante was asking himself what he could have done to make things different.

Of course, Leonora had behaved appallingly, and there was no need to sugar-coat that. She had caused him and her mother incalculable grief, humiliation and embarrassment – all done quite blatantly and with deliberate intent to wound. He felt wronged, disrespected, insulted, et cetera, et cetera. He could think of a hundred synonyms to describe his feelings, but the time for listing those had passed.

Dante began to think less about what Leonora had done and more about why she had done it. Was her behaviour not a symptom of the sickness of the household in which she had been raised? Now perhaps was the time to start to consider the subject he avoided thinking about; the cross which he bore day in, day out, year after year – his wife, Leonora's mother: Ortensia.

Had she ever been quite right in the head? Dante wondered. That initial timidity and child-like naïveté which had so endeared her to him at the start, was that not just a sign of her mental fragility? Maybe he had been over-optimistic to presume that Ortensia would be capable of assuming the duties of marriage and motherhood.

The madness hadn't all come at once, not at the beginning, at least. There had been small, incremental increases, so gradual that they were difficult to spot individually. Ortensia's fear of the outside world became progressively more pronounced. Her silences grew longer and sadder; her fits of unprovoked weeping, more frequent. That had led to those hours, then days, then weeks, closed up in her room, nursing all manner aches and pains – all of them psychosomatic in nature. Dante had no doubt about that.

When Leonora had arrived, he had hoped that having a child to care for would distract Ortensia from her own tribulations, but the pregnancy had been difficult and the birth traumatic. After that, there had only been one direction, and that was down.

There had been times when he had thought about entrusting Ortensia to professionals, but he had always talked himself out of it. Handing over responsibility, even temporarily, would be a mark of failure. He would never forgive himself. His wife would never forgive him. Leonora would never forgive him. But the road to hell was paved with good intentions, as the old proverb said. In his effort to do the right thing, all he'd succeeded in doing was making life far harder than it needed to be.

Dante's mind was drawn back to those excruciating Sundays, which came around just once a week, but which felt so much more frequent.

There would be two hours spent coaxing his wife from her bed, then from her room, followed by his begging that she should get dressed for church. Ortensia owned twice as many clothes as most of the women in Montacciolo put together, and hers were good quality garments which Dante had purchased for her in town; not the cobbled-together hand-me-downs that most of the other Montacciolane sported.

Why don't you put one of your lovely dresses on for church, Ortensia darling? You'll feel better. And after some encouragement, she would, and it would look very nice on her. *Would you like me to help you with your hair? Here, I've polished your shoes for you. Oh, you look a picture! Come on now, or we'll be late. Please, Ortensia, darling, don't make a fuss. It'll be all right.*

He would usher her to the front door. Deep breath. Practise smiling to the world, like an actor preparing for a performance. Pretend that it hasn't taken three hours of negotiation and anguish to get ready. Best foot forward. Here we go. *Ready, darling?*

They'd walk up to church arm-in-arm in their spotless Sunday best, greeting everyone who crossed their path. *Good morning. Good to see you.* They would sit, stand and kneel their way through Mass. *Lord, in Your mercy, hear our prayer.* After the service they'd shake the priest's hand. *Splendid sermon, Don Generoso, splendid sermon.* Then they'd chat with other villagers, exchanging superficial small talk about inconsequential matters. *How are things? Perfect, thank you, perfect.* Back home they would go, still arm-in-arm, still looking immaculate, and with their unflinching smiles screwed onto their faces.

This bubble of perfection would be burst by the closing of the front door. *Pop!* Then the exhaustion of keeping up the pretence would hit Dante. He would stand with his back pressed to the wall, drained of everything – energy, patience, goodwill, hope. How he sympathised with Sisyphus and that blasted boulder!

What had compelled him to keep pushing that boulder uphill, knowing that it was destined to roll back down again, and that on his next attempt it would feel twice as heavy, and it was only a matter of time until it flattened him completely? If he was honest, what had stopped him was the shame of his private failures becoming public. Now he saw that fear for what it was – such a myopic and self-centred way to think.

Dante had convinced himself that he was doing his duty, but what had he really succeeded in doing? Home life had been a miserable torment for him, but that had involved some element of choice. Leonora had had no choice in the matter. He'd just presented her with the boulder and told her to get pushing.

He used to say to himself that Leonora would be all right because he was both her father and her mother, but that was a ridiculous delusion. He'd just been a father struggling to be a father. Leonora had deserved better. He had allowed her to be damaged.

Now that he thought about it, perhaps that was the reason she had found it so difficult to make friends. Leonora had enjoyed only one childhood friendship, but that had ended abruptly for reasons that Leonora would not explain, and she had formed no meaningful connections in Montacciolo after that. She had been a solitary child, always closed up in her room with her books and poems. He had viewed this as a good thing at the time – his daughter was studious and creative. But in reality, had she just been terribly lonely and sad?

No wonder that she resented him so much, and that she had grown up embittered. Those swings of mood, those viperous words, those tantrums at home and those disruptive outbursts at school – they were all proxy symptoms of her mother's sickness. Why had he not seen it for what it was? Why had he let it happen? Why had he punished Leonora for her reactions, rather than dealing with the cause?

Perhaps when Leonora was older and he was long-gone, she might think back and remember dancing in the field of lazy, crazy daisies; eating bite-size pieces of sausage wrapped in leaves; riding on her father's back whilst he clip-clopped like a horse. So easily forgotten were the most important things, mused Dante.

Dante hoped that when the day came that his daughter found herself looking back, as he was now, armed with life experience and the perspective that only the passing of time could bestow, she might understand, dissolve her own anger – perhaps even forgive him as he had forgiven his own father. There had been a long list of wrongdoings in that relationship.

When Dante thought about his father now, he no longer thought of the tyrant whose temper could be inflamed by the most trifling matter. Instead, he concentrated on the times which amused him, or brought him a sense of pride. He remembered the man who sharpened and oiled his tools with such care that he might have been handling glass; and admired the man who had been so rooted in ancient ways, yet forward-thinking enough to have ambitions for his son beyond the stone trades.

Dante didn't dwell on the out-of-the blue fits of violence, the belittling and the beatings. He barely gave those a moment's attention now; not even the time when his two front teeth were knocked out. His father hadn't meant to hit him quite that hard, but Dante had flinched the wrong way and straight into the trajectory of his father's fist, so his own misjudgement was half to blame. Anyway, they were only milk teeth, so they were replaced eventually.

The correspondence from Leonora continued, except that now sometimes there was a letter – although it rarely involved more than a single side of writing. The content was culturally interesting, but never personal. The letters comprised descriptions of foreign places, different foods that she had tried, accounts of customs she found interesting. How infuriating for the postmaster, thought Dante, not to be able to nose about in my business – although one letter did arrive looking suspiciously as though it had been steamed open and pasted closed again.

These letters caused Ortensia new worries – foreigners, foreign food, foreign things. So many dangers to pray about that it was hard to know where to start.

Sometimes, if Leonora was staying somewhere long enough to provide a return address, Ortensia would spend two days in a frenzy of letter-writing and pen several pages of speculation about what she supposed was happening in the village, although she didn't really know because she never went out. The rest was invariably about what she'd been praying for – namely for God to forgive Leonora her sins. It was important to let Jesus into her heart, she told her daughter.

Leonora would write back expressing a false interest in the village hearsay and ignoring the parts about seeking God's forgiveness. She never alluded to letting Jesus into her heart, or to returning home, not even for a visit. Dante found the exchange excruciating, and although he abstained from joining in with it, he read both sides. He preferred to cast his eye over what his wife had written before he posted her letters, just in case she'd said something which might cause Leonora undue concerns. Many times he'd insist that Ortensia should copy out her letter again because she had made such a mess of it. It was not just her handwriting which lacked regular form and clarity, the misspellings, or the ugly, crossed-out corrections. For some reason

Ortensia had adopted a habit of tearing the corners off the page. Dante couldn't bear for something so dog-eared and scrappy to be sent, so he would refuse to post it unless Ortensia re-drafted it neatly and did not damage the corners.

One day Dante did something which previously he had vowed never to do. He wrote back too, in the expectation that Leonora would understand his words to be a preliminary olive branch. He kept his message short, but tried his best to assume a tone of fatherly concern. *He hoped that she was safe. Happy. Fulfilled.* Then he crossed the word 'fulfilled' out and replaced it with: *Satisfied with your choices.* He signed off as *your father, Dante.*

Leonora replied very economically, saying that she was all of the above. She just signed it 'L.B.', as though she had been in a hurry.

This lukewarm, token correspondence continued for seven years – until in October of 1972, it stopped.

CHAPTER 11

'When did you report your daughter missing?' Asked Jubanne Melis Puddu, and the question brought the old man back to the present.

'I didn't,' he replied. 'My wife and I didn't know she was missing until several months after she disappeared.'

Dante rose to his feet, went to the dresser and came back with a bundle of letters and postcards tied with a ribbon, from which he peeled the top envelope and said, 'The last contact my wife and I had from Leonora was this, dated October 3rd 1972. It was sent from Pesaro, where she had been living for a few months.'

He sat back down and slipped the letter from its envelope.

'As with all her previous letters there isn't anything to indicate what was going on in Leonora's private life. She writes that her summer job has ended and that she intends to rest for a couple of weeks, but that she will be remaining in Pesaro as she has been offered another job there for the winter. It was an unusually long length of time for her to spend in one place. She doesn't give any details of the job, and we assumed it was not dissimilar to her previous casual employment in bars, cafeterias and such-like. The subsequent police investigation confirmed that it was indeed in the kitchen of a nearby restaurant.'

Dante contemplated the letter for a moment, although it was clear that he had read it often enough to know its contents by heart.

'We received this final communication around ten days after it had been written and posted back a reply about a week later. My wife was going through one of her more agitated episodes and took a particularly long time composing her response. I could not guess how many attempts it took her. And when she finally managed to produce a coherent letter, I was obliged to ask her to copy it out again because she had torn all four corners off the page.'

'Why did she tear off the corners like that?' inquired the Sardinian.

The old man shrugged, 'This compulsion was just one more expression of her increasingly disturbed behaviour. Now, I must confess, my insistence that she should re-draft her letters seems somewhat pedantic. But I have always had a preoccupation with neatness and order. Once a schoolmaster, always a schoolmaster, I suppose.'

Dante folded the letter carefully, running his finger and thumb precisely along the fold.

'In this region, the winter of '72 to '73 was particularly inclement. The heavy snows came early. Montacciolo was already cut off by mid-November and remained snowed-in until mid-March. Then, when the temperature rose, the rain started. It rained so much that it resulted in part of the road to Montacciolo being washed away in a landslide, so we were cut off for a further six weeks until that was sorted out. The government had to send in the army with emergency food and medicine. Members of the *Alpinisti* regiment came up on foot with backpacks filled with supplies for us. But of course, during all that time there was no post, either leaving or arriving in Montacciolo. Nothing came until the road was re-instated. But when at last the post did reach the village, there were no letters from Leonora.'

Dante put his hand to his heart again.

'My wife was beside herself, as you can imagine. She jumped to the conclusion that Leonora had died. I thought this to be rather an over-dramatic assumption and I tried to remain pragmatic, suggesting that perhaps Leonora had changed her mind about staying in Pesaro and had gone off somewhere where the postal service was unreliable, which was not too outlandish a supposition to make. But I cannot deny that I was concerned, so we wrote to her at that last address we had in Pesaro.'

They had received a reply very quickly, Dante explained, not from his daughter, but from a woman who lodged in the boarding-house where Leonora had been living. She apologised for the fact that she had opened the letter and said that she would not have done so had the circumstances not been as they were.

'The woman informed us that the last time she, or anyone else who lodged in that boarding-house, had seen Leonora was around the 15th of October of the previous year. But, she was at pains to point out, nobody could be absolutely sure of the date. That boarding-house was a transient place. People came and went all the time and most rarely stayed long enough to form any meaningful connections with their neighbours. The woman said that although she had spoken to Leonora a few times, she could not claim that they were anything more than passing acquaintances. When the woman noticed that Leonora was absent, she assumed that my daughter had gone to stay with friends, or family, or perhaps that she had met a new lover. But it was none of her business, so she hadn't given it much thought.'

The old man slid Leonora's last letter back into its envelope and went on to recount how, according to the neighbour, at the beginning of November the proprietor of the restaurant where Leonora was due to start her winter job had called by to see where she was because she hadn't turned up for work as promised. Still nobody had thought anything untoward. Even when Leonora's rent was overdue and the landlord opened up her room, all that concerned him was recovering the rent that he was owed. He had picked through her belongings to see whether she had left any money.

Dante shook his head sadly. 'Is it not astonishing that this did not ring any alarm bells? I find this lack of concern a grim reflection of modern society. Had anybody thought to inform the authorities sooner, the case might have had some hope of being resolved. But it wasn't until early December that the neighbour filed a missing persons report with the police, and when she did, she wasn't taken seriously. She was unusual in appearance, a marginal type and a little unwashed. A vegetarian – by choice, I believe. She was what people called a 'hippy'. I expect you're familiar with the term?'

Jubanne Melis Puddu nodded. Dante continued, 'On learning this I contacted the Pesaro police immediately and I was met with what I can only describe as indifference. I discovered that there had been absolutely nothing undertaken in the way of an investigation. No police officer had even been sent to the boarding-house to interview the other tenants.'

'They'd done nothing at all?'

'Nothing! Except to give the report a number and file it away. As you can imagine, I was outraged. I insisted that the police should begin an investigation immediately, which reluctantly, they did. But by then six months had passed since Leonora had last been seen and there was very little to investigate. Her room had been cleared and her possessions had been put in boxes, and much of it had been rifled both by the landlord and tenants, so it was impossible to say what she might have taken with her which might provide some clue to where she had gone. As for anyone who could provide any other information, over a period of time such as that peoples' memories become unreliable. Details which might have been important are forgotten, or misremembered. Some of the tenants who had been lodging in the boarding-house at the time of Leonora's last sighting had moved away and nobody could be sure where they had moved to, so they couldn't be interviewed. Those who remained simply said that one moment she was there, the next she wasn't, but none of them had really known anything about her. Some had only learned her name once she was gone. Other people were tracked down and spoken to– former friends, acquaintances, ex-lovers, ex-employers – but there was nothing to link any of them to Leonora's disappearance. I demanded that the police should find Fernando and other members of The Collective in case she had been tempted back into the fold, but The Collective had disbanded a long time before. By some miracle they managed to locate Fernando, but there was nothing to connect him to Leonora any more.'

Dante turned the envelope over in his hand. Eventually he said, 'I travelled down to Pesaro to retrieve my daughter's things. There wasn't much – just three boxes, the contents of which could have fitted into two. There was some clothing, some toiletries, a few trinkets and items of cheap costume jewellery, small souvenirs of the places she'd visited. I was relieved to find that her notebooks were still there though.'

The old man set aside the letter, took the volume of poetry and clutched it to his chest.

'It would have been a further assault on my heart if somebody had taken those,' he said. 'Because by then the fear of something terrible having happened to Leonora had become very real. I was ready at any point to be told that she was dead. I was ready to hear reports of a body being discovered somewhere, and for the police to come knocking on my door with the news. I didn't want to be prepared, but I had to be.'

'But she was still alive,' said Jubanne Melis Puddu. 'She was in Sardinia by then.'

'So you claim, my friend, and that is not in itself difficult to believe. It was in her character to up sticks and go from place to place on a whim. But the question remains: why, after years of regular correspondence, would she have severed all contact with us so suddenly?

For that, Jubanne Melis Puddu had no answer, but quite abruptly, his expression changed.

'I'm supposed to take pills with my dinner,' he said with an air of panic. 'Did I take my pills?'

'You did.'

'What did I take?'

'A round blue one and a diamond-shaped white one.'

The big Sardinian furrowed his brow, as though trying very hard, and failing, to recall it.

'Is that what it said I should take on the list?'

'Yes.'

'Are you sure I took them?'

'Absolutely. You took them right here in front of me.'

Relieved, Dante's guest brought the conversation back to the matter in hand.

'Tell me about the police investigation,' he said.

Now Dante's expression turned rancorous and he spoke with his lip curled.

'The police continued with their nominal investigation, but I regret to say that they were more invested in finding out salacious tit bits to snigger at than in finding out what had happened to my daughter. There was no hiding from the fact that Leonora had led a promiscuous life. Every time a former lover crawled out of the woodwork the police's reaction was: "Well, what does a girl expect, running around after all these men? That's just asking for trouble." In their small minds they had already decided that Leonora's life had come to a gruesome end following an altercation with some new man whom she had provoked in some way. Perhaps she had made him jealous because of her past affairs. Perhaps she had said something to anger him. Whatever the catalyst, the case was dismissed as a probable crime of passion, and a young woman like Leonora was its deserving victim.' Dante held up his hands, 'Of course, this conclusion may well have been correct, but the police were unable to prove anything.'

The old man paused, staring down into his empty soup bowl. 'Having lost all faith in the police, I took the initiative and contacted a national newspaper, *Il Resto del Carlino*, to make an appeal about Leonora's disappearance. A journalist came to interview me and I asked for whoever knew anything, however small or insignificant they thought it might be, to please come forward. What they remembered could be the essential piece of information to unlock the puzzle. The article appeared on page six, but it was not what I expected, in either tone or content.'

'What do you mean?'

Dante's jaw trembled. He spoke barely opening his mouth.

'Clearly the journalist who interviewed me had contacts within the police force, and the more sensational parts of the investigation were leaked to him. So, rather than depicting me as concerned father desperately seeking confirmation of his daughter's whereabouts, or her fate, my words were twisted, taken wholly out of context and I was portrayed as a negligent parent, directly to blame for my daughter's immoral lifestyle and therefore responsible for her disappearance. And as if that was not enough, they even had the temerity to question my educational credentials and my teaching professionalism! I was made a pariah in the press, just as I had been made a pariah in the village. Only this time the defamation wasn't confined to Montacciolo. The coverage was nationwide, and twice even reported in foreign newspapers.'

Clearly the emotions aroused by this recollection still vexed the old man. He was icily silent for a moment before adding, 'Perhaps it was naïve of me to suppose that Leonora's disappearance would be taken seriously. In the eyes of the press, missing women were divided into two categories – the virgins and the whores. My daughter was firmly placed in the second category and therefore deemed unworthy of any serious investigation.'

'Were there no answers to your appeal?'

'Nothing of any significance,' said Dante, gesturing vaguely towards the files on the shelves. 'Just a deluge of judgmental correspondence in which I was called some terrible names, and no end of lascivious speculation. Anyway, I refused to be interviewed after that, but by then the story had piqued public interest for all the wrong reasons, and the snowball continued to roll. Several other newspapers and periodicals reported on the original article. There were even photographers sent to take pictures of the charcoal-burner's house. "The House of Sin", they called it. What a sorry circus that was! Various hacks came rapping on my door asking me to comment, which as you can imagine, caused my wife's precarious emotional state to spiral.'

As Jubanne Melis Puddu listened to the old man's account, Dante's expression darkened to a look of disgust. He went on to explain how certain individuals from the village of Montacciolo had seized the opportunity to make a fast buck out of his misfortune. They were at pains to remain nameless, yet eager to sell tawdry tales relating to Leonora and The Collective. The eyewitness accounts were, at best, wildly exaggerated and at worst, entirely made up.

'Those Judases!' Spluttered Dante. 'What easy money it was for them, making those anonymous denunciations! But it wasn't difficult to see who'd sold out. People who previously didn't have two lire to rub together suddenly started parading around the village in new clothes. Silvio, who everyone had always known as "Senzadenti" because he had no teeth, miraculously managed to procure himself a smile like Jean-Paul Belmondo. That Fiat 126 the bar owner bought was not purchased with the profits of selling cups of coffee...I could go on.'

Making an effort to gather himself, Dante steadied himself against the edge of the table.

'I would be the first to admit that my daughter wasn't perfect, and that I did not approve of the way she chose to live her life, but to have her name and reputation slandered in such a way when she was not there to defend herself was a grotesque and unjust thing to behold.'

The Sardinian tilted his head in sympathy, 'I remember. Some of the things that the newspapers said weren't kind.'

Now the old man was close to tears.

'And when you saw those malicious articles, you would have seen the indecent photograph which accompanied them.'

'The picture on the beach?'

Dante nodded. 'Yes. As I was unable to provide a recent photograph of Leonora, one was furnished by that beast, Fernando. It had been taken on the South coast of France not long before Leonora left The Collective. I could hardly bear to look at it, with all that flesh on display. That two-piece swimsuit could hardly be called an item of clothing. Leonora might as well have been pictured naked. And it was all the worse because the very part of my daughter which was essential for people to recognise her, namely her face, was almost entirely obscured by sunglasses and the wide brim of a straw hat. I am certain that photograph was responsible for the countless false sightings.'

Dante made a spitting sound. 'Having lost all faith in the police and the press, the only route open to me was to commission a private investigation, which was a very expensive enterprise. I was not a rich man, you understand. My teaching salary covered the basics, and that was the only salary I had left. Since being stripped of my other duties, I had been obliged to tighten my belt. However, whilst in my previous teaching post in Ferrara, I had purchased an apartment in the city. In those days, right after the war, one could buy a property for next to nothing. I lived in that apartment only briefly, before returning to follow my calling in Montacciolo, but I had the good sense not to sell it when I moved away. I installed tenants and scrupulously saved the modest rent they paid each month. Over the years, a reasonable nest egg had accumulated. Originally it had been destined to complement my pension as I knew that my miniscule teaching salary in Montacciolo would reward me with a miserly provision to cover my declining years. One's pension is not necessarily proportional to the sacrifice of one's labours.'

'Is that how you paid for the private investigation?'

'The saved money was not sufficient to cover it. I was obliged to sell the apartment too. That money funded a year of private investigation before running out. But it uncovered nothing useful.'

Then suddenly, as though the trauma of those past events had fallen back upon him, the old man buried his face in his hands stammered, 'The smearing in the press was not the worst thing, nor was the financial ruin and loss of a secure future for myself and my wife. Not knowing whether Leonora was dead or alive was worse than all of that.'

Dante took out his handkerchief again, dabbed his cheeks and blew his nose loudly.

'I realised that although I should not give up hope of finding Leonora alive, the best I could do was to come to terms with the fact that my daughter was probably dead. It is an abhorrent thing, picturing the death of one's own child, but it was a process which I had to go through. All I hoped was that Leonora's end, if indeed it had happened, had been quick and that she had not suffered. That was the *only* thing I could hope for.'

The old man sniffed, swallowed hard and continued in a choked voice, 'It was another matter entirely for my wife, Ortensia. She did not have the capacity to process difficult feelings. By this time, with the emotional and financial strain of

128

everything which had happened, I was finding looking after her impossible.'

Dante's expression betrayed the fact that he was not comfortable with what he was about to confess.

'Things had become so untenable that I resorted to medicating her, which was something I had pledged never to do, but I could see no other way. The sedatives which Ortensia took were relatively mild, but at least with those she slept, often until late in the morning, and they kept her calm for the remainder of the day. I could come home from work and be assured a few hours of peace and a full night's sleep.'

'Medication is necessary in some cases,' said Jubanne Melis Puddu, referring just as much to himself.

'Indeed it is. And it was effective,' continued Dante. 'Those interminable fits of weeping stopped altogether and Ortensia's prayers were not so frenzied, although I was under no illusion that she was healed. I was aware that the sedatives simply gave the impression of calm. But that temporary solace, illusory though it was, allowed me to save myself from disintegrating, and I was most grateful for it. I know that must sound terribly selfish.'

Dante was silent for a few moments. Resting his head in his hands he concluded, almost inaudibly, 'What I did not realise was the extent to which that medication pushed my wife's pain deeper inside her.'

CHAPTER 12

Dante woke up late on the morning of the 6th of April 1975 – a highly uncommon occurrence. He had not had any nightmares, which was even more unusual. Yet he felt terrible; nauseous, with a thick head a mouth so dry that his lips were stuck to his teeth. He must be going down with something, he thought. There had been a few cases of influenza going round. Maybe it was that. When he tried to get out of bed, the room spun. He called out to his wife repeatedly, but she did not hear him, which was not a surprise. Ortensia's bedroom was at the opposite end of the house and the sedatives often knocked her out until lunchtime. Dante lay back down on the bed to try to settle his vertigo and although he had not intended to, fell back to sleep.

He was jerked awake just before midday by a persistent knocking at his door.

'Dante! Dante! Are you there? Open up!'

He had hauled himself out of bed, still dizzy, and had fumbled his way downstairs to discover Don Generoso accompanied by half a dozen solemn-faced villagers at his door. The priest was the only one to come into the house. He sat Dante down at the kitchen table and told him to prepare himself for some bad news. Dante, despite feeling as though his head was filled with cotton wool, had braced himself. He knew by the priest's expression that this was a moment he'd been expecting, and he was ready for it.

'Your wife's body's been found,' said the priest. 'I'm very sorry for you, Dante.'

Dante had faltered, thinking that either the priest had misspoken, or he had misheard.

'You mean my *daughter's* body?'

'No, Dante. Your wife's body.'

Still Dante couldn't process the information. Surely Don Generoso was talking nonsense. He must have been at the Communion wine.

'No, no, Don Generoso. Ortensia's upstairs in bed. She hasn't been feeling too well. There are a few cases of influenza going around. We think it's that. Here, come with me. I'll show you.'

Still unsteady on his feet, Dante had ushered the priest upstairs, stumbling as he went and all the time calling out Ortensia's name. He had opened the door to reveal his wife's room; empty and with the bed neatly made.

Exactly how the sequence of events had been explained to him, Dante could not recall. In his shocked state, it was hard to remember who had told him what, and in which order. One minute the priest was in his kitchen, then there were several different policemen and a mountain ranger, two official-looking men in suits and a woman who apparently was some sort of social worker.

The previous night Ortensia had dressed herself smartly, in a nice dress, as though she was going to church, and had left the house for the first time in almost ten years. She had walked a long way under the cover of darkness, down the road which led out of Montacciolo and as far as the bridge which spanned the gorge at Pontenuovo – a distance of around six miles.

Nobody knew what time she had left home, or how long it had taken her to reach her destination, therefore initially it was not clear at exactly what time she had jumped from the bridge into the torrent below.

A fisherman who had found her at 8 a.m. said that her body was cold, but that was no surprise as the water in the torrent was icy. Subsequently, the *Medico Legale* who carried out the autopsy estimated the time of death to have been between two and four in the morning. Ortensia Bacchetti had not drowned, he concluded. It was the thirty meter fall onto the rocks that killed her.

The reason behind Dante's uncharacteristic over-sleeping and thick-headedness that day was also explained. So that he wouldn't wake up and realise that she was gone, Ortensia had drugged her husband's dinner with a mighty dose of her sedatives.

The days which followed were hazy. The police returned to take a statement, although because no foul play was suspected, it was a just a formality. The social worker came back, accompanied by a second social worker. They asked a few sensitive questions about Ortensia, followed by a whole list of questions aimed at Dante, which he found uncomfortably personal under the circumstances. Once satisfied that he was not about to follow his wife's example and take himself down to the bridge at Pontenuovo, the social workers left and didn't come back.

The effect of the sedatives lingered. The doctor who examined Dante said that he was lucky to have woken up at all considering the amount he'd been given – ten times the normal dosage, at least. Dante thanked providence that he had not finished the drugged dinner which Ortensia had prepared, as without a doubt, it would have killed him.

Some villagers took pity on Dante and turned up on his doorstep with offerings of food. He did not eat a single morsel of it, but threw it away as soon as it arrived. He didn't trust anybody not to spit in his supper, or worse.

Still not feeling at all well, Dante went to see Don Generoso to make funeral arrangements. Ortensia wouldn't have wanted anything fussy, he said – just a simple send-off – but she would probably have wanted to be entombed as close to her parents as possible.

The priest squirmed and looked down at his feet. 'I'm sorry, Dante. I can't do that,' he said.

'Ah well,' sighed Dante, 'if Ortensia can't be close to her parents, that can't be helped, I suppose. Having such a modestly sized cemetery at our disposal, there isn't an awful lot of choice. You pick the spot, Don Generoso. I don't think I could bring myself to do it.'

The priest, who had turned a pasty grey colour, continued to look at his shoes as he spoke.

'Ortensia can't be laid to rest in the cemetery, Dante, in view of the circumstances of her passing.'

'What?'

'Suicides can't be entombed on consecrated ground. You know that, Dante.'

'But Don Generoso, this is Ortensia – my wife, Ortensia!'

Still the priest shook his head.

'I'm sorry. It's not allowed. *To wilfully destroy one's life is to wrongly assert dominion over God's creation.* It is a mortal sin.'

Dante stared at the priest, dumbstruck. Don Generoso continued in his most unctuous tone.

'Difficult though it must be, I would urge you not to despair, Dante. I have been praying for your wife, as have many others. Ortensia may still have a chance at salvation in view of her *morbus animi.*'

'Her *morbus animi?*' Bellowed Dante. 'You have the effrontery to refer to her "disease of the mind"? What would you expect when a woman has suffered everything that Ortensia has endured?'

'Indeed, Dante. And had you attended Mass yesterday, you would have heard me speak of the situation with great sorrow and regret. I urged the congregation to put aside past differences and to pray not only for Ortensia, but for you too.'

'Pray for me too? What, in case I also succumb to a fit of *morbus animi?*'

Don Generoso clasped his hands, doing his utmost to maintain an expression of priestly compassion.

'Everybody appreciates how difficult things are for you, Dante. I think that after she has been laid to rest, a memorial service would be the most appropriate way to remember Ortensia. I don't have any objection to that.'

Dante shot a direct look at the priest. He understood that there was something else that Don Generoso had not yet dared to say.

'A memorial service *after* the burial? You're even going to deny my wife a proper funeral aren't you?' He growled.

The priest's lips quivered. He pressed them together to steady his voice before he spoke. 'The same premise applies for the funeral service as for the burial. In view of the circumstances, I could not administer the rites *in corpora presente*.'

On hearing these words, *in corpora presente*, meaning that Don Generoso would not even allow Ortensia's body into the church, Dante experienced a surge of rage so intense that he grabbed Don Generoso by the bib of his cassock and shoved him hard against the wall. The priest made a startled noise, like the air being stamped out of a squeezebox.

'You won't permit my wife the basic dignity of a funeral? You won't give her a Christian burial in the cemetery?' Dante hissed into his face.

'I-I can't Dante. I'm sorry. I don't make the rules,' stammered the terrified priest.

'After everything I've done for you, you servile, cowardly, bible-muttering bastard!' Spat Dante, letting go. Don Generoso slumped to the floor, shaking.

Nothing could be done to convince the priest to break the rules.

Dante, insulted and aggrieved to the very core of his being, insisted that Ortensia's memorial service should be held *before* the burial, not after. So as not to offend the Good Lord by bringing the perpetrator of a suicide into His house, Ortensia's coffin would be carried into the church and placed before the altar – as was befitting of any dignified funeral – but it would be empty. To further emphasise the point, Dante demanded that the casket should remain open throughout the Mass. There was nothing in the rules to say that he couldn't do *that*.

The black-clad Montacciolani filed into the church in uneasy silence. With their hands clasped and chins pressed to their chests, they circled in a slow procession around the empty box, glancing at one another without moving their heads.

Dressed up in his best funerary purple robes and clearly in a state of acute discomfort, Don Generoso went through the ritual of the memorial Mass and offered up a cautiously worded sermon on suffering, perseverance and hope.

Dante limited himself to a simple five minute eulogy, filled with the customary clichés about loss and grief, and refrained from using over-complicated language or too many long words. The mourners listened. Then, whilst still at the lectern and whilst he had the congregation's full attention, Dante turned a fiery glare towards Don Generoso and demanded in a loud, strident voice, 'Where were *you*, Don Generoso, priest and shepherd of Montacciolo, when one of your flock was in need?'

The priest swallowed so hard that his gulp echoed around the church. He was at a loss to answer. Dante continued.

'Did you ever try to call in on Ortensia, Don Generoso? Did you ever once walk the fifty steps from this church to the door of my house to see how she was; to ask why she wouldn't come out, or why she was no longer attending Sunday Mass, which you knew had been so important to her? Did you think it unworthy of investigation that a woman should lock herself away like that for ten years?'

The priest, unblinking, clutched at the fringe of his funerary stole. No response was forthcoming.

'And during those ten long years, did you ever ask me, "Dante, how's your wife?", "Dante, how are things at home with Ortensia?" No, you did not. There was not the faintest murmur of concern from you. I ask you, Don Generoso, is it not a priest's basic duty to visit the sick, and to offer comfort and succour not just to them, but also to their families?'

Again, there was no reply from the priest. Dante turned back to address the stunned congregation.

'And you, people of Montacciolo, did any one of *you* ever trouble yourselves with a little neighbourly concern? Where was the Christian premise of loving thy neighbour? *Carry your neighbours' burdens and you will fulfil the law of Christ*, it says in Galatians, chapter six, verse two. What neighbourly burdens did you carry? You carried nothing. You fulfilled nothing. You were too busy spreading your slanderous calumny and your dirty tittle-tattle.'

As he spoke, Dante cast his eyes along the pews, row by row. Many parishioners looked down at their Orders of Service. The rest just remained frozen and stupefied and staring straight ahead.

'There's an awful lot you people don't know, but I'm pretty certain that you have a basic grasp of the Ten Commandments. *Thou shalt not bear false witness.* You've all heard that one before, I'm sure. Do you not think that the lies you invented concerning my daughter, and which some of you had the audacity to sell to the press, were not instrumental in my wife's decline and tragic demise?'

Then, addressing everyone present, the pitch of Dante's voice rose, and thumping his fist down hard on the lectern, he bellowed, 'Every soul in this church has had some part in my wife's death!'

As the congregation shrank back into their seats, Dante pointed at the open, empty coffin and gave a loud, disparaging laugh.

'And to add one final insult to the lengthy catalogue of injuries suffered by my wife, Ortensia is denied being present at her own funeral! It seems that it would be somehow offensive to God if her dead body was here in this church – yet it is perfectly acceptable for you all to be in here, pretending to mourn her, whilst you, Don Generoso reluctantly offer a few lame words on perseverance and loss and hope. If we're looking at offending the Holy Father, I put it to you, people of Montacciolo, and to you, Don Generoso, that all *your* actions are infinitely more egregious to God than my wife's desperate final act!'

With that, Dante took his seat again.

The priest was so disconcerted that he forgot all about communion, but the congregation's relief at being dismissed early was quite obvious. They wouldn't have cleared the church any faster if it had been on fire.

Following this most memorable of memorial services, Ortensia Bacchetti was buried on a small plot of un-consecrated ground, just behind the back boundary of the cemetery, which was reserved for the unworthy and the unbaptised. She was laid to rest beside the newborn baby boy who had been left on the church steps in 1963 and the fifteen year old girl called Tina, who was presumed to be his mother.

Initially, Dante was granted compassionate leave from his job and a supply teacher was brought in to take over his school responsibilities. After a month, still feeling unable to resume his duties, he asked for an extension and was awarded a further fortnight. When he requested longer, a representative from the Ministry of Education came to see him.

The representative spoke very sympathetically. He offered Dante the option of early retirement, not on a full pension, of course, but the Ministry could assure him a pension of sorts. Although this was being proposed as a choice, it wasn't really a choice. Dante guessed that if he turned the offer down, the

Ministry could find a reason, probably more than one, to fire him anyway; and then he'd have no income at all. Certain in the knowledge that he could not possibly live on the pauper's pension being proposed, Dante accepted the offer there and then. He had no fight left in him to argue for a better deal.

Dante's only request, which was more of a humble plea, was that perhaps the Ministry might name the village school after him to commemorate his years of service to education. A small plaque bearing the Bacchetti name would suffice. It would have meant a lot to his late wife. The representative said that he would see what he could do.

Shortly after his enforced retirement, Dante received a letter from the tax office requesting the payment of capital gains pertaining to sale of the apartment in Ferrara. This demand did not come as a surprise because Dante knew that taxes would be due, but he had spent the money on the private investigation. Trying to find Leonora had been more important that stuffing the government's coffers.

He wrote back explaining his predicament and there followed a period of to-and-fro correspondence where the tax office would demand the money in ever more stern language; Dante would write back to say that, regretfully, he was unable to pay it. The tax office would send another unyielding letter, still demanding payment, and Dante would reply that he still did not have it. A total of twenty-two letters were exchanged. Eventually the tax office threatened to take possession of his house in Montacciolo to cover the debt.

The house had been in the Bacchetti family for many generations. It was one of the better houses in the village; quite substantial and in good order. Had it been situated elsewhere, it would have fetched a handsome price. But property was cheaper than cheap up in Montacciolo. When the assessor from the tax office's debt recovery department came to value it, he remarked drily that it was worth 'approximately two sacks of onions', and certainly not enough to cover the tax bill owed. The tax office said they would take it anyway and Dante would have to pay the outstanding balance through some other means. Dante threw the letter into the fire and pledged never to correspond with the tax office again.

What next? thought Dante. Surely, no man could be burdened with quite so many misfortunes. He was by nature so careful. During his entire life, he had never lost his keys, or his wallet, or any of the other things which people so commonly lost. He had never even mislaid his hat. Yet he had managed to lose his daughter, his wife, his money, his job, and now even his house – not to mention his status and his reputation. He had to do something before he also lost his mind.

The only thing he could think to do was to go up into the mountains.

He walked the route to the little house far more quickly than he had ever done, as though propelled along those steep paths by some desperate, furious force. Up he went, barely noticing the ivy-covered oak, the lighting-struck maple, or the waterfalls. He did not pause to rest on the moss-covered rock. It was only when he reached the field of daisies that he stopped.

There, he lay amongst the flowers, breathless and spent. It was difficult to say how long he remained there – two, perhaps three whole hours – waiting for the energy from the earth to fill him, but this time he could not feel that sensation of energy pouring upwards into his body. All he could feel was the hardness of the earth and the uncomfortable prickling of his mattress of daisies and grass.

The visit to the house was relatively brief because Dante had already made his decision. It was time to leave Montacciolo. He would live out the rest of his days, which he hoped would not number too many, at the little mountain house.

Thus began the process of emptying his old family home in Montacciolo.

He did not inform anyone of what he was doing, but seeing him make his daily trips laden with possessions, the Montacciolani worked it out for themselves. Clearly they thought he had gone quite mad – a man of his age, going to live in the mountain wilderness, alone? He wouldn't last long. Quite apart from the ice storms which raged up there, what if he got ill? What if he fell and broke his leg? What if he got bitten by an adder? But anyone who questioned his plan was told to mind their own business.

Maybe it was a fool's errand. Maybe he wouldn't last until Christmas in the little house. Maybe even survival until Christmas was ludicrously optimistic. But it was the only option which Dante saw open to him.

By early summer, Dante had transferred all that he needed. It pained him to have to abandon most of his books, and choosing which to leave was the most difficult decision he had to make. He took Leonora's collection of poetry, a few old favourites and several practical reference books relating to nature and wildlife.

Many things remained in the house in Montacciolo, including almost all the furniture, most of his personal possessions and any clothing which did not have a purely practical use; but Dante had neither the need nor the space for it up in the mountains. The tax office could have all that too. Dante left the key under a flower pot, turned and left, making a point as he walked away of not looking behind him.

At last, removed from everything which had cursed him, Dante's misery gave way to the rapture of having released himself from the shackles of his wretched existence. Whatever time was left for him on earth would be spent living free.

He was away from people, but by no means alone. The mountains were full of life. Every morning Dante was awoken at first light by the birds. He would remain in his bed for a while, listening to the chorus of different calls and songs. A blackbird would perch outside his window and whistle the most complex tunes, as though rejoicing that at last he had a human audience. What a showman!

Then there was the spectacle of the birds of prey which would circle on the thermals at midday, when the sun was at its highest in the sky. Every time Dante saw them he would stop whatever he was doing to admire their dives and their acrobatic manoeuvres.

Being unaccustomed to humans, the animals were not overly afraid of him. The foxes were curious and observed him as he went about his daily routines. He could probably have tempted them to come and eat from his hand, but he wasn't in a position to share his supplies. The wild cats were more wary and watched him from behind the tall grasses. Occasionally a ferret-like creature would cross his path, as well as all manner of other little rodents.

Even the insects proved to be pleasant companions. Dante loved to observe the bees going about their business; to watch the crickets jump impossibly high; to admire the different butterflies. He spoke to them all, encouraging the bees to make plentiful honey, cheering the crickets' most spectacular leaps, and complementing the butterflies for the beauty of their colours.

He found himself inspecting the plants far more carefully than he had ever done. Now every leaf and every flower had a potential use – culinary, medicinal, or both. If Dante did not know a particular plant, he would look it up in his encyclopaedia of mountain flora, by far the most useful book that he had brought to the little house. Before then he'd had no idea that poppies were edible. He'd never heard of the plant called capsella which tasted like mustard, although he must have trampled it plenty of times. He was astonished to learn that the daisies which grew close to his little house in such abundance could be made into a tea to treat coughs, bronchitis and even disorders of the kidneys and liver.

He hoped that he would make it through the winter ahead so that the following year he could watch the progress of each of these plants from bud, to bloom, to fruit.

Living without running water and electricity was not too difficult to get used to. Dante would collect his water from the stream every morning. Whilst the daylight hours were long, he refrained from using the oil lamp, and only lit a candle at night for as short a time as possible. He needed those for the winter ahead.

His principal concern was food. The tins and dried goods which he had carried up from the village would not last him, so he dug over a vegetable plot and planted cabbages, onions, potatoes and beets, then came across some wild strawberry plants and put those in too.

Dante could not eat all the bounty of raspberries as they ripened, but picked them all anyway and laid them out on a sheet to dry in the sun, as he'd seen his mother do. She had made jam as well, but he wasn't sure how to do that and he knew he'd need quite a lot of sugar, which he didn't have. Perhaps that could be a project for the following summer, assuming he was still alive.

When he came across a walnut tree in the next valley, he was so thrilled that he let out a triumphant cry. Stripping the walnuts turned his hands black, which gradually faded to purple and left his palms and fingertips stained for weeks. One of the greatest discoveries was a small copse of chestnut trees, not far from the little house. Dante filled sack after sack with chestnuts, making several trips per day. He only stopped when he ran out of room to store them.

Firewood provision was as important as food. Fortunately it was plentiful up there. Dante didn't even have to fell any trees. He collected fallen deadwood and spent an hour or two every day cutting it to a size to fit the stove. That ever-growing, neatly-stacked wood-pile filled him with satisfaction and gave him more of a feeling of security that any money in the bank had ever done.

A pleasant tiredness overcame him every evening. Dante would eat his dinner and sit on the front step of the little house picking the splinters from his fingers with absolutely nothing troubling him. It was as though his brain had been washed of all worries. Even when a thought of Leonora, or Ortensia, or some hateful Montacciolano entered his mind, he no longer found himself stewing over past sufferings. Gone were the nights spent awake, tossing and turning and twitching in his bed. Gone were the nightmares. Gone were the abrupt awakenings. The move to the mountains felt like deliverance.

The only other human being he saw that summer was Ermenegildo the goat-herder, who came up at the end of August. The first sign of his approach was the jangle of the goat bells in the distance. Dante was not unhappy to see him. Ermenegildo was one of the few Montacciolani for whom he still had any level of respect. The goat-herder had never slandered him, or jumped on the scandal bandwagon. He was a simple soul who cared nothing for gossip. He just cared about goats.

Ermenegildo said that he'd come up so that his herd could graze on the raspberry bushes. Something in the leaves made them pee a lot, and it was particularly good for the nannies if they were in kid. Dante looked this up in his book of medicinal herbs and learned that the same benefits applied to humans.

The goat-herder had brought with him half a dozen letters – two from people proposing random theories about Leonora and four from the tax office. Dante read the letters pertaining

Leonora, but they were nothing beyond a bit of flimsy specula-tion, so he put them aside to be filed later. The letters from the tax office were filed immediately, in the firebox of the stove, still unopened.

'If you want a bed for the night, there's a bunk in the kitchen,' offered Dante, but Ermenegildo declined, saying that he was grateful for the gesture, but his dog wasn't used to sleeping inside and she would get nervy if she was a distance from her herd, and so would he. Dante sensed that this was not untrue, but it was more of an excuse than a reason. He didn't take it per-sonally. The goat-herder liked his own company – and now, more than ever before, Dante respected that. Ermenegildo pitched up his goat-skin bivouac at the edge of the raspberry field.

For their dinner, Dante pulled a few new potatoes from his vegetable plot. He had been intending to leave them in the ground a little longer so that they could grow to full size, but having a guest was a special occasion, so he made an exception. Ermenegildo contributed the butt-end of a salami. It was as hard as a stone. Dante rinsed the goat-hair off and put it in the pot to flavour the water. The resulting dish, served with wild parsley and the mustard-tasting capsella, was very tasty. The two men dined together sitting on the steps outside the little house. Although Dante had offered to set the table inside, the goat-herder said that he'd prefer to eat in the fresh air. It always made the food taste better.

When Dante offered Ermenegildo coffee, the goat-herder de-clined.

'That's kind, but it's too late for coffee for me now. I'd rather have a tot of *Ballerina* by the fire. Come along too if you want. Bring your own cup.'

Without asking what *Ballerina* was, Dante took a cup and ac-companied Ermenegildo back to his camp where, with well-practiced efficiency, the goat-herder lit a fire of pinecones by his bivouac.

'It's nice to sit out under the stars for a while last thing at night,' he said, 'Clears your head of your troubles. A man sleeps well when he's only got stars in his head.'

Dante smiled at this snippet of goat-herder wisdom and took his place on one side of the fire whilst Ermenegildo sat cross-legged opposite him, with one hand absent-mindedly ruffling the neck of his dozing dog. In his other hand, he held a small clay pipe.

The goat-herder loaded his pipe with a pinch of tobacco, then, from a battered tin flask, he began to decant a rather pungent-smelling substance – too thick and lumpy to be called a liquid, yet too slack to be a solid. This, he explained, was *Ballerina*, a concoction of home-distilled alcohol, fermented goats' milk and a secret ingredient.

'A secret ingredient?' Repeated Dante, intrigued.

'Ah, yes,' replied Ermenegildo, tapping the side of his nose. 'And I can't tell you what it is, or it would bring bad luck on both of us.'

'I think I've had enough bad luck.'

'Not many would argue with that, Dante, so I'll keep the secret to myself.'

Whatever it contained, the drink was not enticing in either smell, or appearance, but Ermenegildo assured him that it was good stuff.

'Just a bit should do as you're not used to it and there's not much of you,' he said, pouring a little into Dante's cup. 'You wouldn't want it if your belly was empty. It can make you sick then, but if you can hold it down, it'll get you pissed as a cricket. It's called *Ballerina* because it does something to your legs. Makes you dance around all night.' He swilled the flask and poured a more generous tot for himself, then added, 'Not that I have any objection to a night like that once in a while. But you've got to be in the right company.'

Obviously Ermenegildo did not consider Dante to be the right company for a night of drunken revelry. Dante didn't take offence. He probably wouldn't choose to get drunk in his own company either.

Dante found that he could stomach the *Ballerina* quite well. It repeated on him a bit, but it tasted better than he had expected. Perhaps the goat-herder had over-sold its potency. He didn't feel the need to dance. All it did was to give him a pleasant warmth and an appreciation of how beautiful the flames of the fire were.

This, he thought, was a little glimpse into the goat-herder's world, and what a wonderfully simple world it was. Ermenegildo sat opposite him, sucking pensively on his clay pipe and blowing small wisps of smoke towards the stars. The dog rolled over and stretched out across her master's lap, belly-up. Dante felt honoured to have been invited, even briefly, into this very private space of man and dog and fire and stars.

For a time neither spoke. They just sat in quiet contemplation before the crackling flames. It was the goat-herder who broke the silence.

'Now my pa's too old and my cousins have found work in the town, it's just me left with the goats, although my brother comes sometimes when he's not busy. But back in the old days, when the men used to work bigger flocks and herds, there'd be three or four of them out together. Every evening on the mountain, they'd make a fire like this to cook up their dinner and they'd sit round it after. Their fireside talks were a time to think about life.'

In a small but significant way, something did happen that night by the fire which made Dante reassess the course of his existence. It came about accidentally, as a result of a bit of small-talk, during which Dante mentioned his walk to Santa Croce.

'Santa Croce? I don't like to call it that. That spot's always been Filomena's Place to me, and always will be,' said Ermenegildo.

'Who's Filomena?'

The goat-herder took a draw of his pipe before replying, and when he did, it was not in his usual tone of voice, but in that of a veteran raconteur who had told the story many times.

'Filomena was my cousin's great great grandmother on his mother's side. Her father was a shepherd. He was a widower and she was his only child. They didn't live in Montacciolo, but not far away, in a hamlet which isn't there any more. But one night, when Filomena's father was up on the mountain by himself, a pack of wolves attacked his flock and killed his dog. And as he was trying to defend his animals, the wolves got him too. It was a terrible business.'

Ermenegildo sucked contemplatively on his clay pipe.

'And being as the sheep were the only thing she had, and she was the only child, it was up to young Filomena to take over the care of what was left of the flock. But one night when she's on the mountain by herself, she hears the wolves coming. The poor girl's so scared that the only thing she can think to do is to pray. So she drops to her knees and suddenly, out of the night sky, a bright light comes down and lands on the mountainside opposite in a flash, like a column of white fire. And from this light, an angel appears, and although the angel doesn't speak, Filomena understands that he's come to protect her and her sheep. Then as quickly as he'd come, the angel vanishes. Sure enough, those wolves came nowhere near her ever again.'

The goat-herder paused, allowing Dante to take in the story.

'That spot where the angel appeared has always been known as Filomena's Place to us shepherds and goat-men. Our forefathers arranged a pile of stones there so it wouldn't be forgotten, although it was easy to find because the trees never grew back.'

Now Ermenegildo's voice hardened.

'But then, years later, that priest we had before Don Generoso got wind of what had happened and thought to himself that Filomena's vision could be good for the village. I hope you won't mind me mentioning your pa's part in this, Dante, but between them they decided that it was time to make some money from it by organising a few pilgrimages and suchlike.' Ermenegildo, rubbed his thumb and forefinger together in a you-know-what-I-mean kind of way, then added, 'But there weren't any takers. That place was only special to us shepherds and goat-men, and we weren't going to be paying for the pleasure of visiting it.'

Dante could not disguise his surprise. The goat-herder continued, 'So the priest and your pa decide that there should be a cross there to make it a bit more official, which us goat-men and shepherds wouldn't have minded, although it would have been good manners if they'd asked us before going ahead with it. But changing the name of the place was wrong. Disrespectful to that young girl, Filomena.'

Dante was immediately compelled to apologise for his father's insensitivity. He also apologised on behalf of Don Generoso's predecessor.

'Nothing for you to be sorry about. You were nothing to do with it. But what I'm saying is that there was a miracle up at that spot well before your pa claimed he had his vision. Now, I'm not saying that your pa couldn't have had a vision too, but there was many folk that never really believed it.'

This, of course, threw a whole new light on the event for Dante. Had the whole thing been an act of collusion between his father and the priest and nothing more than a money-making scheme? If it had, the trajectory of Dante's life had been based on a lie. How he wished that his father's vision, whether genuine or a scam, had been that his son should be not a priest, but goat-herder. Life would have turned out so much simpler.

Within the hour, Ermenegildo was dampening down the fire, which was Dante's cue to take his leave. He wove his way back to the little house via a slightly meandering route. Ermenegildo was right. *Ballerina* did affect the legs.

During his stay the goat-herder offered Dante two nanny-goats. They were good milkers, he assured Dante. And they had nice characters too. Some goats could be grumpy, but this pair were quite agreeable and they got on well. They would cost him nothing to keep up here where there was so much grazing, although he would have to put aside some feed for winter. And they'd have to be penned in securely, or they'd go trotting off down the mountain looking for the herd.

Dante was keen to have the goats, but doubted whether he could afford to buy them, unless the goat-herder agreed to staged payments. Ermenegildo said he didn't want any money. He'd feel better knowing Dante was up there by himself if he had a supply of milk. And when it got really cold, he could bring the goats into the house, like people used to. Livestock gave off a fair bit of heat. Dante accepted the offer gratefully.

Ermenegildo helped him to build a goat pen with a shelter, then showed him how to milk his new charges; after which he taught him how to make cheese, by heating the milk slowly, until it was frothy, and adding vinegar and salt. Dante could add other things too, Ermenegildo explained – more salt and herbs for a savoury cheese, and fruit if he wanted something sweet. Honey was the best. He promised to bring him up a jar or two when he came back in the spring.

Dante was thankful for each one of these acts of practical kindness, and also heartened by the fact that Ermenegildo seemed confident enough that he'd last the winter to promise him honey in the spring.

As he was leaving, the goat-herder said, 'All the best, Dante. Stay safe and stay warm.'

'You too, Ermenegildo.'

'And look after those two nannies. You look after them and they'll look after you.'

'I will. Thank you.'

Dante watched Ermenegildo make his way down the mountainside, whistling to his dog above the jangle of the goat-bells, aware of the fact that those might be the last words he would ever speak to another human being.

That first summer in the mountains faded quickly. Shortly after Ermenegildo's departure, from one day to the next, the temperature dropped. There was a cool quality to the light, with the sun lower in the sky. It hovered just above the mountains, lengthening the shadows cast by the surrounding peaks. One by one the deciduous trees turned gold and red and shed their leaves, until the only green left was the grass and the pines.

With the autumn rain came generous quantities of mushrooms. Every morning at dawn Dante gathered those which he knew for certain to be edible – *porcini, piopparelli* and *chiodini*. He put some aside to dry and the rest he cooked up with onions and wild garlic. The dish had a certain mossy, earthy taste to it. An omelette would have gone down very well. He wished he'd had the presence of mind to procure himself a couple of chickens.

The winter warned Dante of its approach with frosty winds. Nights were considerably colder and most days were chilly, but clear and sunny. There was no proper snow until almost the end December.

When those first feathery snows fell, Dante stood at his window watching the beauty of the landscape being engulfed in white and enjoying the pleasure of being inside; cosy, with plenty of firewood. Thanks to the provisions he'd gathered, the harvest from his vegetable plot, the milk from the goats and the industrial quantity of chestnuts he had collected, he had sufficient food.

The potatoes ran out in early January and many other things had run out by February. Although his diet became more restricted, Dante never went hungry, thanks in great part to the two nanny-goats.

He became very proficient at cheese-making. His specialities were a cheese made with wild parsley and garlic (a delicacy worthy of the finest restaurant menu), and another to which he added walnuts and dried raspberries. Otherwise, Dante lived on vegetable soups and chestnuts.

During his visit Ermenegildo had mentioned fattening up a sheep through the following spring and summer and slaughtering it when the snows came. The meat would stay fresh in the cold. Dante doubted whether he could bring himself to despatch a sheep, but by the end of the first winter, when he had grown weary of vegetable soups and felt his body crave the nourishment of meat, he had almost come round to the idea. He would also ask Ermenegildo about setting a few traps. The thought of roasting a rabbit over the fire made Dante's mouth water.

The thing that he wished he had more of was books. In his state of semi-hibernation, time that was not spent dealing with the day-to-day chores, or sleeping, Dante spent sitting by the range, reading. He had memorised every poem of Leonora's, and was now an authority on mountain flora and fauna. The handful of other books which he had brought with him, although long-time favourites, felt dull after the umpteenth re-reading.

Intellectual stimulation was the only thing Dante yearned for. Now he had the quiet, solitary space needed for study and learning, he lacked the material for it, and as a result, suffered bouts of boredom. He missed his regular visits to the library in the nearest town, where he could pick out books on philosophy, or science, or history, or any number of subjects with which to broaden his mind. Still, he tried not to dwell on it too much and told himself that what he lacked, he would simply have to learn to do without.

All things considered, that first winter did not drag on. Dante had experienced far longer winters in more comfortable circumstances. He certainly did not feel robbed of the benefits of domesticity, such as companionship and love, because over the years he had grown accustomed to living entirely without them. If one looked at life objectively, those things, Dante had come to understand, were wholly dispensable luxuries.

At the start of the winter he had been very tired, ground down by the catalogue of calamities, then further exhausted by the move and all the preparation. But now, after a winter of rest, both physical and emotional, he felt energised and ready to welcome the spring. Letting the body tick over to the natural rhythm of the seasons was what human beings had been designed to do, after all.

As the snow melted, the green pastures reappeared, followed soon after by the spring flowers – aquilegia with pink and purple flowers like geometric bells, and an abundance of violets and white orchids sprouted all around his house.

When Dante happened upon a crop of saponaria rosa, he remembered that in his youth, his mother had made soap from the leaves. He boiled up an amount, just as he had seen his mother do and strained the thickish liquid. The resulting soap was not as he had imagined in appearance, but it did make his beard very soft. Dante had not shaved once since his move to the mountains and now his beard almost touched his chest. He was intending to let it grow long, so that in the cold weather he could wrap it around his neck like a scarf.

Ermenegildo appeared in early March, just with his dog.

'How are you, Dante?'

'Still alive,'

'Just as well, because I didn't think to bring my shovel.'

'Are you staying?'

'No, no. I just came by to tell you that the track's clear now if you need to go down to the village, and to bring you this.'

He pulled a jar of honey out from somewhere in his layers of clothing.

'I went to see about your honey, but it's too early in the year. There was a bit of last season's left, so you can have this to keep you going a while.'

Ermenegildo stayed long enough to drink a cup of coffee sweetened with honey, then disappeared again down the mountain, whistling to his dog.

CHAPTER 13

The combination of good nursing, a wholesome diet and fresh air led to a marked improvement in Jubanne's recovery. As his balance improved he was no longer confined to his spot under the fig tree. He still had to be careful and he relied on a stick to steady himself, but walks around the paved terrace became more and more manageable. It was not long until he felt sure-footed enough to venture further. Once he had gained the confidence to tackle a few steps, he was able to wander through the garden, along the paths between the rose bushes and lavender beds, the aloes and the prickly pears, stopping here and there for a rest on one of the benches. He took great pleasure in these leisurely walks. There was so much to see in the garden that he had been too busy to pay proper attention to before his accident.

In particular, it gave him great satisfaction to walk down to the end of the wooden jetty to meet the fishing boats which came to deliver the fresh fish most days. The fishermen would invariably comment about how good it was to see him up and about, to which Jubanne would always reply something along the lines of, 'I'll be taking my wife out dancing before you know it.' Then they would exchange a few pleasantries about the conditions out at sea, which led to the usual question from Jubanne, 'What have you got for me today?' And the fishermen would either reply that they had some amberjack, or some red snapper and as many sardines as he wanted – there was always a glut of sardines; you couldn't throw a stone into the sea without hitting one. Sometimes they'd say that they'd had a good catch of bream, or albacore – and how about a piece of the hundred kilo blue-fin tuna they'd hauled in?

During Jubanne's stay in hospital, Signora Melis Puddu had employed a new cook. She was a woman from the Italian mainland, but she could prepare all the traditional island dishes as well as any Sardinian, if not better. She had a way of adding a little twist to her creations to make them even more delicious. Whenever Jubanne went to meet the fishing boats, the cook would go down with him to select the best of the catch for her kitchen.

Jubanne found himself nervous around most people now, but he was comfortable in the cook's company. She would often come to sit with him under the fig tree when she was on her break, and they quickly became very amicable. Admittedly, at first she had been a little reserved with him, but Jubanne was used to that. Before his accident, people who didn't know him could be intimidated by his size and it might take them a while to realise that he was a giant of the gentle variety. Now, he understood that some felt awkward because he didn't always make sense, and people found that difficult to deal with.

His friendship with the cook had started when she had begun to bring him her creations to try, and she would ask his opinion on this or that aspect of the dish. She called him her 'taster-in-chief'. They would even share a joke about it.

'Could you try this for me, Jubanne?' She would say as she appeared carrying a bowl or a platter of something which he knew would be delicious.

'Are you experimenting on me again, cook?'

'Well, nothing's killed you yet.'

'Then I suppose you'd better keep trying.'

The cook brought him semolina gnocchi, risotto with saffron, *fregola* with clams, fried cinnamon dumplings filled with sweetened ricotta and vanilla; and all of these, he was able to recall. Often he could remember quite correctly what he had eaten the previous day, or even the day before that. The thing that

Jubanne could not do, no matter how hard he tried, was to re-member the cook's name correctly. He knew he'd been told it umpteen times, but it just wouldn't stick. He'd embarrassed himself often enough by calling her Linda, Maria, Sabrina, Alessandra, Elena and by many other names – none of them correct – sometimes he had even called her 'Nora'. In the end, he just called her 'Cook', which she said she didn't mind. At least he'd managed to fix it into his unreliable brain that she was the cook, so that was something.

One afternoon she'd made a glazed tart using lemons picked from the trees in the guesthouse garden, and it was the most exquisite thing that Jubanne had ever tasted. He had wanted to complement her, but a filthy swear word had fallen out of his mouth instead and he'd been utterly ashamed of it. In his attempt to apologise, he'd sworn again, even worse, and then the sentence that he'd spoken had been a garbled mess. And to cap it all, he'd called the cook by the wrong name. He'd been so frustrated with himself that he had wanted to beat his thick head with his fists; but he refrained, because he was still cogent enough to know that was the last thing he should do.

The cook had leaned across, placed her hand gently on his forearm and said, 'Jubanne, it's all right if there are things you forget, and if you swear when you don't mean to, and if you can't remember my name. I know you can't help it, so I don't take it personally. Stop trying to pretend that you haven't banged your head.'

Those words – *stop trying to pretend that you haven't banged your head* – had actually stuck in his head and he found the honesty of them reassuring.

'We all know that this is hard for you, but you have to get used to life being different, Jubanne,' continued the cook soothingly. 'It's the same for your wife and for your children. Everybody has to come to terms with things being normal in a new way.'

Hearing this, and particularly the mention of his children, had brought a lump to Jubanne's throat. He was missing his children very much.

'When will I see my kids?' He asked, even though he knew that he'd be told many times that he'd already seen them. He was sick of arguing that he hadn't, and really, he couldn't be absolutely sure that he hadn't. The cook smiled sympathetically.

'I'm sure you'll see them soon.'

'I expect they've grown.'

'You can be certain about that.'

Jubanne opened his mouth to say something about his son and felt his heart sink. What was his son's name? Of course he knew it, but where had it gone?

'Sometimes I think about taking him out fishing at sea. He'd like that.'

'Who do you think about taking out fishing?'

Still the name escaped him, so Jubanne said, 'My little boy. He's probably big enough now. Do you think he's big enough?'

'Definitely,' replied the cook. 'But it might be a while before you're well enough to be out at sea.'

Her hand was still on his forearm, and she gave it a reassuring squeeze. This small gesture meant a great deal to Jubanne because people rarely touched him now. He had always been tactile with those he loved and he missed the contact. Before, his wife had sought him out so that he could envelop her in his enormous arms and hold her against his chest. He would kiss the top of her head. She didn't do that any more. She sought no physical closeness whatsoever. If anything, she gave him the impression that she was avoiding it at all costs.

Jubanne had always hugged and kissed his children, swung them into the air, carried them on his back and on his shoulders – often both together. He remembered the funny play-fights with his son, where he would feign being overpowered, or he would pretend to lose at arm-wrestling. He'd promised to give his boy the medals he'd won at the regional championships one day. Memories of his daughter were still fresh and clear too. He recalled when she was still very small, how she would call him 'Papá Juju' and seek him out with her hands outstretched to be picked up. He also thought of her as she had been just before the accident, when she would come out on the boat with him and if the sea was calm enough, he would unfurl the sail and help her steer the rudder. He would be the captain and she would be the first mate.

These were once such ordinary things, but now any kind of physical contact with anybody was a rarity. All Jubanne ever heard was that he had to be careful, so people treated him like a fragile, broken thing which might shatter at the lightest fingertip touch.

The cook kept her hand on his forearm as though she had understood what was going through his mind. Jubanne thought what a remarkably perceptive woman she was. She didn't look old, probably somewhere around his wife's age, maybe a little bit younger, but there was a wisdom about her. There was something that made him think that she was experienced in life and had survived difficult times. Perhaps one day they would talk about it. Not yet, though. He'd have to be more confident in his memory first.

He meant to say 'Thank you,' but it came out as 'Fuck lemons.'. The cook laughed and Jubanne laughed with her, although really, he felt like crying. He might have let the tears escape had his wife not come out to bring him his medication at that very moment, but he was very careful that she should not see him upset if he could help it. She had enough to deal with without him blubbing because he felt sorry for himself, so he swallowed down his sadness and greeted her with a determinately cheerful smile.

Signora Melis Puddu sort of returned the smile and handed him his pills. The cook said to her, 'Have you had lunch?'

'No, I haven't had time.'

'You can't go all day on fresh air. I've made a lemon tart. If I were you I'd have a slice before Jubanne polishes off the lot.'

His wife sat down and kicked off her shoes. Her feet were red. She'd been on them all day. She looked overworked and Jubanne felt guilty for not being able to help her.

When he looked at Signora Melis Puddu, she was hard to recognise. Of course he knew who she was, and he was very grateful that the accident hadn't stolen that; but she was definitely different, and it wasn't just her hair, which was threaded with grey and which she had cut shorter since he'd been in hospital. It seemed as though she had aged by a decade in the space of a few months.

Jubanne sat back, watching his wife as she ate the lemon tart. He had always been in awe of her, but now 'awe' didn't even begin to describe the way he felt. A weaker-spirited woman might have crumbled when faced with her husband's life-changing situation, but Signora Melis Puddu had remained resolute and level-headed. Jubanne could see that the guesthouse ran with the efficiency of a Swiss train timetable. Of course he was glad about that, but it also saddened him that everything was carrying on without him. When he had been well, he had been useful, but now that he was no longer useful, he realised that he had never been indispensable.

Signora Melis Puddu and the cook were talking. It was just guesthouse chatter – everyday practicalities and the odd reference to particular guests – but Jubanne could see that theirs was more than just an employer-employee relationship. His wife had always kept a professional distance between herself and the staff, but with the cook, it was different. The two women were comfortable in each other's company, as though they had been friends for a long time.

During those years of hard work to get the guesthouse up to scratch and with all the family commitments, his wife had had little time to dedicate to friendships, not that she had ever said that it bothered her; but it was nice to see that now she had someone with whom she got on so well.

Signora Melis Puddu and the cook often took their meals together. Some evenings Jubanne had seen them sitting in the garden enjoying a glass of wine, then going down to the beach and coming back with their shoes still in their hands. Often they would be arm-in-arm, walking slowly with their steps in rhythm, their heads bowed in conversation. They would stop occasionally and laugh.

Jubanne's mind wandered back to the time when he had been the one arm-in-arm with his wife, returning from the beach at night with his shoes in his hand. He could see that the cook had filled some of the space which he had occupied before. He didn't mind. On the contrary, he was grateful for it, if it made his wife happy. The guilt of having let her down weighed heavily on his conscience. He could, to some extent, rationalise that feeling of culpability. The fact that things had changed was not entirely his fault – 'just one of those things' his wife called it – but nevertheless, he felt guilty that she had had to take over all the responsibilities.

The tiredness overcame him very suddenly, as it often did, and in a way that it was pointless to resist. Jubanne could no longer make out the words of the conversation taking place opposite him. The figures of his wife and the cook blurred, lost their contours and dissolved away. Jubanne blinked, and they disappeared entirely.

Instead, sitting where Signora Melis Puddu had been just seconds before was Nonna Maria-Annoriana, daintily eating a slice of lemon tart.

CHAPTER 14

The old man hadn't wanted to appear ungracious by interrupting the Sardinian's story, but he was not very interested in learning about an un-named cook, however amenable the woman might have been, and however delicious her lemon tarts, and however friendly she was with Signora Melis Puddu. He also had no patience to hear about another ghostly manifestation of the long-dead Nonna Maria-Annoriana when the whole point of the Sardinian's long journey was to speak about his missing daughter, Leonora.

'I'm heartened to hear the progress of your convalescence,' he said politely. 'But what of the other situation?'

Jubanne Melis Puddu gave him a look of incomprehension. 'What do you mean?'

'The situation with my daughter.'

Jubanne Melis Puddu did not speak immediately, but stared straight ahead, aloof and unaware of where he was, or of Dante's presence just a few feet away. When at last he snapped out of his dream-state he said, 'There was nothing to be done. The accident changed many things, but it did not change the fact that I had fallen in love with Nora.'

'Is that what you would call it?'

'I loved my wife, and I loved her very much, but I had never felt about her the way I felt about Nora. I had never truly fallen in love before then, I suppose.'

'Dangerous sentiments for a married man.'

'Yes, and I tried my best to fight them, but it was impossible. Nora would come to find me whenever she had a quiet moment and we would sit and talk, sometimes for hours. All my life I had never met anybody who I could talk to quite like that. She would tell me all about her travels and the people she had met and the things she had seen. Then she would ask me about myself.'

The big Sardinian's eyes glistened like those of a star-struck lover as he went on, 'Although my head was muddled about some things, other things from before the accident I could remember perfectly clearly. Nora liked to listen to stories from my past, even though I didn't have a string of adventures to tell her about. My life had been content, but not exactly exciting. But everything I spoke about just delighted her. She liked to listen to stories about my grandmother, and she liked me to speak about my children and even about my wife.'

Dante raised an eyebrow and asked, 'And how did your wife feel about this association now? She had expressed some concerns before your accident.'

Jubanne Melis Puddu shrugged his huge shoulders. 'It didn't trouble her after the accident like it had before. I think that she was glad I was being kept occupied. All Nora and I were doing was talking. And we weren't meeting secretly. We'd sit together under the fig tree and in plain sight of everybody. From time to time my wife would appear to remind Nora that something needed doing in the guesthouse, but she wasn't jealous.'

The Sardinian reflected for a moment and the volume of his voice dropped. 'It wasn't my wife's jealousy which was the problem. It was mine. Nora affected me so deeply that sometimes it was hard to think straight. If she wasn't with me, all I could think about was where she was and who she was with. When she was serving the guests I'd see her through the dining room windows and whenever she talked to a man, I felt terrible. I hated the thought of anybody paying her any attention.'

'Were you still concerned about Corrado?'

Jubanne Melis Puddu made a gesture to indicate both yes and no.

'The feeling that something might happen between them never really went away, even though nothing did happen as far as I know. They were just good pals and they'd lark around together, and sometimes Corrado would give Nora a lift into town on the back of his Vespa. I did ask my wife if she thought there might be a romance between them.'

'And what was your wife's opinion on that?'

'She told me to stop being so ridiculous. My wife was sharp when it came to things like that. There would have been no reason for her to lie to me about it.'

All at once Jubanne Melis Puddu's face flushed and he said, 'But as soon as I'd calmed down about Corrado, there was the doctor, and that was another thing entirely.' He then fell silent.

'The doctor?' prompted Dante after a while.

The big Sardinian nodded and his countenance remained dark.

'There was a doctor who used to come to check up on me – a good-looking young fellow who drove an Alfa Romeo. I liked him at first. He even showed me his car. It was red. One of those little sporty models where you could take the roof off. He let me sit in it and we laughed because my legs were too long to fit and you'd have had to take out the front seat for me to drive it – not that I was allowed to drive, even though I could remember perfectly well how it was done. But then one day Nora brought him something to drink after he'd examined me and he mentioned some sort of event that was happening in town, and it sounded to me as though he was asking her out.'

Jubanne Melis Puddu's nostrils flared and he made a growling noise. 'And then he paid Nora a compliment and he looked at her in a way that just made me want to punch him.'

'And how did she react to this compliment?'

The big Sardinian began to crack his knuckles finger by finger. 'She looked back at him.'

'Was that all?'

'No. That wasn't all. She smiled, as though she was pleased.'

'Well, I would imagine that a compliment from a handsome doctor would please most young women,' said Dante, then immediately wished that he had kept his opinion to himself, for suddenly Jubanne Melis Puddu swelled with anger, which was a most frightening spectacle.

'I mean,' Dante backtracked anxiously, his voice unsteady, 'Surely it would have been churlish to scorn a polite compliment?'

The big Sardinian was making a snarling noise with each breath.

'There was something going on with that doctor. I could feel it. And it made me so angry.'

The old man shrank back and kept quiet. Once he had composed himself, the Sardinian said, 'I just couldn't stop myself feeling that way. I loved Nora so much.'

'And did she understand how you felt?'

'Oh yes,' replied Jubanne Melis Puddu, nodding with absolute conviction. 'Nora knew because I told her.'

'You told her?'

'One day she said that she hadn't renewed her contract to go back and work on the yacht because she wanted to stay in Sardinia permanently, so that she could be close to me. And not just while I was getting better, but after that too. Well, that overwhelmed me, as you can imagine. I didn't know what to say, except to tell her that I loved her. It just came out of me.'

Uncertain whether what the Sardinian was saying corresponded in any way with reality, or was an imagined scenario like the apparitions of Nonna Maria-Annoriana, or simply a case of wishful thinking, Dante chose his words carefully.

'And how did she react to that?'

'She put her arms around my neck and kissed my face and told me that she loved me back.'

The old man raised his eyebrows, not looking at all convinced. 'Really?'

'Yes. And not just once. She said it many times after that. And I would say, "but I'm married and I love my wife" and she would reply, "You can love your wife as well as me.".'

Dante considered this, but his expression remained doubtful, 'How very avant-garde. And not altogether out of character, I suppose, in view of her indoctrination at the hands of The Collective. Although perhaps not a very workable situation and probably doomed to heartbreak.'

Jubanne Melis Puddu was staring straight ahead, seemingly right through Dante, as though in that moment he was transported back to those hours on the terrace with Nora.

'Part of me felt so happy. But the other part felt terrible. What of my wife, my children? If I allowed myself to get involved with Nora, however wonderful she was, I would destroy my family, and they did not deserve that. I did give it some thought though. I shouldn't have done, because it messed up my head even more. And then everything went wrong.'

The big man relapsed into silence and retreated into his own brooding thoughts. Dante allowed him a few moments before asking, 'Are you going to tell me what happened?'

Jubanne Melis Puddu reddened with embarrassment.

'Some of it is...intimate.'

'You think that I am unaccustomed to hearing intimate revelations concerning my daughter, both real and fabricated? And in any case, have you not travelled all this way specifically to tell me what happened?'

'Yes. But now that I'm here, it feels awkward.'

'Please,' implored Dante. 'You are increasing my anguish by leaving me in doubt. And I would ask you to be candid with me. Tell me everything, however unpalatable you think I might find it.'

CHAPTER 15

Jubanne retired to his ground floor room one night to discover his wife there, wearing her dressing gown and in the throes of preparing herself for bed. He was rather surprised when she said something along the lines of, 'Shall I take the left side, like I used to?' But he didn't want to seem rude, or divulge that he had absolutely no idea that a return to marital sleeping arrangements had been agreed, or even discussed, so he smiled as though he had been looking forward to it and said, 'That would be nice.' Signora Melis Puddu had smiled back, but her eyes had betrayed her unease.

'Don't feel you have to,' he told her, trying to sound as reassuring as he could, as much for his own benefit as his wife's.

'I know. But with this new medication you're starting, the doctor says you shouldn't be by yourself at night until we know the dosage is right for you.'

'Oh yes. Of course,' replied Jubanne, who had no recollection of the doctor ever saying such a thing, nor that there had been any proposed change in his medication. And which doctor was it? Was it Doctor Bow Tie, or Doctor Alfa Romeo? Had he even seen Doctor Bow Tie since he'd come home? No, of course he hadn't, so it must have been that weasel, Doctor Alfa Romeo.

'Here,' said Signora Melis Puddu, handing him an orange pill, which he swallowed without question. 'If you feel strange during the night, you must wake me up and tell me.'

Jubanne promised that he would, although 'strange' was the way he felt all the time. It was certainly strange to think about being in bed beside his wife again.

She took off her dressing gown, under which she was

wearing a floor-length nightie. The neck was so high that the collar brushed her earlobes. Only her fingertips were visible poking out of its long sleeves. The message broadcast by the nightie was loud and clear. This bed-sharing was a sleeping arrangement only – not that Jubanne would have expected anything else. Anyway, even if Signora Melis Puddu had been amenable to a little *you-know-what*, he couldn't have done much about it. He hadn't had so much as a twinge in his loins since the accident.

Once each had inquired politely whether the other was ready and confirmation was given that they were, both lay down cautiously and pulled up the covers, being careful not to take more than half. The light was turned off and they lay rigidly on their backs with a wide space between them.

'Good night.'

'Good night.'

They fell asleep without changing position.

When Jubanne awoke the following morning, Signora Melis Puddu was gone. He had not been aware of his wife getting up. He could hear the breakfast service being cleared away in the distance, so he must have been by himself for several hours. He didn't usually sleep that late. Perhaps it was the new medication. Aha! He'd remembered that he was on new medication, so that was a good thing. He even remembered that the pill was orange. *Congratulations, Jubanne!*

The joint sleeping arrangement continued for a time following exactly the same pattern. The fact that Signora Melis Puddu turned up in her dressing gown and wore a nightdress not dissimilar to a nun's habit, spelled out clearly to Jubanne that she was not comfortable with undressing in front of him now. Out of respect, Jubanne always ensured that he was already in his pyjamas when she arrived, and he also made certain that he'd been outside for a fart before retiring for the night.

The only thing that changed as the ritual was practised was that they both became less nervous about it. Signora Melis Puddu would offer up the orange pill and Jubanne would take it. They would get into bed altogether more comfortably, sometimes even exchange a few words. Lights off, then they would lie with the wide space between them until they fell asleep.

There was only a little time before the pill took effect, but during those few conscious moments Jubanne would always think the same thing. He would have liked to have held his wife – nothing more than that – just to feel her warmth; to be close enough to feel her heart beating; her hair tickling his nostrils; and to give her a chaste kiss when he wished her good night. He missed that so much, and having her there, just an arm's reach away, yet so unobtainable, aroused in him a feeling of tenderness mixed with despair, because he didn't feel brave enough to ask whether he could hold her, just in case she said 'no', which he feared that she probably would.

Then one night, a moment after the light had been switched off, Signora Melis Puddu reached across and briefly squeezed his hand.

'Good night.'

'Good night.'

Jubanne wanted to return the gesture; desperate to hold onto his wife's hand for a little while – a minute, even half a minute, would have been enough. But she moved away too quickly. He was just left with a fistful of nightie.

When Doctor Alfa Romeo asked Jubanne how he felt on the new medication, he said, 'All right.'. Then he added that he was sleeping in more. He knew he was because before he used to wake up just as they were setting the breakfast tables, but now he woke up when they were clearing away.

Signora Melis Puddu, who was always present whenever the doctor came to check on him, concurred that she hadn't noticed any negative side effects, but it was true, Jubanne was sleeping longer in the mornings.

Doctor Alfa Romeo spoke about the brain repairing itself through sleep and then explained a whole lot of things containing an alphabet soup of medical jargon, which Signora Melis Puddu understood because she asked a lot of clever technical questions. Jubanne didn't even try to make sense of it. There was no point. The brain of which they were speaking would forget it anyway.

The doctor seemed satisfied and increased Jubanne's dosage to two orange pills, plus a green one which looked like a jelly sweet.

After that, everything went strange. Very strange.

Rather that the customary easy slide into sleep, Jubanne would lie awake, trying to quell the agitation that he felt. It was a sort of pins and needles sensation, but over his entire body. He didn't know whether it was normal, or whether the doctor had mentioned that it might happen, but as he grew accustomed to it, he found it not to be unpleasant. In fact, if he relaxed, it could be quite enjoyable. It was not dissimilar to being out on the boat, where he could feel the roll of the waves beneath him and the vibration of the engine through his body.

He was dreaming more, but he didn't mind because to a certain extent he could guide his dreams by keeping himself in a semi-woken state. Nonna Maria-Annoriana was his most frequent visitor, and Jubanne was always pleased to see her. They would have their unspoken conversations, reminisce about this and that, laughing at so-and-so, or such-and-such. He often dreamt about being out on his boat with his children. They would drop anchor at the horseshoe reef, swim together, and if they were lucky, even see dolphins. Other times he dreamt about very ordinary things, such as doing odd jobs around the guesthouse, changing the beer kegs, driving into the nearest town to run an errand. These dreams were comforting in their everyday ordinariness.

One morning Jubanne awoke and found himself alone in bed as usual, with the sounds of the breakfast service being cleared away in the distance, yet something was different. He was aware of a familiar, yet almost forgotten sensation and he understood perfectly well what it was, but peered under the covers to check. Yes. As he suspected – he had an erection.

Jubanne put the covers back down delicately. His manhood hadn't raised its head since his accident. He wasn't sure what he should do about it. There was the obvious, of course, but that probably wasn't a good idea. Everyone was always telling him to be careful, not to exert himself, not to get over-excited. But that just applied to the day-to-day things, like climbing the stairs, or walking beyond the garden. Nobody had ever mentioned what he was supposed to do in case his cock woke up. The sensible course of action would be to wait until it passed.

He lay still staring at the ceiling and thinking of mundane things, and eventually managed to convince his unexpected guest to leave. The following morning, it was back; and the morning after that. Each time Jubanne willed it to pass.

Then, having done this for several days in a row, he began to wonder – what was the harm? Maybe just a stroke with his hand would be all right. Surely a little caress wouldn't over-exert him, and clearly this was a sign that he was getting better. This was progress.

He checked that his grandmother had not just appeared in his room, and satisfied that there was no sign of Nonna Maria-Annoriana, or anybody else for that matter, he slid his hand into his pyjama trousers.

There was no denying that it was very nice. In fact, it was particularly pleasurable because the pins and needles sensation was quivering through him like the buzz of a mild electric charge, extending through his entire body, even as far as his fingertips. Still, Jubanne limited himself to a few minutes of self-soothing and refrained from letting his mind wander into territories which might cause him to forget his limitations.

He decided that he would not mention it to the doctor. He would not mention it to his wife either, or she might no longer feel comfortable sharing his bed. When Doctor Alfa Romeo asked how he was doing on the new medication, he said, 'Great.'

'Are you experiencing any agitation Signor Melis Puddu?'

'No, no, nothing like that.'

'No disturbed sleep?'

'I can assure you that I'm sleeping like a dormouse.'

To Jubanne's relief, his wife concurred that there was nothing untoward to report as far as she could tell. Doctor Alfa Romeo was satisfied that all was in order and nothing more was asked. Jubanne's medication was increased to two orange pills and two green jellies.

Signora Melis Puddu must have sensed that something of her husband's old vigour had returned because that night she arrived, not bundled into her usual convent-style nightwear, but wearing her silvery blue silk robe. Jubanne had always had a bit of a thing about that robe. The way his wife's bottom quivered under the thin fabric as she moved had always excited him. But it was not just the alluring silk robe and the quivering bottom – that night Signora Melis Puddu had brushed her hair in the way that made it soft and Jubanne could smell the rose oil on her skin.

She smiled at him seductively and said, 'Shall we?' and Jubanne had been both thrilled and terrified at the prospect.

'We'll have to be careful,' he said.

'We can take it gently. Promise you'll tell me if you don't feel right.'

They got into bed, lay in an awkward, out-of-practice embrace and tentatively began to kiss. Jubanne had always made a point of being a gentle lover, mindful of his considerable size and weight; careful not to make any thoughtless, clumsy moves. Now their roles were oddly reversed. It was his wife who was the cautious one; the one asking, 'Is this all right for you?'

Jubanne was transported back to their first nights together. They had waited until they were married before sharing a bed, not because either of them was religious, but it just wasn't the done thing to have the dessert before the main course in those days. Anyway, they had only been together for six months, so the wait had been bearable.

Before meeting his wife, the sum total of Jubanne's sexual experience was little more than a bit of awkward teenaged canoodling. Later, in his early twenties, he had been unofficially engaged to a girl who was so terrified of falling pregnant that she wouldn't go beyond a bit of manual relief, and only on specific days and under certain conditions, most of which were based more on superstition than the biology of reproduction; so Jubanne could count those experimentations, lovely though they were, on the fingers of one hand.

When the matter of sex had come up with his future wife, at first he had been shy about owning up to the fact that he was still a virgin; but she had said that she didn't mind at all. In fact, she found it rather endearing.

Jubanne knew that he was not her first lover, but Signora Melis Puddu hadn't said whether there had been more than one. Jubanne had not pried into this private part of her past because it made him uncomfortable thinking about his wife being intimate with somebody else. He hadn't wanted to be told anything beyond the fact that he wasn't her first.

Now back in the marital bed all these years later, sharing their tentative reunion, Jubanne found that despite the fact that he was enjoying the closeness very much, there was nothing useful happening in his loins. Perhaps it was down to nerves, or the unexpectedness of the situation, but he could summon none of his morning vigour. Signora Melis Puddu said that he wasn't to worry and he knew that she meant it. Perhaps it was a bit of a relief for her too to take things slowly.

In the end, they had done nothing more than kiss and fondle. Jubanne fell asleep with his wife in his arms, and that was enough. It was really all that he wanted.

But as each night passed, they grew a little braver, and it was not long before Jubanne's loins caught up with what was going on. The couple began to make love every night, which was something that they had never done previously, even in the early days, before the kids came along.

If Jubanne was really honest, things had become a little stale in the conjugal intimacy department well before the accident. Since the arrival of their second child, Jubanne had sensed that his wife tolerated his sexual attentions rather than enjoying them – not that he would ever have imposed himself upon her. Jubanne had never liked to inconvenience Signora Melis Puddu too often, or for too long. She was never the one to make the first move, and often she would turn him down, saying that she needed her sleep, which was not unreasonable – and he always respected her wishes without question or complaint. He never quite knew if he had satisfied her. If he had failed to, she hadn't ever mentioned it, and he didn't want to embarrass her, or himself, by asking. They could go weeks without making love, especially in the summer when the nights were so hot and the guesthouse was so busy. Now he understood that before the accident their love-making had been little more than another household duty.

On that particular night, Jubanne lay awake beside his sleeping wife wondering what time it was – two, perhaps three a.m.? What he did know was that it was August and the summer heat was at its peak. Jubanne was perspiring so profusely that the sheet on which he lay was soaked. He was anxious about disturbing Signora Melis Puddu. This was nothing new. It had been an issue since they had first shared a bed, but previously, Jubanne had simply decamped to his boat. Now that was not an option. The *Lavandula* had been taken away to have the boom peg repaired. Anyway, even if she had been moored up in her usual place, he wouldn't have been allowed aboard. His balance had definitely not returned enough to be clambering around on a boat by himself.

He lay still for as long as he could. Now, to add to the discomfort of the heat and his sweat-soaked pyjamas and wet bed, he could also hear the high-pitched whine of a mosquito, which was bothering him too much to ignore. Eventually he slid out of bed and tiptoed barefoot out of the room. He would go to the terrace for a while to cool down. Perhaps he might manage to fall asleep in his chair under the fig tree.

Jubanne padded quietly through the sleeping guesthouse and through the dining room onto the terrace. It was cooler outside. A light breeze was blowing in off the sea. Jubanne stood with his arms outstretched, drying off his drenched pyjamas.

The night was not entirely dark. A three-quarter moon cast a silvery light that threw shimmering patterns on the sea and smudged soft contours around the plants in the garden, making even the spiky aloes seem less sharp.

Suddenly Jubanne became aware of somebody behind him. He looked over his shoulder and to his surprise, there was Doctor Alfa Romeo. His hair was wet.

'Are you all right, Signor Melis Puddu?'

Jubanne was confused. Doctor Alfa Romeo had no business being there in the middle of the night, so this could not really be happening. This must be an apparition, like Nonna Maria-Annoriana. Jubanne replied anyway, 'I'm fine. Just hot. I didn't want to wake my wife up.'

'I see,' acknowledged the doctor. 'It might be the medication too.'

It then struck Jubanne that whereas he knew his grandmother to be dead, as far as he could recall, Doctor Alfa Romeo was still very much alive; and unlike the conversations with Nonna Maria-Annoriana, which were carried out telepathically, with this apparition of the doctor, both were speaking out loud.

'Do you want me to stay here with you Signor Melis Puddu?'

'No, no. I'm just cooling down, then I'll go back to bed.'

Doctor Alfa Romeo seemed disinclined to leave. Jubanne didn't want him there. Even in his supernatural state, he didn't like the doctor, so he decided that the best thing to do would be to ignore him. Jubanne turned away and moved to the edge of the terrace, but the doctor followed him and asked, 'Have you had any more headaches?'

'No.'

'Any nausea?'

'No.'

'Indigestion?'

'No.'

'Would you let me take your pulse?'

Jubanne felt his heart rate quicken at the prospect, and replied again with a very firm, 'No.'

'Are you feeling agitated?'

This question caused Jubanne to feel very agitated indeed.

'Yes, but only because you're asking me stupid questions! I'm perfectly all right. I told you, I'm just out here to cool down.'

'I'll stay with you a little while anyway, just to make sure.'

The doctor came to stand beside him and started talking in an overly chummy kind of way, making irritating small-talk about his car. The model was a Giulietta Spider, he said, designed by Pininfarina. Four cylinders. 80 horsepower. Top speed of 155.

Eventually Jubanne told him to go away. The doctor shrank back into the shadows. A minute later Jubanne heard the engine of the Alfa Romeo start up, then the car drove off.

This apparition was unsettling. The doctor had seemed so real, as though Jubanne could have reached out to touch him. He had been able to smell a spicy, soapy, freshly-showered aroma, which was still lingering. Jubanne pinched his arm hard to make sure that he wasn't dreaming and found himself to be perfectly awake. He stood for a while with his elbows leaning on the terrace balustrades, calming the feeling of animosity he felt towards Doctor Alfa Romeo.

The smell of the lavender was intense and Jubanne watched the great clouds of scent floating in a fine grey mist just above the garden and mingling with the resinous perfume of the pinewoods, which appeared as a heavier, deep green vapour. What was that word for being able to see smell? He'd have to get Nora to tell him again. Maybe it would be a good idea to write it on his hand and keep repeating it. Then, as Jubanne continued to sniff the air, he became aware of something else – a waft of smoke. What smoke was that? Not tobacco. It was pungent, like herbs – unusual, but not unpleasant. When he spotted the glow of a cigarette at the far end of the terrace, he made his way towards it.

Nora was sitting up cross-legged on one of the lounging chairs, wearing a man's shirt half buttoned-up over her yellow swimsuit. She didn't seem surprised to see him.

'Can't you sleep?' She said, flicking the ash from her cigarette.
'No. It's too hot.'
'Aren't you going to tell me off for smoking?
'No.'
'Do you know what I'm smoking?'
'A cigarette.'
'Do you know what kind of cigarette?'

'No.'

'Probably just as well. Don't tell anyone.'

Nora re-arranged herself on the lounging chair and patted the space beside her, inviting Jubanne to join her.

They sat in silence for a while, looking out over the sea. Something in the smoke was wrapping itself around Jubanne's brain. He was feeling peculiar, but nicely so. A flash-back of being in hospital – *another two milligrams* – was followed by a pleasant sensation which made him feel both light and heavy at the same time. The patterns of moonlight on the sea began to move in a kaleidoscopic kind of way, spinning, dividing and merging into each other. The moon was more detailed than usual. He could see craters within craters. And there were so many stars. More stars than sky.

Nora was speaking, but Jubanne couldn't make out all the words, despite trying hard to focus.

'Maybe you shouldn't be breathing this in,' she said, fanning away the smoke with her hand.

'It's nice,' replied Jubanne, and without asking whether she minded, he leant over and rested his head on her lap murmuring, 'Another two milligrams.'

'What?'

Then it was as though he could hear two voices – Nora's voice beside him and another voice, still Nora's but different, as though she was speaking underwater. It was that underwater voice which said, 'I can smell your wife's pussy on you.'

Jubanne flushed. Surely she couldn't have just said what he thought she'd said. He opened his mouth, but no words came out.

'Lucky Signora Melis Puddu,' said Nora's voice, 'Is there any left for me?'

Jubanne sat up with a start and the pleasant feeling he'd been enjoying left him instantly.

'You mustn't say things like that!'

'Do you think I'm joking?'

'I don't know what you're doing. But I'm a married man-'

'A married man who thinks about how it would feel to fuck me every time he sees me. I've seen that look, when your eyes glaze over. And don't think I haven't noticed your cock get hard when I'm around you. I've seen it bulge so much it's almost burst out of your trousers. I expect it's hard at this very moment.'

Jubanne did not reply. He got up and walked away because Nora was right.

That meeting on the terrace changed the way Jubanne allowed himself to think about Nora. He had been so careful before, tiptoeing delicately around the edges of sexual fantasies, mindful of not overstepping the mark. But now the situation had changed. Nora had confirmed that she wanted him in *that way*. She could not have made it any clearer.

Jubanne's waking mind raced with new fantasies of Nora, which spilled into his nighttime dreams too, merging with the fragments of other memories. He had seen some things, a long time ago, which had stayed with him. He'd been twenty years old and working in his parents' tavern, and sleeping in an upstairs room, which he shared with the barman, Michele. Michele was a ladies' man – a self-confessed scoundrel who traded on his handsome face and drew women in with a combination of witty charm and free drinks.

One night they'd ushered out the last of the patrons as normal, at around eleven-thirty. Michele had said that he was going outside for a bit of air. He wouldn't be long. He'd see to locking up and turning off the lights.

Jubanne had headed upstairs to their shared room and got into bed, but he hadn't been able to sleep straight away as the lamp which hung above the tavern sign outside was shining in through the window. Although his half of the room was in darkness, Michele's end was brightly lit.

He was still half-awake when Michele had come up and Jubanne had wanted to tell him that he'd forgotten to turn off the lamp above the sign – but Michele hadn't been alone. There was a woman with him, and Jubanne knew her. She was the widow who ran a haberdashery shop at the end of the road; and she was undressing herself with some urgency.

Should he make a noise, wondered Jubanne, maybe just clear his throat to alert the widow of his presence? No. The widow was in a state of undress, so he decided that he should save her the humiliation and keep his eyes shut. He'd have to have a stern word with Michele in the morning.

He closed his eyes just as the widow, now wearing only her stockings and garter belt, was bending over Michele's bed; but even though Jubanne couldn't see anything with his eyes screwed up tightly, there was no way of ignoring what was going on at the far end of the room – the low rumble of Michele's voice, punctuated by grunts, and the widow, gasping and moaning and using some shocking language. Jubanne half-opened one eye. The lamp above the sign was illuminating the goings-on like a theatre spotlight. He knew he shouldn't watch, but the widow was a very attractive lady, still not yet fifty and very well-preserved. Of course, he'd never tell a soul, or make it known to the widow that he'd been party to her indiscretion; so if he did spectate secretly, it wouldn't matter because nobody would know, except Michele, and Michele knew already.

Perhaps, Jubanne thought, he could learn a thing or two. He'd always assumed that sex was supposed to start with kissing, but as far as he could tell, Michele and the widow hadn't kissed at all – unless they'd got that bit out of the way downstairs.

The widow was making a noise like a fox caught in a trap and Michele was pulling on her hair and calling her a 'filthy slut' and 'dirty bitch'; and this, Jubanne found alarming. He tensed, wondering whether he should leap out of bed to rescue the widow; but her cries, ever-increasing in volume, were cries of encouragement, not distress. In fact, she was letting it be known in no uncertain terms that Michele should not stop what he was doing, and rather than offending the widow, the disgraceful names that he was calling her seemed to be escalating her enthusiasm.

This continued for quite some time, until the widow let out a howl, and with one final grunt, Michele disengaged himself. He stepped back and as he turned, his profile was silhouetted against the lit window. Sainted Sardines! Michele was hung like a horse!

Jubanne felt too awkward to bring the subject up with Michele and this turned out to be just the first of many episodes. At least twice a week, Michele would bring a companion back to the room, and the number and variety of women willing to give themselves to Michele was quite astonishing to Jubanne. There were the regulars, like the widow, and a woman called Gilda who sold oysters; and the wife of Pio, the merchant-seaman – she only visited when her husband was away at sea. In addition to these were several women who were invited back a handful of times, and various who only came once.

How could Michele convince all those women to engage in all that hanky-panky? Jubanne marvelled. And the spectacle was not the same every time. Michele was like a different man with each individual woman. With some, his voice would growl, he would demand, give instructions, blaspheme, thrust away in a tangle of limbs and sweat and spit. With others, he was a gentle lover, murmuring sweetly and barely creasing the bedsheets. How did he know? How could Michele guess what each woman wanted? It was a mystery.

Now Jubanne looked back on these memories as an education. When he thought of the widow bent over the bed; or Gilda the oyster-seller who was more inclined towards oral pleasures; or the wife of the merchant-seaman who would straddle Michele and ride him so vigorously that she made the floor tremble – or any of the others – onto each of these women Jubanne would superimpose a vision of Nora.

He woke every morning hard as rock, and whilst still holding the image of Nora in his head, Jubanne would run his hands over his sleeping wife and wake her with his caresses, and always, she was receptive. She would moan, stretch back and open her legs for him. It was only ever like that, because that was the only way Signora Melis Puddu enjoyed being pleasured. She was soft and pliant in his arms, and she would seek out his mouth and kiss him.

Yet this sensuality masked the simmering lust inside Jubanne. Nora would not be supine, docile and compliant, like his wife. Nora would be a wild cat – a combination of all of the women in Jubanne's bank of memories and more. She would howl like the widow; devour like Gilda; ride rodeo-style like the merchant-seaman's wife.

So outwardly, as Jubanne made love to his wife, kissed her, penetrated her tenderly; inwardly, he was fucking Nora.

One night, after they had retired to bed, he remained wide awake with that electric pins and needles feeling vibrating through his body. Signora Melis Puddu was asleep, curled up with her back to him. Thoughts of Nora made sleep impossible, and in a fervent state of arousal, Jubanne began to caress his wife. She didn't stir for quite some time, and this didn't displease him. It was easier to hold the image of Nora that way. He eased his fingers between his wife's buttocks and felt between her legs, but she was dry, so he spat on his hand, as he had seen Michele do, and as he began to rub her, she made a sound somewhere between a sigh and a groan -but still, she remained

181

asleep. As he worked his fingers inside her, she turned not onto her back as was her usual habit, but onto her front, and still not awake, she made that sound again.

Maybe this time they could do it differently, thought Jubanne. Maybe this time he wouldn't be so tentative and gentle. Maybe it was time to take a leaf out of Michele's book of tricks. Now that he thought about it, had his wife's pre-accident sexual indifference been because she knew that she would not be satisfied by his efforts? Perhaps the years of deliberate tenderness had been terribly dull for her. This question now became a certainty. Of course! She must have been so bored by the prescriptive monotony of their lovemaking. He'd been bored too – he just hadn't recognised it at the time. Signora Melis Puddu moaned quietly. Jubanne undid the cord of his pyjamas and mounted her.

His startled wife woke abruptly and cried out, just as he pushed himself hard inside her with a single, sharp jab.

'Jubanne, what are you doing?' She gasped, her voice muffled by the pillow.

He pinned her down. His size and his weight felt powerful, dominant, and he liked it.

'No! Stop! Get off me! Stop! Stop! Stop!'

That irresistible compulsion to swear overcame him. Michele's words to the widow sprang from his mouth with each thrust. *Filthy slut. Dirty bitch. Filthy slut. Dirty bitch.* Jubanne had never used language like that in bed and his wife's shock excited him. When he felt her fight back and resist, it excited him further. He yanked hard on her hair and began to pound into her, and it was over in no time.

Signora Melis Puddu struggled to disentangle herself and slapped him so hard that his ears rang, which brought Jubanne back to reality very quickly indeed. The look on her face was one of fury and terror and confusion.

She kicked him first out of bed, then out of the room, and

locked the door behind her. Jubanne stood for a time with his nose an inch from the door. On the other side, he could hear his wife's broken breathing. He knocked. Signora Melis Puddu shouted at him to go away.

Dazed and wearing only his pyjama trousers, Jubanne made his way out onto the terrace trying to make sense of what he had just done. He felt terrible now. The thrill of virility and dominance had vanished, leaving only a feeling of disgust at his behaviour. What on earth had come over him? His wife wasn't one of Michele's conquests. She was his wife; his wonderful, beautiful, beloved wife. The mother of his children. How could he have done such an appalling thing to her?

Jubanne sat down on his chair under the fig tree and cradled his head in his hands. The salt in his tears made his slapped cheek sting. The spermy smell of his pyjamas revolted him.

As he was formulating an apology, Doctor Alfa Romeo came out through the dining room again. His hair was wet this time too, and although he was dressed, he had a slightly dishevelled air about him – as though he'd thrown his clothes on in a hurry. His shirt was not tucked into his trousers. But how the doctor looked was beside the point. He was the last person Jubanne wanted to see, so he pretended not to have noticed the apparition and wiped his face dry.

'Signor Melis Puddu, is everything all right?'

Jubanne ignored him.

'Are you feeling unwell, Signor Melis Puddu?'

'Go away!' Warned Jubanne, shaking his fist. 'Mind your own business!'

The doctor did not move.

'I heard shouting,' he said.

'You'll hear a lot more of it unless you fuck off right now.'

Jubanne leaned his head back and shut his eyes tightly until he heard the engine of the Alfa Romeo start up and the car drive away.

Then, just as had happened after the previous manifestation of the doctor, Nora was there wearing a man's shirt, unbuttoned – only this time she was not wearing her modest one-piece swimsuit underneath, but a skimpy two-piece. She was smoking one of her strange cigarettes.

'Your wife's certainly getting a lot of your attention,' she said and pulled up a lounging chair, placing it directly opposite Jubanne.

Embarrassed, he covered up the crotch of his pyjamas with his hands. He couldn't tell Nora the awful thing that he had just done. He certainly couldn't admit that she had been the fuel of his fantasy, so he said nothing.

She half-reclined on her lounging chair, letting the shirt fall open, and took a long suck on her pungent cigarette. Jubanne felt the smoke envelop his brain.

'Your wife's got secrets,' Nora whispered.

'What secrets?'

'Oh, you have no idea! Your wife's done things that would make your hair stand on end. And she's had so many different lovers that even she doesn't know how many there have been. And not just men, women too.'

Jubanne had no idea how he should reply. All he could do was to stare dumbstruck at Nora, and as he did, her features began to change – not all at once, but in a gradual, yet perceptible way. It was like watching the minute hand move on a clock. A small lifting of her eyes, a little less length to her nose, a broadening of her mouth. This was Nora, but with Signora Melis Puddu's face. Jubanne continued to stare. Now her eyes were different. Her pupils contracted to two little slits, like those of a cat.

It was too much for Jubanne. He got up and hurried away into the darkness of the garden, where he stood trying to calm himself. His teeth were chattering, despite the heat.

Could it really be that his wife had had so many lovers that she had lost count? Exactly how many was 'so many'? And women, as well as men? Surely not. He couldn't imagine how that might work. And how did Nora know? Had Signora Melis Puddu told her? Jubanne shook his head. No, of course she hadn't. His wife's interactions with the staff were rigorously professional. There was absolutely no way she would have confided such a thing to a girl who worked in the restaurant, even if it was true, so it couldn't be true. Nora was making things up.

Just then, Jubanne's attention was diverted by two fishing boats moored up at the end of the jetty. How strange, he thought. The fishing boats never came at night. They always arrived in the early afternoon with their morning's catch. He glimpsed a figure coming towards him. It was Nonna Maria-Annoriana with a basket on her hip, and she was singing one of her half-hummed songs.

'I've got sea urchins,' she said without speaking. 'I'm going to take them to the cook.'

She walked past Jubanne, through the garden and across the terrace which now, inexplicably, was filled with people sitting at the tables. That was odd. How come they were all awake in the middle of the night?

Jubanne followed his grandmother and made his way through the tables. A few people gave him funny looks because he was only wearing his pyjama trousers. One was the widow from the haberdashery shop. Another was the nurse who had injected his neck in hospital. Then he spotted Michele, sitting with both Gilda the oyster-seller and the merchant seaman's wife. He had an arm around each of them and a big grin on his face.

He would have said something to Michele had he not spotted his parents. They were going from table to table serving lemon tea with mint and ice from huge carafes. His mother and father acknowledged him, but they were too busy to stop and talk, so Jubanne made his way into the guesthouse.

Jubanne found Nonna Maria-Annoriana in the kitchen, where she had said she would be. She was preparing something with the cook. He watched the two women, trying to understand how it was possible that the cook could see Nonna Maria-Annoriana. They were talking about the benefits of whisking beer into the batter to make apple *frittelle*. Just a little, Nonna Maria-Annoriana was saying, and fry the apples in butter first. Mix cinnamon with the sugar. Sprinkle it on as soon as you take the *frittelle* out of the pan, whilst they're still sizzling hot, that way it'll caramelise.

'Oh, hello Jubanne. Can't you sleep?' Said the cook, as though meeting in the kitchen in the middle of the night was a perfectly normal occurrence.

Jubanne shook his head and looked down at his feet. He was wearing his best shoes, the ones he wore for weddings and funerals, but couldn't remember having put them on. When he looked up again, the cook was by herself.

'Where's Nonna Maria-Annoriana?' He asked.

'Who?'

'Nonna Maria-Annoriana. My grandmother. She was here just now, showing you how to make apple *frittelle*.'

The cook shrugged her shoulders as though she didn't understand.

'There's nobody else here,' she said. 'Just me. I've made a lemon tart.'

Jubanne looked around the kitchen, but could see no trace of his grandmother. When the cook passed him a slice of lemon tart, the dish was covered in sea urchins, which, still being alive, began to circle around the plate before scuttling off in a little procession and finally settling on the ceiling.

He must have gone back to his bedroom, although when he awoke the following morning, he had no recollection of having made his way there. There was no sign of his wife, or of her things. He lay for a while, summoning the pluck to get up. He had a very, very sincere apology to make.

When he found Signora Melis Puddu, to Jubanne's utter horror, she had a black eye. He didn't need to ask whether he had been the cause of it. He knew by the frightened and betrayed way she looked at him.

'I don't know what got into you,' she said.

'It was a dream, I think.'

'A dream?'

'I believe I had a dream, then in my half-woken state-'

'I don't want to hear about a dream like that. But whatever it was, let's do our best to forget about it, shall we?'

Jubanne gave a remorseful smile and moved to kiss his wife's cheek, but she flinched and held up her hand to stop him.

'You're not forgiven,' she said firmly. 'And I think it would be best if you stay in the room on the ground floor and I'll move back into our old room in the attic.'

From that night onwards, Jubanne refrained from going out onto the terrace, even if he woke up hot. In any case, he wasn't suffering quite so much from the heat now that his wife had returned to their former bedroom and he was sleeping alone.

One morning he noticed the doctor's Alfa Romeo parked next to Corrado's Vespa. At first he thought nothing of it, except that the doctor must be there to examine him, so he had gone back to sit under the fig tree and waited to be found.

Some time had passed, but there was no sign of the doctor. Jubanne went to check whether the car really was there and that he hadn't imagined it; and it was. He'd even knocked on the bonnet with his knuckles to make sure. Jubanne returned to his seat under the fig tree. Still Doctor Alfa Romeo did not appear.

Eventually Jubanne went to locate him, but happened upon Signora Melis Puddu instead.

'Is that the doctor's car parked at the back?' He asked.

'Yes,' she replied.

'I haven't seen him.'

His wife gave him a look which he couldn't quite read and said, 'I don't suppose we'll be seeing either of them much before lunch time. They went to a concert last night. They didn't get back until very late.'

This statement made no sense to Jubanne. Who were 'they'? Who had the doctor come to Villa Zuannicca with?

'The doctor's staying here?'

'Yes.'

'Oh. So he's not here to see me?'

'No.'

Satisfied with this answer, Jubanne would have left it at that, had his wife not added, 'Nora asked whether I minded him staying over and I said it was fine. I know he's been sneaking up to her room anyway and creeping off in the early hours. But it's not the nineteenth century any more and Nora's a grown woman and it's not as though he's just some casual boyfriend.'

Jubanne heard exactly what his wife said, but initially he was unable to understand it.

'Who's boyfriend?'

'Nora's boyfriend.'

'Nora has a boyfriend?'

'Well, I'd say he's a bit more than that.'

Now Jubanne was confused, like someone trying to understand the gist of a conversation spoken in a foreign language. He repeated, 'Nora has a boyfriend?'

'Yes, Jubanne. Nora's had a boyfriend since before she left to work on the yacht.'

'Is it Corrado?'

'What?' Exclaimed his wife. 'No, of course it's not Corrado!'

Whatever else Signora Melis Puddu might have said was lost on Jubanne. His pulse began to hammer and such a raging, furious jealousy consumed him that he thought his heart might explode out of his chest. Suddenly those night-time 'apparitions' of the freshly showered Doctor Alfa Romeo made sense in a way which he did not like one bit.

'That bastard!' He bellowed, feeling a burst of violent energy rush to his clenched his fists.

His wife blanched, clearly alarmed by his reaction, but she kept her voice as composed as she could. 'Nora's a grown woman. If she wants to-'

Jubanne stormed away, out through the kitchen to where the Alfa Romeo was parked and snatched up the first thing that came to hand – a garden spade, which had been left by the door.

In a fit of rage the likes of which he had never known to be possible, he raised the spade above his head and began to beat great dents into the car. But this was not just anger aimed at the doctor, or at Nora. This fury was fed by everything – by the stupidity of the accident, where one moment, one split second of inattention, one crack to his skull had changed everything.

His wife didn't love him any more – not really, not like she had before. Now she tolerated him, showed him nothing more than duty-bound charity. He was useless to her, just a great time and energy-sapping burden. And where were his children? Why hadn't he been able to see them? Maybe they didn't love him any more either. Maybe they were frightened by the bumbling, punch-drunk freak who had once been their father.

And to compound it all, the exhausting confusion, the constant questioning of what was real, the crazy, illogical way his brain cherry-picked what to remember. He wished that the accident had taken it all. *Whack!* Gone! He would rather have been a dribbling wreck left to vegetate in a hospital bed than to be this tortured, half-existing man.

Now everything was fucked.

Over and over again Jubanne drove his boot into the car

doors, wielding the spade and bringing it crashing down onto the bonnet of the Alfa Romeo; smashing the lights, the windscreen. Sparks and shards of glass flew out in all directions.

For exactly how long his rampage continued, he could not say, but when at last he paused, gasping for breath like a panting dog, sweating, bleeding and still furious, the car looked as though it had rolled down a ravine.

A terrified crowd stood cowering by the kitchen door. There was Signora Melis Puddu, pleading for him to stop; the cook holding onto his wife's arm; Corrado, looking stunned; Nora, pale and crying and wrapped in a short dressing gown. And Doctor Alfa Romeo, with wet hair and wearing only a towel around his waist. Guests who had been alerted by the commotion gathered at a distance. Jubanne shook the spade at them, warning them to keep away.

'Do you love me, Nora?' He demanded.

'Yes, yes, of course I love you.'

'And *him*?' cried Jubanne, jabbing the spade towards the doctor.

Nora, fearful and wide-eyed replied, 'Yes, I do. I love you all.'

Jubanne swung the spade and hit Doctor Alfa Romeo with a slapping sound and a dull, bell-like ring. The doctor fell to the floor and Jubanne raised the spade again, ready to beat every drop of life out of the man, when in a sideways tackle, Corrado pounced on him, knocking the weapon out of his hand. There was blood on his face. 'Stop!' Corrado was shouting. 'Stop! Stop!'

Suddenly, with all the effort of his frenzy, Jubanne's head began to pound. He doubled over, clutching his skull in his hands and howling, 'No, no, no, no, no!'

CHAPTER 16

'I realised what was going on,' snarled Jubanne Melis Puddu, rocking in his seat. 'It was that doctor giving me those green and orange pills. He wasn't trying to make me better. He had a plan to make me act like a crazy man because he wanted Nora all for himself.'

Dante was now feeling more than a little unsettled by the enormous man, who was bearing forwards menacingly, snorting the air in through his nose and blowing it out again through his mouth in sharp puffs. His eyes flashed with a primordial look, threatening imminent violence, then rolled back in his head until only the whites were visible. From somewhere deep within him rose a rumbling noise so intense that it buffeted the fire to the back of the hearth.

Terrified, Dante gripped the edge of the table. If the big Sardinian chose to attack him, it would be a David and Goliath situation, except that under these circumstances David could not be the victor. To say that he was at a disadvantage would be an understatement.

Dante had pictured his own death many times, but never had he imagined himself murdered. A man the size of Jubanne Melis Puddu could knock him down with one finger and snap his neck like a toothpick. Disposal of his corpse would be easy. His murderer could tear him apart and scatter the pieces on the mountainside, and by the time the spring thaw came, the wild animals would have devoured the meagre amount of meat on his body, gobbled down his organs and crunched up his bones. There would be nothing left. 'What became of Dante Bacchetti?' people would ask. Nobody would know. 'He disappeared without a trace, like his daughter,' they would say.

Dante waited, trembling and expecting an attack, but the Sardinian remained static in his chair. Gradually the deep rumbling abated. An expression of calm returned to Jubanne Melis Puddu's countenance. He wiped a veil of sweat from his upper lip and when he spoke again, his tone was regretful.

'The doctor had me taken away after that and I had to stay in hospital. And my wife said it was for the best and I didn't want to cause her any more upset, so I went without making a fuss.'

Then, as though a satisfactory end to the meeting had been reached, the Sardinian retrieved his shoes and said, 'That's what I came to tell you.'

'That's it? What happened to my daughter?'

Jubanne Melis Puddu shrugged, 'I can't be sure, because people don't tell me things to my face, but I think Nora married the doctor and they had a child a couple of years back. A boy. They called him "Jubanne".'

The old man stared open-mouthed and repeated slowly, as though the idea was having trouble sinking in, 'My daughter married the doctor and now has had a child named "Jubanne"?'

'I'm pretty sure that's correct. I overheard a few conversations when my wife was on the telephone, and there were some pictures of a baby in the dining room.' He then added, almost matter-of-factly, 'If you want to know for certain, you'll have to ask my wife.'

By this time the Sardinian was lacing up his shoes.

'You'll find my wife at Villa Zuannicca. You'll have to take the ferry from Livorno to Olbia and go up the coast as far as Baia Sanna. Don't go in peak season though because my wife will be very busy and you'll inconvenience her.'

With that, he went to collect his coat.

'What are you doing?' Asked Dante, for surely the Sardinian could not be considering leaving now, in the dark and with the storm still raging. 'You can't go back out in this weather.'

His guest did not seem at all troubled by the conditions. 'I can't stay,' he said. 'They'll be wondering where I've gone. My wife will be worried. I have to go back.'

The enormous man patted his pocket to check for his pills, thanked Dante for dinner and calmly walked out into the storm. Dante dared go no further than the porch. The blizzard was blowing so hard that he couldn't see to the end of his small garden, and it was so cold that it hurt to breathe. Within a few strides, Jubanne Melis Puddu had vanished entirely from view.

'Come back!' Called Dante. 'You won't survive a night like this!' But the enormous man had disappeared deep into the icy darkness.

Dante paced the floor until the clock struck three and tiredness drove him to his bed, but he lay with his eyes wide open for most of the rest of night, kept awake in part by the blizzard and the clonking chimney pot and in part by everything he had just learned.

All at once, that unexpected evening, the feelings which he had so carefully managed and put in their place had returned – anger, outrage, despair; the anguish of uncertainty. All of his losses came crashing back down upon him. The misery of his life, which had in many ways been tempered, opened up again, like a bottomless chasm. Why now? he thought. Why now, when he was so near the end and he might have gone to his grave if not at peace, at least not in turmoil...and to crown it all, did he really have a grandson now? A grandson called Jubanne?

During two or three hours of broken sleep, the nightmares of insects and fields of knives haunted him again, only this time, accompanied by the wailing cries of a baby.

When Dante awoke at first light, the chimney pot was no longer making the clonking noise. He pulled on his boots, wrapped himself in the sheepskin and ventured outside. The storm had subsided and the wind had died away. The snow which had fallen overnight had crystallised into a thick, white, glistening mass. Great icy spikes hung from the pines. The leafless branches of the deciduous trees were frosted white like lacework. There was no birdsong; not even a breeze murmuring through the trees. There was nothing but blinding white and utter, utter silence.

The furrow gouged out by Jubanne Melis Puddu's passing through the snow had in part filled in with fresh snowfall, but it was still discernible, leading out in a curved line from the door of the little house to where the terrain dropped away sharply. Dante laboured through the furrow, waist-deep in snow, but stopped at the edge of his garden. He did not dare go any further in these conditions. He made his way back inside, stoked the fire and sat alone with his turbulent thoughts.

*

The thaw came quickly in March, with the sun providing an early burst of heat which melted the snow into the mountain torrents, filling the rivers in the valleys below. By April there was hardly a scrap of snow to be seen around the little mountain house.

Dante ventured out, scouring the immediate vicinity for evidence of a dead body, certain that Jubanne Melis Puddu could not possibly have made it back down the mountain alive. But he found nothing – no body, no bones, no rags of clothing torn apart by wild animals. Surely, he thought, the Sardinian could not have survived the night; but then, he had ascended the mountain in conditions which even the most experienced *Alpinisti* would consider impossible.

At this time of year, Dante would normally have been keen to go to the village to refurbish his supplies and collect his pension, but as he hadn't completely run out of food, he kept putting it off. The prospect of the trek to the village, followed by the return trip laden with provisions felt like an impossible prospect.

He had developed a terrible ache, which began at the base of his back and travelled down his hip and right leg as far as his knee. His daily chores, which he had tackled with increasing difficulty every year had now become unmanageable. His thoughts too seemed painful and slowed in pace. Dante's clothes were even looser now. He knew that he had not eaten enough those past few weeks, but not because of scarcity of provisions. His appetite had been spoiled by the Sardinian's visit.

Ermenegildo turned up accompanied only by his dog. Before he said anything, the goat-herder leant on his crook and looked Dante up and down, as though assessing what damage the winter might have done to the old man. Dante knew by Ermenegildo's expression that he wasn't looking good.

'How are you, Dante?'

'Still alive. Just about.'

Satisfied that this was the case, Ermenegildo did not stay long – just long enough to tell him that the track was clear and to give him the village news, which was that the mayor had died the week after Epiphany. He'd gone in his sleep. 'You couldn't hope for a better end than waking up dead,' the goat-herder said.

Ermenegildo did not mention finding the remains of an enormous man, but Dante thought it best to check anyway.

'No fools venturing out into the wilds this past season then?'

'I haven't tripped over any bodies this year,' replied the goatherder.

Dante made his way down to the village the following day, and as he had feared, the trek was far more arduous than it had been previously. The pain in his back and his leg caused his knee to buckle every few steps. He lost count of how many times he had to stop to rest and tried not to think about the prospect of retracing his path to go back up the mountain. Nevertheless, eventually he made it to Montacciolo.

His old house was still closed up. After all these years, there was no sign of the tax office having carried out their sequestration. Maybe they'd changed their minds and decided that a house valued at 'approximately two sacks of onions' wasn't worth the paperwork. Dante didn't care either way.

They key was still under the flowerpot, although not exactly as Dante had left it because now the flowerpot sat slightly askew beside the door. Out of curiosity, he let himself in. The place was very damp and there were a few things missing, the most obvious of which was his kitchen table. Either the tax office had decided that they could do with some supplementary dining arrangements, or one of the villagers had helped themselves to it.

Dante locked up again and replaced the flowerpot the way it was meant to be. He had no feelings towards his old house any more, and he was glad of it. It had never felt like home, as the little house did. It was too full of unfriendly ghosts.

Every spring, whenever Dante made his first trip down to the village, he would allow himself the luxury of breakfast at the bar. It was a very small treat, but he always looked forward to a sweetened *caffè latte* frothed up with cows' milk, to fresh bread with butter and jam, and even a custard pastry if the bar owner's wife had been up to the task.

As soon as he entered the bar, he located his old kitchen table and the bar owner looked sheepish about it.

'I hope you don't mind, Dante. It's just at the mayor's send-off there was a bit of a to-do in here and someone ended up going through one of my tables, and as yours was just sitting there in your house doing nothing...'

Dante made a dismissive gesture to show it didn't matter. The bar owner looked relieved and mentioned a few other things in the house which could be useful to him. Dante told him to take whatever he wanted. He then ordered his breakfast.

The two remaining Montacciolo councillors were seated at his old dining table and enjoying a mid-morning communion of crackers and red wine. One was wearing Dante's best suit, although minus its buttons and with the breast pocket torn off. The jacket was fastened with bits of wire. Dante didn't mention it, although he didn't pretend not to have noticed.

'Did you get a visitor a couple of months back, Bacchetti?' asked the first councillor.

Dante had no wish to give anybody present any fuel for gossip, nor did he want to be questioned about Jubanne Melis Puddu's visit, so he feigned surprise.

'A visitor? Up at my place in February?' he laughed. 'Have you forgotten where I live?'

'There was a big foreign fellow looking for you, but we told him your place was cut off.'

'Did he say who he was?'

The first councillor shook his head, 'I don't remember. I might have had a glass or two already that day. But he was foreign.' He then turned to his colleague for confirmation.

'He was foreign, wasn't he?'

'I think so,' replied councillor number two. 'He spoke Italian, but he had a funny accent. He didn't seem much in the mood for a chat though, so I didn't want to get his dander up by asking where he was from.'

Dante's breakfast arrived, served on a plate which he recognised as being his own. It was chipped from where Ortensia had accidentally knocked it against the draining board. His enjoyment of the breakfast was somewhat spoiled by the councillors, who began to pick his brains about council matters. As he had predicted, Montacciolo's administration was in a mess, but that was only to be expected if one left the monkeys in charge of the zoo. In this village, it would be hard to pick the idiot.

Dante finished his bread and jam quickly, swallowed his coffee, wrapped the custard pastry in a piece of paper and put it in his knapsack for later. He made his way to the post office, crossing paths with various villagers along the way. As always, most couldn't hide their astonishment that he'd made it through yet another winter. Nobody mentioned having encountered Jubanne Melis Puddu, either alive, or dead.

Dante hadn't been able to draw his pension since the previous November and was relieved to find that the postmaster had not spent the money which had accumulated. It was enough to stock his larder and to buy some of the other things he needed, but he stuffed most of it into his pocket and bought only a few basic supplies, which he found had risen quite sharply in price. His pension had certainly not increased in line with inflation.

He didn't remain in Montacciolo any longer than necessary. As he plodded his way slowly back up the mountain track, his small selection of provisions weighed down heavily on his shoulders. His burden was a quarter of the amount he'd been able to carry in previous years, yet it felt ten times heavier. The pain in his back and his leg was ever-present.

When he reached the ivy-covered oak, which had always been his half hour milestone, he knew that he had been walking considerably longer than that. It must have taken him a further hour to reach the zigzag path, and when he finally came to the hollowed-out maple tree his exhaustion was such that his legs shook with the exertion of every step and his lungs rattled with each suck of air. But if he stopped, he thought, he might not be able to start again. Eventually he made it to the waterfalls. He was still only half way.

Dante knew for certain that there was a probably a summer left in him, maybe and autumn, but definitely not another winter. The end was close. Before, he had thought about it, but now, he could feel it.

As he struggled up the mountain, every step he took brought him closer to that moment. Would he know it was happening, he wondered, when death came for him? A sleep death, like the mayor's, was the one that everyone wanted. People would sign up for that one if they could. Just go to sleep and wake up dead, as Ermenegildo had said. However it came, Dante would not fight it.

Purely for the sake of argument – what happened if you did indeed you wake up dead? mused Dante. If you believed what you were encouraged to believe, that there was a Saint Peter and a set of pearly gates and all the other amusement park attractions that heaven promised – wouldn't that be grand? All as perfect as a picture in a catalogue – a sunlit garden of fragrant flowers and sparkling fountains, filled with family, old friends, good-looking angels. Ha! The flowers and fountains and pretty angels were all very well, but as for the family and old friends, if there was any justice in the heavenly admissions system, the handful of people Dante could count in those categories would have been sent to the alternative destination, down below.

But Saint Peter and the Heavenly Father and whoever else was on the committee were reputedly a forgiving lot and you could get in as long as you apologised for having been a liar, or a cheat, or a thief, or a general nuisance, and if you promised to mend your ways. Even murderers had a chance if they said that they were really, really sorry.

Maybe his father had managed to elbow his way in by showing contrition for his fits of violence and was now living out the rest of eternity as a benevolent spirit who wouldn't dream of making a child feel worthless, or knocking the same child's front teeth out with his fist. Maybe Ortensia had managed to find some loophole in the celestial legislation and was enjoying the fruits of all that time spent praying. Perhaps now she was cheery and well-disposed, and as sane as sane could be.

Dante snapped out of his reverie. Why was he wasting his energy thinking about all that heavenly hogwash? He didn't believe in it any more than he believed in fairies or Father Christmas. Heaven was nothing beyond a spurious promise made to comfort and control the gormless, and if that applied to heaven, then it also applied to hell. Burning fires and lakes of sulphur, indeed! Bah!

The old man took a moment to pause and steadied himself against a tree. He was feeling sick and light-headed. His mouth tasted of metal. Every fibre of his body was telling him that he should not be walking up the mountain, but he couldn't stop now. There were fewer steps ahead of him than behind him to get to the little house, so he had to continue.

'One last push, Bacchetti,' he wheezed and withdrew back into his own thoughts. Now, where was he? Ah, yes. Death. The eternal question: So, what happens next, after you cast aside your human costume?

The most likely thing, Dante mused, dragging the air into his lungs with the effort of the climb, was that nothing happened. Sweet oblivion. Lights out. *Buonanotte*. With your last breath, everything you'd ever said, done and been, was gone. You might live on in other people's memories for a while. If you hadn't upset them too much, they might mourn you. Some might like to make themselves feel better by tending your grave until their turn came. But expecting anything more than that was a delusion.

If you were a king, or personage who had done something memorable – whether that be good, or bad – you might be captured for posterity in a history book and people would look back on your life. But there would be no such commemoration for Dante Bacchetti. The Ministry of Education had never named the village school after him. There was no plaque on the wall.

Within no time ordinary men were entirely forgotten, or at best their lives would be reduced to a few hand-picked anecdotes shared between those who had known them. They might remember you more easily if you'd had an amusing talent. Apparently Dante's great uncle had been able to juggle five oranges whilst balancing a sixth on his nose – and that was the only thing Dante knew about him, although there must have been more to the man than that.

So that was it. Everything that used to seem important because it pertained to you was gone. All that was left was the carcass, and that carcass would go back to the earth and feed the worms– at least then you could say you'd done some good.

If you'd gone to the trouble and expense of having offspring, your job as a human being was more or less complete. Nothing else mattered, really, in the great, eternally boiling cauldron of life. Impregnate, propagate, beget. Done! Just try to keep your progeny alive for long enough so that they can keep the cycle going. If you measured it by those parameters, Dante's life had probably had no point at all...or had it? Was what the Sardinian had told him true, that Leonora had had a child?

One thing which Dante could be pretty certain of was that it would be Ermenegildo who'd find him dead, but that was something he had been anticipating since he'd moved to the little house. Dante had written the goat-herder a note before the first winter, which he kept in a prominent position, pinned to his dresser, in preparation for the day when Ermenegildo came across his remains.

Firstly, the note apologised for the inconvenience of discovering him dead. It then specified that Ermenegildo need not put himself to the trouble of procuring a coffin, nor of moving his corpse to the village cemetery. Instead, Dante wished to be buried in the field of daisies, and the book of poetry entitled 'The Little Boat' was to be interred with him. Dante had already dug the hole, but included an annotated, to-scale plan to ensure that there were no misunderstandings. Once his body had been committed to his grave, he requested that Ermenegildo should scatter it with quicklime, which he would find in the porch, to the left of the woodpile. Dante had also left a shovel there for his convenience.

To this, Dante had added a short post-scriptum to say that upon his death the little house was Ermenegildo's to do with as he pleased – not that there was much which could be done with it. There were no deeds, or official documents. Probably best not to mention it to the tax man, or to the land registry.

Dante's most heart-wrenching concern, and that which weighed heaviest on his conscience, was what would happen to Gineprina when he died. He couldn't bear the thought of the goat being trapped in her pen, uncared for, unfed and unwatered, whilst his remains lay waiting to be discovered. All he could do was to trust that the goat would have the presence of mind to break out of her enclosure. Whether she would survive out in the wilds alone was uncertain. Hopefully her instincts would lead her down the mountain in search of human companionship and she would be cared for in a new, loving home. Dante had shed many tears over the uncertainty of Gineprina's fate.

By the time the old man reached the little house, the light was fading. He tried to chew his way through the custard pastry which was left over from his breakfast, but he was too dry-mouthed. It was like trying to eat sawdust. He gave it to the goat and went straight to his bed without taking off his boots.

Dante's exhaustion was so profound that he wondered whether the walk to the village and back might have used up those final few drops of life left inside him. Yes. This was it. Death was coming to claim him right now. He could not only feel death's gentle beckoning, but he could hear it too, whispering into his ears, like the sound inside a seashell. Maybe he should have stopped in the field of daisies and lain down in the hole he had dug and perished there quietly. That would have saved Ermenegildo the trouble of moving his corpse.

Dante closed his eyes. His mind felt numb. He was already dead inside – surely his body would not take long to catch up. In fact, his heart was barely beating. He was looking forward to the end. Oh, the sweet release! He had never looked forward to anything so much. Dante fell asleep for what he was certain would be the last time, if not at peace, at least grateful that his end was neither painful, nor protracted, nor violent.

But when he awoke, just as the new day was dawning, he was still alive.

Now he didn't feel so bad. The few hours of sleep had been very restorative, and not only that; unbelievably, the previous day's long walk had eased the pain in his leg, as though the movement had somehow unblocked something. It was not completely gone, but certainly vastly improved.

Dante felt for his pension in his pocket. There was no point in spending it on provisions. No point planning for a future which was not going to happen.

He knew that he had one final mission in life, and that was to go to Sardinia to speak to Signora Melis Puddu.

PART 2

THE GUESTHOUSE BY THE SEA.

CHAPTER 17

Dante spent a week resting and eating his way through everything in his larder. Satisfied that he was as physically prepared as he could hope for, he packed a small bag with a few essentials and left an amended note for Ermenegildo, still bequeathing him the house and thanking him for his assistance over the years, but minus the apology for the inconvenience of finding his remains and minus the burial instructions.

His farewell to the little mountain house was brief. There was no reason for long-drawn-out sentimentality. Dante made his bed, washed up his breakfast dishes and left the place tidy, then walked down to the village at first light with Gineprina tethered to a length of string. He left her tied up outside Ermenegildo's brother's house. The fellow would recognise who she was. Men like him never forgot a goat.

'All the best, old girl,' he said, patting her flank. He didn't say '*arrivederci*' so as not to give the goat false hope, because he knew he would not see her again. This was the only good-bye Dante said in Montacciolo. He made his way out of the village of his birth without a backward glance.

As luck would have it, he didn't have to walk much further, and he was glad of it, as the trek from the little house had already fatigued his old legs considerably and the pain which afflicted him from his spine to his knee had started bothering him again. A man who had been delivering supplies to the general store gave him a lift in his van down as far as Pontenuovo.

This was the first time Dante had been to Pontenuovo since Ortensia had taken herself down there on her final outing. He stopped for a moment on the bridge and peered over the side.

The torrent was full of meltwater, just as it would have been when his wife had jumped. It was surprising that she'd hit the rocks with all that water to aim for. Maybe she'd misjudged her position in the dark, or maybe the wind had caught her on her way down. Anyway, no point in mulling over the macabre details, especially now, a full sixteen years after the event.

Dante had intended to visit her grave after he'd dropped off the goat, but had changed his mind. All that visiting the dead business was meaningless if you believed as he did, that death held no mystical or religious significance. He had never commissioned a gravestone because it would have been an unmanageable expense – and in any case, what would a gravestone have commemorated? *Here lies Ortensia Bacchetti – unworthy of a Christian burial.* He had planted a hydrangea there instead, which was the flower that Ortensia was named after, but had rarely been back to prune it.

Just beyond Pontenuovo, Dante flagged down the first car that passed him travelling in the right direction. A quiet, ripe-smelling fellow set him down in the nearest small town.

This was a place familiar to Dante, although he had not been there since before his move to the little house in 1975. The streets and most of the buildings were as he remembered them, but there was a visible change in style to the place. Progress moved more quickly in towns than it did in remote little villages like Montacciolo, and certainly faster than in places like Dante's mountain house, where it didn't move at all. Here, in this small, ordinary, provincial town, the 1990s were very different in appearance to the 1970s.

The volume of traffic was intimidating and the lay-out of the junctions was incomprehensible. Dante stood on the pavement as cars raced past him, waiting for a light to change so that he could cross the road. He waited and waited, not daring to attempt a dash through the stream of traffic as he was certain that if he tried, his knee would buckle and he'd end up on his backside in the middle of the road. Still, he waited. How did people cross roads these days? The answer came eventually, when a woman with a pram came up beside him and pushed a button on a bollard. Five seconds later, the lights changed and the traffic stopped. Dante crossed over and assuming he must now change the lights back, pushed the button on the bollard on the opposite side. The lady with the pram gave him a quizzical look.

Very few of the old shops remained, and those that did looked outmoded beside the new plate-glass shopfronts. The stationer's where Dante had previously bought school supplies now sold electrical goods. Dante stood before the bewildering display of items. Televisions had grown in size. Radios had changed in appearance and sported more switches and buttons than he could imagine uses for. He could not fathom the purpose of some of the other items.

People looked different too. The youth, the girls as well as the boys, were dressed in blue jeans and jackets of the same fabric. Few men wore suits and many women had abandoned skirts and pretty dresses in favour of trousers. Dante was intrigued by some of the footwear. There were people of all ages wearing what appeared to be sports shoes, in every possible colour and pattern, although clearly they were not engaged in any sport.

He became aware of passers-by staring at him just as much as he was staring at them. Hardly a surprise, he thought. He knew of how out-of-place he must look in his shabby clothes, wearing a jacket that was all patches and mends, and with his beard hanging past his navel. When he caught sight his reflection in the window of a shop, he saw a wild man escaped from the mountains.

Just then, a group of youths rode past on scooters and yelled some sort of mocking insult at him. Well, well, well, thought

Dante. The clothes and the cars and the shops have changed, but people haven't.

Not wishing to attract attention, Dante found a barber's where he requested a haircut and parted company with his most of his beard. He asked to keep a little length, neatly trimmed. After all this time he reasoned he would feel uncomfortably naked with no beard at all. It was many years since he had looked at his face properly in a mirror. How hoary and withered his features were now! He had been quite handsome once – distinguished, one might say – but time had not been kind. The barber, despite his best efforts, was unable to work any miracles. Nevertheless, the end result was an improvement. With his freshly cut hair and cropped beard, Dante surmised that he looked a good twenty minutes younger.

He emerged from the barber's doused so profusely in some sort of balsamic cologne that his eyes were watering, and crossed the road to a gentlemen's outfitters which still looked reassuringly old-fashioned. He knew the shop as he had purchased clothing there twenty years before. Nothing much had changed except the prices. Dante bought two pairs of trousers, two shirts, a light sweater and a jacket, new underwear and new socks; and left the establishment wearing half of his purchases. He then located a shoe shop and acquired a pair of sports shoes. Their rubber-soled springiness took a little getting used to, but once he had adjusted his gait, Dante found them to be extremely comfortable and rather beneficial to the pain in his leg. He dropped his ragged old clothes and ancient hobnail boots into a dustbin and made his way to the bus stop.

Within the hour he had boarded a bus to Bologna; and within another hour, he had alighted outside the grand neoclassical edifice of Bologna Centrale railway station.

As he wove his way through the jostling ants' nest of humanity, Dante did his best to quell his anxieties and reminded himself that catching a train could not be any more difficult now than it had been back in his teaching days in Ferrara, when he had caught many trains to and from this very station. He knew where the ticket office was and where to locate the departures board. He hoped that they hadn't been moved, and once inside the cavernous atrium of Bologna Centrale he found, to his great relief, that both were still exactly where he expected to find them.

Dante's one-way ticket to Livorno was considerably costlier than he had anticipated, but there was nothing he could do about that. With his ticket clutched firmly in his hand, he spent some time gazing at the wizardry of the arrivals and departures board. Gone was the old mechanical board. This was a new thing – a great electronic screen of digital numbers – and Dante found it to be quite mesmerising. He watched the numbers and letters flashing in different colours and constantly changing. It was a most wondrous technological vision to behold. He would have lingered longer if had he not had a train to catch. The board informed him that his train would be leaving from platform nine.

He followed the signs, which led him down into the underpass, and navigated his way back out to platform nine. To reassure himself, he asked two ladies whether they were waiting to catch the train to Livorno, and they confirmed that they were. Relieved, Dante sat down on a bench with his bag on his lap. So far so good.

Although Dante had already experienced journeys on diesel trains, the train which pulled in a short while later was not like those he'd ridden on before. This was a slick, long-nosed locomotive pulling a serpent of modern carriages. Quite miraculously, all the doors slid open simultaneously and of their own accord. Dante took his seat in the emptiest carriage he could find.

Thus far the journey had gone as well as he could have hoped;

probably better than he'd expected. He'd managed to make it out of Montacciolo, as far as Bologna and now he was on the correct train to Livorno. He had feared that he might have wrongly ended up on a train to Trieste, or Taranto, or not even have been able to make it to Bologna Centrale station at all.

The train pulled away, slowly at first, and trundled its way through the maze of tracks. Bologna Centrale was, as its name indicated, a central hub where many lines intersected. The backstage part of the station was nothing like the grand theatre of the arrivals and departures hall. This was all pylons and signal boxes and miles of criss-crossing electric wires.

Now to his left and to his right were freight sheds and warehouses and sidings where carriages were being cleaned and repaired. Beyond, two dozen locomotives were parked up. They were all diesel now. He saw just one steam locomotive, three, or even four decades out of service – just a rusted relic abandoned outside a shed. Dante could sympathise with that redundant, time-worn steam engine. If Leonora was the Little Boat, he was the Old Locomotive. He began to make up a rhyme in his head, and he found himself reciting it to the rhythm of the moving train.

I am an engine that once was the king – now an Old Locomotive, a discarded thing.

After a time, the freight yards gave way to the suburbs, where blocks of flats had been built, rising higher and higher. It astonished Dante that people could live so tightly packed in those human rookeries. Within a few minutes, the habitations became more sparse and the train picked up speed. Eventually they were slicing through the countryside, and from what Dante could see as he passed fruit orchards, farms and fields, that had not changed at all.

He had intended to enjoy the landscape, but worn out by the morning's travel and rocked by the motion of the train, Dante felt his eyelids grow heavy. He fell asleep and re-awoke just ten minutes from Livorno with a very stiff neck and dribble down the lapel of his new jacket.

Here, despite having been built in a grand style, the station was far smaller and less labyrinthine than Bologna Centrale. Finding a bus which would take him to the port was very easy. There was one parked just outside the station with *Porto di Livorno* sign in its window. Dante was the only passenger to board.

During his seventy-three years Dante had only been to the coast twice. The first time had been when he was still a school-boy. The Jesuits had taken his class on a trip to Piombino to visit the cathedral of Sant'Antimo – the reason for which Dante could no longer remember – but it had been deemed of some impor-tance to their education at the time. The Jesuit schoolmasters had granted the class half an hour of paddling in the sea under certain strict conditions. The boys had been allowed to take off their shoes and socks and to roll up their trousers no higher than just below the knee. No running, jumping, splashing or horse-play was permitted. Dante recalled that time as having been nothing more than thirty minutes spent walking carefully through ankle-deep seawater, but an enjoyable distraction nonetheless. The class had filled their pockets with shells and got into trouble for the sand they had taken back to school. The beating for this transgression had been moderate, but the trove of seashells had been thrown away by those in charge.

Dante's second encounter with the sea had been when he had travelled to Pesaro to collect Leonora's things. That time he had had no appetite to dip his feet.

Now, as the bus driver announced, 'Porto di Livorno!' Dante found this to be a very different kind of coast. He could see no pleasure beach here, or even a passenger ferry terminal. This place was all cranes and containers and freight and noise. Even from inside the bus, he could smell the diesel and the old fish, mixed with a pungent tarry odour.

When he asked the driver nervously, 'Is this the port? Can I catch a ferry to Olbia from here?' the man didn't answer his question. He just looked at Dante as though he was stupid and said, 'I'm not the travel information service,' then told him it was the end of the line, so he had to get off the bus.

Dante was unprepared, not just for the appearance of the port, but also for its vastness, and for the size of the vessels moored there. Great leviathans of merchant ships registered to places all over the world. *La Guapa* – Veracuz. *Anastasia* – Kavarna. *Princesa do Mar* –Lisbon. The sea lapped dirty, greasy tidemarks against their hulls.

Assailed by panic, feeling very vulnerable and utterly unprepared for his voyage, Dante almost turned back. He had come to the wrong place. Catching a train from Bologna Centrale railway station was one thing, because he had been on trains before; but he had never been to a port, or on a boat of any kind. This was new, a frightening unknown, and he was afraid to ask the people he encountered for help. Those whose paths he crossed were rough types, tattooed and wind-burned seamen, and others whose appearance was unnervingly foreign.

If he turned back, he could be safely in Montacciolo by sunset. He could forget about the whole thing. Nobody need ever know about his ridiculous escapade. He would go and retrieve the goat and carry on with his original plan to die up in the mountains. The prospect of the hole in the ground in the corner of the daisy field was as comforting as the thought of a feather bed.

Just as he was about to head back to where the bus had dropped him off, Dante happened upon a group of men and women dressed in olde-worlde rural clothing, clearly the traditional dress of wherever they were from. The women wore shawls and headscarves and long, full, skirts with ruffled hems.

The men wore their trousers tucked into their boots, coupled with waistcoats which almost reached their knees. They looked as though they had disembarked from a previous century, but it came as a relief to Dante to encounter people who were more of an anachronism than he was. Each was carrying a great bundle wrapped in a blanket and they spoke to each other in a dialect which Dante neither recognised nor understood.

One of the group spotted Dante and asked in Italian whether he might have a cigarette to spare. After being told that he did not, the wily fellow asked whether Dante would like to buy some for a good price. The sales pitch had been unsuccessful, but the ice had been broken and they had fallen into a conversation.

The man was from Sardinia and referred to himself as a 'transporter'. The group of Sardinians were all transporters, he said. Every month they would travel to the mainland loaded with traditional arts and crafts; basket-ware mainly, such as *corbule* and *crobededda*. They weren't worth two gobs of phlegm back at home, but on the mainland they fetched a good price because city folk liked things made by hand. They didn't use the baskets for storing food, like they were supposed to be used, the transporter explained. He'd been told that they just hung them on their walls for decoration. He seemed to find this rather amusing.

For the return journey, the transporters would stock up on certain goods which were cheaper on the mainland, like branded soap and cigarettes and various tinned foods. His wife sold it all from her market stall. The business didn't make them rich, but it kept their three children from going to bed with empty bellies.

The transporter was keen to point out that what he was carrying wasn't contraband – not this time, anyway – but the reason he always carried cigarettes was in case one of the customs men gave him grief.

'Customs have got no business poking their nose into our stuff because when we leave Italy for Sardinia, we're still in Italy, but they do anyway. Most of the time if we offer the officer a few packs of smokes, they let us through without busting our balls.'

The problem with carrying real contraband – the 'naughty stuff' as he referred to it, making his hand into the shape of a pistol – was that unless you had a friendly customs man on your side, you were screwed. And those types of friendships didn't come free. And sometimes they took your bung and then they took your goods as well. Some people had no scruples.

'See that fella there?' said the transporter, indicating a paunchy man in an official-looking uniform. 'Slippery as a greased eel, that one. I wouldn't trust him any further than I could spit. He goes on holiday every summer to Portofino. Don't tell me he can afford that on a custom officer's salary.'

It was then that the transporter mentioned that he and his colleagues were due to catch the next ferry to Olbia, which couldn't have come as more welcome news to Dante. They would be boarding from a neighbouring dock. Where they were standing now was the freight end of the port. He and his colleagues were only there because they'd hitched a ride in the back of a truck.

'Just tag along with us,' said the transporter, and Dante was very grateful to have his guidance.

Clearly the load which the man carried was extremely heavy, but he bore it without complaint. His back was bent by the burdens of his occupation and he walked with a lop-sided, irregular gait, with one shoulder stooped and his body at an angle. Dante cast his eyes over the other transporters. The eldest was a woman, who Dante surmised must have been well into her seventies. Her ankles, just visible beneath the hem of her long skirt, were swollen with oedema.

The ferry-passenger terminal turned out to be a large tin shed in the middle of a car park. Inside it was almost entirely empty, except for a smeary glazed-off section at one end which served as a ticket office, and at the other end, a bar – at least, that was what the handwritten sign said.

The 'bar' comprised a shelf made from a plank supported by empty beer crates. Lined up along it was a row of dusty bottles with their labels faded beyond legibility, and coffee machine connected to a bucket. Thinking that it would be polite to offer the transporter some refreshment as he'd been so friendly and helpful, Dante asked if he could buy the fellow a drink.

'Kind of you, but what you're looking at right there is the worst cup of coffee in the whole of Italy. You'd think there'd be laws against that sort of thing.'

There was a wait of three hours for the ferry. The transporters set down their bundles and fell asleep on them, but Dante's new companion seemed more than happy to chat. As there was no seating in the place, they sat on the floor with their backs against the tin wall and the bundle between them.

When the transporter inquired what business Dante had in Sardinia, he hesitated before answering. He did not have the inclination to explain the whole story, so he said, 'I'm going to try to find an old friend.'

'Where does your friend live?'

'I'm not exactly sure,' replied Dante, and he admitted that he had only the name of a guesthouse and a neighbouring cove to go by. The transporter said that he had never heard of Baia Sanna, or of a guesthouse by the name of Villa Zuannicca, but he came from a place inland. He didn't know the coast well.

'How are you getting back home?' Asked Dante.

The transporter gave a little shrug and cast his eyes heavenwards.

'It's in the hands of God,' he said with a hopeful half-smile. 'When we disembark, we'll catch a lift on a truck if we can. We'll butter up a few of the drivers when we're on the boat. It's not usually a problem. Truck drivers are pretty sound. None of us travels alone any more though, because you just don't know who you might come across. There are people who look out for folks like us, offer a lift and then rob us of everything.'

The transporter glanced both ways to check that they weren't being observed and opened his long waistcoat to reveal the handle of a knife tucked into his belt.

'Better safe than sorry,' he said, giving Dante a knowing wink and then buttoning up his waistcoat again. 'There are brigands and bandits out there, you have to be careful.'

Dante was suddenly very concerned. He had not accounted for Sardinia to be full of brigands and bandits, although now that he thought about it, in the past he had heard stories of kidnappings being relatively common on the island. There had even been a movie made about it back in the '60s. On seeing Dante's anxious frown, the transporter laughed.

'I don't think you've got anything to worry yourself about, not with that little suitcase in your hand. And please don't take offence, friend, but you don't really look like a fellow worth the trouble of robbing.'

Dante laughed with him, not disguising his relief, but wondering whether it might be prudent to avail himself of a weapon of some kind too.

The transporter began to rummage around in his bundle and pulled out a package wrapped in oiled paper which, when he opened it, revealed itself as a huge slab of *schiacciata* bread stuffed with salami. He gestured towards Dante, 'Want some?'

'I wouldn't want to deprive you of your food,' replied Dante, licking the spit from his lips as a delicious savoury waft filled his nostrils.

'It's too much for me. Have some, or it'll go to waste.'

'Well,' said Dante, whose mouth was now watering so much that he had to swallow his saliva, 'if you can spare it, I wouldn't say no to a few bites.' Then, thinking it would be discourteous to over-exploit the transporter's generosity, he reached into his pocket and added, 'Here, let me pay you for it.'

The transporter scoffed, 'Don't offend me by offering me money!' and broke the enormous sandwich in half.

As they ate, their conversation continued.

'So where are you staying when you get to Sardinia?' Asked the transporter.

'I don't know. In hotels, I suppose. I presume there are many along the coast?'

The transporter then gave Dante a very useful piece of advice.

'Yes, there's plenty of hotels, but if you can get so much as a whiff of the sea, they double their prices. And if you can actually *see* the sea, well, then they double them again and some even more than that. Same goes for places to eat. If you can see the sea, you get charged the tourist price. If you want a cheap bed for the night, stop in a village a couple of kilometres inland and ask in the bar whether one of the locals has got a decent room. They'll probably give you dinner and throw in some breakfast for less than you'd pay in a hotel just for the room. But tonight when you get to Olbia, it'll be late and there won't be any more buses out of town, so try the Hotel Lux. It's the cheapest place in Olbia. It's not fancy and you probably shouldn't drink the water, but you won't have to share your bed with too many cockroaches either.'

Once they had finished their food, the transporter took a pack of greasy-looking playing cards from the pocket of his waistcoat and made a gesture to Dante inquiring whether he fancied a game. Dante agreed and the transporter began to shuffle.

As they played without paying any attention to the score, and as they chatted about this and that, Dante sensed his heart lightening. The feeling of somebody enjoying his company was unfamiliar and not at all unpleasant. How liberating it felt to speak with a man who knew nothing about him, who didn't judge him on the lot that life had dealt him. This fellow didn't look at him and think: *Dante Bacchetti, Leonora's father. His errant daughter disappeared. His crazy wife jumped off a bridge.* The transporter just took him for what he saw – a dotty old man on a harebrained quest. It was a relief not to feel manacled to the baggage of his life.

When the transporter asked him what he did for work, it crossed Dante's mind that he could invent any occupation that he fancied. He could claim that he was a poet, or a philosopher; he could confidently pass as a university professor. But Dante replied honestly, saying that he was a retired schoolteacher. He didn't mind admitting that. When the fellow inquired after his family, Dante bent the truth a little and told him that he had been widowed for many years, and that sadly he and his late wife had never been blessed with children. Respectfully, the transporter changed the subject to that of Sardinian food and began to describe all the dishes which he recommended that Dante should try. It was easily the most pleasant conversation that Dante had enjoyed in decades.

The ferry arrived on time. Once aboard, the transporter said he was going to go for a sleep because otherwise he'd get seasick. His stomach could go funny just crossing a pond.

Dante made his way to the top deck, where he stood holding onto the rails, feeling the sway of the sea under his feet and looking out across the great expanse of water before him. He felt both a sense of trepidation and excitement at the thought of leaving Italy, even though, as the transporter had pointed out, the place he was heading for was still technically part of Italy.

Despite the early start, the trek down the mountain and the whole day spent travelling, Dante felt his exhaustion dissipate. Maybe it was the invigorating effect of the sea air, but the moribund feeling which had been consuming him lifted and gave way to a sensation of being rather more alive than dead.

He told himself to enjoy the novelty of the experience. Now, standing on the top deck of the ferry to Olbia, for the first time he understood something of Leonora's wanderlust. Perhaps he was not just an Old Locomotive, he too was a Little Boat, but an ancient one now, leaky and patched up and soon to be useful for nothing but firewood.

A sharp blow of the horn was followed by the shudder of the engine as the ferry left its dock, escorted by a flock of squawking seagulls. Within a short time, mainland Italy was reduced to a distant, hazy strip on the horizon. Soon that too disappeared and there was nothing to see in any direction except the sea.

Dante remained where he was, watching the play of the afternoon light on the water and the wash of the vessel as it cut through the waves. He should have travelled as a young man, he thought. Back in the days before he had a wife and a daughter and responsibilities, why had he bowed to duty when he could have been exploring the world? Why had he submitted to the drudgery of teaching, when he could have lived to ride the oceans? He had wasted his finest years. Who would Dante Bacchetti be now if he had made off to catch a ferry to somewhere at the age of twenty? His life would have been immeasurably enriched, no doubt, by visiting places which he only knew by descriptions written in books and in Leonora's letters. Oh, to have lived a life un-moored! Perhaps, if fate had dealt him a lucky hand, he might have lost his heart in some little tavern in some pretty foreign town and spent long, sultry nights making love to beautiful, brown-eyed girls with soft, young hair. His life seemed nothing more than a long series of missed opportunities. '*Regret not what you have done; regret only what you have not done,*' the saying went. How true, how true, mused Dante ruefully.

Day was fading into dusk when the island of Sardinia came into view. The sea took on a violet hue. By the time the vessel docked, the water was as black as an oil slick. The port of Olbia was small, nothing like the great industrial agglomeration of Livorno, and Olbia itself was a quaint harbour town. A few lights were beginning to come on, their luminous crowns throwing glittering reflections on the sea.

Dante felt a sense of accomplishment for having made it so far and disembarked with the transporters who all said something which sounded like '*Bai in bon ora,*' which he presumed meant 'good luck' in their dialect. With one final wave, they lined up by the roadside with their bundles on their backs to wait for their lifts.

Dante navigated his way through the streets of Olbia as per the transporter's directions. There were few people about. The shop blinds were down, but the bars and restaurants were open and the streets were beginning to fill with enticing smells. He stopped for a moment to read a menu on a blackboard outside a trattoria. He wasn't hungry, but he could have eaten, and the transporter had whetted his appetite with his descriptions of all manner of Sardinian delicacies. No, thought Dante. His funds were limited and he shouldn't fritter them away on food which was not absolutely necessary. Besides, he'd had a good breakfast at home and he was still quite full of *schiacciata*.

He located the ironically-named Hotel Lux, but Dante was hardly accustomed to luxurious accommodation, so he found its run-down grubbiness perfectly acceptable. As the transporter had promised, it was cheap and cockroach-free. He didn't drink the water, as advised, just in case.

The following morning Dante paid almost as much for breakfast in a café overlooking the marina as he had for his budget room at the Hotel Lux, which he realised was a silly trap to have fallen into because it was the very thing that the transporter had warned him against. Before the waiter could clear his table, Dante slipped the butter knife into his bag. It was a pitifully dainty weapon with which to defend himself from potential brigands and bandits, but knowing that he had it made him less uneasy.

Dante found a public library and requested to see a detailed map of the island. The only information he had on the location of Villa Zuannicca was that it was situated beside a cove by the name of Baia Sanna, and that on a clear day Isola Spargi could be seen from there. Yet despite locating Isola Spargi and scouring the map for over an hour, he could see no cove by the name of Baia Sanna. As for a guesthouse by the name of Villa Zuannicca, when the helpful librarian telephoned the tourist board, she was told that no guesthouse by that name was listed on the official register of accommodation, either in the northeast of Sardinia, or anywhere else along its almost two thousand miles of coast.

Discouraged but by no means beaten, Dante took a bus which followed the coastline from Olbia heading North and worked his way along, stopping in every village to ask whether anybody knew of a Baia Sanna, a Villa Zuannicca, or a family by the name of Melis Puddu. The first day yielded no results, but the transporter's tip to ask in an inland village for accommodation proved invaluable. That first night, for the same price as he'd paid for his room at the Hotel Lux, he was fed and lodged like a king.

Assuming that the generous platter of cured meats, pickles, olives and flatbreads was to be his entire dinner, Dante ate without restraint, only to discover that this was just the *antipasto*. In addition to this, Dante was served spaghetti with pecorino cheese and black pepper, followed by roast pork with gravy and freshly picked beans; and then, when he thought he might burst, he was presented with a plate of sweet fritters, still sizzling from the pan. The feast was washed down with wine from his host's own vineyard. To a man whose palate had grown accustomed to a lean and dreary diet, every flavourful bite was intoxicating, and by the time he left the table, he felt quite food-drunk. Before retiring to his very comfortable bed, Dante enjoyed a long soak in a hot bath, and was sent on his way the following morning stuffed to the gills with breakfast.

His first week followed much the same pattern. Dante made his way from village to village using a combination of buses and thumbed lifts. Thankfully he did not encounter any brigands or bandits. On the contrary, locals were friendly and happy to furnish him with all sorts of information, although none of it useful to his quest. The answer to the Baia Sanna and Villa Zuannicca questions was always a blank look, or a shrug of the shoulders and a shake of the head.

By the second week of going village-to-village Dante was beginning to lose his optimism. Now he had used up over half of his money, so he could not go back home even if he wanted to, and he was no closer to finding the place he was looking for. He might actually be further away from it than when he'd started. He had no way of knowing.

The matter of the dwindling funds did not preoccupy him. He was destined to run out of money and there was nothing he could do about that. He would leave his fate for fate itself to work out.

On day twelve of his travels the bus dropped him off in yet another village, just past the town of Porto Pollo, and as usual Dante made his way to a bar and asked the customary questions.

'Baia Sanna?' Said the barman, nodding. 'Yes. I know Baia Sanna. It's a little way up the coast. But you won't find it on any maps because it's just the locals who call it that. The Sanna family used to live there until part of the cliff came away and crushed their house. Now you can only get there by boat because the cliff path's been condemned. But why would you want to go there? There's nothing to see. There isn't even much of a beach.'

'I'm looking for a guesthouse near it, Villa Zuannicca. It's run by Jubanne Melis Puddu and his wife.'

And then at last, much to Dante's relief, one of the patrons who had overheard the conversation chimed in with, 'Melis Puddu? Isn't that the big chap who was in a coma?'

'That's right!'

'Oh, in that case the place you're looking for is Villa Lavandula. It's the wife who's called Zuannicca, not the guest-house. You've got all your names mixed up.'

Dante juggled this information in his head. 'Are you sure?'

The man said he'd bet his shirt on it, adding that his cousin could probably tell him more, because now that he thought about it, he was pretty certain he'd heard it mentioned that his cousin's godmother had worked at Villa Lavandula at some point, but going back a fair while. He could give his cousin a shout if Dante wanted to ask the godmother in person. And as luck would have it, his cousin drove a taxi, so if Dante needed a ride up there, it shouldn't be a problem. He wouldn't be able to get there by bus. It was too out of the way.

Both the taxi-driving cousin and his godmother were summoned and concurred with everything that had already been said. The guesthouse by the name of Villa Lavandula was owned by Zuannicca Melis Puddu, and she was indeed Jubanne Melis Puddu's wife. The taxi driver didn't know that much more about it, apart from its location.

'It's on the other side of the next town and a fair bit up past that,' he said. 'It's a good hour's drive from here, but I don't think it'll be open yet. The season doesn't start for a couple of weeks.'

Dante said that he did not envisage staying there. He had an errand to run, that was all.

The godmother was more broadly informed. Years ago, when she had worked there, she said, it was during the time that

Zuannicca's aunt had owned Villa Lavandula, and the place had been a bit run down then. It was a much better place these days. All the rooms had their own modern bathrooms and cooling fans and radios and all those types of things. And the restaurant had an excellent reputation. People liked to go there to eat even if they weren't staying in the hotel. She herself hadn't been. It was a bit pricey for her pocket, but it must be very good if people went all that way for the food.

'It's Zuannicca who's really made something of the place,' said the taxi driver's godmother admiringly. 'She's a sharp lady, that one. And I mean that as a compliment. She's got a clever head on her shoulders. Her aunt would have been very proud of her.'

The godmother didn't know Jubanne personally, although she'd encountered him at a few local *feste* back in the day. He'd won the regional arm-wrestling championships when he was young. He was already two meters tall by the age of fifteen. She had been acquainted with his grandmother, Maria-Annoriana. She was a strong character.

Dante felt both a sense of accomplishment and trepidation as he took his seat in the back of the taxi. The driver took him out of the village and through a neighbouring town, then up into the hills, where the road was narrow and full of hairpin bends which twisted their way through a rugged, wooded land-scape. Dante turned his head away from the precipitous drops. Very few habitations were visible – just the occasional meagre-looking smallholding and plenty of tumble-downs. This felt like a wild part of the island, as yet undiscovered by the tourist hoards.

The taxi slowed as they approached a set of tall, wrought iron gates. On one gatepost the name *Villa Lavandula* was etched into a stone plaque. They turned in and proceeded down a long driveway, flanked on either side by pinewoods, but these were not the Christmas tree mountain pines familiar to Dante. These were *pini marittimi* with great boughs like outstretched limbs and umbrella-like canopies.

At the end of the winding driveway a large Napoleonic-style villa came into view, and Dante was taken aback by its grandeur. It was a far more impressive place than he had expected, with broad steps leading up to an arched colonnade.

The building was painted a very pale pink, which provided a rather pleasing backdrop to the grey-green foliage of the lavender beds all around it. How magnificent it must look when those shrubs flowered!

Clearly Villa Lavandula was not yet open for business. All the shutters were shut on the top two floors, and most on the ground floor. The place had an out-of-season look about it, with garden tables and chairs stacked up under tarpaulins.

The taxi driver made a sign to Dante in the rear-view mirror and asked, 'Do you want me to wait?'

'If you wouldn't mind.'

'I'll have to charge you for the time I'm waiting.'

Dante replied that wouldn't be a problem.

He did not need to knock to announce his arrival. The front door was opened by a handsome, dark-skinned woman of Mediterranean appearance. She was probably no older than fifty, but her hair was entirely grey.

Dante introduced himself and said, 'I'm looking for Signora Zuannicca Melis Puddu.'

'That's me,' replied the woman with a cordial nod. 'How can I help you?'

'I believe that my daughter, Leonora Bacchetti, worked here some years ago.'

Zuannicca Melis Puddu considered this for a moment, then shook her head. 'Leonora Bacchetti? No, I don't recall anyone by that name working here.'

'It was during the summer of 1973. She worked in your restaurant.'

Zuannicca Melis Puddu continued to shake her head and repeated, this time more firmly, 'No. There was never anybody by that name working here. Who told you that there was?'

'It was your husband, Jubanne.'

This appeared to take her by surprise.

'My *husband*?'

'Yes. Perhaps you could ask him to confirm it.'

What followed was an uncomfortable pause, where Zuannicca Melis Puddu seemed to be sizing Dante up and considering the most appropriate way to respond. Eventually she replied curtly, 'My husband no longer lives here.' Then she added in a voice which indicated that she was dreading the answer, 'When was it he told you this?'

'At the beginning of the year, in February. He came to see me.'

'Where?'

'At my home near Montacciolo, in the Apennines.'

'The Apennines!' She gasped, the colour draining from her face. 'Good grief! Is that where he went...' but then the tone of her voice dropped and changed to one of great concern. 'How was he?'

'He seemed in very good form. He made it up the mountain in the dead of winter.'

'I mean his head. How did he seem in his head?'

'Well enough, I'd say...I suppose,' replied Dante, although now with all this matter of the mixed up names and Zuannicca Melis Puddu's denial that Leonora had worked at the guesthouse, he couldn't be certain of anything.

'I trust your husband was able to return safely to Sardinia?' Inquired Dante. 'I have been very concerned as he left my house at night during a particularly harsh storm.'

'Yes, yes. Jubanne came back.'

Dante expressed how glad he was to hear it. Then, thinking it best to clarify the situation, and to justify having turned up unannounced as he had, he explained the details of Leonora's last known sighting in Pesaro and the unsolved mystery concerning what happened after she left there. He followed this with a brief account of what his Sardinian guest had told him. As Zuannicca Melis Puddu listened, her expression softened to one of sympathy.

'I'm very sorry to hear about your daughter. I can understand how you would want to follow up any new piece of information, however obscure, in the hope that it could bring you closure. But I'm afraid that my husband, who is not of sound mind, has spun you a nonsense tale. Further than telling you this, I cannot be of any help to you. I fear you've had a wasted journey, Signor Bacchetti.' With that, she stepped back, as though to close the door.

'Please!' Implored Dante. 'Perhaps you could look through your employment records? Your husband was certain that my daughter was here in 1973 and gave me a number of details which convinced me that –'

Zuannicca Melis Puddu did not let Dante finish his sentence. She interrupted him with, 'My husband can be certain of many things, Signor Bacchetti. He might have told you that a dog was a cat, or that the sky was green, and been entirely convinced that it was true. But I can assure you unequivocally that my husband could not possibly have known who was employed here during the summer of 1973. At that time he was lying unconscious in a hospital bed. He'd had an accident.'

'Yes, he told me about that. He said that he was in a coma for ten days.'

'Ten days? No, no, not ten *days*, Signor Bacchetti. Ten *years*! My husband had his accident in 1970 and did not regain consciousness until 1980.'

Dante's mouth dropped open, but no sound came from it.

On seeing the look of consternation on the old man's face, Zuannicca Melis Puddu conceded, 'Perhaps you should stay for some refreshments, Signor Bacchetti. You can explain to me in more detail what my husband told you and I can try to clarify for you, or discount, his claims. Your journey here might not hold any of the answers you hoped it might, but I will do my best to ensure that you leave less confused.'

Zuannicca Melis Puddu did not invite Dante into the guest-house, but instead led him around the building, to the side which faced the sea, and gestured to him to take a seat on the veranda – a rather beautiful semi-open construction, which had been ingeniously-built to incorporate a fig tree. Then, in the congenial tone of a well-practised hostess she said, 'What can I offer you, Signor Bacchetti?'

'I've been told that you serve a particularly fine lemon tea with ice and mint.'

Zuannicca Melis Puddu gave a little amused smile, 'Of course,' she replied, 'It's a Villa Lavandula speciality. I'm most flattered that the reputation of our tea has reached as far as the Apennine mountains. If you'll excuse me, I'll be back in a moment.'

As Dante waited for her return, he took in his surroundings. This place on the veranda beneath the fig tree was the very spot which Jubanne Melis Puddu had spoken of. Dante tried to peer in through one of the windows which he reasoned must belong to the dining room. Although the window was open a crack, the curtains were drawn and he couldn't see inside.

Here, there was no discrepancy between what Jubanne Melis Puddu had described and the reality of what he could see around him – the paved terrace; the gently sloping garden with its rose beds, enormous spiky aloes and prickly pears, and banks of lavender bushes, which dropped away to the half-moon of sandy beach. The sea was more emerald than sapphire today. In the far, far distance Dante could see the outline of a small piece of rocky land, which he concluded must be Isola Spargi. At the end of the wooden jetty, two small rowing boats were moored, but there was no vessel which resembled the *Lavandula* – if that was indeed the boat's name.

Zuannicca Melis Puddu came back with a carafe of lemon tea and a glass on a tray and set it down on the table. Dante thanked her and asked, 'Did your husband own a boat?'

'Yes, but I sold it years ago. The children were particularly upset about letting it go, but I had no choice. Boats require constant maintenance.'

'What was the boat called, if I may ask?'

'*Maria-Annoriana.* Jubanne named his boat after our daughter, who was herself named after his grandmother.'

The discrepancy in the boat's name did not surprise Dante. So far the name of the grandmother was the only one which corresponded to anything which up until earlier that day he had assumed to be fact.

'Tragic, that such a well-loved boat should have been the cause of the accident,' he mused.

Zuannicca Melis Puddu tilted her head to one side and frowned.

'The cause of his accident? Well, indirectly, I suppose. But not directly.'

'Your husband told me that the boom of the sail swung around and hit him on the head.'

'Is that what he told you? No, no, Signor Bacchetti, that's not at all what happened.'

CHAPTER 18

Jubanne had done a lot of work to the guesthouse over the winter before the accident. He had redecorated all the bedrooms, which had been no small feat, and worked hard in the grounds too. Now that he'd grubbed up that patch of scrub and planted more roses, the garden looked so much better. His wife was talking about putting up a covered veranda next year if the finances allowed. Jubanne said it shouldn't be too costly because he could do most of the work himself. All he would need was a day or two of hired help for some of the awkward lifting. What a shame it would be to cut down the fig tree though. If he could incorporate it somehow, it would be quite a feature. He was still thinking about exactly how to do that, but he had time. The veranda was a project for the following winter.

The season had started well. The guesthouse was about three quarters full, which was full enough because they were a bit tight on staff, as usual.

Shortly after school finished in June, the children, Corrado aged eight and Nora aged ten, were due to leave for their annual stay with their cousins, so Jubanne had promised them a trip out on the *Maria-Annoriana*. Nora in particular was keen to go to the horse shoe reef, because sometimes they could see dolphins there. The pods liked to go to rest in that spot as it was sheltered and shallow. But really, she wouldn't have cared where they'd gone, or whether or not they saw dolphins. She just liked being out on the boat with Papá Juju.

Now that Corrado was bigger, he would sometimes come along too. Nora said that she didn't mind because Corrado wasn't a nuisance, like most of her friends' little brothers were.

Still, she treasured the times when Papá would take her out by herself.

When it was just the two of them, he was the captain and she was the first mate, and because she held this position of responsibility, she would assist with all the pre-sail checks. Boom peg first, without exception, before absolutely anything else – Papá was super strict about that. He knew a man who'd been knocked into the sea by a swinging boom, and if someone hadn't seen it happen and jumped in to rescue him, the man would have drowned. Nora had been told that cautionary tale more times than she could count. After that, it was water, oil, fuel checks; then sails, whether they were planning to use them or not.

Usually they would motor out because it was quicker and easier, and often their whole trip would be engine-powered; but sometimes, if the sea was right and the wind was right, Papá would unfurl the sails. That was Nora's favourite thing in the whole world – when the shudder and noise of the engine would stop, and in a smooth, rustling sweep, the wind would belly out the sail and begin to power them along. For a little while the engine noise would still be ringing in her ears, and she usually felt a little bit queasy from the smell of the fuel and the fumes, but then all that would fade away until all there was was the sound of the sea and the occasional slap of the sail and the taste of salt spray. Nora loved to lie on her tummy right at the front, like a real life nautical figurehead, watching the prow slicing through the waves, and she was always so thrilled by it all that she couldn't stop herself from laughing and swallowing the spray.

Since the age of nine she'd been strong enough to take charge of the rudder whilst her father manned the sail. 'Watch the boom, Nora!' he'd always say, 'Watch the boom, sweetheart!' She must have heard it a hundred times every time they went out.

That June day in 1970, Jubanne was preparing for the children's promised trip on the boat. He carried out all the pre-sail checks by himself because it was quicker – first the usual double-check that the blocking peg was well-secured in the boom, then all the other things – oil, fuel, water. But when he had started the engine, there had been a terrible noise.

'Cursed Cauliflowers!' He'd exclaimed, cutting the engine immediately. He knew what that racket was. Something was stuck in the pump, probably some piece of rubbish, like one of those awful plastic shoes the tourists wore. Those were constantly getting washed up on his stretch of beach. Whether the culprit was a plastic shoe or not, unblocking the pump wasn't a long or complicated procedure, but being in such an awkward position, it was a two-man job.

It was then that the children came skipping down the wooden walkway, loaded up for their day out at sea. Nora was carrying a basket of food and a bundle of towels. Corrado had his fishing rods and a ball.

Jubanne watched their approach. It wouldn't be too long before they weren't kids any more. How quickly time passed! It felt like the blink of an eye since they were babies. Another ten years and they would both be adults. It didn't seem possible. How would it feel being the father of two adult children? Jubanne wondered. That would be a whole bunch of different delights and different worries. If one, or both of them, wanted to take over the guesthouse, that would be magnificent; but Jubanne had already agreed with his wife that they shouldn't make it an expectation. The children must be free to find their own paths in life. And one day they'd probably both get married and have children of their own. Grandchildren – Holy Horseradishes, imagine that! Jubanne wasn't looking forward to prelude though. The thought of Corrado having a girlfriend didn't trouble him at all, but he did dread the day when the boys would begin sniffing around Nora. He knew he'd turn into one of those irrationally over-protective Papás – the type who had chased him off when he was a lad and sweet on somebody's precious daughter.

Now the children were almost half way down the jetty. Corrado had grown again. He was all arms and legs. Bets were off as to whether he'd end up taller than his father. Nora didn't seem to have inherited the Melis Puddu stature. She looked more like her mother every day.

Jubanne wished that the children weren't going to their cousins' for so much of the summer. He always felt as though he was missing out when they were away, and a bit guilty too. But it was the sensible thing to do. He and his wife were so busy during the peak season that there wasn't time for proper parenting; anyway, the kids loved staying on the farm with their cousins. It was no sacrifice for them.

Nora and Corrado had reached the mooring now. Jubanne gave them an apologetic smile.

'Sorry kids. We can't go out. There's something jammed in the pump,' he said.

'Can't we sail, Papá Juju?' Suggested Nora, grinning at the prospect.

Jubanne licked his index finger and held it in the air to check the direction of the wind. 'Not today, sweetheart. The wind won't get us out far and if we get stuck, we can't rely on the engine to get us out of trouble. What's the first rule of going out to sea?'

Nora and Corrado replied in unison, 'Always ensure that your vessel is seaworthy!'

Jubanne gave a little salute.

'That's right, shipmates! Now run along, First Mate Nora Melis Puddu, and Second Mate Corrado Melis Puddu, and find something else to amuse yourselves with. If I can get some help today, we'll go out tomorrow.'

The children made their way back up the wooden walkway, discussing alternative arrangements for the day's entertainment.

Luckily, Jubanne's brother-in-law turned up barely half an hour later and helped sort out the pump. The culprit was, as Jubanne had suspected, a plastic beach shoe. It was still only eleven o'clock in the morning, so there was plenty of time to go out for a jaunt at sea that day.

Jubanne went to locate Nora and Corrado. They weren't in the guesthouse, or in the garden. Thinking that they had probably gone to the beach, he made his way down, but there was no sign of them there either. The only other place they could be was in the woods, where Jubanne had built them a rather fine tree house. As he was approaching the pinewoods, he crossed paths with one of the guests returning from a walk.

'Did you happen to see my children in the woods?' Asked Jubanne.

'I saw them up on the cliff about an hour ago, heading down the path to the next cove.'

'What?' Exclaimed Jubanne, feeling the blood rush to his head. 'They were going to Baia Sanna? Are you sure?'

'Yes. It was definitely them. They were heading down to the beach with a ball.'

'And you didn't think to say anything to stop them?' Exclaimed Jubanne, stunned at the guest's total lack of common sense. 'That place is dangerous! Didn't you read the signs? You shouldn't even have been there yourself!'

Jubanne didn't give the guest time to answer. He stormed past him, calling him a 'damned fool' and sending him to the devil for being so stupid. He also wished boils and haemorrhoids upon him, which caused the guest to turn pale with fright. As Nonna Maria-Annoriana would have said, 'big dogs don't need to bite', but the occasional snarl sent the message very clearly.

The children were free to ramble beyond the guesthouse grounds, but within certain well-defined limits. The places that were absolutely prohibited to them were the cliff top and Baia Sanna, and they knew it. The erosion and instability of the cliff meant that another piece of it could come away at any moment without warning – and it wasn't a case of *if*, but *when*. A couple of idiots had got stranded there the previous year and Jubanne had had to haul them to safety with a rope, risking his own neck in the process. After that incident, Jubanne had put up a sign to warn people about the rock-falls and telling them to keep off the cliff-top. He had also promised his wife that if anything of the sort happened again he would not put himself in any danger, but would call the coast guard instead.

Jubanne hurried through the pinewoods which rose beside Villa Lavandula, stumbling over roots and kicking up the springy carpeting of fallen pine-needles. He was more dismayed than he was angry. The children were not usually disobedient like that, and it wasn't as though they didn't have other places to swim. There would be consequences. There would certainly be no boat trip. He was still formulating a list of sanctions as he emerged from the pinewoods. The view from the cliff-top across the sea was spectacular – deep blue dotted with little white sail boats; the silhouette of Isola Spargi was clearly visible in the distance – but Jubanne didn't stop to admire the vista. He paused for a moment to catch his breath. It was already quite hot and he'd ascended rather too quickly. The sweat was collecting at the base of his neck and trickling in rivulets down his back.

Jubanne picked his way through the scrub, past his sign which read *KEEP AWAY! DANGER OF ROCK-FALL*. He could see exactly where the children had passed, as the gorse branches had been snapped and the rough grass was trodden flat. As he descended, the path crumbled underfoot. Several times it gave way entirely, sending a cascade of rocks and pebbles tumbling down the cliff. What did those kids think they were doing, taking such a dangerous route? Nora, in particular, was old enough to know better than to take herself and her little brother somewhere so perilous.

'Maria-Annoriana Melis Puddu, what on earth were you thinking?' Muttered Jubanne, picking his way gingerly along a section of path which was barely thirty centimetres wide. He only ever called Nora by her full name when he was cross with her, which wasn't very often.

At last Jubanne came to the big rocks known as the Balzi, which were relatively easy to clamber down, but he wasn't as nimble as he used to be. Those few extra kilos he was carrying around his middle made a difference. Little pieces of rock, which he had loosened during his descent, came away from the path above and bounced past him.

He could feel the sun blistering his skin. Jubanne's sweat-soaked clothes stuck to him and even his eyes were stinging with sweat. It was as he reached to dry them with his shirt that a section of path disintegrated under his foot and he almost went head over heels down the cliff-side. He was saved by a gorse bush, which hooked into him, breaking his fall, but driving two dozen thorns into his arm. This time a real curse escaped from him.

Finally he reached a level plateau, and it was from there that he first heard the children's voices. As he edged his way around a jagged shard of cliff, he saw Nora and Corrado some twenty to thirty meters below, splashing around in the shallows and knocking a ball back and forth between them. He called out their names, but they didn't hear him, so he shouted again as loudly as he could:

'Nora! Corrado!'

Just then, a rock-fall missed him by a whisker and suddenly it dawned on Jubanne that having descended the cliff had been very foolish. He had further damaged the path and he did not want his children using it now that it was even more dangerous than before. He should have gone round in the boat. That would not only have been safer, but quicker too. Why, in the name of the Father, the Son and the Holy Cabbage had he not done that? He'd been so angry with that daft guest that he'd suffered a lapse in common sense. If he could get the kids to see him, he'd signal to them to stay where they were. He'd go round to pick them up on the boat.

It must have been then that the big rock hit Jubanne squarely on the side of the head.

The children found him when they returned from their prohibited escapade, lying unconscious on the plateau below the Balzi in a pool of sun-blackened blood. They tried to shake their father awake, but he remained utterly unresponsive.

It took nine men from the coast guard service to haul Jubanne back onto the cliff top. They bound him to a stretcher and hoisted him up with a winch. He remained unconscious throughout and was rushed to the hospital, where he was operated upon immediately.

Zuannicca Melis Puddu was warned to expect the worst and to prepare her children for it. The next few days were touch-and-go. The blow to the head had fractured Jubanne's skull and his brain was bleeding. The first operation was only partially successful, and although he had woken up very briefly after it, the doctors considered a second operation to be too risky at that time. All they could do was to try to keep him alive. A priest was called to perform the traditional rites in case the doctors were unsuccessful.

CHAPTER 19

On hearing this version of events from Jubanne's wife Dante *really* didn't know what to think. It was like trying to find his way through a hall of fairground mirrors, where everything was distorted.

'Nora and Corrado are the names of your children?' he asked.

'Yes. Nora and Corrado are our children.'

'So who are the Nora and Corrado your husband described to me?'

'The same children, just grown up. When Jubanne had his accident, they were eight and ten. When he woke up, they were eighteen and twenty.'

'And he didn't understand that they were his children when he woke up?'

Zuannicca Melis Puddu shook her head.

'It was more complex than not understanding, Signor Bacchetti. Jubanne absolutely refused to believe that Nora and Corrado were his grown-up children, despite having been told over and over again.'

'And your husband wasn't hit by the boom on his boat?'

'No, although I have heard him tell various versions of that story. He has also claimed to have had an accident on a Vespa. There have been other times when he's recounted falling off a ladder, or down stairs. The list goes on. But what he never says is what actually happened. He has erased that from his mind entirely, and I believe that to be a deliberate choice.'

'A deliberate choice? Why?'

'To protect his children. Never, *ever* in any of his imagined accident scenarios are his children mentioned as having a part in how he came to be injured. Jubanne always takes the blame fully. And although there are many things which I cannot begin to explain to you, I believe that the reason for the erasing of the truth is quite simple. Jubanne does not want his children to think that he holds them in any way responsible for what happened to him. Despite the injuries to his brain, his unreliable memory and the skewed versions of reality which he believes to be fact, his sense of paternal protection remains intact.'

Dante sipped his tea, thinking back to everything the Sardinian had told him; and now, trying to comprehend it all from a new perspective. After a time he said, 'I don't understand where my daughter fits into this.'

'I will do my best to unravel that for you, Signor Bacchetti. But first I should explain to you in more detail what happened when Jubanne woke up.'

Zuannicca Melis Puddu settled herself in her chair and began to recount how, against all the odds, her husband did not die after the second operation, but instead remained in a deep coma. The doctors thought that the likelihood of Jubanne ever waking again was very slight, and if he did, they couldn't say how he might be. The worst case scenario was that he would be in some sort of conscious but unconscious state.

Even if some of his faculties remained, Zuannicca Melis Puddu was warned that he might not recognise her, or his children, or have any memory of who he was, or the life he'd had. The doctors couldn't even be sure whether Jubanne would be able to speak, or walk, or have any control over his own functions. But really, it was all just guesswork. The doctors had no way of knowing what long-term damage had been done. All that they could be certain of was that in the unlikely event that Jubanne should ever regain consciousness, he wouldn't be the man Zuannicca knew as her husband and he wouldn't be the man Nora and Corrado knew as their father.

'My heart goes out to you, Signora Melis Puddu. It must have been an impossible prospect.'

'It was difficult to know what to hope for, Signor Bacchetti; whether to pray that Jubanne would wake in whatever state, or to pray that he should never wake up.'

'Uncertainty is a most wearing condition,' said Dante, speaking just as much about his own situation as Zuannicca Melis Puddu's.

'Indeed it is, Signor Bacchetti. Uncertainty can devour you from the inside. There were times when I would torment myself with "what ifs". I didn't know whether to feel like a wife, or a widow; to hang on, or move on.'

Zuannicca Melis Puddu gestured towards the guesthouse.

'At first I thought I might have sell this place. Running it alone, as well as looking after the children was too much for me under the circumstances. I venture to say it would be too much for most people. But then I thought, if sell up, what then? Villa Lavandula was built by my great-grandfather on land which has been in my family since the 1700s. My family's roots are here, and that is important to me. And what kind of message would it have sent to my children if they saw their mother give up in the face of adversity?'

'Clearly you are blessed with extraordinary fortitude, Signora Melis Puddu,' said Dante, who could not help but be impressed by the woman seated opposite him who, despite the trials she had faced, appeared so decorous and so in charge of her own emotions. Zuannicca Melis Puddu acknowledged the compliment with a dignified nod.

'I cannot claim to have done it all alone. I will be forever grateful to those who rallied round me. But one year passed, then two then three and so on. After the third year things became easier.'

'And what about your children? I cannot begin to imagine how difficult it must have been for them.'

Zuannicca Melis Puddu leaned forward, rested her wrists on the edge of the table and laced her fingers together.

'For Nora and Corrado the first thing was to come to terms with the fact that it was their actions which led to which led to their father's accident. It was particularly hard for Nora, whose idea it had been to go to that prohibited place. Of course, nobody pointed the finger of blame at either of them. It was just one of those things, a little act of childhood disobedience which had consequences that nobody could have foreseen. I honestly don't know why Jubanne chose to go and retrieve them via that perilous cliff path when it would have been both far quicker and far safer to go round to Baia Sanna in his boat. But there is little point in dwelling on the way things might have been. The simple fact concerning the children was that their father was lying unconscious in a hospital bed with life-changing injuries, and that had come about because of them, and they were reminded of that all the time.'

'I have taught many children during my career,' offered Dante, hoping that his words would be of some solace. 'And if teaching taught *me* anything, it's that children are adaptable creatures.'

'Yes, indeed they are,' agreed Zuannicca Melis Puddu. 'Once the preliminary shock had passed, both Nora and Corrado got used to the fact that their father was in a hospital bed and totally unaware of them, or anything else. Sitting by his bedside, holding his hand and having one-way conversations with him became normal.' She paused for a moment, as though transported back to those hospital visits and said quietly, 'It will always weigh heavily in my heart that Jubanne was not able to witness such formative years of their lives, because they would have delighted him. He did not have a close relationship with his parents and he had vowed that should not be the same with his own children. He was a wonderful, loving, attentive father.'

The pain was clear in Zuannicca Melis Puddu's expression. She lowered her eyes and gathered herself before returning to the subject of her husband's recovery.

'When the doctors called me and said that Jubanne was regaining consciousness, terrible as it might sound, Signor Bacchetti, I prayed that they were wrong. Ten years is a long time, and during those ten years I had re-adjusted my life, and done it well. I had found a new balance and I was not unhappy. And it might sound selfish, but I thought to myself, "What now? After the years of work I've put into this place, will I have to let all this go and dedicate myself to looking after an invalid husband?" And what about the children? Corrado was just finishing his final year of high school and was enrolling at university, and Nora was on the other side of the world. All I could think was, "Oh Jubanne, of all the moments to choose to wake up, please, not right now!" But he did wake up.'

'So, how was he?'

'Well,' said Zuannicca Melis Puddu, as though recalling that moment with mixed feelings, 'In many ways, he was surprisingly like his old self. Confused, of course, but then who wouldn't be? The doctors kept him on some very strong sedative medication to prevent the risk of convulsions and strokes, but to everybody's astonishment, he was still more or less Jubanne. He knew who he was, and he knew who I was, and the first thing he did was to ask after the children and the guesthouse. It all seemed miraculous, to begin with, anyway.'

Dante nodded as he listened, for he too had been fooled into thinking that his Sardinian guest had been perfectly rational, to begin with, at least.

'*But*,' continued Zuannicca Melis Puddu, emphasising the word, 'what became clear very quickly was that Jubanne had lost all concept of the passing of time. When he first saw me, he looked utterly horrified. Over the space of ten years I had aged, naturally. And without a doubt the hard work and the worry had taken their toll on my appearance. My hair had greyed significantly over that decade. But of course, to Jubanne, it seemed as though it had gone grey almost overnight.' Zuannicca Melis Puddu smiled wryly, with an expression of great affection. 'He never mentioned it, and I'm certain that was so as not to hurt my feelings, but I could see by the way he looked at me that he was thinking that I'd really let myself go.'

For the first few weeks she had been the only person allowed to see her husband as the medical professionals were concerned about not over-taxing him, or causing him distress. The doctors suspected that he might be hearing voices, although when he was asked, he would deny it.

'All-in-all, a slow and gentle approach was advised. I had to be very tactful. I never spoke to Jubanne about any subject which might worry or upset him, and when he showed signs of confusion, or said something which was outright untrue, I was instructed by the doctors not to contradict him, just to prompt him when he misremembered something, particularly when it concerned the children. It was a very delicate approach, and it did not work at all. But honesty, I don't think anything would have worked because it was evident that Jubanne would only believe what he wanted to believe.'

'So what happened when he was reintroduced to the children?'

'Corrado was first, and nobody was quite sure what to expect. Of course, we all hoped that there might be some recognition, and there was, just not any recognition of what was true. Jubanne decided that Corrado was somehow related to my sister's husband and nothing – no explaining, no prompting, no contradicting – would convince him otherwise.'

'That must have been very difficult for your son.'

'Yes, it was, but he was prepared for it. Having grown up

under the circumstances that he did, Corrado was very mature for his age. He played along and Jubanne behaved like a benevolent uncle towards him, inquiring about his interests, whether he had a girlfriend, how he was doing at school. He asked him all manner of perfectly rational questions; so rational, in fact, that if anyone had been listening who did not know the reality of the situation, it would have been easy to believe that there was nothing wrong with Jubanne's cognitive functions whatsoever.'

'And when your husband was reintroduced to your daughter, how did he react then?'

Now Zuannicca Melis Puddu's expression changed. She furrowed her brow and pursed her lips and when she spoke, her tone of voice was strained.

'Jubanne didn't see Nora until some weeks later. I was not able to contact her immediately.'

'Your husband mentioned that she was working on a private yacht in the Caribbean.'

'Yes, that is correct. Nora was due to come home anyway to help for the peak of the tourist season after her contract on the yacht ended. Of course, on hearing that her father had regained consciousness, she wanted to return immediately, but I dissuaded her and asked her to be patient. I knew that out of all of us, seeing Nora would probably affect Jubanne the most. The bond they had shared was a very special one, Signor Bacchetti. I'm sure you will appreciate how precious the bond between a father and daughter can be. Nora had always been a daddy's girl.'

Zuannicca Melis Puddu lapsed into silence for a moment, as though recalling those past, lost, tender moments.

'In view of this, the doctors recommended that Jubanne should be back at home and settled before any reunion with Nora, and I agreed that this would be best, hoping also that once he was back in familiar surroundings, his general grasp on reality would improve. But I didn't realise that they were intending to send him home quite so soon. I believe that he was discharged far too early. The doctors were still experimenting with different medications to find a combination which worked.'

Zuannicca Melis Puddu continued her account, describing to Dante how she had implored the hospital to keep Jubanne until the end of the tourist season, when she could dedicate herself properly to his rehabilitation, but the hospital had insisted on discharging him in May, when the guesthouse was almost full to capacity, and right in the middle of Corrado's final exams. They couldn't have picked a worse time.

'When Jubanne was returned home, it was not just his mental state which remained fragile. Having been confined to a bed for a decade, despite the physiotherapy that he had received in hospital, he was very physically weak. He weighed only seventy-six kilograms, which for a man of his stature was not very much at all. He would say to me, "Look, Zuannicca, I'm as skinny as a gypsy's dog," and he would look down at his body as though he couldn't quite believe that it was his own. Then he'd say something like "It's amazing how much weight you can lose by spending a few weeks in bed." He'd also joke about the lengths he'd had to go to get a bit of time off work.'

Zuannicca Melis Puddu had arranged a bedroom for Jubanne on the ground floor of the guesthouse and had engaged the services of a private nurse, but often he would wake up and believe that he was still in hospital.

'We suspected that he was seeing people who weren't there,' she said.

'You refer to the visions of his grandmother?'

'Yes. Clearly he told you about those. Nonna Maria-Annoriana had been a very influential figure in his life. They had been very close; but she had been gone a long time. She passed away the week before our wedding. Thankfully my husband's hallucinations became less frequent after the doctors decreased his anti-seizure medication. He was also happier once he was well enough to be outside, so that helped his progress. He liked to sit exactly where you're sitting, Signor Bacchetti, and he was quite content to spend his days watching the world go by. And gradually, as he became stronger and steadier on his feet, he would take short walks, and with the increase in physical activity, his appetite returned.'

'Ah, yes. He told me about the cook and her excellent food.'

Zuannicca Melis Puddu looked questioningly at Dante.

'The cook?'

'Yes, he described how a friendship formed between himself and the cook, and he mentioned a particularly fine lemon tart.'

Zuannicca Melis Puddu shook her head.

'That's the first time I've heard that,' she said.

'He informed me that the cook was a woman from the mainland. Your husband said that they would sit here and talk and that she was very understanding of his condition. He also described the cook's friendship with you, and how you would take walks together on the beach at night.'

'No, Signor Bacchetti,' said Zuannicca Melis Puddu defensively. 'That is an invention. I have never employed a cook from the mainland. The specialities we serve in our restaurant are typically Sardinian and therefore I make a point of hiring only cooks who are from the island. And my relationships with all the staff I have ever employed have been, and continue to be, strictly professional. I do not believe that mixing business with friendship is the thing to do.' Then, laughing at the ridiculousness of the idea, she added, 'I have certainly never taken moonlit walks with my staff!'

'Oh,' mused Dante. 'Your husband described this cook with great affection. He also spoke of them going down to meet the fishing boats together at the end of the jetty.'

'Fishing boats do not stop here, and whilst he was recovering, my husband was certainly not steady enough to be wandering down to the jetty. That would have been far too risky. When he was sufficiently well to walk to the edge of the garden he would often look out to where the *Maria-Annoriana* had been moored, and he seemed to sense that something was missing, but he never actually asked what had happened to his boat. There seemed little point in telling him that I'd sold it. It would only have upset him.'

'I apologise if I have caused you to digress, Signora Melis Puddu. You were recounting what occurred when your daughter returned from the Caribbean.'

'Part of me hoped that Nora would be the magic key which would unlock the confusion in Jubanne's brain, but he did not recognise her as his daughter. The effect Nora had on him was to remind him of old feelings, but his muddled mind took those feelings and distorted them.'

'How do you mean, Signora Melis Puddu?'

'Jubanne fell in love with his own daughter – obsessively, and in a monstrous way.'

CHAPTER 20

The four hour journey from the airport in Cagliari back to the guesthouse had seemed even longer to Nora than the three different flights she had taken to get to the Sardinia. Why, of all the times for flights to be delayed or re-routed did it have to be this time? The past seven days, stuck in airport terminals and hotels had been unbearable.

Nora knew that she should have gone to find her mother first, but she couldn't stand the wait any longer and she ran from the taxi straight to the terrace, where she supposed her father might be. There he was, standing under the fig tree and watching a handyman re-laying a stone slab, but he was so engrossed in watching the man at work that he didn't notice her.

How strange it was, she thought, to see him standing. He was leaning on a stick. She approached him slowly, just in case her mother's warning had been wrong, and her father *did* recognise her. She hoped with all her heart that he would; that seeing her now as a young woman and remembering her as a child would click everything into place in his bruised, confused brain – but still, she didn't want to shock him. Her mother had been explicit about it. She must not, under any circumstances, cause him any agitation.

Now Nora was really close, and her father still had absolutely no idea that she was there, so she took the time to inspect him. It was good to see some colour in his cheeks. For the past decade she had only seen him under the glare of hospital lights, which had turned his skin a yellowish grey. All-in-all she thought that he looked all right, considering. Mamma said that he'd been eating well – making up for lost time. He had certainly put on a bit of weight, and spending most of his day outside on the veranda was clearly beneficial. His forearms were quite brown. That was the only bit of him that tanned.

Still, her father hadn't seen her. He was saying something to the handyman about the cement in the wheelbarrow. Then he laughed, and hearing that booming, big man's laugh again brought back a thousand happy memories and the sting of tears to Nora's eyes.

The handyman finished what he was doing, and it was only once he'd left that Nora's father glanced up and saw her. And when he did, he just stared. Nora smiled, hoping for a small glimmer of recognition, but all he did was gaze at her so intently that she felt as though he was looking inside her.

'Hello Papá Juju,' she said, but that didn't seem to register anything, so she made her way towards him slowly, as though approaching a frightened animal which might bolt. He didn't move. He just kept his eyes fixed on her. Once they were touching distance apart, Nora held out her hand and said, 'It's me, Nora,' at which point her father blushed, seemingly assailed by embarrassment. He opened his mouth to say something, then closed it again and looked away. She could see by his bewildered expression that he was trying to focus his thoughts.

Still, Nora was mindful of her mother's warnings. Whatever was going on in her father's mind, she must play along with it, so she did her best to hide her disappointment at not being recognised.

'You're here to work in the restaurant, aren't you?' he said in an affectedly serious voice.

'Yes,' replied Nora.

'You'd better go and speak to my wife. She'll show you round and tell you what needs doing.'

'Can't I stay out here with you a little bit first?'

His response to this was to appear both delighted and aghast.

'Re-laying slabs is no job for you, young lady. Run along inside and find my wife.'

Run along. That was exactly what he used to say to her when she was small. *Run along now, sweetheart.*

Nora leant in towards him, looped her arms around his neck and kissed his cheek gently. Maybe that would jog something in his memory; but instead he responded with a panic-stricken look, then put his fingertips to his face where her lips had touched and told her she must go – quickly. She did as he asked, and when she turned around to wave at him, he pretended not to see her.

Her mother was not pleased that Nora had gone straight to her father, having requested to be present during the initial reunion, just in case his reaction was negative.

'Nora, darling,' she said. 'You have to understand how fragile Papá is, and how sometimes his confusion can lead to angry outbursts. What if he'd reacted badly? What then?'

Nora said that she was sorry, but deep in her heart she couldn't conceive of her father ever reacting badly to her. Papá Juju was all love and laughter and fun and bear hugs. On the very rare occasions that he had been cross because she had been naughty, he would call her by her full name – that atrocious mouthful, 'Maria-Annoriana'. That was usually punishment enough.

Nora's mother put her to work straight away, ironing tablecloths for the restaurant. Nora set up the ironing board in the dining room and pulled back the curtains. She could see her father dozing in his lounging chair under the fig tree. When at last she saw him stir, by which time she was thoroughly sick of ironing, she went back out to him, taking with her a carafe of cold lemon tea with ice and mint. Apparently he had developed quite a taste for that since regaining consciousness. He had never cared for it before.

Now he seemed very pleased to see her, and Nora was heartened by the fact that he remembered her from before his nap. That had to be something. He was keen to chat, so she sat down beside him and began to tell him about her travels.

'Amazing,' he said as she described the places she had been. *Amazing. Amazing. Amazing.* Then, when she complained about the some of the rude, entitled people she had worked for on the yacht, her father made a joke about throwing them overboard, and they both laughed about it together.

He noticed the rose pendant which she wore on her ankle bracelet, her lucky charm, and he commented on how pretty it was, then seemed embarrassed by the fact that he'd looked at her legs.

He'd always been so polite, so proper, and that hadn't changed. What a sweet man, thought Nora. She could understand why her mother had chosen him. He would never be as he was before – Nora was perfectly aware of that – but maybe, little bit by little bit, if they spent time talking, more of him would come back. Memories must still be there, stowed away somewhere in his head. He could not have completely forgotten their trips out on the boat, or how he would carry her on his shoulders, or how she called him 'Papá Juju'. Surely, she could convince him that she was that little girl.

But more than anything in the whole world, Nora wanted her father to love her again.

CHAPTER 21

Dante sat back, turning his glass of lemon tea around in his hand as Zuannicca Melis Puddu took up the story again.

'Nora's arrival threw Jubanne into a tailspin. She couldn't help but be affectionate towards him. Nora was just being Nora. And despite my insistence that she should not overwhelm him emotionally, she was determined that her father would recognise her as his daughter again. I know that she resented me a little because he knew who I was, but he wouldn't accept who she was.'

Zuannicca Melis Puddu's expression remained pained. 'But Jubanne took this daughterly love and warmth to be something else. I cannot emphasise enough how wholly uncharacteristic this behaviour was, Signor Bacchetti. *Never* before had my husband behaved in any way inappropriately towards our daughter, and never during our entire marriage had he shown interest in other women in that way. But suddenly, finding himself with this beautiful, intelligent young woman who hung on his every word and paid him boundless attention, well, he misread that as the possibility that there might be some sort of romantic interest between them. And that is when his behaviour became very bizarre. To my enormous regret, I did not grasp what was happening to begin with. It did not enter my mind that what my husband was experiencing was a monstrous twisting of his paternal love.'

'That is indeed a hideous thing, Signora Melis Puddu. Your husband mentioned to me some hostility towards you son as a result of his feelings towards Nora.'

'Yes, he turned against Corrado, thinking him some sort of

rival for Nora's affections and that unleashed a very ugly jealousy. Jubanne would ask me incessantly where Corrado was, what he was doing and whether he was with Nora. And of course, not understanding the reasoning behind his questions, I would tell him. Nora and Corrado have always been very close. They enjoyed each other's company as children and that continued through adolescence into adulthood. When they worked here during the season, they would also spend their leisure time together. Often they would go to the beach, or into to town. But if Jubanne knew that they were together in circumstances other than the workplace, he would become angry about it. It was only when he asked me directly whether they were lovers that I realised quite how skewed his grasp on reality had become. Quite frankly, I was flabbergasted. I sat him down and against the doctors' advice, I explained to him very, very clearly that Nora and Corrado were not only brother and sister, but also his children.'

'And how did he respond to being told?'

'He just looked at me as though I was speaking nonsense, or wilfully misleading him, then got up and walked away. After that, Jubanne's attitude towards me changed entirely.'

'I was told that there was an incident of violence of a most abhorrent kind when you returned to the marital bed. I understand that you suffered a black eye during the course of a sexual assault.'

Zuannicca Melis Puddu immediately straightened her spine and cast a sharp look at Dante, indicating that he had overstepped the mark. When she replied, her tone was prickly.

'Not that it's any of your business, Signor Bacchetti, but I can assure you that there was never any return to out pre-accident sleeping arrangements.'

'My apologies,' retracted Dante. 'I didn't mean to cause offence by bringing up such an intimate matter.'

The apology was acknowledged with a steely nod, then Zuannicca Melis Puddu conceded, 'However, I do know to which incident you refer, and it was nothing to do with sharing a marital bed. Jubanne suffered a period of somnambulism, triggered by a change in his medication. One night I was awoken by shouting and I found him here on the terrace, ranting and thrashing at the air with his arms. He was cursing and using the most obscene language. I don't know who he thought was here, or why he was so angry with them, but there was definitely nobody else here. Instinctively, I reached out to calm him, but not before he had delivered quite a punch to my face. Well, you've seen the size of my husband. He's a man who can do a lot of damage with very little effort. He not only gave me a black eye, but also fractured my cheekbone.'

Dante was aghast. 'How terrible for you, Signora Melis Puddu!'

'In the moment, Jubanne was wholly unaware of what he had done. But of course, when he saw me injured the following day, I told him.' Zuannicca Melis Puddu swallowed hard. 'He was devastated to have hurt me. Never in my life have I seen a grown man weep so wretchedly.'

She raised her fingertips to her face, as though recalling the pain of the injury, both physical and emotional. 'I should have heeded that alarm, but I did not act upon it the way I should have done. I was afraid that if the doctors learned what had happened, they might insist on institutionalising Jubanne. At the time I believed that putting my husband away, even temporarily, would have been most detrimental to his wellbeing, and that it would have erased the progress that had been made with his recovery. I discussed the matter at length with Nora and Corrado, and they agreed with me, that their father should remain here with us and that we would keep the incident to ourselves. Our decision was made with the best of intentions, but sadly, Jubanne's outbursts became not only more frequent, but also more violent. It was only a matter of time before things escalated.'

'I was told about an incident involving the vandalism of his doctor's car. An Alfa Romeo, I believe.'

Zuannicca Melis Puddu nodded, 'The Alfa Romeo did not belong to a doctor. It belonged to Nora's fiancé, who is now her husband. He would sometimes stay for the night, which I had no objection to. But when one morning Jubanne noticed his car was parked here, he asked why and I told him.' It was obvious that the recollection of this moment was still unsettling. 'This information caused my husband a fit of rage so dangerous, so intense and so frightening that I could not risk it being repeated. He not only vandalised the car beyond repair, but also set about Nora's fiancé with a garden spade. It was only thanks to Corrado's intervention, at great personal risk to himself, that he was stopped.'

'Was your daughter's fiancé badly injured?'

'Thankfully not. He was hit on the arm, and although the force of the blow knocked him over, it left nothing beyond a large bruise. It could have been far, far worse and I fear that it would have been if Corrado had not intervened. I would go as far as to say that Corrado probably saved his life.'

There was a pause as Zuannicca Melis Puddu collected herself. After a moment, she said, 'Following that incident, I had no choice but to place Jubanne in the hands of professionals. And that is where he has been since 1982. My husband resides in a facility for the victims of brain injuries, situated about half an hour inland from Porto Pollo. He understands that he is being looked after for his own good and he never complains about it. The facility has a well-equipped workshop and Jubanne fills his time doing woodwork. He has not lost his practical skills. The correct medication has been keeping him coherent enough

257

to function day-to-day, which is the best we can expect. Physically, as you were able to see for yourself, Signor Bacchetti, he has returned to very good form.'

'Are you able to visit him?'

'Oh yes. I drive down at least once a week. My husband is not a prisoner, but a patient, and as a result is allowed a certain amount of freedom. He is free to walk around the hospital grounds, and even beyond, under supervision. When the guest-house is closed, and if the doctors consider him well enough, I go to collect him for the day and bring him back here.'

'Are you not afraid that he might harm you, Signora Melis Puddu?'

'Not at all. Now that he is appropriately medicated, with me, Jubanne is very docile. We sit in this spot and drink tea, just as you are doing, then we have some lunch, and we pass the time together, then I take him back to the facility for his supper. Sometimes he quite talkative, other times he is more subdued and just wants to watch television. He likes it when I hold his hand. There are times he barely lets go of my hand, from the moment we say hello to the moment we say good-bye.'

Zuannicca Melis Puddu looked towards the sea, blinking away tears. When she was able to turn her face back to Dante and to speak again, it was in a regretful, restrained tone. 'That is our marriage now, and we are still married. I would never petition for a divorce. That would feel like a terrible betrayal, not only to Jubanne, but also to our children.'

'Does he see the children?'

Zuannicca Melis Puddu shook her head sadly, for clearly speaking of it caused great emotion to well up inside her.

'No. And that is the hardest thing, Signor Bacchetti. Jubanne was party neither to Corrado's graduation from university, nor to Nora's wedding. He has no idea that he has a grandson now, also named Jubanne. We could not risk another violent incident. As I mentioned before, my husband is a patient, not a prisoner, but if he was to hurt someone, or worse, his prospects would change entirely. He might not be criminally prosecuted in view of his medical condition, but he would certainly lose the small amount of freedom which he has now.'

'Does he still ask after his children?'

'Oh yes. How they are is the first question he asks every time I see him. I tell him that they are well and happy, which is the truth. But Jubanne still believes they are small, so we leave it at that. Nora is thirty-one years old now, happily married and enjoying motherhood. She works here at Villa Lavandula during the season and when the day comes that I am no longer willing or capable of running the business, she will take it over. Corrado will soon turn thirty. He lives in Cagliari and has a very promising career in engineering. Yet in their father's mind they are little children, and he still believes that they are staying at my sister's.'

Dante frowned, perplexed. Having learned about the secure facility in which Jubanne Melis Puddu resided, the question arose of how he had been able to travel all the way to the Apennines to see him. Zuannicca Melis Puddu pronounced herself equally baffled.

'That, Signor Bacchetti, is a mystery. How a man of Jubanne's size managed to evade the staff and leave a secure hospital; and how a man in his confused state could have travelled across the sea and to a place he had never been before is beyond anything I could explain. And there's also the question of how he funded his journey as surely he must have had to pay fares. My husband's access to money is limited to the small amount I give him. He doesn't have much use for it as everything is provided by the facility. Occasionally, if a member of staff accompanies him to the local shop, he'll buy a packet of biscuits. But now at least I know where he went last February, and I thank you for

259

that, Signor Bacchetti, because when he returned from his venture he would not say where he had been.'

'How long was he absent?'

'He was gone just over a week. Search parties were sent out because we assumed that he was wandering lost somewhere and without his medication. Part of me feared that perhaps he had decided to take his own life. But eight days after he vanished, he walked into a police station in Porto Cervo, told them who he was and asked them to telephone me to say that he was safe and well. He then asked whether they would mind taking him back to the facility.'

With that, Zuannicca Melis Puddu placed Dante's empty glass on the tray, which he understood was his cue to take his leave. But still, the fundamental question remained unanswered.

'Grieved as I am to hear about this ordeal for your family, there's something I still don't understand,' said Dante. 'Where does my daughter fit into all of this? Why would your husband confuse his daughter, Nora, with my daughter, Leonora, who you say was never even here. How did he know my daughter? How did he know where to come and find me?'

'There was some reporting in the newspapers about your daughter's disappearance, was there not, Signor Bacchetti?'

'Yes. Extensive reporting over a considerable period of time.'

'I confess that when you first mentioned Leonora's name, something about it was vaguely familiar to me. Although I can say categorically that she was never employed here, I'm reminded now that I did read some reports on her disappearance. I can only suppose that my husband might have read something in the newspaper and that stuck in his head. Maybe it was the similarity in their names.'

Although this answer was less than satisfactory to Dante, he understood that it was probably the most rational explanation for something which had no rational explanation.

'Perhaps our daughters are similar in appearance,' he conjectured.

'Never having met your daughter, I wouldn't be able to tell you that.'

Dante reached into his pocket and took out a copy of an article which had appeared in one of the national newspapers. Beside the tawdry speculation, which he folded back carefully so that it could not be seen, was the picture of Leonora in her swimsuit, taken by Fernando. Dante presented it to Zuannicca Melis Puddu. She looked at it only briefly before saying, 'Honestly, Signor Bacchetti, it would be difficult for anybody to identify Leonora from that photograph. Her face is entirely obscured by the hat and sunglasses. But from what I can see, there is no obvious similarity between your daughter and mine. In fact, I would say that they are very different physically.'

'Would you allow me to see a picture of Nora? Do you have one from the time that your husband came out of his coma?'

Zuannicca Melis Puddu seemed reluctant to satisfy Dante's request.

'I don't see how that would help, Signor Bacchetti.'

'Please, Signora Melis Puddu. If I could just ask that of you. Then I will impose on you no longer and be on my way.'

Zuannicca Melis Puddu excused herself, returning a few minutes later with a colour photograph of a striking, dark-haired young woman. Dante thought that he recognised her face from somewhere, but of course, that was impossible. He looked from the photograph of Nora to Zuannicca Melis Puddu. There would be no mistaking them as mother and daughter. Perhaps that was the familiarity that he perceived, or perhaps now, having had his view of the whole situation turned upside down, *his* mind was playing tricks.

But Zuannicca Melis Puddu was right. One couldn't say that Nora Melis Puddu resembled Leonora Bacchetti at all. Both were attractive and had long, dark hair, but the likeness ended there. There was no similarity in their facial features, plus Leonora was of a petite build and pale-skinned. Nora had inherited her mother's Mediterranean colouring and some of her father's height. The two would not have been easily confused.

'Thank you,' said Dante, returning the photograph and placing the article back in his pocket.

He presumed that the meeting had now reached its conclusion. He couldn't be certain whether he knew any more or any less than before, or whether he was any more or less confused, but as he rose to his feet, Zuannicca Melis Puddu inquired, 'If I may ask, Signor Bacchetti, what of your wife, Leonora's mother? Surely her daughter's sudden disappearance must have been an ordeal for her.'

'Ah,' replied Dante, lifting his eyes skywards, 'indeed it was, and I hope that now she is in a place where she has found her peace. My darling Ortensia left this world some years ago.'

For a moment Dante wondered whether he should explain the circumstances of his wife's departure, but quickly decided against it. There was no need for Signora Melis Puddu to know the grisly details. Instead he said, 'The end was mercifully brief and I take comfort in knowing that she is in a better place. I believe that it won't be long until we are reunited. The sand has almost finished running through the hourglass of my life, of that I have no doubt.'

They made their way back to the waiting taxi, exchanging a few sympathetic formalities. As Zuannicca Melis Puddu helped Dante into the car, she wished him a safe journey back to Montacciolo. Dante did not tell her that he had neither the means nor the intention to return home.

'Shall I take you back to town?' Asked the driver.

'No,' replied Dante, feeling his breath falter and exhaustion overwhelm him in that same paralysing way as it had when he had walked from Montacciolo back up the mountain. 'I want to go somewhere out of the way, where there aren't any people.'

'How far do you want to go?'

'Wherever this will take me,' said Dante, taking out his few remaining notes and a fistful of change, and handing it all to the driver.

Leonora, hidden from view, watched as Zuannicca helped the frail figure of her father into the taxi. He looked so very old now. He had shrivelled and he didn't move in the same way. His walk, which had once been so confident and sure-footed was hesitant and limping. She had only managed to glimpse his face briefly when he had turned back to glance at the guesthouse. His face was shrunken beneath his grizzled beard. Would she have recognised him if she had passed him in the street? Probably not.

Leonora had listened to her father's exchange with Zuannicca from behind the dining room curtain. What had not changed was how convincing Dante Bacchetti could be. Despite his advanced years and slightly shabby appearance, he still displayed a carefully cultivated image – those restrained manners, that false empathy accompanied by all that affected self-deprecation; so many finely crafted phrases and scholarly words, spoken as if they were sincere. How well he played the frail old man, desperate to learn of his disappeared daughter's whereabouts! He should have been an actor.

Still, the foul feeling that he gave her was the same. It didn't take much, she thought, to bring old emotions to the surface.

Leonora nudged the curtain back a little, still mindful of keeping herself well-hidden, just as the taxi pulled away. It was then that she heard Zuannicca come back into the guesthouse, and a moment later she was by her side. Before anything was said, the two women held one another.

'How did I do?' Asked Zuannicca. Her heart was beating fast.

'You did magnificently,' replied Leonora, pressing her cheek to Zuannicca's.

'Do you think your father believed everything I told him?'

'It was all the truth, except the part about me.'

'Do you think he realised who I am?'

'The last time he saw you was in 1965. I don't think he made the connection today.'

'I didn't think he'd recognised me either, until he asked to see a picture of Nora. I wondered whether he have seen something of me in her.' Zuannicca looked down at the photograph which was still in her hand. Nora was so like her in appearance that even she might have mistaken the photograph of her daughter for herself, aged twenty, when her face still bloomed with youth and her hair was still black.

Both women remained quiet as the events of the past half hour percolated through their minds. Zuannicca broke the silence.

'Of all the people who might have told your father where to find you, I never thought it would be Jubanne.'

'Well, I suppose that for once his confusion has worked in our favour.'

Another moment of silence ensued. Leonora's eyes met Zuannicca's. They knew that they were both thinking the same thing.

'I'm so very sorry about your mother's death, darling.'

Leonora nodded with her head bowed. 'At least now I know,' she replied. 'I can stop worrying about her.'

'You did all you could, under the circumstances.'

'It will never feel like enough.'

To that, there was little that Zuannicca could say. Concerning her mother, Leonora had made a heart-wrenching choice in an impossible situation. They could speculate for ever as to whether it had been the right one. The answer to that was unknowable.

'Are you going to be all right, darling? Is this going to bring all the old feelings back?'

'It might,' replied Leonora, leaning her head on Zuannicca's shoulder, 'but it's all right. I can deal with them now.'

CHAPTER 22

'Don't go near those people,' Leonora had been warned, and to begin with, she had done as she was told. The Montacciolani were visibly hostile whenever any of the group of newcomers ventured into the village, and the girl couldn't really understand why. Sure, they were strangers, and they dressed differently, but there didn't seem to be anything threatening about them – quite the opposite, in fact. They appeared to be very gentle people.

One of the women, who was probably not much older than her, had caught her eye crossing the piazza and smiled, and Leonora had smiled back, although she hadn't dared to approach the young woman, and certainly not there, in the middle of Montacciolo where some busybody would witness it and word might get back to her father. It was impossible to know who to trust in the village. Gossip spread like a wildfire in a drought. The last thing Leonora wanted was to fuel it.

This encounter, if one could call a split-second exchange of smiles from a distance an 'encounter', stuck in Leonora's mind. How exotic the young woman had seemed to her, with those waves of gleaming black hair tumbling down her back and that fluttering, flower-patterned dress. Leonora glanced down at her own dowdy brown dress and buckled shoes – all perfectly good quality and bought new in town by her father – but not her choice. She wished that she too could be dressed in jewel colours and flamboyant patterns, but she knew that her father would never allow such gregarious clothing. He would say that it was vulgar.

One morning, about a week after the newcomers' arrival, Leonora's father had announced that he had to attend a meeting with the Regional Council in town. Knowing that he would be absent for a good part of the day, Leonora's curiosity overtook her reticence and she decided to go to the charcoal-burner's house, only to say hello, of course. She wouldn't stay long. What could be the harm in that, as long as nobody found out?

Taking great care not to be spotted as she made her way to her forbidden destination, she had gone via a circuitous route, firstly crossing the village as far as the earthquake scar and doubling back on herself several times when she encountered one of the Montacciolani.

'Morning, Leonora. Where are you off to?'

'Nowhere special. I'm just taking a bit of air.'

She skirted round the side of the church, all the time checking that she was not being observed, then cut through the cemetery and out via the back entrance, where she stopped, wondering whether she really did have the courage to approach those unusual people. Should she? Shouldn't she? What would be the consequences if she was found out? Leonora sat on the grass and began to thread together a daisy-chain whilst she made up her mind.

Eventually she decided that yes, she was brave enough – brave enough to creep up to the boundary of the charcoal-burner's property, anyway. Whether she could summon the pluck to walk up to the house and introduce herself was another matter. She would see how she felt when she got there.

Leonora made her way through the chestnut woods until finally she came to the boundary, where she stopped, half-hidden by thickets. From there she could see the group, sitting in a circle in the garden. They appeared to be having some sort of meeting. One man was reading aloud to the others from a book. Leonora hesitated, uncertain whether she should interrupt, or just turn around and go back home. The decision had been made for her when, as though she had sensed her presence, the woman who had smiled at her just a few days before looked up and saw her and beckoned her over.

The group of newcomers had all welcomed her warmly, despite learning whose daughter she was. What a joke they had thought it to have given those made-up names to her father! The whole pantomime had amused Fernando so much that he had made a declaration: That summer, whilst in residence in Montacciolo, all members of The Collective were to use their adopted names and to address him as 'Forest Wolf', or risk being exiled into the mountains for the rest of eternity.

When, much to her surprise, Leonora had been asked to choose a name for herself, without thinking she had said, 'Little Boat'.

'Why "Little Boat"?'

The question was asked by the beautiful dark-haired woman, who went by the adopted name of 'Wild Rose'.

'Because,' Leonora had replied, astonished by her own boldness in the company of these unusual strangers, and hoping that they wouldn't think her silly, 'I feel like a little boat. I yearn to be out at sea, sailing away, travelling and seeing the world. But instead I'm stuck on a mountain, where a boat is pretty much useless.'

'Genius!' Forest Wolf had exclaimed, applauding, and everybody else had followed suit. Still feeling consumed by an unusual burst of bravery, Leonora had then added that she had written a poem on the subject.

'Let's hear it then, Little Boat!'

The girl had hesitated, now wishing she had thought of the consequences before opening her mouth. She didn't mind reciting the first couple of verses, but the rest of the poem was deeply personal and they might ask uncomfortable questions about it. She only performed the first twenty or so lines and pretended that was it.

They had all voted unanimously for Leonora to be The Collective's official poet. She was one of them now, and the thrill that this gave her – the sense of acceptance and belonging – filled Leonora with such joy that she found it hard not to grin like an idiot.

For almost three hours they had sat together on the grass outside the charcoal-burner's house, drinking bergamot tea and eating sticky honey cake. Forest Wolf had talked about making the world a better place, quoting passages from esoteric books and explaining the various conditions of mankind, both physical and spiritual. Silver Fox had played ethereal tunes on a copper flute, accompanied by Moonbeam on a wooden whistle. Wild Rose had sung. They asked whether Little Boat had any more poems to share, and Leonora had recited a humorous one called 'Synaesthesia', which was all about mixed-up senses. Mighty Oak had then taken a few lines and strummed an accompaniment on his guitar.

They told her about places they had been and of the things they had done there – lavender-picking in France; walking the *Camino di Santiago* in Spain; visiting the souks in Morocco. Leonora listened, wide-eyed and bewitched. How deep and rich and free these people's lives were compared with her stifling, shut-up existence in Montacciolo, where a trip into the nearest town to borrow a book from the library was like a foreign expedition.

Much as she would have loved to, Leonora had not dared to stay too long in the company of her new friends. She knew it was imperative to get home before her father returned from his meeting and to pretend that she had been there all day.

Forest Wolf said she could come back to see them any time she wanted. Sensing that Leonora was not going home happily, Wild Rose had added, 'Remember we're here if you need us,' and she had walked Leonora back to the boundary of the garden.

Then, as they said good-bye, Wild Rose had undone a chain around her neck on which a rose pendant hung, and she had fastened it around Leonora's.

'This came from a market in Marrakesh,' she said. 'It was my good luck charm, and now it's yours.'

Leonora hurried away with her hand pressed to the rose pendant, but took it off before she arrived home and stuffed it into her pocket. It must under no circumstances be seen, or questions would be asked.

She let herself into the house quietly, in case her mother was asleep, but the house was not silent. Her father's voice boomed from the kitchen, 'What in the name of Jesus Christ do you think you're doing, Ortensia?'

Leonora's heart sank. She stood with her back pressed to the wall, feeling the grim claustrophobia of home displace the joyous freedom of the charcoal burner's house.

A wail from her mother was followed by her father's voice echoing down the hallway, 'You stupid half-wit, Ortensia!' Then there was the crash of something being thrown on the floor.

Leonora did what she could to protect her mother from her father's onslaughts. She would mediate, attempt to play the referee, the rescuer, or the distracter – not always successfully. She had to tread the tightrope carefully, for if anything, her interference risked making the whole thing worse and she would end up embroiled in her mother's punishment – but her father knew that. That's why he did it. Living under the roof of Dante Bacchetti meant that there was always a punishment waiting to happen; not a physical one, but some sort of mental torment – the threat of rage, or disapproval; or some demeaning, caustic judgement. Even his periods of silence were steeped in menace.

Over the years, Leonora had become skilled in the art of keeping out of her father's way and of moving through the house as lightly and silently as a feather, but this time she did not feel as though she could slip upstairs to the relative safety of her bedroom. She made her way to the kitchen and discovered that the argument was about something which her mother had been attempting to cook. A potful of pasta was spilled across the floor, still steaming. Her father was in the midst of it, puffed up to his full height and circling her mother, his footsteps squelching in the mess; and he was still spitting insults.

'Look at you!' He was sneering, wrinkling his nose as though there was a bad smell. 'Look at the state of you, Ortensia! You disgust me. You're an embarrassment!'

Leonora's mother, accustomed to these indignities, was absorbing them in silence with her head bowed. She accepted them as if they were owed to her. She would never answer back, and on the occasions that her husband demanded a reply from her, Ortensia would speak almost inaudibly, opening her mouth as little as possible, like a ventriloquist. Her responses were usually limited to 'yes' and 'no'. If ever she dared to utter a sentence which was not a plea for forgiveness, she would be viciously cut off.

Leonora assessed the situation, trying to figure out the best way to deal with it. She did not dare to shout at her father. She had tried it twice and it didn't work, and only served to upset her mother further. Asking him to stop was pointless, because then he would make a point of not stopping. The best course of action was to switch the attention onto her.

'I'm home,' she announced, clutching the rose pendant in her pocket.

Her father rounded on her, still snarling, 'Where have you been? You didn't tell me you were planning to go out.'

'I went to put flowers on Tina's grave,' Leonora replied calmly, and this was not a lie as that was precisely what she had done on her way to the charcoal-burner's house, when she had stopped for a little while behind the cemetery and looped her daisy chain over the little cross which marked the spot . This seemed to throw her father. He fell silent and chewed his lips, made a snorting sound, picked his way through the pasta and slammed the saucepan back on the stove, then snatched up his hat and left the house.

He would be striding out onto the street now, smiling and amenable, wishing everyone he met an affable *buongiorno*, as though he had just kissed his wife and daughter an affectionate good-bye. Leonora could see it as clearly as if she was walking by his side. Oh, how artfully her chameleon father changed his colours every time he stepped through the front door of the house and became Dante Bacchetti, the upstanding pillar of the community; and how easily the Montacciolani were duped by his performance. They believed the excuses about Ortensia. *Poor Dante Bacchetti. His wife suffers with her nerves, you know.* They didn't question the things he said about Leonora. *His daughter's not quite right – she must take after her mother. Poor Dante Bacchetti...*but weren't the best lies always based on truth?

Nobody dared, or cared enough, to ask Leonora if life at home was all that it seemed on the surface. In a village where everybody knew everybody's business, there was some business they preferred not to concern themselves with.

Ortensia had not moved a millimetre. She stood in the middle of the kitchen with her head hanging and her hair drooping on either side of her pale face.

'Come and sit down, Mamma,' urged Leonora gently, taking her mother's elbow and guiding her to her chair.

'It was my fault. I put too much water in the pot,' said her mother, wringing her hands. 'It boiled over. That's why he was cross with me.'

'No. It wasn't your fault, Mamma.'

Leonora didn't ask what had possessed her mother to attempt

to cook pasta in the middle of the afternoon. Ortensia never cooked. Leonora had taken charge of preparing all the meals, as well as most of the other domestic chores, since the age of eleven precisely to avoid situations such as this. Leonora took a kitchen cloth, got onto her hands and knees and began to mop up the mess of parboiled pasta from the floor.

Leonora's father did not return that evening to eat the supper that Leonora had prepared. It was another of the tricks he played. He would often leave the house after one of his outbursts without saying a word about where he was going, or how long he would be absent – it could be ten minutes, or several hours, even all day. That was part of the game too; to leave Leonora and her mother unsettled and listening out for the dreaded moment when he came back through the door. Even when Dante Bacchetti was not there, the threat of his presence remained, infusing every gasp of air in the house.

Later that evening, with her father not yet home, as Leonora was giving her mother a bath, she said, 'I think I've found a way for us to leave, Mamma.'

Ortensia stared at her and mouthed the word 'leave' silently, before saying out loud, 'Leave? How?'

Leonora soaped the sponge and began to wash her mother's back, Wild Rose's words echoing in her head. *Remember we're here if you need us.*

'I've met some people, Mamma, and I think that they can help us. They're good people. They believe in kindness towards humanity and in sharing, so I'm sure they would help us if I asked. When they leave here, we could go with them and stay with them for a while, just until I've found a job and a place for us to live. We can go a long way from here, Mamma. Somewhere where we can't be found.'

Her mother made little agitated splashes in the bathwater with her fingertips.

'He'd find us,' she said.

'What if he did? I shall be eighteen years old at the end of the month and then he won't have any say at all in what I do. And if you choose to leave him, there's nothing he can do about that either.'

Leonora wished that it was that uncomplicated, and that she was as brave as her words sounded.

'I don't know,' said her mother, without looking up, and Leonora knew that what her mother really meant was 'no'. Leonora felt her hope and enthusiasm dissolve into exasperation, then into despair.

'But Mamma, this is an opportunity which won't come again! We've spoken so often about leaving and making a nice life. Just you and me. Remember how we said we'd get a little flat with a balcony so that you could sit outside? Remember how we said we'd go somewhere warm enough to grow a lemon tree in a pot and I'd make you lemon tarts with our own lemons? Remember that, Mamma? Remember how we said- ' but Leonora didn't finish her sentence because her mother had screwed her eyes up tightly and begun to pray.

'*Hail Mary, full of grace, the Lord is with thee...*' The words were spoken frantically and almost inaudibly, but Leonora knew the prayer by its rhythm. '*Blessed art thou amongst women and blessed is the fruit of thy womb, Jesus...*' A pause. A faltering breath. '*Holy Mary, Mother of God, pray for us sinners, now and at the hour of our death. Amen...Hail Mary, full of grace, the Lord is with thee...*'

As the *Ave Maria* was repeated a second, a third and a fourth time, Leonora's heart thudded heavily, like a lead pendulum swinging back and forth in her chest. She had broached the subject in completely the wrong way. She had been too excited, too eager, and now her mother was panicked by the idea and had shut herself in.

274

Leonora squeezed the sponge and watched the trickles of soapy water run down her mother's bony back. Every vertebra and every rib was clearly-defined, pushing up through her skin. Leonora reached for a towel and held it open for her mother. 'All done, Mamma.'

Still reciting her *Ave Maria*, Ortensia Bacchetti slowly drew herself up to a standing position and stepped out of the bath. She was a pitiful sight. Her body was pallid, fleshless and loose-skinned, like that of an under-nourished old woman; although in actual fact, Leonora's mother had not yet turned thirty-five.

Leonora was already in bed when she heard her father return home. She listened to his footsteps moving from the hallway, to the kitchen, to the study, and he was making no effort to be quiet. She lay in the darkness with the rose pendant clutched in her hand, too agitated to sleep.

'Take me with you, Wild Rose,' she whispered under her breath. 'Take me with you. Take me away from here.'

When Leonora looked out of her bedroom window the following morning, she saw that her father's car was not there. Good. That meant that he had gone into town again and should be away for most of the day. She could go back to the charcoal burner's house without fear of being questioned.

Leonora helped her mother to dress and persuaded her to have some breakfast, which Ortensia ate in such miniscule mouthfuls that by the time it was chewed, there must have been little left to swallow.

As Leonora was leaving the house, Don Generoso arrived. Leonora had ambivalent feelings towards the priest, but she was grateful for the time he spent with her mother. That, at least, gave her some respite. The priest visited her mother every time he saw that her father's car was gone. He also made his house-calls during term-time when he knew Ortensia would be alone. These clandestine visits were an absolute secret, if you didn't count the fact that most of Montacciolo knew about them. At Don Generoso's behest, they were kept carefully hidden from Leonora's father. The priest didn't want to land himself in hot water with the deputy mayor. On more than one occasion, his surreptitious visit had been cut short by a villager rapping on the window to warn of the imminent return of Dante Bacchetti. Don Generoso would slip out of the back door like some illicit lover.

What confidences and confessions were exchanged between the priest and her mother, Leonora did not know. Ortensia never spoke of the visits and Don Generoso would not betray the inviolability of the Sacramental Seal.

Leonora had learned at a very young age that secrets were a part of life – not just those kept within the four walls of the Bacchetti house, but outside in the village too. Secrets were secret for a reason. Some had many faces and only certain ones could be exposed to certain people. Some could not be exposed at all. And woven within this snarled web of selective silences, her father's secrets were the most cleverly camouflaged. Dante Bacchetti was righteousness and morality personified, and he made himself too useful to warrant uncomfortable questions being asked about his private life. Without him, who would educate the children? Who would see to all the administration? Montacciolo would wither and die. Clearly her father understood this. Indispensability was a solid shield behind which to hide.

It was only a quarter to nine, probably too early to turn up at the charcoal-burner's house, so Leonora took the same circuitous route and stopped as she had the previous day on the patch of land behind the cemetery. The daisy-chain which she had placed on Tina's grave had withered overnight. Leonora looped Wild Rose's pendant over her head and sat on the ground beside the stubby wooden cross, the only indication that anything lay beneath.

As the church clock struck nine, Leonora became aware of somebody approaching from the chestnut woods. A moment later, Wild Rose emerged through the trees. A moment after that, she was sitting beside Leonora on the grass. The first thing she said was, 'There was more to that "Little Boat" poem, wasn't there?'

'The rest of it isn't very good,' replied Leonora, although she did not believe this to be true.

'By whose judgement?'

Leonora shrugged and looked down at her dung-coloured dress and ugly shoes and muttered, 'Mine. I've never let anyone else hear it.'

'Would you let me hear it?'

'I don't know,' she said uncertainly.

Wild Rose reached out her hand.

'You seem to me terribly sad, Leonora, and terribly lonely. Don't you have any friends?'

'Not any more.'

'Why? What happened?'

Leonora looked up at Wild Rose and now, for the first time in her life, dared to speak the truth out loud.

CHAPTER 23

There weren't many children in Montacciolo. Leonora and Tina had been born just a few months apart, so their friendship was inevitable. The two girls got along quite well, although in truth, they had few shared interests. Leonora was inquisitive and bookish. Tina was not. What united them was circumstance, age and gender, which, for the first few years of their young lives, had been sufficient.

Tina had no father, and this was not a secret in Montacciolo. There were rumours that he had been a married door-to-door salesman from Modena. Whoever he might have been, wherever he might have hailed from and whatever his marital status, his romance with Tina's mother had been short-lived. Once she had fallen pregnant, he was never seen again in the village.

Consequently, Tina and her mother existed in a state somewhere between poverty and destitution. They were poor even by Montacciolo standards. Sometimes Tina's mother did a little domestic work, or washed glasses in the evenings at the bar, but her meagre income barely covered the basics. Had it not been for the charitable assistance of Dante Bacchetti, Tina would not have had schoolbooks, or a sturdy satchel in which to carry them; neither would she have had a warm coat or good boots for the winter. During particularly lean times, or when the weather was especially cold, it was not uncommon for the deputy mayor to call in with a parcel of food, or a wheelbarrow of firewood.

The friendship between the two girls continued until around the time that they turned twelve when, for reasons that she would not explain, Tina stopped speaking to Leonora. She even asked to move desks at school.

This breakup did not go unnoticed by Leonora's father, of course. He made no inquiry as to how or why it had come about, but simply mentioned to Leonora that she was better off not associating with a girl from 'that sort of background'. He did not elaborate on what he meant by this, and Leonora did not ask, because she knew that people said mean things about Tina's mother. The brief dalliance with the door-to-door salesman had remained an indelible stain on her reputation. Leonora assumed that it was probably something to do with that.

Since Tina had requested to be moved, Leonora had found herself seated beside a boy called Enrico, a tiresome idiot whose company she found hard to tolerate. He teased her incessantly about being the teacher's daughter, despite the fact that this position made life harder for her, not easier. Everything she did had to be perfect. To the outside world, her father boasted of Leonora's academic abilities as though they were simply an extension of his own brilliance, and consequently, he viewed even her smallest errors as a personal affront. In school, he insisted that Leonora should address him formally, as 'Maestro Bacchetti'; not that she liked to call him 'Papá', even at home. It seemed an ill-fitting title. The word stuck in her mouth and when she had no choice but to utter it, it left a nasty after-taste.

Without Tina, outside school Leonora was alone much of the time. Once she had completed all her domestic chores and had seen to her mother's needs, she filled the void with writing poetry. The process of fitting words into formats of rhythm and rhyme soothed her and distracted her from the eternal chaos of home. Her writing was carried out in secret, of course, for if her father had known, or even suspected, that she expressed her innermost feelings in such a way, he would have put an end to it in pretty short order. Leonora kept her poetry notebooks hidden under a stack of blankets in her wardrobe.

One solitary Sunday Leonora was enjoying an unusually

peaceful afternoon of poetry-writing. Her father had gone to the little mountain house – a place he went to regularly, and always on his own. Neither Leonora nor her mother had ever been allowed to accompany him there. It was his private space, he had warned, and nothing to do with them.

Ortensia, exhausted by that morning's expedition to Mass, was asleep in her room. Leonora loathed Sundays and the ordeal of preparing for church, but her father insisted that they should attend. What would people think if they, the Bacchettis, did not show their smiling faces and parade about in their town-bought clothes? They had to be seen. Their perfection had to be admired. They were Montacciolo's Royal family.

When Leonora searched through her satchel looking for her pencil-sharpener, there was no sign of it. Perhaps it had been stolen by her idiot classmate, Enrico. It wouldn't be the first time he'd helped himself to her things. Leonora tried using various kitchen knives to sharpen her pencil, without success, as they were all too blunt. She even attempted to use the cheese-grater, but all that did was mash up the lead. Hoping that there might be an appropriate implement her father's desk, she began to search through the drawers. She wasn't supposed to access the desk without his supervision, but her father wasn't there to ask and all she was doing was trying to find a pencil sharpener.

One drawer jammed. Leonora wiggled it, but it wouldn't shift. It was only just open enough for her to slip her hand in, and she felt a piece of paper wedged in the runner. Bit by bit, she managed to ease it out and free the drawer, but there was nothing useful for pencil-sharpening in there.

The piece of paper which had caused the problem turned out to be a letter, written on thick, old-fashioned linen paper. A quick glance at the letterhead showed an emblem in the shape of a shield, divided in four by a cross. Below it was the name of the school in Ferrara where her father had been employed before his return to Montacciolo. The letter was dated 1946 and addressed to Maestro Dante Bacchetti.

Leonora thought nothing of it as her father never threw away any correspondence, however old or inconsequential. She might have put it back in the drawer without looking further than the fancy letterhead had something not caught her eye in the first paragraph. It was three words – *gross moral turpitude* – and on seeing the word 'turpitude', which she had never encountered before, the girl felt compelled to find out its meaning. She loved new words, and this looked like a good one.

The next lines read: *So as not to cause their daughters more suffering than they have already endured, the parents remain resolute in their decision not to press criminal charges...*

The second paragraph sharply admonished her father for the shame that he had brought upon the name and reputation of the school and concluded with a demand for his immediate resignation. It also specified that Maestro Bacchetti was not to seek alternative employment within less than one hundred kilometres from Ferrara.

Leonora went to fetch the dictionary and looked up 'turpitude'. It meant 'wicked or depraved behaviour'. She had then looked up the definitions for several other words which appeared in the text – 'perverted', 'corrupt' and 'sordid'.

Now Leonora sat with the letter open on her lap, staring at the writing. She thought she understood what it meant, but could it really mean that? Her father was awful in many ways, but he was a good teacher. Surely he would not do perverted, depraved, sordid things with his students?

Leonora didn't know much about sex apart from the fact that, generally speaking, it was forbidden. She was familiar with the biology of reproduction because she'd read about it in a book, but she realised that there was more to sex than that. It was no secret that Pierino Ciocca shared the same father as his own mother, and that was very much frowned upon. Germano Pozzo was the rapist's brother, and that had something to do with sex, but not the kind that the biology book had shown in its diagrams. The problem was, there was nobody to ask.

Perplexed and with many questions turning over in her head, Leonora moved to put the letter back where she had found it, then hesitated. Something was telling her to hold onto it, so she took the letter to her room and hid it under her mattress.

The following day at school she had consulted the map of Italy which hung next to the blackboard. Taking her ruler and measuring from the city of Ferrara to where she knew Montacciolo to be, she scaled up her reading and found the distance to be just over one hundred kilometres.

Leonora glanced up from her schoolwork as her father did the rounds of his students. In the classroom, when he was playing the part of Maestro Bacchetti, he put on a show of kindness and of special interest in each pupil. Leonora watched as he leant over each child with his reassuring hand resting gently on their shoulder, praising their work, or suggesting improvements and corrections, speaking in his encouraging, teacherly voice. *Well done, Enrico. Very good, Tina.*

Thoughts of the letter invaded Leonora's head. Was anybody in Montacciolo aware of the reason why her father had been dismissed from his position in Ferrara? Surely, they would not have given him a job if they had known about his *gross moral turpitude.*

As she continued to observe him, different thoughts began to join up in Leonora's mind. She had occasionally heard whisperings not meant for her ears – comments about a time before she was born. People made observations about her parents' hasty marriage, about their considerable difference in age. Leonora sensed that there had been some sort of scandal. It was no secret that Ortensia had been one of Maestro Bacchetti's pupils.

The letter remained hidden under Leonora's mattress for

many months. Every so often, she would take it out and read it again. It felt valuable – not valuable like gold, or diamonds – but valuable like ammunition, although how she would use it, she did not know.

Then, one evening, almost a year since she had discovered the letter, her father came into her room. As usual, he walked straight in. He never knocked.

'Leonora, have you been in my desk?' he demanded.

The girl hid behind an expression of innocence and lied, 'No. Why? Have you lost something?'

Her father grunted irritably and said that it was of no consequence, then turned and exited the room. Leonora let out the panic breath she had been holding in her body. Her heart was beating so hard she could hear it. Moments later Dante Bacchetti's voice exploded up through the floorboards.

'Where is it?' He was shouting. 'Where have you put it? What have you done with it?'

Whatever reply her mother gave was not audible to Leonora, so she crept from her room and tiptoed half way down the stairs. Although she could not see into the kitchen, the door was ajar and now she could hear both her parents. Her father was continuing with his accusations, shouting, 'I know you've taken it Ortensia!' Her mother, tearful and trembling was denying it.

Leonora felt an awful, guilty pang. Should she say something? Should she admit that she had taken the letter? Would it be better to put it back exactly where she had found it; or perhaps slip it behind the desk, to make it look as though it had accidentally fallen out? She probably had enough time to creep down into her father's study whilst he was distracted in the kitchen.

Then, unusually, her father fell silent and only her mother's voice could be heard.

'Dante,' she was saying, her voice choked and small and stuttering, 'D-Dante, please. Don't shout at me. I don't know. I haven't seen any letter.'

The pleading voice continued, 'Why must you be so cruel with me, Dante? What have I ever done to you, except to try to be what you wanted me to be? I've tried. I've tried for such a long time. I've given you twenty-two years of my life!'

Dante Bacchetti did not reply. He stormed out of the kitchen and shut himself in his study with a violent slamming of the door, clearly too consumed with anger to notice Leonora standing half way up the staircase with her back flattened to the wall.

Twenty-two years? thought Leonora. Had Ortensia really been suffering Dante Bacchetti's attention since the age of twelve? How had it started? she wondered. How had Maestro Bacchetti first gained the confidence of young Ortensia? Was it that reassuring hand placed on her twelve-year-old shoulder as she wrote out her poems and sums? Was it that encouraging, teacherly voice saying, 'Very good, Ortensia. Well done.'? Had it been the same for those girls at the school in Ferrara?

Leonora waited long enough for her father to settle himself in the study. She heard the metallic clang of the poker hitting the fire grate, then the scrape of his chair on the flagstone floor as he sat down. He would be reaching for his newspaper now. Give him a moment, she thought. Wait for a minute's silence. Leonora counted to sixty under her breath, but slowly, stretching out each second. Now? No. Wait another minute, just in case. *One, two, three...fifty-eight, fifty-nine, sixty.* No sound from the study. The coast was clear. Leonora tiptoed down to the kitchen.

Her mother was standing at the sink with her back to the door, staring out of the window into the darkness.

'What was that about, Mamma?'

Leonora's mother remained fixed in her position and did not turn her head when she mumbled, 'I don't know.'

'It was about a letter?'

'I don't know about any letter.'

Was this true? It was difficult to determine. Leonora couldn't see her mother's face.

'It sounded important.'

Again, her mother replied, 'I don't know anything about all of that.'

Yes, Leonora thought. She knows. She knows about the girls in Ferrara. She knows.

'Were you already with *him* when you were my age?'

No response.

'Mamma, did he start touching you when you were still at school?'

The silence remained unbroken.

'Mamma-' began Leonora, but her mother cut her off with, 'Don't ask me such questions! I have confessed my sins and I repent for them every day.' With that, she bowed her head and began to repeat the *Ave Maria*.

As Leonora listened to the prayer being repeated, something revealed itself, like a light being switched on in her brain. In that moment she understood the value of the letter. Unless her father stopped tormenting Ortensia, Leonora would make the letter's contents public, and not just in Montacciolo. She would go straight to the top, to the Ministry of Education.

She crept back to her room and lay on her bed, curled into a tight ball with her knees drawn up under her chin, mentally pronouncing the words she would use when she confronted her father. This in itself was nothing new, for every time Leonora was obliged to talk to her father about anything, however small or seemingly straightforward, first she would go through her script in her head. It was imperative to craft her words carefully; to adopt the correct tone of voice; to structure her sentences in just the right way. And that was just half of it. Gauging her father's responses was every bit as complex. She would go through a thousand different versions, trying to predict what he would say to try to derail her, because invariably that is what he would do, sometimes blatantly, and other times so subtly that Leonora would be left questioning her own sanity.

This matter was far more serious than any she had confronted her father with before. The girl was plagued with doubts. What if threatening him just made everything worse? Several times she approached her father, then lost her nerve and shrank back into herself.

Finally, one evening, Leonora stood on the threshold of her father's study, clutching the door frame so tightly that her knuckles turned white. Her hands were ice-cold, but her cheeks were burning. Her father, who was sitting by the fire and engrossed in his newspaper, had not noticed that she was there. Leonora had gone through every conceivable variation of the confrontation, but now, faced with the reality of it, all her well-rehearsed lines abandoned her. How stupid, illogical and tongue-tied she felt in her father's presence. She wished that she didn't doubt herself so much. Perhaps she spent too long alone, closed up in her own head, arranging and re-arranging her thoughts. Maybe she wrote too many poems and somehow they distorted reality. That's what her father said – that she didn't remember things right, that she imagined things, that she made things up. *You're as mad as your mother, Leonora.*

The girl let go of the door frame, turned and began to tiptoe away, then stopped. No. She couldn't keep putting it off. It must be done. What was the sentence she'd decided to launch her speech with? She couldn't remember. Perhaps it would be better not to open with a direct accusation, but to try to start with a question.

'Why did you leave Ferrara and come back to Montacciolo?' She asked.

Dante Bacchetti looked up from his newspaper with a surprised expression, then a puzzled frown creased two lines over the bridge of his nose.

'I beg your pardon, Leonora. What did you say?'

'Why did you leave your job in Ferrara and come back to Montacciolo?'

'You know why I came back. The village school was threatened with closure and I wanted to prevent that.'

'Wasn't there another reason?'

He folded his newspaper carefully and set it aside, then removed his reading glasses, placing them on top of his newspaper with the same deliberate care.

'Why do you ask, Leonora?'

She managed to blurt out just three words, 'Gross moral turpitude.'

Her father remained impassive.

'What precisely do you mean by that?'

'You did bad things to girls in Ferrara.'

'I did bad things to girls in Ferrara?'

For this, Leonora was prepared with her evidence. She pulled the letter from inside her cardigan sleeve and held it up for her father to see.

'It says here that the things you did to those girls were perverted and depraved and sordid. You lost your job in Ferrara because of what you did. And then you came back here and you started on Mamma.'

Her father remained with a steely gaze fixed on Leonora and the letter, neither confirming nor denying the accusation. The girl braced her legs to stop them from trembling, reminding herself that she was in the right. She had evidence. Now her father was standing up. Don't step back; stand your ground; do not yield, Leonora told herself.

He moved closer. His expression had not changed. Now the

trembling had risen from Leonora's legs and taken over the whole of her body. Don't be afraid, the voice inside her kept repeating, but all she heard was *afraid, afraid, afraid.*

He moved so quickly that she barely had time to flinch, but his intention was not to strike her. With one deft movement, Dante Bacchetti plucked the letter from Leonora's hand and with a single, precise flick of his wrist, sent it spinning into the fire. It was like skimming a flat stone across Lago Stretto. There, the letter smouldered for a moment, then caught a flame and almost instantly disintegrated and disappeared up the chimney in a blizzard of black ash.

To a person who did not know Dante Bacchetti, the minute change in his expression could well have gone unnoticed, but Leonora saw it. For a second, no longer than that, her father's eyebrow lifted almost imperceptibly. His mouth did not move, but the shallow dimple which briefly dented his cheek betrayed the fact that he was smiling. It was a smug smile, intended just for his own personal satisfaction, and kept inside. This was her father's victory smirk.

'Leonora,' he said, keeping his voice low, 'That is an *opinion* which you will keep strictly to yourself.'

'Only if you stop hurting Mamma.'

After a moment Dante Bacchetti made a quiet snorting noise. 'You're as mad as your mother,' he whispered, and then he repeated it several more times, each time just a little louder, and each time inching just a little bit closer to her.

'Mamma only suffers because of you!' Spat Leonora, now feeling unexpectedly brave. 'How old was Mamma when you first put your hands on her? She was only twelve, wasn't she? Twelve years old. That's younger than me!'

To this, her father replied with a moment of silence, then shot her a warning look and said, 'Leonora, do not make accusations which you do not understand.'

'If you don't stop, I will report you to the Ministry of Education!'

'Well,' said her father, stepping away – and now the tone of his voice changed. It was lighter and not so menacing. If anything, he gave the impression of being amused by the absurdity of his daughter's threat. 'You'd better trot off and tell the Ministry of Education then, hadn't you, Leonora? Off you go and spill your unsubstantiated story. See where it gets you. You suppose they'd believe a crazy thirteen-year-old girl, one with a history of making trouble at school? Or would they be far more likely to believe a respected, experienced teacher with not one blemish on his record? Of course, they would also be obliged to question your mother and I can't imagine to what point that would distress her. Obviously your mother, the woman I *married*, would confirm that your allegations are wholly unfounded.'

Dante Bacchetti paused and gave his daughter a look of mock pity. 'They would take you away, you know, Leonora. They'd insist that you should attend a special boarding school for making up wicked stories such as those. I would have no say in the matter. It would be a shame, of course. Not so much for me, but mostly for your mother. As you are aware, your mother is fragile and weak of mind. Goodness only knows what effect it would have on her nerves.'

Still, Leonora stood firm, determined not to be crushed by threats which involved her mother.

'I'll contact your old school in Ferrara. I'll get them to write another letter.'

This time her father's smirk was not hidden. He gave a nasty, smug chuckle and said, 'Good luck with that. The accursed place burned down in 1951 and never re-opened.'

Now Dante Bacchetti began to circle her, pacing with his hands clasped behind his back and articulating his words with icy clarity, just as he did when he was tormenting his wife.

'Leonora, should you be misguided enough to consider not doing as I have asked, I would remind you to think carefully about consequences. If you were to report your allegations to the Ministry – and if for some reason some low-grade jobsworth should decide to investigate your spurious claims – I would find myself suspended without pay. And as the investigators are likely to be a bunch of idiots, I could not begin to guess how long an inquiry might take them. It could be years. And who knows whether I could keep my other paid positions here in Montacciolo whilst under such an investigation? I would also risk being suspended without pay from my administrative duties whilst I fought to prove my innocence. I'm asking you to think about that, Leonora. How would we live if I was suspended without pay? You see how your actions would affect not only me, but they would affect you and Mamma also?'

With that, he returned to his fireside chair and calmly collected his newspaper. Then, waving Leonora away with it, added, 'There is nothing else to say and nothing more will be said on this matter. Go to your room. I don't want to see you again today. Kindly close the door behind you.'

He settled his spectacles on his nose, shook open his newspaper and resumed reading.

Despite the apparent failure of the confrontation and the destruction of the only piece of physical evidence, three things did change immediately after that. The first was that Leonora was constantly in trouble at school – not that she had changed her behaviour in any way. But now, every time she glanced up from her work, or spoke without raising her hand, or made even the slightest error, her father reprimanded her for it. Every infringement, every misdemeanour, however inconsequential, was logged in the class ledger by Maestro Bacchetti. Leonora understood that this was an insurance policy for her father, for if the day came that she did attempt to expose him, he would be armed and ready with his defence. After all, as he had so point-edly said, who was more likely to be believed – a teacher with not one blemish on his record, or a girl with a history of making trouble at school?

The second consequence was that Leonora's notebooks of poetry disappeared from their hiding place. Her father did not deny that he had taken them, but he refused to say what he had done with what he called her 'mendacious, made-up nonsense'. She did not give him the satisfaction of showing that she was upset. Anyway, Lenora knew all her poems by heart. Every word was engraved into her brain.

The third thing to change, for which the first two did not seem an unreasonable price to pay, was that although life in the Bacchetti household continued with its exhausting cycles of chaos and silence, her father's attacks on her mother became a little less frequent. Rather than a prolonged taunting of his wife, Dante Bacchetti would simply silence her with, 'I swear, Ortensia, that you'd do us all a favour if you jumped off a bridge.'

CHAPTER 24

On the morning of the 17th of March 1963 two policemen knocked at the door of the Bacchetti house, and as her father was still upstairs dressing, Leonora had answered.

'Is this the deputy mayor's residence?' They asked. 'We need him to come with us.'

When her father finally appeared downstairs, freshly-shaved, but still minus his cufflinks, jacket and tie, he had greeted the policemen cordially and asked how he could be of assistance.

One of the policemen had gestured uncomfortably towards Leonora, indicating that the reason might not be suitable for the ears of a fifteen-year-old girl.

'It would be best if you came with us, Deputy Mayor Bacchetti.'

Leonora's father had calmly gone to finish dressing and seemed not to be in the slightest hurry, but on his way out to join the policemen, he shot Leonora an accusatory look. She stared back at him blankly. She had no idea why the police wanted to speak to him. It was nothing to do with her.

News of what had occurred spread around the village at great speed. A newborn baby boy, a very small one, probably barely at six months' gestation, had been left on the steps of the church. It was uncertain whether he had been placed there lifeless, perhaps still-born, or whether he had perished in the cold. Nobody knew whose this infant was. There was only one pregnant woman in Montacciolo at that time, and she was still most evidently pregnant.

Leonora's father was absent for several hours. When he returned home he explained how, as deputy mayor, he had been obliged to assist the police by filling out all sorts of paperwork, both on behalf of the Council of Montacciolo and on behalf of Don Generoso, who really was extraordinarily inept at dealing with any sort of crisis. The priest had been in mute shock since happening upon the dead baby, which was all very well, but any person in a position of authority, whether that be administrative or ecclesiastical, should have the ability to pull themselves together in a time of emergency.

Of course, Leonora's father had continued pompously, the police had asked him whether he had any idea who the mother of the unfortunate child might be. Charges would be pressed if her identity could be proven. The crime of infanticide carried a hefty prison sentence.

'No,' Dante Bacchetti had replied with great regret. 'I'm afraid that I am at a loss to help you, Officers. But for what it's worth, my instinct tells me that the mother of this child is not from this village. I suspect that the infant's body was left in Montacciolo to throw you off the scent.'

After agreeing that he was probably right, the policemen had thanked the deputy mayor for his assistance and let him return home to comfort his wife and daughter during this difficult time.

Over the following days there was talk of nothing else in the village. Speculation as to the mother's identity was rife. Every woman of child-bearing age was questioned. Many were asked intrusive questions about their menstrual cycles. Others had their bellies prodded. Leonora's father petitioned for calm and warned of the danger of this sort of inquisition becoming a witch-hunt.

On day four, early in the morning, the two policemen were once more at the door asking for Deputy Mayor Dante Bacchetti. He left with them, seemingly as unruffled as the previous time, but he shot the same look at Leonora. Again, she looked back at him blankly.

Just as it had before, news of what had occurred reached Leonora within minutes of her father's departure. A girl had been found hanged in the chestnut woods. The girl was Leonora's former friend, Tina.

It did not take the Montacciolani long to link this tragedy to that of four days previously; and this was confirmed by a doctor who stated that the dead girl's body showed clear signs of very recent forced *partus*. No details were given as to how Tina had rid herself of her baby, but folk were familiar with the various grisly techniques and the barbarous home-made implements involved.

Shocked and grieving, the villagers asked how it was possible that nobody had realised that Tina, still herself little more than a child, was with child. Her mother, whose inconsolable cries could be heard from the far end of Montacciolo, swore upon all that was Holy that she had had no idea. Tina had claimed to be suffering from a stomach upset.

Questions were asked of Maestro Bacchetti too. Had he not noticed anything different about Tina as she sat in his schoolroom? And what of her classmates? Did nobody sense that something was amiss? The answer to all of these questions was 'no', except perhaps now, with the benefit of hindsight, it could be said that Tina had been a little distracted recently, and bundled up in more clothes than usual, and absent more often with gastric complaints.

There was also the other burning question: Who was the father?

In this matter the Montacciolani were divided. Some asked what feckless monster had put young, innocent Tina in that shameful condition. Tina was a good girl. She wouldn't have done anything forbidden of her own volition. She must have been forced. Eyes turned to Germano Pozzo, the rapist's brother, but he vehemently denied any involvement.

Others, whilst expressing sympathy for the girl, were not altogether surprised that Tina had got herself into that sort of trouble. After all, her own mother's tryst with the door-to-door salesman was no secret. These moral failings often ran in families.

The hideousness of these tragedies was further compounded when Don Generoso announced that regrettably, in view of the circumstances, he could not lay either Tina, or her baby, to rest in consecrated ground. He was also unable to celebrate a full funerary mass, so he proposed that there should be a memorial service instead, once the two bodies had been interred outside the boundaries of the cemetery. Despite Tina's mother's anguish-wracked pleas to Don Generoso, he would not be moved to bend the rules.

Tina's mother implored Dante Bacchetti to use his position of authority to do something to change the priest's mind. She avowed that if Don Generoso refused to perform a proper, Christian burial, she would throw herself into the un-consecrated grave to be buried with her daughter and grandchild. If they were condemned never to be admitted to heaven, she deserved to suffer the same fate. She had failed to protect her daughter in life, so she would do all that she could to defend her in death.

Dante Bacchetti appealed for restraint, saying to Tina's mother that such histrionics and melodrama were unhelpful under the circumstances. There was nothing he could do to alter the priest's position. It was unfortunate, he said, but rules were rules and they were there for a reason. He reminded the woman that to wilfully destroy life was to wrongly assert dominion over God's creation. It was mortal sin, and even he, in his official position as deputy mayor, was powerless to go against the Word of God.

Two days later Tina's mother was found dead in her bed. She had swallowed a cocktail of red wine and rat poison.

Tina, her mother and her baby were interred on a scrappy plot behind the cemetery where villagers more commonly buried their domestic pets. The three generations were condemned to spend the rest of forever in Montacciolo's knackers' yard of dead cats and dogs – which, according to the accepted terms and conditions, had more chance of getting into paradise than their human neighbours.

When the memorial service had taken place, Leonora's father had been tasked with delivering the eulogy. It was a carefully worded, oblique address, which purposely avoided any reference to what had occurred. He spoke of 'a dedicated mother' and 'a well-behaved student'. There was no mention of the baby.

But it was there, as Dante Bacchetti stood delivering that evasive eulogy, that Leonora's revelation had come. She knew by the oily-voiced words of pseudo-sympathy; by the breathy, dramatic pauses; by the tearless eyes rising heavenwards; the hand on the heart. Her father had fathered Tina's child. Then she saw that expression for a fraction of a fraction of a second – the lifted eyebrow, the cheek-dent – the victory smirk.

It was *him*.

Dante Bacchetti might not have twisted the wire hook inside Tina. He might not have tied the noose around her neck. He might not have dosed out the rat poison for her mother. But Dante Bacchetti had blood on his hands, and that cynical victory smirk confirmed that he knew he had got away with murder.

Leonora sat paralysed in the lugubrious silence of the church. Only her eyes moved as she glanced towards the priest. Don Generoso, stone-faced and unblinking, was clutching at the fringe of his funerary stole. Their gazes met for an instant and Don Generoso looked away, but Leonora understood. The priest knew too.

CHAPTER 25

Sitting by the spot beneath which the three bodies lay, Wild Rose, who had not spoken through the entire time that Leonora had been recounting her story said, 'Did you share your concerns with the priest?'

'I tried to,' replied Leonora, 'But Don Generoso didn't want to listen. He told me that it was a matter for my father's conscience and that the day of my father's judgement before God would come.'

'That was it? He said just to wait for God to sort it out?'

Leonora shrugged, 'Pretty much.'

'And what about the question of your poor mother? Obviously the priest was aware of her wretched situation.'

'He wouldn't discuss that at all. Don Generoso said that if he broke the Sacred Seal of Confession, he would be excommunicated.'

'And you?'

'Me?'

'Clearly the priest understood that you were suffering your father's abuse too.'

Leonora hesitated before answering. 'My father isn't abusive towards me. He just requires me to behave and to do as he says and to-'

'Leonora, stop!' Exclaimed Wild Rose and Leonora immediately clamped her mouth shut. She looked at Wild Rose fearfully, her mind scrambling to understand what she might have said that was wrong, or what she might have mis-explained. The girl hadn't expected to bear her soul in such a way, so she hadn't written a script in her mind, let alone edited it.

She hadn't done that thing of preparing her argument, of structuring her sentences, of practising her tone of voice; and because of that, she hadn't gone through the process of predicting reactions, calculating possible questions, rehearsing appropriate answers. Her father was right. She talked foolish nonsense. She should shut her trap.

But unlike Dante Bacchetti, Wild Rose did not cut Leonora down with a handful of insults and dismiss everything she had said as idiocy. Wild Rose looked at her with an expression of overwhelming concern, and when she spoke, the tone of her voice was gentle.

'Leonora, how can you be so accepting of your father's treatment of you? How can you not see the way he intimidates you and controls you as abuse? He has made you so uncertain of yourself and so afraid of your own thoughts that you defend him, but you cannot make excuses for such a contemptible man.'

When Leonora opened her mouth again, at first no words came out. She had never considered it quite that way; yet in just a few sentences, Wild Rose had plucked the scrambled thoughts from her brain and rendered them coherent. Eventually she admitted, 'I'm afraid that if I say anything, I'll just make everything worse.'

'That's exactly how your father wants you to think. Open your eyes, Leonora! He is holding a knife to your throat and you have grown so accustomed to it that you don't even feel it.'

'Would anyone believe me though? The whole village thinks that my father is a great man. He's a good teacher. He helps people.'

'Two opposing things can be true at the same time. A person who is cruel can also perform acts of kindness. A person who is selfish can show great generosity. A wicked person can demonstrate great virtue. Even a coward can hide behind a mask of courage.' Wild Rose paused, as though she was contemplating a question. After a moment, she asked, 'What do you suppose your father's greatest fear is, Leonora?'

'Being exposed for what he really is.'

Wild Rose looked directly into Leonora's eyes. 'Exactly,' she said. 'And everything he says and does is carefully choreographed to maintain his outward veneer of respectability, no matter how damaging it might be to those around him. Your father preys upon the vulnerable and the gullible and feeds upon the admiration of those who are taken in by his lies.'

Wild Rose gave Leonora a moment to process her words, before asking her next question, 'What do you want out of life, Leonora?'

The girl had no immediate answer for this because nobody had ever asked her. It was a question that she had never even properly asked herself. In a place like Montacciolo, ambition was pointless, unless that ambition was to leave.

'I want to get away from my father and from this place and never come back.'

'What about your mother?'

Leonora looked down at her ugly shoes and sighed, 'I don't know if she would ever agree to come with me.'

'Would that stop you leaving?'

The girl felt the guilt for what she was about to say tightening her throat. 'No,' she replied under her breath. 'But it would be hard because my mother needs me and I would worry that it would make my father worse.'

'If you think that your father would punish you by punishing your mother, you're probably right, and that is just another expression of the grotesque hold he has on you. Between a parent and a child there should be a loving bond, not this blackmail based on fear and control.'

'What should I do?'

'If you want your life to change, you have some difficult

choices to make, Leonora,' Wild Rose replied gravely, then the tone of her voice lightened. 'But to start with, you can stop calling me by that silly, made-up name.'

'What should I call you?'

'Call me by my real name. It's Zuannicca.'

*

Leonora's surreptitious visits to the charcoal-burner's house did not remain secret for long. When the word spread around the village that Bacchetti's daughter was consorting with the new-comers, it excited lively interest. Gossip flew from window to window and doorstep to doorstep, punctuated by sharp intakes of breath. There was talk of nothing else. Oh, how the Montacciolani loved a scandal!

Of course, Leonora's father was furious. How *dare* she disobey him? How *dare* she embarrass him in front of all the villagers who held him in such high esteem?

Leonora could not have foreseen the enthusiasm with which those who had previously bowed in deference to her father de-lighted in the thrill of knocking him off his pedestal. People who had never had the courage to utter a word against the deputy mayor now professed never to have liked him. Who did he think he was, anyway? Just because he knew a lot of fancy words, it didn't make him better than them. Bacchetti was an arrogant, vainglorious bully. The bad blood gushed through Montacciolo's narrow little streets with the force of a mountain torrent.

With the flood-gates open, certain rumours about Dante Bacchetti's private life began to circulate. Don Generoso denied being the source, but did nothing to stem the flow. The Montacciolani understood the message behind his sermon, taken from a verse from the Gospel of Luke. *There is nothing concealed that will not be disclosed, or hidden that will not be made known.*

Was the deputy mayor really all that he portrayed himself to be? The villagers asked. Perhaps he was in some way responsible for his daughter's errant behaviour. And was he not the cause of his wife's so-called 'nervous condition'? Ortensia had been a vulnerable, orphaned child. If her parents had been alive, surely they would never have permitted her to be married at such a tender age. And when exactly had Ortensia's relationship with the schoolmaster begun? Had Maestro Bacchetti's taste for the unripe been a singular incident, or was there more to it than that?

Nobody admitted to writing the graffiti which appeared on the door of the church one morning; but there, scratched out in bold chalk letters were the words: *Bacchetti's baby was left here.* And beneath, to emphasise the point, was an arrow pointing to the step. Leonora guessed by the slight backward slant to the letters and the irregular joining-up of the double 't' that the author was her former classmate, Enrico.

Demands were made that a letter should be sent to the Ministry of Education, requesting an investigation into the schoolmaster's conduct. As he could neither read nor write, the mayor requested the help of Don Generoso. The priest agreed to assist on condition that his name did not appear on the document, citing some obscure edict of Canon Law which forbade his official involvement under such circumstances. A response from the Ministry of Education stated that the appropriate department would look into the allegations.

In the meantime, it was agreed by the villagers that the deputy mayor's position was untenable. The campaign to divest Dante Bacchetti of his administrative duties was brief and brutal and the decision to de-throne 'King' Dante was unanimous.

Exposed and deprived of power, Dante Bacchetti's wrath was overwhelming. He railed at the stupid, gossip-mongering Montacciolani; at the moronic, illiterate mayor; at the duplicitous, pigeon-hearted priest. He, a man who had dedicated his entire existence to the care of the less fortunate had been tried, convicted and condemned by a kangaroo court and given no opportunity to defend himself.

Most of all, his outrage was directed towards Leonora. 'See what you have done?' He thundered. 'See how your disobedience and your twisted falsehoods have caused these half-witted imbeciles to deride me, to insult me, to chew me up and spit me out?' It was all her fault, he roared. Everything was her fault.

Faced with these accusations, and knowing that she could count on the support of Zuannicca and of The Collective, Leonora was seized not so much by bravery, but by an absence of fear. She did not break at her father's fury because here it was at last, the long-overdue retribution, or at least, the beginnings of it. Perhaps one day Dante Bacchetti would be judged before God, as Don Generoso had declared; but in the meantime, he was being judged by the people of Montacciolo, and that was judgement enough. This monstrous, corrupt man, absent of morals, soul or conscience, was finally being made to face the truth.

Leonora had no doubt that she would leave with The Collective at the end of the summer. The only question remaining was whether her mother would agree to come with her, but as Leonora had feared, Ortensia was too afraid.

'Go, Leonora. Go and live your life,' her mother had said. 'Don't tie yourself to me. I have made my choices, and I am resigned to them. The only thing which would bring light into my heart would be the knowledge that you are free and away from your father.'

'I'll write to you, Mamma.'

Her mother had warned her sorrowfully, 'Be careful what you write, or I shan't be allowed to see it. As long as you're safe and well, tell me that in your letters. Tell me about the places you visit and I shall feel as though I'm there with you. I will be comforted to read your words, but please understand that I will be limited in what I am able to write to you.'

Still, Leonora made one final attempt to encourage Ortensia to leave, if not now, later.

'Mamma, if the day comes that you change your mind and you want me to come and get you, when you write me a letter, tear a corner off the page. That will be our sign. Can you remember that, Mamma? Will you do that? If I receive a letter from you, whatever its contents, if a corner is torn off, I will know that you want to leave. I will come and get you as quickly as I possibly can.'

Ortensia agreed that she would.

'You promise, Mamma? You promise you'll do that? Just one torn corner and I'll know.'

'I promise,' replied her mother, and Leonora knew that was the best she could hope for.

Leonora packed a bag of belongings and left the Bacchetti house. This time she did not take her circuitous route, being mindful not to be seen. Instead she strode across the piazza, wearing her rose pendant and a flower-patterned dress which she had borrowed from Zuannicca. She didn't care that her father had said that she looked like some filthy, beggarly charm-peddler.

A group of villagers was gathered outside the bar, watching the daughter of the disgraced Dante Bacchetti in her public act of defiance.

'Where are you going with all those things, Leonora?' Somebody had asked, and she had replied that she was moving into the charcoal-burner's house, and after that, she would be leaving Montacciolo forever. Her words were met with wide-eyed shock. 'What does your father think?' came the question. 'I don't care,' came Leonora's reply. Her joy was such on uttering these words that she could have sung them.

*

Freed of her father's control, Leonora grew to understand that it was acceptable to hold an opinion, to speak her mind, to feel her own feelings; and she no longer wrote scripts in her head before daring to open her mouth. Gradually she taught herself not to filter her every thought and every action through the prism of how Dante Bacchetti might judge it. When, from time to time, his caustic words criticisms echoed in her head, she learned to consign them to where they belonged, to the back of her mind, where the things of no consequence lived.

During quiet moments of reflection, Leonora looked back at the sad, friendless girl who sought solace in poetry. It was hard to recognise her. She shuddered to think to what she would have been reduced to if The Collective had not turned up at the charcoal-burner's house that fateful summer. *You're as mad as your mother, Leonora.* Those words might well have come true.

Now The Collective were her family. Being related by blood meant nothing. Love, support and respect was all that counted. With Zuannicca, Leonora discovered true friendship. They shared new experiences. They laughed together, confided in each other. Sometimes they got drunk. Sometimes they got high. Resources were pooled – money, food, clothes – even lovers were shared, occasionally. With The Collective, the two young women lived nowhere and everywhere. It didn't matter where they stayed, or whether they slept in a soft bed in a grand house, or on a hay bale in somebody's barn. Having little or no money rarely bothered them. As long as they had enough to get them to the next adventure, that was sufficient.

Over a period of three years, they visited countless places, but one by one the members of The Collective drifted away to pursue their individual dreams. A few new faces came and went.

None stayed long, but that was the nature of living unconstrained by society's conventions.

'This life is temporary for me too, Leonora,' Zuannicca had warned more than once. 'There will come a day when I will be obliged to go back home and to settle down. I have committed to taking over my aunt's guesthouse when she is no longer able to run it.'

That day arrived far sooner than either young woman had expected. At the end of their third summer together Zuannicca received news that her aunt was gravely ill. Her travelling days had come to an abrupt end.

Zuannicca's sudden departure was a wrench for Leonora, but they kept in touch by letter. Zuannicca would write and tell her about her plans for Villa Lavandula. There was so much to do, she said. The place was a mess. Within a year of her return to Sardinia she wrote to say that she had met a man by the name of Jubanne Melis Puddu, and barely six months later they were married.

Leonora and Zuannicca's lives had converged for a time, and that time had been precious and would never be forgotten, but now each had taken a separate trajectory. Perhaps, Leonora thought, destiny would reunite them again one day. That thought comforted her during the times that she most missed the love and warmth of their special friendship.

Gradually the frequency of the correspondence dwindled. Leonora moved so often that many of Zuannicca's letters reached their destination after Leonora had left, so eventually, Zuannicca stopped writing.

Looking back over those years after their parting, Leonora described herself as mostly aimless, but not unhappy with her lack of direction. She thrived on the feeling of being able to do as she pleased; of packing a bag and going somewhere new on a whim; of seizing any appealing opportunity presented to her. She had experienced enough insufferable cold to last her a lifetime, so never remained in places where the winter was inclement. Where the sunshine went, she followed.

The work she took on to support herself was mostly in restaurant kitchens, and she enjoyed it. Leonora learned to cook paella and gazpacho in Spain; moussaka and taramasalata in Greece; caponata and arancini in Sicily. By the time she left Tangiers she could whip up a tajine as well as any Algerian.

A stream of interesting acquaintances and curious characters crossed her path. Bohemian types had a way of finding her. She was comfortable amongst the gentle souls, the dreamy musicians, the starving artists and the pot-smoking philosophers. Leonora enjoyed a handful of brief love affairs, almost exclusively with men, but nothing was serious, or permanent. She decided that until the day came when the life of a perpetual vagabond no longer suited her, she would continue to drift from one place to the next. After that, she didn't know. She trusted in fate to carry her like a seed on the breeze to wherever she was destined to be.

During those nomadic years, the longest period of time Leonora spent in one place was when she enrolled at the prestigious Château de la Villandière cookery school in the South of France. By then, she was twenty-two years old. After twelve months, she qualified with distinction. Now she could take on better-paid jobs, in case the day came when she needed to provide for her mother. That thought never left her mind.

Her connection Montacciolo continued by means of more or less monthly correspondence. Leonora only kept in touch for her mother's sake, waiting for a letter to arrive with a corner torn off, but no such cry for help ever came. Ortensia's letters became evermore repetitive, filled with flimsy village gossip and pitiful appeals for repentance before God.

Leonora was under no illusion that her mother's letters were probably dictated by Dante Bacchetti. When he had started to write too, she had done him the courtesy of responding, but only because she knew that if she ignored him, he would put a stop to any contact with her mother. Thinly-disguised hostility was woven into phrases such as: *I hope that you are satisfied with your choices.* Although Leonora tried not to let his words unbalance her, they still had the power to worm into her head. Even the handwriting – so clear, so precise, so elegant, so school-masterly – affected her. It rankled that still now, the hold of Dante Bacchetti lingered, like a rotten stench. Leonora's replies to her father were polite, but impersonal and deliberately short. She kept her mother's letters; but those written by her father, she read once and threw away.

About six months after leaving Montacciolo, Leonora had contacted Don Generoso in the hope that he might act as an intermediary; that through him she and her mother might be able to communicate more freely. Don Generoso had replied stating that he could not, in good conscience, be complicit in view of the dissolute lifestyle choices she had made. He quoted a chapter from Romans which described God's wrath on the subject of shameful lust and unnatural relations, and pontificated at great length on the matter of sexual depravity; after which he warned of the dangers of drunkenness and of substances which altered the mind and were irreparably damaging to the soul.

In his letter, the priest had concluded by saying that there was the possibility of redemption in these matters, and if the day came when Leonora sought forgiveness for her transgressions, he would reconsider. However, Don Generoso stated, in the meantime Leonora could be assured of the fact that he continued to visit her mother whenever possible. He even heard Ortensia's confession and performed Holy Communion, and this, he maintained, was a source of great comfort to her.

Leonora had written a rancorous response, shaming the priest for his gutlessness, wilful blindness and inaction. The day of *his* judgement would come too one day, she said, and she hoped that it would be severe. Don Generoso had never found the courage to reply.

CHAPTER 26

It was whilst she was living in Pesaro in 1972 that Leonora had a dream about Zuannicca, which in itself was not unusual, but this dream seemed to have a particular gravity and Leonora felt compelled to write to her old friend. She addressed her letter to Villa Lavandula, hoping that after all this time, Zuannicca would still be there.

A reply came quickly and started as Leonora had hoped, warmly – *I'm so happy to hear from you. It's been too long. I'm so sorry we lost touch* – then the tone changed entirely. Zuannicca's husband, Jubanne, had fallen victim to an accident. He was in a coma and nobody could say whether he'd ever come out of it. She was thinking of selling the guest house because she was finding it hard to cope on her own. It was so difficult, Zuannicca said, running the business and parenting single-handed. She felt that she was doing neither well. Apologies, did Leonora know about the children? She'd written to tell her about them and never received replies. Numerous letters had been returned to sender.

Corrado was the younger of the two, she wrote, a real sweetheart of a child. She'd had a daughter first, and they had given her Jubanne's grandmother's name – Maria-Annoriana. Her husband hadn't been so keen to start with. Maria-Annoriana was a mouthful, and very old-fashioned – nobody called their children names like that these days. But Zuannicca had said that their daughter could be known as 'Nora'. She had explained to her husband why she was so set on that name. The reason was her dear friend, Leonora. She hoped that it would please Leonora that her daughter was named, at least partly, with her in mind.

Zuannicca had concluded her letter with: *If you have access to a telephone, call me on the number below. My darling Leonora, I have missed you more than I can describe. I would take great comfort in hearing your voice.*

The telephone call was made later that day, and the following morning Leonora packed a change of clothes in a knapsack and left for Sardinia. She told nobody where she was going. There was nobody to tell, anyway. She had not formed any meaningful friendships in Pesaro.

The two women laughed at how time had taken the edge of their youth. Zuannicca's jet-black hair was threaded with grey. Too many worries, she said. Leonora had lines on her face. Too much sun, she said. Yet nothing of the connection between them had changed, except for the fact that now their roles were strangely reversed. It was Zuannicca who needed the support of a friend.

Zuannicca had said, 'Can you stay?'

'I'll stay as long as you want.'

'Stay forever, Leonora.'

Leonora did not need to be asked twice to take over responsibility for the kitchen at villa Lavandula and she set to work immediately. Now the prospect of a settled life no longer unsettled her. She was with Zuannicca and that was all that really mattered. It was then that Leonora decided that she would make another big change in her life. The masquerade of corresponding with her parents must stop. She said that she would not contact them again.

'Shouldn't you just write to your mother one last time and tell her that you won't be in touch any more?' Zuannicca had urged. 'You don't have to say where you are. You could get someone to post a letter from the mainland.' But Leonora had made up her mind. She must sever herself completely from her old life. Not soon. Not in one last letter's time. *Now.*

'There is nothing more I can do for my mother, Zuannicca. I cared for her for as long as I could. She has always known that all she had to do was to give me the sign and I would go and get her, and she has never asked. I cannot live the rest of my life tied to an empty hope.'

Zuannicca had nodded, if not in agreement, in understanding. It was Leonora's decision to make.

But supposing that no part of Leonora's old life would follow her to Sardinia was wishful thinking. Half way through the summer the first newspaper article was published. Beneath the headline *DISAPPEARED* was a photograph of Leonora which Fernando had taken on the beach near Cannes years before, and below that was a report briefly describing her last known movements in Pesaro. There followed a sensationalised resumé of her life with The Collective. The term 'fee love' was used four times. Leonora was described as 'wayward', 'troubled', 'promiscuous' and the issue of 'irresponsible parenting'.

'Darling, you must contact the police and tell them you're safe and well,' said Zuannicca.

Leonora shook her head, 'No. I don't want to be found.'

'You can tell them that. But just let them know you're not missing, or kidnapped, or lying dead in a ditch somewhere. What's more, the newspaper has printed some nasty things about you which simply aren't true, doesn't that bother you?'

'I honestly don't give two figs how they describe me. Let them write as much nonsense as they want.'

'Why?'

'Don't you see, Zuannicca? All those lies my father has told about me have come back and slapped him in the face. Can't you imagine what this is doing to him? Can you imagine his ongoing humiliation? The great Dante Bacchetti, former King of Montacciolo, now being called an "irresponsible parent" in the national press.'

An article which appeared a few days later in a different newspaper showed the same photograph and paraphrased the original article. For a time, the story was published every week. Leonora was amused by the string of reports from 'reliable sources' – Montacciolo's gossips and Peeping Toms – who gave wildly exaggerated descriptions, or utterly fictitious accounts, of the devil-worship and degenerate acts they claimed to have witnessed. Then came the photographs of the charcoal-burner's house – 'The House of Sin', the headlines called it. There was barely a mention of finding a missing young woman.

As Zuannicca finished reading yet another report, she looked up at Leonora with a wry smile and said, 'They've made your life as part of The Collective sound far more exciting than it actually was. All we did was to smoke the odd joint and sit around listening to Fernando droning on.' Then her expression had turned serious again. 'But what will you do if someone recognises you and reports it, darling? One of our guests might realise who you are.'

'Not from that old picture,' Leonora had replied. 'It could be half the young women in Italy. Thank goodness for the sunglasses, for the hat and for Fernando's poor photographic skills.'

Leonora cut out the articles and pasted them into a scrap book. There was something deeply satisfying in seeing Dante Bacchetti's continuing punishment in print – the best that she could hope for, anyway. Of course, those reports would never redress the harm done to the girls in Ferrara. Of course, they were no recompense for the abuse inflicted on his wife. Of course, they would never bring Tina back, or her baby, or her mother. But they were a permanent symbol of her father's fall from grace. Leonora put the scrap book away in her bedside table drawer. She rarely took it out to re-read any of the articles. Just knowing that it was there was satisfaction enough.

After a time, there were no more reports, or if there were, they appeared in publications which did not reach Sardinia. Leonora continued her life at Villa Lavandula, hidden in plain sight. Nobody suspected that Leonora the cook was the missing woman, Leonora Bacchetti. But perhaps nobody was really looking for Leonora Bacchetti. Who would care about finding *that* sort of woman?

The years passed and business boomed. Zuannicca had private bathrooms installed in all the guesthouse bedrooms and had a veranda built which incorporated the fig tree. Villa Lavandula's restaurant earned an excellent reputation and people came from miles away for the food prepared by Leonora. The children grew up. Corrado decided that he wanted to be an engineer. He had those sorts of practical skills, like his father. Nora finished school and chose to travel before settling down, just as her mother had. Leonora gave her the rose pendant as a good luck charm and they had waved her off as she set sail on a yacht bound for the Peloponnese.

Life continued, busy, stable and serene, until the thing that was not supposed to happen, happened. Jubanne woke up.

Leonora's heart broke for Zuannicca. She could see the anguish in her dear friend's eyes whenever she looked at remnants of her husband. In a way, she was as confused as he was. The doctors did their best to assure her that there would be some improvements as soon as the correct balance of medication was found. Hopefully, over time, Jubanne would understand that the accident had robbed him of ten years and perhaps, eventually, he might recognise his adult children. Maybe his life could return to some sort of normality. *Hopefully, perhaps, maybe, over time* – those words preceded everything the doctors said.

At first, Leonora was uncertain how she should act around Jubanne, but it was less complicated than she had feared. She gained his confidence through food. She would bring him things to taste as he sat outside under the fig tree, and each time she would stay and talk with him for a while. He liked to speak about his children, saying that he couldn't wait for them to come back from their cousins'; but he never referred to them by their names because clearly he had forgotten them. Names muddled him, and that applied to Leonora too. Jubanne could never get it right, but she didn't mind him calling her 'Cook'. At least he remembered that.

One afternoon, after she had finished the lunch service, Leonora had gone upstairs to the attic bedroom she shared with Zuannicca and found Jubanne there. It was not a place he was supposed to be. He wasn't allowed to climb stairs. He was standing in the middle of the room looking disorientated.

'Was this my bedroom before?' He asked.

'Yes, it was.'

'It looks different now. Do you know where my medals are?'

'Your medals?'

'I won them at the regional arm-wrestling championships. They were in a drawer.'

'Zuannicca must have put them somewhere.'

'She wouldn't have thrown them away, would she?'

'Absolutely not. She hasn't thrown away any of your things.'

'Good. I wanted to give them to-' Jubanne faltered and he screwed up his eyes in the way he did when he was trying to remember a name. Finally he focussed hard and said, 'I wanted to give them to my little boy when I see him. I promised him I would before I went into hospital.'

'That would be nice,' began Leonora, but before she could add anything else, the enormous man's mouth let out a dismal howl. His face collapsed into an expression of abject distress and he crumpled onto the floor, cradling his head in his hands.

'When will I see him, Cook?' He sobbed. 'When will I see my little boy? When will I see my little girl? Why can't I see my kids?'

Leonora crouched down beside him, wrapping him in her arms as far as they could reach.

'Soon, Jubanne. Really soon,' she said because that was the only thing that she could hope to soothe him with. There was no point in explaining that he'd spoken with Corrado within the past hour and that Nora had been by his side most of the morning.

Leonora held Jubanne close, feeling his hot, stuttering breath on her neck and his tears dampening her shoulder. Instinctively, she rocked the big man gently, like a small child. 'It's all right, Jubanne. It's all right,' she said, even though it wasn't. For all the talk of recovery and progress, it was becoming increasingly evident that even if the doctors managed to find a medication regime which improved his day-to-day life, Jubanne would never be properly 'all right'.

He was so immensely heavy, sinking into her shoulder. Still, Leonora held him. She understood that Jubanne needed to feel the warmth and closeness of another human being. It was as though in that moment she was assuming the weight of his despair and hoped that he would feel, for a short time at least, the burden was not only his to bear.

Zuannicca had described Jubanne as such an affectionate man before the accident. He would reach around her waist and her feet would leave the ground when he kissed her. Then he would fold her into those enormous arms which could have snapped her in two with one squeeze – yet he would hold her so tenderly, so delicately, with such love.

That was one of the hardest things now, Zuannicca had confessed to Leonora. She was frightened to let Jubanne hold her, even though she understood that was what he was desperate to do. She was afraid that he might lapse into some other world for a moment. There were times when she had seen an expression in his eyes – a predatory, sexual flash – which she had never known before, and that terrified her. Yet in that moment,

Leonora feared no aggression from this giant of a man. All she felt was his anguish, his helplessness, his insufferable torment.

Jubanne must have sensed that his weight was pressing down on Leonora, but Leonora sensed that he was not ready to be let go. She re-adjusted her position on the floor and Jubanne curled up in a foetal position with his head resting on her lap. He seemed a little calmer now. His breathing had quietened.

'Are you comfortable, Jubanne?' Leonora asked softly, and he made a sound to say that he was, then he mumbled, 'Another two milligrams,' which was something he often said, but nobody was quite sure why.

Leonora could feel the cross-shaped scar on Jubanne's skull as she stroked his hair to soothe him. X marked the spot – a permanent reminder of where the rock had hit him.

What an unknowing sacrifice this sweet, kind, gentle giant had made. How unjust life can be, thought Leonora. How unfair that you, Jubanne Melis Puddu, a good man who did everything right, who adored your wife and your children, who would have moved heaven and earth to assure their happiness and their protection, were cut down as you were. Without that awful, senseless accident, I would not be here, in this beautiful place, in the bedroom you once shared with Zuannicca. I thank you, Jubanne, but I'm sorry that I have to be thankful to you in this way.

After a time – it could have been half an hour, or more – Leonora's legs were numb.

'How about we go down to the kitchen, Jubanne? I've made one of those lemon tarts you like. It'll still be warm. Or if you fancy something else, I'll make it for you.'

'Do you know how to make apple *frittelle*?'

'Of course.'

'Nonna Maria-Annoriana, used to make them for me a lot. She'd coat them in sugar and cinnamon as soon as they came out of the pan.'

'Would you like me to make you some now? You can watch me. Make sure I'm doing everything just the way Nonna Maria-Annoriana used to.'

'She put beer in the batter. And she fried the apples first in a little bit of butter.'

'Then that's what I'll do too.'

In the kitchen, Jubanne polished off a good part of the lemon tart as he watched Leonora prepare the *frittelle*, then suddenly he stopped mid-mouthful and put down his fork. His gaze fixed upon something to Leonora's left and he switched into an otherworldly state.

'Jubanne?'

Still he remained transfixed, but now he was blinking rapidly and vaguely mouthing something, as though there was a conversation happening in his head.

'Jubanne?'

He snapped out of his trance and his focus returned to Leonora.

'Where's Nonna Maria-Annoriana?' He asked, looking around the kitchen.

'There's nobody else here. Just me and you.'

'But she was here a minute ago, showing you how to make the *frittelle*.'

There was no point in distressing him by denying his apparition, so Leonora played along.

'I expect she'll come back later,' and Jubanne replied confidently, 'Yes, she will.'

Leonora plucked the sizzling apple *frittelle* from the pan, coated them in cinnamon and sugar and arranged them in a circle on the plate. Jubanne looked at them, frowning, and said, 'Sea urchins.'

'Sea urchins?'

He stared at the plate for a few seconds, shut his eyes tightly and opened them again. Then, with a look of relief, he smacked his lips and rubbed his hands together. 'They smell really good!' He exclaimed, drawing the scent of the apples and cinnamon into his nostrils.

'Well, I can't promise that my *frittelle* will be as good as Nonna Maria-Annoriana's, but they should be really tasty.'

Jubanne confirmed that they were, ate them all, and even gathered up the crumbs of caramelised sugar and cinnamon with his fingers; then he announced that he was tired. He went to his spot under the fig tree and fell asleep in his lounging chair almost as soon as he had sat down.

Everyone had been very concerned by Jubanne's expedition to the top of the house. It was the first time he had forgotten the no-stair-climbing rule, which was not an easy rule to forget as he was aware of his instability. He kept away from steps instinctively, as one would keep away from the edge of a ravine. How he had made it all the way to the attic floor without losing his balance and toppling headlong down the stairs had been little short of miraculous.

That night, when Leonora had retired to her room, she had gone to fetch something from the wardrobe and found that her things had been moved. On further inspection, she discovered that not only the contents of the wardrobe, but also the chest of drawers and bedside table had been disturbed. She concluded that Jubanne must have been looking for his medals.

There was just one item missing – Leonora's scrap book of newspaper cuttings. But when Zuannicca had asked Jubanne about it, he had looked mystified and replied, 'Of course I haven't taken anything from Cook's room. I can't go up to the attic. I'm not allowed to climb stairs, remember?'

Why Jubanne had taken the scrap book, and what he had done with it, never came to light.

CHAPTER 27

It was exactly a week since Dante Bacchetti had turned up at the guesthouse. Both Leonora and Zuannicca had half-expected him to come back, but he had not. Whether he had recognised Zuannicca from the photograph of Nora and made the connection to Wild Rose was unknowable. Had he suspected that Leonora might be at Villa Lavandula? It was impossible to say.

They were almost ready for the seasonal re-opening. Zuannicca was running about in the way that she always did during that fortnight before the guests arrived, giving everyone their orders and fretting that they didn't have enough staff. In the kitchen, Leonora was making her preparations. Nora was there, complaining that her mother was a slavedriver and tackling a mountain of ironing whilst little Jubanne kept escaping out through the dining room doors and onto the terrace. They were expecting Corrado to arrive at any moment. He had promised to come up from Cagliari to help out. His mother had a long list of jobs for him ready and waiting.

When they heard a car pull up on the driveway, they assumed it must be Corrado, but Nora's voice rang out from the dining room, 'Mamma, Leonora, the police are here!'

'I'll go,' said Leonora, sensing that the police were probably there for her; and indeed, the moment she opened the door a young officer announced, 'I'm looking for Leonora Bacchetti.'

This is it, she thought as she confirmed her name. My father has joined the dots. Will I be in trouble now, for hiding for so long?

The policeman held up a small leather-bound volume asked, 'Is this yours, Signorina Bacchetti?'

Leonora did not recognise the book, but there, embossed in gold on the cover was her name, and below it, the title – *The Little Boat*.

Respectfully, the policeman removed his hat and explained that the body of an old man had been discovered by a shepherd in a very isolated spot, about twenty kilometres inland. An exact date and time of death had not yet been determined, but it was estimated that the remains had lain undiscovered for a week or so. For the moment, the death was being treated as unexplained; but there were no signs of violence, or of any sort of self-inflicted injury. It appeared, the policeman surmised, as though the old man had simply lain down and died. There were no documents on his person and his identity was yet to be officially confirmed. All they had to go on was the book of poetry.

'We believe that this might be your father, Signora Bacchetti,' the policeman said gravely, and Leonora conceded that he was probably right.

'How did you know where to find me?' She asked, and the policeman gestured that Leonora should open the book. Inside was a note containing a brief instruction:

Please deliver to my daughter, Leonora, at Villa Lavandula. With thanks, Dante Bacchetti.

The policeman offered his most sincere condolences and said that he would contact Leonora in a day or two as there would be certain formalities to undertake.

Later that evening, Zuannicca found Leonora sitting outside and leafing through the collection of poetry.

'Are you all right, darling?' She asked.

Leonora looked up at her with an expression which was difficult to define.

'It's not my poetry,' she said numbly.

'What do you mean?'

320

'These *were* my poems, but my father has altered them all. He's glorified everything which pertains to him and he's omitted all the truth about his treatment of my mother and his treatment of me. There's no word at all about Tina, or the girls in Ferrara. These poems are entirely about his magnificence.'

Leonora cast her eyes over the pages, taking in the false life history of the great Dante Bacchetti, neatly told in verse and rhyme. After a moment, she snapped the book shut.

'Let's go down to the beach,' she said.

The two women made their way together down the path. When they reached the edge of the garden they stopped for a moment to look across the twilight blue sea. The setting sun streaked through the clouds and suffused the sky with a coral-coloured light. In the distance, only the silhouette of Isola Spargi broke the horizon. Kicking off their shoes, they stepped onto the beach and stood in the shallows, feeling the soft, cool sand underfoot and the waves lapping their ankles.

One by one, Leonora ripped out the pages of the book, casting each into the air and watching as Dante Bacchetti's unblemished autobiography fluttered down into the water and was carried away by the outgoing tide.

Finally, with every page torn out and with one last effort, Leonora launched the empty leather binding, sending it spinning into the sea, where it floated for a moment and then sank below the surface.

'The last of Dante Bacchetti's lies have died,' she said, the relief evident in her voice.

Zuannicca stroked Leonora's cheek and kissed her. They left the beach arm-in-arm and walked back slowly through the garden, passing between the beds of roses and lavender, aloes and prickly pears, with their shoes still in their hands. Nora, Corrado and little Jubanne were waiting for them on the terrace under the fig tree.

Printed in Great Britain
by Amazon

48564358R00189